Picture Perfect Autumn

ALSO BY SHELLEY NOBLE

The Tiffany Girls

Summer Island

Imagine Summer

Lucky's Beach

A Beach Wish

Lighthouse Beach

Christmas at Whisper Beach (novella)

The Beach at Painter's Cove

Forever Beach

Whisper Beach

A Newport Christmas Wedding (novella)

Newport Dreams (novella)

Breakwater Bay

Stargazey Nights (novella)

Stargazey Point

Holidays at Crescent Cove (novella)

Beach Colors

Picture Perfect Autumn

A Novel

SHELLEY NOBLE

An Imprint of HarperCollinsPublishers

HarperCollins books may be purchased for educational, business, or sales promotional use. For information, please email the Special Markets Department at SPsales@harpercollins.com.

FIRST EDITION

Designed by Renata De Oliveira
Chapter opener graphic © Sanches11/shutterstock.com

Library of Congress Cataloging-in-Publication Data has been applied for.

ISBN 978-0-06-314154-4

23 24 25 26 27 LBC 5 4 3 2 1

To Jim and Paul

Picture Perfect
Autumn

1

Dani Campbell was headed for a gigantic fall. She knew it. She could feel it lurking close by, waiting for her to blink. So she just wouldn't blink, not tonight anyway. Tonight she was riding high, the darling of the New York art world. Basking in the limelight of her success and celebrating her first solo photographic opening at a Hamptons art gallery.

It was exciting and fun, being the center of attention. Schmoozing with other avant artists and networking with the movers and shakers of the East Coast art world. Smiling and laughing; saying outrageous things about art, being insightful and clever, as the champagne flowed and the canapés disappeared from trays as fast as they appeared.

Across the room, her agent, Manny Rodriguez, was already talking up her next show, lining up possibilities, upping the ante.

Self-taught and only twenty-eight, Dani was the bright young star of the season. She was young, but not naive. She knew that all these friendly well-wishers could turn into enemies faster than their smiles could follow. She'd already seen careers disintegrate practically overnight. Like Jake Carras, whose rising star had burned out but who refused to let go. He was here tonight, standing just outside the action, pretending he wasn't being ignored. His career as fleeting as the ice sculpture in the foyer already beginning to melt under the lights.

Dani turned away. That wouldn't happen to her. She was good. Everyone said so. Still, in a stolen quiet moment she'd recite her mantra. *Fake it till you make it.* Because Dani had no idea what she was doing or how she'd gotten here. Or, more importantly, how to stay.

She upped the wattage, stood a little more confidently; smiling, successful, her spiked hair sharper than the cutting edge her work "defined," while quaking on her stilettos, knowing it might all come crashing down without warning.

And she couldn't help but think she was missing something important.

The next morning on her way back to the city, she drove past a sign for Ye Olde Antiques Barn. Dani knew better than to associate with anything with "Ye Olde" attached to its name, but she was a sucker for a junk store. She loved how everything was all jumbled together regardless of period or style or use. She loved how she could photograph odd objects and turn them into something wonderful with just a few manipulations of a graphics app. She suspected that her life could use a good app right now.

She turned off the main road and pulled into the parking lot of what had actually once been a barn. She got her camera case from the mesh cargo hold of her SUV, set the alarm, and went inside.

The barn was dark and smelled of old age, with rows of shelves, stacks of magazines, boxes spilling over with the castoffs of castoffs. Cheap as dirt and just waiting for Dani to turn them all into celebrities.

She spent the morning shooting doilies and oil cans, jars of buttons and headless action figures. Then, just as she decided to get back on the road, she spotted a dented metal Chinese checkers board sticking out from a box of misshapen chalkboard erasers.

Just one more shot. She pushed away a moldy nine-by-twelve envelope blocking her view.

The envelope split open, revealing a tantalizing peek of photographs inside.

Enlargements, years old, probably of some forgotten family vacation. Dani looked anyway—how could she not look? It was what she did.

The first was a nest, half hidden among the weeds, and a duck, head tucked beneath its wing in sleep or protection. A black-and-white shot that told everything in one perfect moment.

She felt tears well up. She blinked them away.

It's just a duck, she told herself. But it was more than that. That one simple photo had something none of Dani's had—ever. She recognized it right away. She didn't know what it was, but she knew she needed it if she was going to stay on top.

She turned the photo over but found only stains, as if it had been sitting on a wet table. She looked at each photo, carefully turning each over before placing it to the side, as excitement and wonder grew inside her.

A cactus standing like a sentinel in the desert. Maple syrup dripping from a tap into a wooden bucket. A nightgown wafting from a clothesline like a ghost, like a spirit, like the soul of whoever had worn it last.

A woman standing on a rocky cliff overlooking the sea, a house several stories tall, balanced on the earth behind her, as if a breeze could send them both over the edge. The woman, thin as a wraith, her hair gossamer fine, lifted her face to the sky, as if she might take off and fly. For a moment Dani flew with her. Then an overwhelming sadness or happiness or maybe both encompassed her.

She turned it over. And on the back: "Lawrence Sinclair, 1964," and a contact number. And she knew she had to find him. Because he had something she lacked. Something she had to get.

As soon as she got back to her Lower East Side apartment, she Googled him. And found zip. Lawrence Sinclair had dropped out of sight decades ago, leaving a smattering of incredible photographs in galleries across the country and no forwarding anything.

She closed her laptop. He might be dead. But she had to find out.

The next day, she sent out a flurry of emails, made phone call after phone call. For the next few weeks, she scoured newspaper archives, knocked on doors, interviewed several prospective Lawrence Sinclairs. None of them had panned out so far.

She was down to her last chance.

And that was why she was driving down a rutted, barely recognizable car track somewhere in Rhode Island, wearing clothes she'd had on for two days, and her heart racing like someone had spiked the milkshake she'd just had for lunch.

She'd finally traced the contact number to a photography studio in the town of Old Murphy Beach. The studio had shut its doors decades before and was now a newly opened dollar store. The clerk there didn't remember it, but the guy at the laundry next door dropped words she wanted to hear. "Used to be a Sinclair family about a mile and a half down the road."

She was down that road now, and it wasn't looking good. The car track was so neglected and overgrown that she'd begun to wonder if maybe she'd just been punked. Though it had once been paved, big chunks of asphalt now heaved from the earth, creating a moonscape in her path.

She reached over and touched the envelope that sat on the passenger seat beside her. The path suddenly jigged to the right; Dani yanked the wheel; the SUV spewed sand as she turned; and the envelope slid to the floor. She leaned forward, gripping the steering wheel, and crept along for another fifty feet before coming to an abrupt stop just as her GPS went blank, then a No Data Available warning popped onto the screen.

Dani stared in dismay, then dropped her forehead to the steering wheel. She'd counted on this being the right place, the right Lawrence Sinclair, who would unlock the meaning of photography for her. Who would save her career while it was still a career. Who would teach her that thing she needed.

She lifted her head just enough to risk a peek. If Lawrence Sinclair was still alive, he was living in the gothic horror beach house from hell. Without a beach in sight.

But surely no one could live here. A turret sans several roof tiles clung to one corner; a wraparound porch anemically hugged the first floor. Gables and finials perched precariously, seemingly at random, and paint that must have once been blue or gray peeled like a bad sunburn.

The whole monstrosity seemed to be sinking from the center outward like a soufflé pulled from the oven too soon. Not that Dani had ever made a soufflé. Scrambled eggs were about as gourmet as her cooking talents ran.

She inched the SUV forward and stopped at the porch. She'd made it this far on her own, but now she needed a mentor. She needed Lawrence Sinclair. And she wouldn't find him sitting in her car.

She cut the engine. Then she picked the envelope off the floor, got out of the car, and quickly clicked the lock. She had a bunch of expensive equipment and she didn't leave her car unlocked even at a stoplight.

Keeping the keys in her hand in case she needed a quick escape, she took a look around, searched the dark windows of the old house. Nothing. Only slightly daunted, Dani strode up the steps, across the uneven floorboards of the porch to the double front door, walnut or oak, with oval panes of gloomy stained glass, that might as well have proclaimed, *Abandon hope.*

After a brief confusion, she pulled the old bell knob. She could hear it ring inside, but no footsteps or cheery "just a minute" followed.

She rang again, and when that elicited no response, she banged on the wood.

She looked around for a mailbox, saw that someone had added a brass mail slot to the door.

She knelt down to peek inside; the door opened a crack.

Dani bit back a yelp of surprise and stood up.

She waited for the door to open all the way but it didn't. She couldn't see who stood behind it.

"Yes?" The voice was low, rough, as if unused.

"I'm looking for Mr. Lawrence Sinclair."

"Who are you?"

"Dani Campbell. I'm a photographer and I saw—"

The door slammed shut.

It took a second for her to realize that he'd actually closed the door in her face. Not the first time it had happened, but not lately. She knocked again. "I don't want to bother you . . ." Which wasn't exactly true; she wanted a lot more from him . . . *if* he was the Lawrence Sinclair she was looking for.

"Are you Lawrence Sinclair? I'm running out of Sinclairs. Are you the photographer?"

No answer, but she could feel him standing behind the door.

"I've sent out dozens of emails."

No response.

"Look. I've interviewed four other Lawrence Sinclairs. A high school teacher, a car salesman, a night watchman who didn't appreciate being bothered at home on the weekend, and an inmate of the Hartford police station, where he was being held for breaking and entering. None of them were who I was looking for."

"Go away."

And she knew. "You are, aren't you? I found an envelope of your photos. I had to find you. I need you to—"

"Go the hell away. I'll sic the dog on you."

There hadn't been any barking when she rang the doorbell. She bet he didn't have a dog.

"Will you please just talk to me? Just for a minute? I have your photographs with me."

The door didn't open. She pulled the duck photo out of the envelope.

"Did you take this?" She knelt down and slid the photo into the mail slot.

He didn't take it. She didn't let go.

She rattled it just to get his attention and hoped she wasn't making a huge mistake.

It was snatched from her hand.

She half expected it to fly back out of the slot in tiny pieces. He had to be the man she was looking for. Anyone else would have looked at it and sent her packing.

She opened the slot and spoke into the darkness inside. "That photograph is my property, and I want it back. I'm staying at the hotel in town." She knew they had one. The Excelsior. She'd seen it as she drove past. "I have others if you want to see them."

Still no answer.

She was losing her patience, something she'd never had much

of to begin with. "You can slip it back through the mail slot now, or I can come back later—as many times as it takes."

When no photograph slid back to her, she stood up. "Fine, but I'll be back."

She reluctantly started down the steps toward her SUV. Maybe she shouldn't have shown him the photograph so quickly. Let him stew longer. If he was stewing. Maybe he'd already gone back to whatever he was doing, the photograph forgotten.

Fine. He might be used to getting his own way, but so was Dani. And her life, certainly her livelihood, depended on him. She hesitated before getting into the car, giving him one last chance, giving herself one last hope.

"Where the hell are you going?"

She couldn't stop the smile of satisfaction that crept up her face, but managed to compose herself before turning to face the source of that raspy voice. He stood in the doorway, a tall man, old and slightly bent, ascetically thin, with long white hair that reached to his shoulders, and a long, thin face with a pointed wisp of beard that made it seem even longer.

To Dani, in that moment, he was her Gandalf.

"Where did you get these?"

"An antiques barn. They were all together in this envelope." She held it up and took a few steps toward him. "I just stumbled across them. And I need you to mentor me."

He raised his hand to his mouth and convulsed with an attack of coughing. Not coughing. He was laughing.

Was the man stark raving mad? And was she crazy to approach him?

"Well?" He opened the door wider; she bounded across the porch and slid past him into the house before he could change his mind. Or she could change hers.

═

Peter Sinclair stifled a yawn and shifted in the plush leather conference chair. He hadn't been tired until he sat down for the board meeting. But it happened every time, an enervating heaviness that made his eyelids droop, his shoulders slouch, and his interest plummet. He knew he shouldn't complain, and he didn't, not out loud. He'd known what he was in for all his life. Through boarding school, prep school, college; through internships and law school. Everything was set for him. His legacy as a Sinclair. It was downright archaic.

But it was the way it was. And now that he'd passed the bar, there were no excuses.

Since the death of Peter's father, his mother had been designated as proxy co-chairman of the board with his great-uncle James, until Peter was ready to take over his half of the company. No way was Peter ready for that position; they'd at least all agreed on that point. Actually, the whole situation held no interest for him. Just walking into the building made him feel forty years older.

But he didn't have a choice. Just look what had happened the last time someone had bucked the chain of continuity, the family tradition, or as Peter was beginning to think of it, a fate worse than about a thousand other jobs he could think of.

Now they all seemed to be on edge over the question of who would hold the controlling shares, currently controlled by his absentee grandfather. By right they would come to Peter now that he had joined the firm. They were the last thing he wanted.

"And I'm sure you'll all agree . . ."

Peter straightened up. At some point in his stupor, his mother had taken the floor, currently holding the voting shares for his grandfather and waiting for her son to assume his responsibility. She was speaking eloquently, the only way she ever spoke, about something, probably the fiscal state of the company.

". . . will add a depth that most of you realize . . ."

Why was it when his mother talked like that, Peter was certain she was directing her words solely to him. He straightened even more, put on an interested expression.

Peter just wanted to practice law. He liked practicing law. His two years clerking with Judge Wembley had been a little slice of heaven. Law that made a difference to people it was made to protect. He'd be a happy camper if big corporations would stop suing each other or skimming the books and hiding their assets, and he was left to help those who really needed it.

Too bad Sinclair Enterprises didn't have an underdog department. Though Peter suspected that he was the underdog in this organization.

He glanced up to see everyone looking at him, and he realized he'd been tapping his ballpoint pen on the table. He stopped. Slipped the pen into his jacket pocket.

"Do you want to comment?"

No, Mother. I don't have a clue as to what you're discussing. "Not at this time. Please continue."

He knew he was one of the lucky ones, born to money in a somewhat loving family. Never had to do without. He wasn't ungrateful. It was just sometimes he wanted to yell, *I hate this job.*

Those times were when he remembered his grandfather.

His grandfather had handed over the "keys to the kingdom" to Peter's father the day Elliott Sinclair passed the bar. Everyone was scandalized except Elliott, who had plans and was hot to implement them. Lawrence Sinclair had merely said, "I'll be in touch," and moved himself and his wife to the original family homestead in Rhode Island.

Unfortunately, Peter didn't have an heir waiting in the wings. He didn't even have a steady girlfriend. He'd just have to wait it out.

The meeting was breaking up. Several of the partners gathered around his mother and Great-uncle James. Peter calculated how quickly he could get out the door and down the hall.

His mother caught up to him at his office door. She practically pushed him inside and shut the door.

"What is wrong with you? Can't you pay attention for two hours?"

He could; he just didn't. He tried. At least he thought he tried. At least for the first few minutes. Maybe it was just a form of passive aggression.

"You're going to have to take your place as head of this company soon. It's your . . ."

Please don't say "legacy," thought Peter.

". . . duty to make the transition as seamless as possible."

His mother was the one who should be running the company—permanently. She was good at it, and it gave Great-uncle James more time to perfect his golf game. But she wasn't born a Sinclair, had only married into the name, as if she didn't count for anything else. Something she never let herself forget.

She pursed her lips.

Peter braced himself.

"Please try harder, darling. Everyone is anxious for you to get up to speed."

Except for me, Peter thought despondently. "I will."

"This is a pivotal time in the firm. We're about to make some huge decisions. And from all I'm hearing, your grandfather is not as sharp as he used to be. You need to be in a position to take over his votes."

"I think that may be a bit premature," Peter said as diplomatically as he could. He might have his own issues with his grandfather, but he never questioned Lawrence's intelligence or his integrity. "He's never refused to give you his vote." That had been the deal; he would have nothing to do with the family or the business, except to send in his vote when needed. In return they left him alone.

"Let's talk about this later, Mother. I have another meeting."

"Very well, tonight, then." She strode off down the hall.

Peter grabbed his folders for the Donovon-Schickley merger and took the elevator to the second floor.

He opened the meeting room door, nodded at the others, and sat down. His eyelids grew heavy . . .

2

Dani couldn't see a thing, not even the old man who had just shut the door behind her. Shutting out the sunlight, the brisk September air, her escape route.

She repressed the idea that maybe she had just stepped into a too-stupid-to-live moment. Then he slowly came into focus. He towered over her, but she was pretty sure she could take him. She hadn't spent her childhood navigating the Brooklyn public school system for nothing.

Hell, he was so thin a heavy exhale might blow him away.

He walked past her, a mere rustle of wind. Definitely, she could take him. So she followed him through a door to another room.

A click, and a table lamp flickered light into the depressive shadows. She could make out old furniture and heavy drapes covering what must be windows.

He moved over to another lamp. Turned it on. Then turned on her.

"You said you had others."

She clutched the envelope with the remaining four photographs to her chest.

"I do. Where is the one I slipped through the mail slot?"

He shrugged, all bony shoulders beneath a moth-eaten cardigan.

God. This was Lawrence Sinclair? What had happened to him? He'd been at the beginning of what could have been an illustrious career, and then nothing.

She tried not to think that maybe she was in jeopardy of fading as quickly as this old man.

"Are you him?"

"I was." He stretched out his hand, also bony and beginning to creep her out.

Dani swallowed. "First tell me what happened to my duck."

"My duck," he rasped. His throat rattled. "Now a dead duck."

"No!" Dani whirled around as if she could locate it in the dim room of shadows. "What did you do with it? That was my property."

He didn't answer; she could feel him taking her measure, though she couldn't really see his face.

"I want it back."

"Too late. Not very bright of you to slip it through the door like that."

"I wasn't trying to be bright."

"Obviously. But I got the picture. How much do you want? I'm not a rich man."

"What are you talking about?"

"You were savvy enough to recognize them as Lawrence Sinclairs, I'll hand you that. But don't even think of gouging me. I'm flat-out broke."

She could believe that. No one who had two cents would choose to live in this dreary old termite fest.

"So what's it gonna be?"

"Stop it, you arrogant old geezer. I'd never heard of you before. I just saw them and . . ." Dani tried to swallow, but for some dumb reason she felt like bursting into tears. Just like when she'd first seen his photos. She sank down on a hard dusty couch. "I can't believe you destroyed my duck."

"I'll pay for it, seeing as how you were so attached to it."

"I don't want your money, I want my duck, and wanted . . . I was hoping . . ." She slumped. All those weeks of searching—for nothing. "I just want to see what you see."

This time it was a recognizable laugh, but it made her skin crawl. This was one bitter man, not what she'd expected at all. She didn't know what she'd expected, but if he'd been fat and happy and a crossing guard at the local elementary school, she wouldn't have been more surprised, and never this disappointed.

She should leave, but something kept her pinned to the scratchy old sofa.

"Why?"

She looked up. "Why what?"

He placed the tips of his fingers on his forehead and shook his head.

"I fell in love with these the moment I saw them. I think maybe I fell in love with the photographer who took them, and I knew I had to find him."

"You weren't even born when these were taken."

"It didn't matter. I just knew it, you know?" Did he know? She sure as hell didn't. She never talked like this. She never felt like this.

He threw out his hands, almost skeletal in their thinness. "Behold him now."

And she did. She itched to run out to the SUV for her camera, or even reach for the cell phone in her pocket. But she didn't dare.

She could see history written in his features, in every movement, though brittle. Even now they spoke of a youthful grace.

And she decided at that moment she wanted to hear him. Wanted to know him. Wanted to learn from him.

It was weird. She had gone from exasperation, to trepidation, to total acceptance in a walk from the front door to this cold, abandoned room.

Because the room wasn't just dark and dusty, it was barren, unused. The sparseness, the obviously missing pictures on the walls, where gaps among the other paintings stood out like the sign of dwindling wealth in old horror movies.

She could pay him for the duck photograph that she'd already paid for and leave him to his misery. She actually had money thanks to her sudden popularity among the graphics collectors.

She'd be turned away, he would spend the money, and they'd both be back where they started. Was any of that magic she'd seen in the photographs left in this old man? She'd come this far. She wouldn't leave without even trying to find out.

"I need you."

He jumped.

"Look, I'm a photographer, too."

"Ah." He started to walk toward the front door.

"A real photographer. I get paid, I'm in galleries and everything."

He kept walking.

"Dani Campbell. Maybe you've heard of me? I'm kind of famous."

He'd almost reached the front door.

Dani jumped up. "Do you have a computer? I can show you."

Of course he didn't have a computer; he probably didn't even have a cell phone. But if she left long enough to get her laptop out of the car, she knew he'd never let her back in again.

At least he'd stopped and turned back to her.

"Famous, huh?"

She nodded, feeling stupid and not at all cutting edge and trendy up against Lawrence Sinclair.

"I guess I could see them." He turned and walked in the opposite direction across the foyer and through a smaller doorway. She hurried after him.

It wasn't any lighter in this room than the other. How could anyone live in such gloom?

But he turned on a lamp or two as he had done in the first room, disclosing a large wooden desk and a streamlined desktop computer with external keyboard and mouse.

"Are you still taking photos?" Dani asked as she followed him behind the desk. He closed out of a spreadsheet, clicked a few keys, and a search engine sprang immediately onto the screen. It was surprisingly quick, considering the lack of everything else in the house.

He gestured to the keyboard and stepped aside. She leaned over and typed in her website. "Ready?"

"Go ahead." He sounded resigned. Or maybe bored.

One press and a giant DANI exploded onto the screen like the Star Trek *Voyager*, racing toward the viewer in a graphic tour de force. The rest of the graphics appeared, then sorted themselves into a horizontal menu.

She glanced over her shoulder to see if he was impressed, but nothing in his stark features had changed. He saw her looking, so he tilted his head, which she read as *Proceed*, so she did.

She scrolled down to a montage of photos. "Here's my latest gallery show."

She clicked on one. "This just sold for . . . enough." It was not his business. "And this one . . . This was featured in an article about new directions in *Art Quarterly*. And this—"

The mouse was snatched out of her hand.

"What?"

"What's the rush? You bully your way in here, with your purple nails and spiked hair, and insist that I look at your photos, then speed through them as if you are afraid for me to really look at them."

"I'm not."

"Then get out of the way and stop the running commentary." He nudged her aside, pulled up the desk chair, and sat down. She leaned over his shoulder.

"Go sit over there."

She didn't move; he crossed his arms. "Go sit over there on the window seat."

"Okay, but click there to see my reviews. And that one to see my upcoming exhibits. And—"

"Go!" He huffed out a sigh and waited until she had backed across the room. "Sit."

She sat down on the window seat and swore dust rose up around her. He should hire a housekeeper. She sneezed, then realized he'd told her to sit so that the computer screen stood between them. She shifted to one side, then the other, but couldn't get a better view. She stood up once, but an immediate command of "Down" made her give it up.

It seemed an eternity of listening to him make the occasional sound, usually a grunt or a sigh, then silence followed by another grunt or sigh.

He was taking his sweet time. Did he hate them? Some people couldn't relate, usually the old establishment people. But most critics were riding her bandwagon.

"I'm told I have an eye," she blurted, when the waiting got to be too much.

His head appeared over the top of the screen. "From where I am, I'd say you have two."

Dani gritted her teeth. "You know what I mean."

He gave her a look that quelled any pretension she might have had, which at this point was minimal, before his head disappeared behind the screen again.

Time passed. Dani pulled her phone out of her jeans to check how much. Though, considering she hadn't looked at the clock when she'd arrived, it was hard to know exactly. It seemed like an eternity.

A profound silence was followed by a series of snorts and grunts, then his disembodied voice. "I hope you haven't been listening to these guys."

"What guys?" Dani asked, and used the question as an excuse to return to the desk.

He tapped a fingernail, in need of a manicure, at the screen. "Critics. They'll eat you alive and have your art for dessert if you let them."

"Is that what happened to you?"

"Me? Nah."

"Then why did you stop showing? You just dropped out of sight. I know because I searched." She looked around the room. She hadn't seen a camera, camera case, or photo anywhere since she'd arrived. No evidence that he'd ever taken a picture in his life. "Do you know how many Lawrence Sinclairs live in this country?"

"I could have been living in South America."

She groaned. "Well?"

"Well, what?"

"Don't be obtuse. My photos. What did you think?"

"First of all, what someone else thinks is beside the point. That tip is free."

"And . . ."

"Oh, for God's sake. What do you want?"

"Your opinion."

"That'll cost you."

"I can pay."

"More than you know." He'd mumbled it, but she heard it loud and clear.

"You don't like them."

"Not much," he agreed. "But someone liking your work is about the most useless tool there is. It's about them, not you."

He hunched forward and clicked through several examples. "I suppose all these were done digitally and with computer enhancements and all that."

She nodded and named a few.

"Greek to me."

"But can you help me? I can do just about anything, but there's always something missing. Not quite right. I can't find it, no matter what I do, how I manipulate the RAW photos. However I present them, it just doesn't come. Everybody thinks I'm great, but I'm not. I'm beginning to doubt my ability to find it. Maybe I'm just not a real photographer."

"I don't doubt it." His words shocked and hurt.

"You mean I'm not really a good photographer." She dashed at her eyes, embarrassed at her sudden, amateurish tears.

"I mean, your problem is you have too many toys. You obviously have the technique, the eye, but you're so busy doing everything and listening to everyone that you missed the main point."

"Which is?"

He shook his head, then tapped his fist to his chest.

When she didn't answer, he said, "Soul. The thing these photos lack is soul, and you don't find that by looking out or even at."

"I lack a soul?" She settled back, deflated.

"That's not what I said." He shut the computer down and stood. "You know, your generation gives up so easily, it's a wonder you accomplish anything at all. Or even try."

"That's not fair. You obviously gave up. I bet you never leave this house. Do you even own a car? How do you even know what 'my' generation is like?"

"I've known a few of you. It was depressing."

"And that's why you sit here all alone in the dark."

"Pretty much."

With a terrible sinking feeling, she scooped up the envelope and the remnants of her hope. "Sorry I bothered you. I'll just take my photos and my lack of soul and go. I won't bother you again."

"See? That's exactly what I mean. One little bump in the road and you're ready to cave. And by the way, those are my photos, not yours."

"They're mine now. I paid for them, and I want my duck back, even if you tore it to pieces."

"And that's the second point. If you can buy it, you're missing the point."

"Well, you're so smart, what *is* the point?"

"Ha . . . and expect someone else to give you the answers. Hell, sometimes you even want us to supply the questions."

"Well, here's a question. Will you teach me or not?"

"You can't teach soul."

Okay, that hurt. This whole trip had been a bust. And the creeping disappointment was almost too big to cope with. "Thanks anyway." She started past him.

He followed her to the door. "What do you plan to do?"

She shrugged. Turned. "Not much I can do, except keep taking my soulless photos. And keep making the money from them."

"God, that's depressing."

"Tell me about it."

"I said you couldn't teach it. But sometimes you can grow it."

She whirled around. "Will you grow mine? I can pay."

"Souls and payment always leads to trouble."

"But can you do it?"

"Who knows? That's the other thing about your generation. You want to know what you're going to get out of it before you put the effort into it. It doesn't work that way. You have to be willing to risk it all. Or you might as well not do it."

He probably didn't even know someone in "her" generation. He was arrogant, and self-important, and a know-it-all. He was completely unlikable and would probably waste her time. And charge her a fortune to boot. Though it did look like he could use some cash. The place was falling down around his ears; he hadn't had a professional haircut maybe in decades. It was pitiful. He probably spent his entire Social Security check to buy that computer.

"Now, now, don't go away mad."

He'd just eviscerated her and now he making fun of her? She could hear it in his voice. "I get it. Don't go away mad, just go away."

He shrugged, was silent for so long that she thought maybe he'd nodded off. She had no choice but to head reluctantly for the front door.

"So you're just going to give up and go back home and keep working the way you always worked."

"I didn't say that." She'd just thought it.

"I thought you wanted to improve your photography. You can certainly do that by yourself. But are you sure the photography is the problem?"

She wasn't sure of anything. Just that something didn't feel right. That was why she'd set out on this godforsaken trek. But after meeting Lawrence Sinclair, and his bitter, acid personality, not only did she not believe in herself, she was pretty sure he couldn't help her. And yet . . .

"Maybe I'll stay around here for a few days, take in the sights."

"What? Suit yourself. But you can forget staying at the Excelsior."

"I can afford it."

"Hooray for you, but it closed up the week after Labor Day."

"I'll find somewhere else."

"Everyplace around here closes up."

"Then I'll . . . I'll . . ." She quickly glanced around the room and repressed a shudder.

He looked, too, and just as she saw him realize what she was thinking, she said brightly, "I could stay here."

"Oh no," Sinclair said, literally backing away from her.

"Why not? Looks like you have plenty of room."

"None of them have been cleaned, don't have clean sheets."

"I could—"

"No washing machine. No cook. No—"

"I can pay. You can use the rent money to hire a cleaning service."

That got his attention, though she couldn't be sure of its reception. His expression was unreadable. Finally he leaned into her. "How much?"

"Well, let's see, a room with, I'm guessing, no amenities, no bellhops, no free Wi-Fi, no restaurant or bar. Off-season—what's the going rate? I'm thinking three hundred dollars a week?"

"Nine hundred dollars."

"That's highway robbery."

He shrugged. "It's been nice. Good luck. I'll see you out." He started toward the door.

"Okay, okay."

He slowed, turned, considered her for a few moments, his eyes narrowing to black slits like some CGI fantasy beast. "You can have the housekeeper's suite."

"Is that like the Lincoln Room?"

"Better. It's off the kitchen, has its own bathroom. I think it still works."

Dani rolled her eyes. "Is it secure?"

"What? You worried that I might walk in my sleep?" He suddenly waggled his thick eyebrows. "You can lock it from the inside."

"I was thinking of my equipment. I have a lot of expensive stuff."

"You won't need it. But if it'll make you feel better, you can bring it inside. Oh, and you'll have to feed yourself."

"I can do that."

"And me."

She huffed out a sigh. He was playing her. She'd been off-balance since she'd looked into the mail slot. But she couldn't resist.

"I can do that, too. I'll just get my stuff." She hesitated. "You're going to let me back in, right?"

He stuck out his bony, long-fingered hand. "Shake on it."

Lawrence stood in the darkness of the foyer, watching Dani Campbell collect her belongings from her SUV—late model, he noticed. Either she was doing okay for herself or mama and daddy were bankrolling her.

He shook his head, laughed quietly at the situation. He was definitely in his dotage to take on this brash young tyro with her spiky hair and deep-set eyes. But he had to admit that she was entertaining. He couldn't remember the last time he'd enjoyed himself so much.

Pitiful old man. Now what was he supposed to do? He'd agreed to rent her a room, hoping to scare the crap out of her so she would run as fast and as far away as possible. She wasn't a dummy. But really, didn't girls these days know better?

Who in their right mind would want to stay in the house with some old dude who looked like him? Some mornings, he scared himself.

She'd offered to pay him rent. And for his sins, he'd agreed. Even bargained with her. He had to be out of his aging mind. Though he had to admit she was a breath of fresh air. Most people were trying to relieve him of his money.

He didn't have any illusions about how long she would last. Her photos were technically sound, even interesting to look at. But they had no depth, nothing that grabbed you by the cojones until you begged for mercy.

She knew something was lacking. That was perceptive of her. Even though she dressed worse than he did, and though she acted all flash, he had a feeling about her.

He might even help her, though what he could actually contribute was questionable. Things had changed radically since he'd given up photography. Something he still tried not to think about. Too many years, too much backstory. If he got bored or started feeling cramped, he'd just tell her to go.

He wiped away the smile that had crept to his lips. She was staggering toward him, loaded down with bags and tripods and a rolling suitcase.

He didn't move to help her, just opened the door wider and stepped to the side as she rattled up the steps and through the front door.

It might even be interesting. It was definitely entertaining. Besides, what harm could it do?

3

Dani looked over the "housekeeper's suite." A bedroom off the kitchen with one window looking over a wooded area—at least it wasn't the driveway. A bed that might have been a double in prestandardized times. A faded quilt and folded comforter that looked like it came from one of the discount stores that dotted the highway into town. Old Murphy Beach. She wondered briefly who Old Murphy was and if there was a new Murphy down the road.

She hadn't seen a beach anywhere, not before the town, near the town, or after she left the town. Maybe it was farther down the road than the Sinclair turnoff.

She hoisted her suitcase onto the bed; the mattress gave under the weight. She looked around for a closet and found an old-fashioned wardrobe. Good thing she'd packed light. Hopefully she could grow a soul before the weather turned cold.

She sighed, screwed up her courage to look into what Lawrence Sinclair had promised was the bathroom. She pushed open the door. It had all the necessary plumbing; she turned on the hot water. It spurted and coughed and ran rust, then clear. Flushed the toilet; same story. Moved on to the tub. There was a permanent rust ring around the drain, but with a good scrub . . . She wandered back into the bedroom. It was even smaller than her bedroom in Manhattan.

But she wouldn't be spending much time here. And she had plenty of photographic "toys" to keep her busy.

Into this moment of optimism, her cell rang.

Manny. "Hey."

"Where the hell are you?"

"Rhode Island."

"You were supposed to email me the shots for our pitch to the publisher next week."

"I know. I just . . . I don't know, ran out of steam. I needed a change of scene."

"You can take a change of scene when this is done. They loved the shots I sent them from the antiques barn. They already have a title. *Gems and Junque.* It will be their lead title for next Christmas season."

"Then I have a year to worry about it."

"That's not how it works and you know it. What's wrong? You're not depressed, are you? I lose more damn artists to depression than I can count. Things are good, but we have to keep branching out. I'm gonna get you a spot on the next PBS arts special."

"Manny, you're making me tired. I'm just taking a few days, okay?"

"Okay, but now's not the time to get complacent."

"I'm not. Promise. I'll get the stuff to you. I just need a couple of days."

"Right. Okay, stay in touch. Damn, I've got another call coming in, Jimmy Wharton. Gotta run. Ciao."

"Ciao," Dani said to empty space, and tossed her cell on the bed.

She washed and changed, quickly wrote out a check for her rent, then grabbed her camera and phone and left her new home away from home. She found Lawrence Sinclair rummaging in the fridge. For a few seconds, she just watched him.

There was something fluid in the way the man moved, though he must be eighty—or close to. Good genes? Or could he possibly be keeping in shape? Exercise even? Somehow she couldn't imagine him running through the woods in his spandex and Nike Airs.

Maybe he had a Peloton in one of the many rooms that the old mansion must possess.

He backed out of the fridge and stood up. "All unpacked?"

Dani nodded, waved her rent check at him, and plunked it down on the kitchen table. "I thought we could get started. I brought my camera."

"Huh, we're out of milk and we need something for dinner." He tilted his head and assumed an expression that she knew he meant to be innocent, angelic even. He did not wear it well.

"I suppose I now have to go grocery shopping."

He beamed a smile at her. "That's a great idea. There's a Shaw's nearby. Just turn right out of the drive past the highway. It's about fifteen minutes."

She returned his smile. Could hers look more fake than his?

"Should I make a list?"

"Good idea."

She pulled up the notes app on her cell and looked at him.

"Oh, whatever you can cook, I can eat." And he wandered away, while Dani began to steam.

But she opened and closed cabinets, even made a foray into the fridge, which was virtually empty and in need of a good scrub, which she had no doubt would fall to her. She had choices; she could complain that this wasn't what she was here for. She could repack and leave.

But the man wasn't clueless; he was definitely trying to push her buttons. Okay. She would play. What she needed from him was that important. She began to make a list, praying that she wasn't just being used, and that his attitude toward her was actually part of her gaining a soul.

When she had a lengthy list, she added stops at the liquor store and bakery. Might as well eat well while she was here, no matter how briefly. She looked into the parlor and the office before she left, but there was no sign of Lawrence Sinclair. He hadn't left money or a credit card for her to find, which she guessed meant she was supposed to pay for groceries as well as rent.

Okay, Mr. Sinclair. I'll play your game. For a bit. You better come up with some pretty spectacular mentoring or I'll put hot sauce in your tapioca.

═

It was after five when Dani finally drove the SUV up the bumpy car track and stopped in front of the house. It didn't look any better the second time around. But her cargo hold was filled with groceries, plus a box of beer and wine from the local liquor store. She couldn't find a bakery. She'd save that for another day. If she lasted for more than a day.

She wasn't surprised when Lawrence was still nowhere to be seen. She'd decided to call him by his first name while she was picking through the green beans—they would never get a rapport if she called him "Mister," and he would probably resent her calling him Larry. She'd reserve that for if things didn't work out.

She started carrying the bags up to the porch, and when he still didn't appear, she carried them through the house to the kitchen. It took several trips and a quick cleaning of the worst messes in the fridge before everything was in its place and there was a place for everything.

She was just brushing out an ancient breadbox when he padded into the kitchen. She almost didn't hear him enter; she'd have to remember that. Very sly.

"What's for dinner?" he asked, and opened the refrigerator door and peered inside.

She started to tell him whatever he was making but she stifled her growing annoyance. She couldn't get a handle on what he was doing. Was he just naturally rude, a bully, and a crotchety old geezer? Or was he trying to wear down her resistance like one of those weird cults or an EST meeting so she would be more responsive to his ideas?

That seemed a bit extreme. All she wanted was some guidance about her photography. No deep metaphysical reckonings.

Or was it?

He was still staring into the fridge.

She nudged him aside. "How about ham and eggs and toast?"

"How about those steaks? Did you buy potatoes?"

She didn't answer but pulled over a rattan basket she'd found under the counter. "Potatoes, onions, garlic."

"Sounds good. Baked, medium rare. Call me when it's ready." He headed for the door.

"Hey!" she called.

He turned, and she saw the glint in his eye before he put on a smile.

"Butter or sour cream?" she asked sweetly.

"Both," he said, and pushed out the door.

Dani grabbed two potatoes from the basket. She had never prided herself on her cooking. It was easier to grab takeout on the way home from a shoot. She could eat internationally anywhere on her block. But she could bake a potato in a pinch, had even learned how to butter the peels first so they got good and crispy.

She put the potatoes in the oven, then uncorked a bottle of wine, found two jelly glasses in a cabinet filled with mismatched mugs and glasses, and poured wine into one of them.

It could breathe while she was drinking it.

She seasoned the steaks, and while they rested, she took a sponge and a spray cleaner that she'd had the foresight to buy at the market and scrubbed off the first few layers of grime from the counters and appliances.

Having lived in the city all her life, she knew the importance of keeping things clean. And being a photographer, she knew the necessity of keeping everything organized and minimal.

Then, since Lawrence hadn't pointed her to an outside grill, she made do with a heavy cast-iron pan and a smoky kitchen.

Dinner went pretty much to plan, including the smoky kitchen, but opening the window helped. While the beans steamed, she searched the cabinets and drawers and found plates and silverware, which she set on the table. She sliced thick wedges of a long loaf of French bread, and was about to call Lawrence to dinner when he strolled through the door and sat down at the table.

She served him his steak and potato, pushed the condiments across the table at him, and served herself.

He was already slicing his steak.

"Shall we say grace?" she asked, her voice dripping syrup.

He glanced up, looked at the cube of meat on his fork, and stuck it in his mouth. "Not bad," he said, chewing.

After that they ate in silence. Dani didn't mind the lack of conversation. She was still trying to figure out what the deal was.

She knew creative people were sometimes bullies, and worse. Was he punishing her for ferreting him out? Why had he kept himself hidden away for so long? He hadn't shown up in any of her Google searches, and she'd searched. Even the Lawrence Sinclair in jail had a Twitter account. Was he trying to drive her away? Then why let her stay in the first place? Maybe she should just leave before it got any weirder.

Then she remembered what he'd said: "One little bump in the road and you're ready to cave."

That must be it. He was her bump in the road, and he was going to make the most of it. She was going to have to fight all the way.

Well, hell, she could do that. She would do that. The stakes were that high.

═

Peter dashed his forearm across his forehead, bounced on his toes, ready for Rashid's serve. He counted on his twice-a-week racquetball bouts to keep him in shape; it took his mind off work, tired him out. Tonight it was doing none of those.

The ball slammed against the wall. Peter lurched toward the rebound and missed.

"Man, what's wrong with you tonight?"

"Sorry." He readied himself to return the next serve. The ball bounced, he moved, managed to return it and clear the floor, but the ball was already bouncing back at him with a crack and the speed of light. He watched it as it flew by.

He breathed a sigh of relief when the hour was finally over.

Rashid clapped him on the back and they walked out of the court together. "Hell, I wish I could take credit for that trounce. What's going on? Wait, I know. Woman trouble."

Peter had just buried his face in his towel, but he looked up at that one.

"No such luck."

"What happed to Natasha?"

"Natalia. She said I didn't fit in with her friends."

"Ouch. Did you want to?"

"Nope. Movers and shakers. Successful, rich, and getting richer."

"What's not to like?"

"I know. She wanted to know the same thing. I fell back on the 'It's not you, it's me' line and that corked it. She agreed with me."

Rashid winced. "You really need to work harder on your relationships and less on your career."

"Maybe. Definitely need to work less at my career."

═

After a shower, followed by a few beers and a burger at the corner bar, Peter turned toward home. It was almost midnight, and with any luck his mother would be in bed. It was absurd that a grown man had to sneak into his own home at night. Of course, most men didn't share their home with their mother. It was a ridiculous situation. Like the rest of his life.

Maybe she'd be in bed by now.

But he'd barely made it to the staircase when his mother's voice sounded from the office.

Peter accepted his fate and went to see what she was saying.

He stopped at the door to his father's study, unchanged since he'd died sixteen years before. As if someday he would be walking through the door again. Something that even his strong-willed mother couldn't accomplish.

She was sitting in the wing chair reading something and looking like she'd been born and bred there. But she wasn't working for her own advancement. She was keeping his father's interests—and Peter's—in firm control.

She looked up and dropped the paper to her lap. "I've been trying to call your grandfather all day; he isn't answering." She finally looked up. "He hasn't answered my emails."

Peter automatically straightened in the doorway. "Maybe he's busy."

"So busy that he can't shoot me a text? He could be dead for all we know. Lying unattended in that old firetrap of a house."

"That old firetrap is the Sinclair family homestead."

"That nobody had lived in for decades until your grandfather did what he did and retired there. I want you to go make sure he's okay."

"Me?" Peter blurted out. "I'm in the middle of the Donovon-Schickley merger disclosures."

"This is company business. Someone in the legal department can cover if anything comes up while you're gone."

She cut him a crosswise look. She would have blitzed right through the holdouts, wrung them up, and had the whole organization trussed up like a Thanksgiving turkey by now. She hadn't practiced law herself for years.

The world had lost a fierce litigator. She could take his place anytime.

"Besides, it's time you made up with your grandfather."

Since when? Peter ordered himself not to react. He knew he was in trouble when his mother started conniving. What was she up to now?

"You will have to deal with him." She paused, looking as

if she had something stuck in her throat. "He's family and he shouldn't grow old alone."

The hell. What was this newfound sympathy? His mother hated her father-in-law. She blamed Lawrence for her husband's death, though Lawrence had nothing to do with Elliott Sinclair insisting on taking the company twin-engine to a meeting in Cleveland even though a storm was approaching. He never made it.

After the funeral, as the family stood graveside, Marian accused Lawrence of murdering her husband and his son. It was a crazy thing to suggest, and yet she delivered the accusation in the quiet, precise manner she was known for, and it was all the more frightening in its control. No one said a word. Even his grandfather was surprised. He'd walked away without a word and cut all personal ties with the family from that moment.

Peter had just stood there as the only person who had let him be himself walked out of his life. And Peter missed him.

"I'm busy this week." If Peter had just gotten an apartment of his own, they wouldn't be having this conversation. It was *his* house, another Sinclair legacy. When he suggested he move out, she insisted that she should be the one to move, then looked so morose that he capitulated. The albatross around his neck.

Something really had to give. No wonder his grandfather had fled as soon as his son was ready to take over. It must skip generations. Because Peter's overriding ambition these days was to get the hell out.

"I'll go this weekend, all right? Though I don't know what you expect me to do. If you're that worried, we could call the local police and have them check the house."

"This weekend, then. Put it on your calendar. I'll tell James you'll be out of the office for a few days."

4

Dani cleaned the kitchen, put the dishes away, and retired to her room, where she found a stack of sheets on the coverlet. She picked them up and took a whiff. Clean; that was a good sign. He must have put them there while she was busy.

She made her bed, opened her laptop, checked her email, then opened her antiques barn folder. *Gems and Junque.* Was there any way to make that title sexy, cutting edge, or even tasteful? The best they could hope for was cute. The thought made her teeth ache.

She sighed, yawned—the next thing she knew, it was morning. At some point she had plugged her laptop into the charger, changed into a nightshirt, and climbed under the covers. She didn't remember any of it. For a brief moment of panic, she was afraid that she'd been drugged by a nutcase, but a turn of the doorknob proved that she was not being held prisoner.

Relieved, she showered and changed into jeans and T-shirt and headed to the kitchen, where she had no doubt she would be expected to make coffee and breakfast.

She was right. The day was sunny, the clock read eight o'clock, and nothing had changed since she'd left the room the night before. She was getting coffee from the cabinet when the back door opened and Lawrence Sinclair strode in, looking bright and energetic and much younger than he'd looked the day before.

Normally sunlight made a subject look older.

"No time for coffee," he said.

Dani considered him. "Does this mean we're going to start my . . . mentoring . . . lessons? Whatever."

He shrugged.

It was maddening. "Why do I feel like you're always laughing at me?"

"I haven't the foggiest. What do you think it is?"

"Could be because you are?"

He shrugged again. His expression was completely guileless. And totally bogus.

"I know what you're doing. You're breaking down my resistance like they do in EST."

"Never heard of it."

"So now I suppose I'll make breakfast, which you'll eat, and then you'll have to take a nap to recover, and then I'll have to make lunch."

"No time for breakfast, either. Better put on some shoes and a long-sleeved shirt. Meet me back here in five minutes."

"Why, what are we doing?"

"Taking a walk," he said, before continuing through the kitchen and out the door to the rest of the house.

Maybe this was it, the beginning of her transformation. Coffee forgotten, she hurried back to her room to change. She didn't dare keep him waiting. He might change his mind. She shoved her feet into sneakers and pulled on a sweatshirt. She slipped her camera case over her head, her travel tripod case over her shoulder, and hurried back to the kitchen.

Since there was no sign of Lawrence she pulled her cell out of her jeans pocket and checked her Instagram and TikTok feeds.

He came in a few minutes later, shrugging into an old corduroy jacket. He was empty-handed.

She slipped her phone back into her pocket and tried not to look too eager.

He flicked a finger toward her tripod.

"You won't need that."

She slid it off her shoulder and put it on the table.

"Or that." He motioned toward her camera.

"But . . ."

He flicked his finger, more sharply this time.

She lifted the strap over her head and put it on the table.

"And that cell phone. Leave them all here. They'll be safe enough."

"I don't understand."

"Surprise, surprise."

"But—"

He yawned. "Or maybe I'll take a nap."

"Okay, okay," she groused, reluctantly adding her cell phone to the other equipment. "But what if one of us falls and can't get up?"

He'd started toward the back door, but he stopped, reached in his jacket pocket. "I'll have this." He flashed his cell before slipping it out of sight.

"Hey, that's not fair."

He didn't answer, but instead of going outside, he turned left down an exterior hallway lined with all sorts of castoffs: waders; fishnets; rakes; old rain ponchos; cast-iron tubs; several bamboo poles, not the fishing kind; old paint cans; haphazardly folded and dusty tarps—all pretty much crusted with dried mud and covered with cobwebs.

She followed, keeping close.

They came to a narrow door that opened onto a thicket of trees. As Dani stepped outside, something darted out in front of her.

She let out a squeak of surprise.

Lawrence merely cast a quick look back at her and struck off through the woods.

"Did you see that?" she asked. "I think it was a fox . . . or a wolf . . . or . . ."

He didn't answer and she hurried after him, sticking close to his heels in case any other feral animals decided to surprise them . . . and hoping that the narrow opening between the trees they were following would soon turn into a well-marked nature path.

Dani wasn't squeamish, though she admitted downtown Manhattan interspersed with trips to the Hamptons or Jones Beach was more her milieu. But she trudged doggedly ahead, wondering where they were going and how soon they would get there.

They were in some kind of forest, heavy with beach brush and bushes and pine trees that rose over her head. Several times she lost sight of Lawrence and hurried ahead, fighting vines and brambles and disturbing a host of flying bugs.

Once, the sleeve of her sweatshirt caught on a mass of brambles, and by the time she fought free, she'd lost sight of him completely. She spun around trying to find the way, but it all looked the same. She had no idea where they might be going or where they had come from.

She was just beginning to panic when his head appeared up ahead and she headed toward him. He was moving so swiftly and easily that she was afraid she would lose sight of him again and find herself completely lost. She was willing to take his abuse, but she wasn't sure she could stand being lost alone in the woods, even if it *was* to teach her some kind of lesson.

And then he was gone again. Damn. She stood perfectly still looking for a glimpse of that white hair, listening for any sound of movement that didn't belong to something feral. The hum she'd noticed earlier was louder now, not an insect or reptile, but she couldn't quite place it, and didn't want to stick around to guess what it might be.

She thrashed forward, swatting away low-lying brush and clinging vines, and was just beginning to get really flustered when she heard voices. She pushed her way through the last of the brush and practically fell into a clearing. She had to blink against the sudden brightness.

At first all she could see was the silhouettes of two figures, but she knew it was Lawrence, and . . . Her eyes gradually made out the other, but she didn't believe it. She blinked again and again.

A nun. A nun in full nun regalia, except for the work boots that stuck out from under her habit.

Okay. There was a rational reason for the appearance of a nun in work boots in the middle of nowhere. Except that it wasn't nowhere. They were standing on a wide lawn. Behind them at the top of a rise was a white wooden house with several wings all protected by a red shingled roof. It was surrounded by a low stone wall opening to a path that led to a gazebo and, farther along, a large picnic pavilion.

And in the distance, a glimpse of the sea.

Dani pulled her gaze back to Lawrence. "Where are we?" she demanded.

The nun just smiled beatifically.

"Just picking up the last of the blueberries." He held up a

wicker basket filled with deep purple berries. "Thought you could make pancakes for breakfast. Saw that you bought bacon yesterday."

Dani didn't miss the nun cut her eyes toward Lawrence, but she didn't say anything to him, and didn't acknowledge Dani except for the smile, which Dani suspected was her natural expression.

Lawrence just nodded to her and passed by Dani before disappearing into the brush again.

Caught by surprise, Dani smiled and nodded at the nun and ran after him.

This time he was traveling on a well-marked, neatly laid-out path. Two minutes later they were standing on the drive of Lawrence's house.

Dani looked back to where they had been, then at Lawrence. "You led me all over creation when we could have just walked straight across to pick up your berries? You could have picked them up yourself while I made coffee."

Lawrence ignored her and walked through the side door and straight into the kitchen.

"I'm covered with scratches and bug bites and—"

"What did you see?"

"What? A nun."

"A nun and what?"

"A nun wearing work boots."

"That's it?"

"And a bunch of irritating green stuff that we could have easily avoided." She frowned at him. "What are you getting at?"

"How many perfect shots did you miss while you weren't seeing anything?"

"I was trying to keep up and figure out what you were doing."

She didn't tell him about the momentary panic she'd felt when she thought he'd left her.

Lawrence did one of those sounds somewhere between a cough and a laugh. "When are you going to give it up?"

Ha, she thought. Now she got it. "You mean how long can you create obstacles before I quit and leave you alone?"

"Wrong. What I mean is when are you going to stop that gerbil wheel that is your brain and start paying attention?"

Heat spread from the pit of her stomach to her cheeks. "You mean that was my photography lesson?"

"What difference does it make? You missed it."

She had missed it. "You could have told me."

"I shouldn't need to."

Dani got down the coffee. She was suddenly too depressed to tell him to get it himself. It was the least she could do. Penance for missing the point. *Penance.*

"You live next door to a nun?"

"Three of them."

"Are they some order that isn't allowed to talk?"

"Only on Wednesdays."

"You're kidding."

"Yep. They live in the world and teach school, what's left of it. Call me when coffee's ready." And he left the kitchen.

She made coffee, even took him a mug. She found him in the study sitting in front of the computer. He clicked out of whatever he was looking at when she entered. Could he be looking at her photographs? She shouldn't flatter herself. And she was glad that she hadn't asked, when he shut a financial register before she approached the desk.

Probably adding her rent money to his monthly account book.

She looked for a place to put down his coffee, but the desk was cluttered with papers and books. She couldn't even pull over one of the small side tables, because they were all cluttered with stuff. Everything had a layer of dust over it.

She hadn't been that aware of it all yesterday when they'd been looking at her photographs, but she was now. How could he live this way? Didn't he have family? Social services? Hell, weren't nuns supposed to take care of the needy?

She was surprised by the pang of sympathy she felt. Old and alone and willing to take on a stranger because he needed money and was too proud to charge her for his knowledge.

Which, she reminded herself, *he has yet to impart.*

"Do you ever dust or pick up things?"

He looked around, frowned, and pushed a stack of papers aside to make room for his coffee.

"Why don't you hire a housekeeper? No. Never mind, no one in their right mind would take the job."

He tapped the desk where he'd cleaned it off.

She put down the mug. "You know, if I weren't such a nice person, you might be wearing this coffee instead of drinking it." And she stomped off to the kitchen to make his breakfast.

Cooking wasn't something she would want to do full-time, but there was something satisfying about it. She hardly ever made food at home. Well, her kitchen in lower Manhattan was about as big as the kitchen table here. And her pots and pans were ancient, dented and stained, mainly handed down or picked up from junk stores like Ye Old Antiques Barn.

Actually, she was kind of enjoying this, Dani thought as she poured water into the bowl of "complete" pancake mix. There was maple syrup in the fridge on a door shelf with a half bottle of ketchup. At least the syrup was real. And the handful of berries she tasted were sweet and succulent.

Lawrence's pans were even older than hers. She fried bacon in the same cast-iron pan she'd cooked the steaks in and found a griddle with a round wooden handle that would be perfect for the pancakes.

She folded the berries into the batter. Then went about pouring and flipping and heating the syrup, until the table was set, the bacon was draining on paper towels, and the pancakes were stacked high and sitting in a low oven to keep warm.

She went to get Lawrence.

They once again ate in silence, but Dani thought it was companionable silence. A notion that she quickly readjusted when Lawrence pushed his plate away—having eaten two stacks of pancakes and half a dozen slices of bacon—and said, "I've been thinking."

Dani stopped chewing. Was this the moment when things changed?

"I think you're right. My office is a mess. It could use some tender loving dusting. You'll find some furniture polish under the sink." He pushed his chair away and headed for the door.

Dani put down her fork. She could feel the steam coming out of her ears. "I know what you're doing."

He slowly turned, the same guileless expression on his face. Which would have earned him a good smack if he were a younger man.

"It's the wax-on-wax-off thing, isn't it?"

"You don't have to wax, just dust."

"I'm not talking about wax."

"You just said—"

"I know but I meant like *The Karate Kid*."

"Never heard of him. Is he one of your avant-garde downtown postconceptual artists?"

Dani snorted a laugh in spite of herself. "No. I mean the movie with Pat Morita."

"Don't know him, either."

"Didn't you ever go to the movies?"

"I got Netflix. You know, instead of waxing you might take a mop to the wood floor. There's some Pine-Sol in the broom closet."

She gave him a look. "Don't push it." But she was no longer annoyed. She remembered that movie, even if Lawrence didn't.

By the time she'd finished cleaning the kitchen, she'd ignored two calls from Manny and a text from the gallery about a recent sale.

She didn't want to deal with either of them, even though she knew an artist of any kind had to take care of business, figuratively and literally, if she wanted to stay a working artist.

But instead of going to her bedroom, making those calls, and dealing with the prints she needed to finish for the *Gems* pitch, she retrieved an old canister of spray polish from under the sink; found the broom closet and got out a mop, several dust rags, and a bottle of Pine-Sol; and carried them into Lawrence's office.

The desk had been cleared of the ledger and most of the papers.

In case she thought about snooping? She smiled devilishly. He knew her so well. But she took a dust cloth and some spray polish and attacked the first surface. Occasionally, the photographic work she should be doing snagged her attention, and she would dust faster and more energetically until it receded into her mental to-do list.

One thing she'd already learned . . . Lawrence was right about her gerbil-wheel mind. Thoughts were popping around all over the place: ideas, to-do lists, favorite lines from recent reviews, grievances over the bad ones, imaginary arguments she would have or should have had with other artists, some with acid personalities and backstabbing tendencies. Her mind was a receptacle for every stray bit of detritus that passed by.

She studied the table she had just polished, returned a couple of books that had been placed there. Rearranged them to make a better shot.

Stopped. There was a lesson there. She just didn't know what it was. Maybe always seeing things in terms of a shot. But wasn't that the way photographers thought, anyway? They were always looking for an interesting subject among the passing humanity, like authors were always looking for a story from overheard conversations or ordinary places.

She wanted to ask Lawrence about it, but he would probably just give her that oh-God-please-save-me-from-this-stupid-girl look he had, and anyway, she'd heard him climb the stairs earlier; he was probably napping.

She had finished cleaning the office and was admiring her handiwork and basking in her sense of accomplishment while she rubbed her aching back. With everything dusted and cleaned and put in place, the room almost looked like it might have once been fairly grand.

She yawned. Today alone had been pretty tiring, and she'd been going nonstop since July. She wouldn't mind a nap herself.

There was a faint crackling, then a disembodied voice that seemed to come from the wall.

She looked quickly around and found the source. There was an intercom system.

"Yes, Lawrence?"

"Do we have any popcorn?"

"As a matter of fact . . ."

"Bring it up and a couple of sodas. Second door on the right."

Okay, that did it. She didn't mind doing her share of waxing on and off, if she got to learn something for it. But she sure as heck didn't see how popcorn could possibly fit into the lesson.

But since he'd signed off before she could say no, she went to the kitchen to microwave the popcorn.

And he did say bring up a couple of sodas. Surely he meant her to have one and not drink them both himself. Maybe she had proved her seriousness by feeding him and cleaning for him. She poured the popcorn into a bowl, stuck a bottle of cola under each arm, and carried it all upstairs.

The hallway, poorly lit and dusty like most of the house, seemed to stretch forever, but the second door on the right was ajar, so she toed it open and went inside.

She was met with delighted laughter. He was sitting on a plush leather couch in front of a giant-screen television and watching—

"I love this movie," he said. "Wax on, wax off. Brilliant. I wish I had thought of that. Sit down. You want me to start over?" He pressed Rewind, and Daniel and Miyagi sped in a comic retrograde until Lawrence stopped it at the opening credits.

"Hand me the popcorn."

They watched the movie twice. At some point Dani went down for cheese and crackers, and Lawrence brought out a bottle of wine.

By the time Dani cried off from a third time through, she was stiff, her back ached, and her arms stung from where she'd been scratched by the jungle that surrounded the house. It seemed like an eternity ago.

She left Lawrence watching the fight scene "just one more time" and managed to get the dishes to the kitchen, where she left them in the sink. She took a quick shower and fell into bed without even looking at her emails or checking her cell.

She slept soundly until the next morning and awoke to an overcast sky. She was tempted to just lie in bed, but the banging of pots and pans had her padding to the kitchen to see what the noise was. Lawrence was kneeling before the cabinet pulling everything out.

"What are you doing?"

"Making breakfast."

5

Except for Lawrence cooking, breakfast was pretty much the same as the other meals, neither of them talking, just concentrating on the food and thinking their own thoughts. At least Dani was thinking hers. Since occasionally a smile played on Lawrence's mouth, she assumed he was reliving the movie. And it didn't take a great leap to realize that she could expect more chores coming her way.

Lawrence wasn't the best cook, but it was edible, and Dani could feel that something had changed. Whether it was the movie or Lawrence cooking, there was definitely a new level of comfort between them.

Maybe it was just time passing and getting used to each other's presence. Maybe it was laughing together as they had over the movie.

Dani did the dishes; she didn't wait to see if he expected her to do them. He'd cooked, she'd clean—a team. At least in her mind. Training moved in both directions.

He didn't leave the kitchen but sat with a final cup of coffee. Was he watching her? She didn't turn around to see. She didn't ask any of the questions she was dying to ask. Not about photography, but about him. Why had he stopped taking photographs, or at least showing them? Why had he retired to this monstrous old house to live alone? Had it been that way for the last fifty years?

What had he done in between? Was it her tenacity or pure dumb luck that had led her here?

Either way, she was here and she was going to make the most of it.

It started raining in earnest, and Dani thought that maybe being stuck indoors, they might get into the photography part of the mentorship, but as she returned the dry cloth to the peg beneath the sink, he said, "Did you bring a raincoat? Boots?"

Dani shook her head as a sinking feeling crept over her.

"Huh," he said, and left the room.

Reprieved, she hurried back to her room. Manny had called three times during the movie last night and again this morning, each message getting a little more hysterical. She absolutely had to make him understand that she needed a little more time. So she missed a few parties, nothing important.

She depended on Manny. He'd lifted her above the other talented photographers and carefully set up her career path, until he deposited her right on top. But she knew it was up to her to keep her success coming.

Product. That's what it was, no matter what medium—art, writing, film, photography. Once it left the creator's hands, it became product.

She texted Manny to call her.

Her cell rang before she even opened her laptop.

"What have you got for me?"

Just the rejects that I didn't send with the first batch. "A few shots. Not totally chill with them, though."

"Send them. I'll be the judge."

She'd anticipated his reaction; she had a folder ready to be emailed. "Will do."

"So are you on your way home?"

"No. I told you. I'm taking a couple of weeks." Hopefully that would be long enough.

"You said a couple of days."

"Selective hearing, Manny."

"You have to be here for the Five X Five gala next Friday. It's your big night. You're heads above the other four. But you miss it and it's a career killer. Capisce?"

"Yes, Manny. Don't worry. I won't let you down. I'll be there."

"Looking expensively outrageous. I'm going to try and get the perfume people there."

"Will do."

"Don't burn out on me, Dani. We've both worked too hard."

Dani flinched, the sick feeling that she was coming to recognize twisting her gut. "I'm not burning out. Actually, I'm working on a new project."

"Why didn't you say so? Great. Give me a hint."

"Later, Manny. Gotta go." She closed the call, dragged a folder to her email, and pressed Send. Then she closed her laptop, determined to wax on and wax off until she was ready to work with her photos again.

Since it was raining, no doubt Lawrence would have some gargantuan housecleaning project. So when he knocked on her door a bit later, she wasn't surprised. But when she opened the door, it was another story.

He was carrying several pairs of rubber boots, which he shoved at her. "See if any of these fit. They're pretty old but they didn't disintegrate when I picked them up so they may keep out some of the water."

So they were going outside. In the rain. Hopefully not to clean the gutters.

"Don't you have any looser jeans?"

Dani looked down at her jeans. "They stretch."

He didn't look convinced.

"A lot." She did several squats while he looked wary.

"Meet me in the kitchen."

"I don't have a raincoat."

"Meet me in the kitchen." He backed out and shut the door.

She glanced longingly at her camera, grabbed a hoodie, knowing it wouldn't keep out the elements for long, then rooted among the Wellies until she found a pair that were only a couple of sizes too big and wondered who they had belonged to. Not Lawrence.

At the last minute, she slipped her phone in her pocket. By the time she reached the kitchen, she'd come to her senses and put the phone on the table.

Lawrence wasn't there, but she heard him rummaging around in the back hallway.

"Aha," he said as she came up behind him. He held up a yellow slicker that looked like it would hold two or three of her, and thrust it out.

"Shake it for spiders," he suggested.

Dani took it between two fingers and gave it a shake.

"Really?"

"Okay, okay." She shook the poncho vigorously, didn't see anything scurrying away; still, she held it open and studied the inside more closely.

"I think it's safe," Lawrence said, pulling another, dark green poncho from a peg and slipping it over his head. He was wearing black Wellingtons that seemed to fit him perfectly.

He strode down the hall and out the door. Dani slipped the hood over her head, hoping nothing was still hiding there, and hurried after him.

She was met with an onslaught of needle-fine rain.

She immediately ducked her head. And caught herself. There was a reason they were out here. It was a test. She looked up and let the rain drench her face.

"Come on," Lawrence ordered. "I'm getting wet."

Jolted out of her momentary exhilaration, she snapped back. "I thought I was supposed to—"

"No thinking."

The gerbil wheel, right. Easier said than done.

They didn't stop until they were past the tall beach shrubs and in the pine forest, where the sound of falling rain was muted by the leaves above them. And the air was so alive it felt raw—not old, just amazingly *there.*

And a thought rose up to ridicule her. *Rain. How can I make it more than itself? Rain but not rain. Rain as something else. More shocking, more ironic, more everything. More. More. More—* She slammed down on the thought and glanced over to where Lawrence had sat down on a decaying log. He turned his head away, but too late.

She was afraid that he could read her thoughts, and was embarrassed for them.

Then he looked back and patted the place on the log next to him.

She clomped over in her too-big Wellies and sat down, not sure if it was rain on her face or tears.

She was suddenly tired. Tired of being cutting edge, of being the wunderkind, tired of not knowing where she was. She sure hoped that this was her making a breakthrough and not her burning out.

They sat there for the longest time, at least it seemed that way to Dani, who never took time, who was always rushing. She tried not to be impatient. Ordered herself to relax. And to see, just see.

She looked around, took note of the slickness of the wet leaves, the branches heavy with the water's weight. Even the tips of her rain boots as they squished into the soggy turf. Was this what she was supposed to do? It didn't seem like it could go anywhere.

She let out a long breath, dogged by the vague sense that she was failing.

She wanted to shake the man sitting beside her. Make him tell her what she was doing wrong. Instead, she kept saying her new mantra—no longer "Fake it till you make it," but "Wax on, wax off"—and wondered if she would ever truly understand.

"It isn't about control," Lawrence said finally, his voice shattering the fragile air between them.

"I feel like I'm never in control. Except in my photos that have no soul."

He raised an eyebrow. Comment, or inviting her to continue?

"So . . . control is bad?" she guessed.

He cracked a laugh.

"It isn't bad?"

His whole forehead lifted.

"I saw that same expression on Pat Morita in the movie last night," she said, crossing her arms.

"It's going to start raining again. What's for lunch?" He pushed to his feet.

"We just had breakfast. Why don't you help me? I'm drowning here."

"Didn't rain that much. Come on."

"Where are we going?"

"Why do you think you should know everything in advance?" He started walking back the way they had come. He didn't look back to see if she was coming. He didn't seem to care.

"Why did you stop taking pictures?"

His step didn't even hesitate, as if he hadn't heard her question. Maybe he hadn't. He just kept walking, and she scrambled up and went after him.

By the time she reached the house, there was no sign of Lawrence. She shrugged out of her outerwear and tossed the Wellies by the wall with the other junk. Then she went straight to the kitchen and picked up her phone.

Manny had texted her twice. Left a voicemail. Must have plenty to say. She listened to it.

"Talked to the perfume people. They're interested. Possible June fashion spread. Big bucks, lots of traffic. So chop, chop." The call ended.

She should really just get some work done, if only to get Manny off her back, and she did have commitments. Something Lawrence Sinclair didn't seem to understand.

She went into her bedroom to get her laptop, but when she got there she hesitated. Her "soulless" photography was inside. What if she opened it and all the bad artistic decisions she'd ever made came flying out like she'd opened Pandora's box? Lawrence didn't want her working on the computer; he'd made that clear. But what did he know? He'd stopped photographing before there was a digital age; maybe he was just too old to understand what she was doing.

And that was a total lie. She didn't even know what she was doing. But Lawrence had known what he was doing—one look at his photos told her everything except how to make it hers.

Around noon, she called Lawrence, but when he didn't come down, she climbed the stairs. There was no sound coming from the den. She hadn't been in the other rooms; she didn't know which one was his, but she was loathe to explore.

She went back downstairs, made herself a sandwich, another for Lawrence that she wrapped up and put in the fridge.

She sat at the table long after she finished her sandwich; watched as the sun came out and brightened the kitchen counters. Finally she went back into the foyer and called up the stairs. And had to finally admit . . . Lawrence was gone.

═

"Just what are you up to?" Sister Mary Catherine, sitting with her hands folded peacefully in her lap, gave Lawrence a look he remembered well. They had grown up together at the local elementary school, when she was Lorna Anderson and most people called him Ren. Funny how clear those memories were, when the nearer ones were often covered in fog.

Today they sat on a bench overlooking the sea. The bench straddled the property line between the convent and the Sinclair estate, but no one had ever thought to move it. The sun was shining, and Lawrence felt like leaning back and lifting his face to its warmth. It would be fall soon, then winter, when the cold would surround them and creep into his bones.

"Lawrence? Who is that young woman?"

"Her name is Dani Campbell. She showed up at my door a few days ago. Looking for . . . me. She'd seen some of my old photographs in an antiques place and decided she had to find me. Told me that she was a photographer and she needed to get what I had."

Sister Mary Catherine smiled that all-seeing, blessed-by-God smile that even after all these years could still irritate him. "Smart young woman."

"That business will devour her."

"It wasn't *that* business that devoured you."

"Touché."

"It wasn't the other one, either."

"I know, I know. But spare this old carcass, please. It's too late for me."

"I believe that it is never too late—for any of us."

Lawrence sighed. "How did we get so old?"

"Speak for yourself, my dear."

Dear Mary Catherine, covered from head to toe in fabric, winter and summer. Most nuns had moved into modern times, relinquishing the old ways for sensible clothing.

But not Mary Catherine's order. He couldn't imagine what she might look like beneath hers. He remembered her as a skinny, freckled girl with big teeth and slightly bowed legs, and wearing hand-me-downs from her sister Olga. These days she had her mother's plump face, the rosy cheeks that spoke of just having pulled a pie out of the oven, and blue eyes that startled you with their understanding and love.

"Did you ever fight with your mother?" Lawrence asked.

"Where did that come from?"

"I don't know. Just wondering."

"All the time. What girl didn't? But not about what I chose to do with my life. Not that. She understood."

"I never understood why you chose the convent."

"I was called. It was too strong to resist. You should understand that."

"Photography isn't a religion."

"It was once . . . to you."

He shook his head. "Do you ever regret your choice?"

She smiled, a little wider this time. "Only on the days when it's my turn to scrub the sacristy stairs. And it's over as soon as I stand up again."

He smiled back at her. It was strange having your best childhood friend grow up to be a nun. And a nun next door. Since first grade, they had planned to grow up and get married, which went out the window in high school when she was sent to the Catholic girls' school and he was sent to a prep school near Boston.

"You're in an odd mood today. Is it because of this young woman? About what people will say?"

"What could they possibly say? I'm old enough to be her grandfather."

"True."

"Though I still have a certain je ne sais quoi."

"You do, and if you ever came out of that musty old house, people could appreciate it more. But that is a subject for another day. What do you intend for her?"

"I intended to send her on her way. In fact I did. She just refused to leave."

"I supposed you used your full armory of standoffishness."

"And more."

"It didn't seem to work."

"She threatened to stay in town. I told her all the hotels closed after Labor Day. Then she said she would live with me. And offered me rent money."

From the movement of the sister's robes, that had set off a laugh.

"I tripled the price and she said yes. It was absolutely insane. Then I made the mistake of looking at her website—not her actual photos, she doesn't actually print them, mind you. I figured, what harm could it do? I would look at them, insult her in the nicest possible way"—he heard Sister Mary Catherine snort—"and send her home."

"Lawrence Sinclair. You wouldn't be so cruel."

"Well, I would. I was. And it didn't faze her in the least. I think she feels sorry for me. And no comment, please. I've made her put away her electronics, sent her out for groceries, which she paid for, made her cook and clean.

"She did it all. Not without a fair amount of back talk and grousing. She caught on right away what I was doing. Only I didn't know I was doing it."

"Sounds intriguing," Sister Mary Catherine said, shifting slightly toward him to give him her full attention.

"Wax on, wax off."

"Ah. The beauty and selflessness of hard work—and art."

Lawrence frowned at her. "Sort of. I can't really explain it . . ."

"Lord bless us. Is it possible that He, in His wisdom, has sent this young woman to teach you a lesson?"

"I'm afraid not. I am, as they say, past praying for." He ignored the small shake of her head. "But this girl, this young woman. I don't know. She has talent. A raw, instinctual, but undeveloped eye. And the intelligence to realize she's missing something. But who the hell—sorry—who am I to mess with that talent?"

"You have much to teach."

"About what not to do with your life, maybe. About photography? What if she takes my advice and it kills any chance of her succeeding?"

═

Dani decided to start dusting the parlor, mainly to keep herself from opening her laptop and falling back into her old habits. And also to keep from thinking about Lawrence and his opinions. She understood what he was doing and she was trying to keep up her side of the unspoken bargain. But it was frightening.

She knew that in the photography business, it was not just out of sight, out of mind, but out of sight, let me take your job and badmouth you to everyone who will listen while you're gone and even after you return. Even though it had been only a few days, she felt it calling to her, demanding her presence. Manny was beside himself, like a week—or two—off was unheard of. It was. Careers could come and go in a matter of weeks. They were both making good money. They were riding high . . . This was no time for her to falter. And yet . . .

She rubbed the dust cloth over the last little table. She didn't really understand why people in old houses had so much furniture. She had just polished five tables and dusted the lamps and stuff that they held. She'd plumped the cushions of the old horsehair couch as well as a club chair and two wingback chairs that faced the empty hearth. One look at the sooty mess in the fireplace and she merely pulled a brass screen in front of it and put off that job until another day.

She paused to scan the room, decided that she'd barely made a dent in what it needed.

A noise screeched from somewhere in the quiet room. It took Dani a minute to realize it was a telephone. Not a cell, but a landline, one that rang with a sirenlike intensity that jangled her nerves. It rang again.

She stood waiting for it to end. Hoping Lawrence had come back and would answer it. But no such luck.

It kept ringing. What if it was an emergency? What if something had happened to Lawrence and they were attempting to get in touch with her?

She spun in a circle, trying to locate the source of the sound. She didn't remember seeing a phone.

When it rang again, she pinpointed the direction it was coming from. Now she prayed it kept ringing long enough for her to answer. She found it under several days' worth of the *New York Times* that were stacked on a table next to the club chair.

Dani glanced over her shoulder, hoping that Lawrence would appear. Which he didn't.

What the hell. She picked it up. Took a breath. "Sinclair residence," she said in her toitiest voice.

"Who is this?" snapped the voice at the other end. A man's voice. A nice baritone—or it would be if he wasn't so bossy.

"This is the Sinclair residence," she repeated, pulling the snobbery up a notch. And they said millennials had no manners.

"I'd like to talk to Lawrence Sinclair."

"May I ask who is calling." It was a question, but Dani spit it out like a demand. When he didn't answer right away, she began to worry. What if Lawrence didn't want to talk to him? He probably never answered his phone. What if it was a bill collector? Or the electric company threatening to turn off their lights? Or the IRS?

He sounded too young to be a friend.

"I'm sorry, Mr. Sinclair is not available. May I take a message?" She probably shouldn't have asked that.

"No!" snapped the other voice. Petulant—and cranky. Maybe he *was* the tax man.

"Who did you say you were again?" he asked.

Typical scammer tactics. Or worse. "I didn't."

"I didn't know there was anyone living there besides my—besides Mr. Sinclair."

Oh jeez, what did she say now? She was still holding her dust rag; she snapped it in the air. "I'm the cleaning lady."

"The cleaning lady," he repeated. He didn't sound convinced.

"Yes, and I'll get in trouble if I'm found lollygagging on the phone." Dani grinned. She'd always wanted to use that word but never found the right occasion. Until now. It sounded just like a cleaning lady. At least the ones in the movies. She'd never had a cleaning lady herself. "Guess it's too late to add a Cockney accent," she mumbled.

"Pardon me?"

"I have to get hopping. You'll have to call back later. Good day." She hung up. Stood holding her breath, waiting for the phone to start ringing again. After a minute or two of silence, she breathed a sigh of relief and dropped into the club chair. That was the last time she'd answer the phone, and she'd tell Lawrence so when he came home.

6

Peter stared at his cell. She'd hung up on him. Lawrence's cleaning lady had hung up on him. He started to call back. Stopped.

Exchanged his cell for a pen and tapped it a few times on his desk.

His grandfather must have picked her up in the village. No service would tolerate that kind of attitude from one of its employees.

She didn't even sound like a cleaning lady. She sounded young and brassy and full of it. He smiled. Even though he was still pissed over the call, there was something about her that just made him smile. She'd bounced from Nob Hill to Beantown without a hitch, keeping him totally off-balance.

And she'd hung up on him. Of course, he hadn't identified himself. He'd felt strange about announcing his name and relationship to a stranger. He and his grandfather had never completely lost touch, but they rarely saw each other. When they did meet, it was usually during one of those awkward business meetings that were absolutely necessary for the firm. His mother refused to look him in the face, and Lawrence left immediately when the meeting was adjourned, both going their separate ways and leaving Peter, as always, caught in the middle, trapped between her anger and his grandfather's remoteness.

And this was exactly what he didn't need. He needed to be concentrating on his work. He needed to be looking for an apartment, a townhouse maybe.

He would do it. He'd drive down and see what the hell was up, make his mother happy, maybe even ask his grandfather for advice—and definitely check out the cleaning lady.

There was something about her that made him uneasy. But she also made him smile. He wondered what she looked like and how Lawrence had ever convinced her to work for him.

He marched down to his mother's office, something James had insisted she keep since she was a "member" of the company and family.

She was on the phone, so he waited at the door until she motioned him in.

As soon as she ended the call, he said, "I called Lawrence."

A momentary silence. "And?"

"He wasn't there."

"He just didn't answer."

"His cleaning lady answered."

"What? Cleaners do not answer phones."

"Evidently, Gran— Lawrence's cleaning lady does."

"What did she say?"

"That he wasn't in and would I like to leave a message." That betraying smile forced its way to his lips. "Then she hung up on me."

"And you're amused by that? I'll make sure she's fired immediately."

"Mother, she's not your responsibility."

"She is now. What if she's robbing him blind? She could be carrying out antiques by the carload, and he wouldn't even notice."

She might be, Peter thought. She sounded tough, though not criminal, and had a sense of humor—nobody had used "lollygagging" since the thirties. "What, Mother? Sorry."

"I said, what did she sound like?"

Not like a cleaning lady, he had to admit, but not to his mother.

"What do you mean?" he asked as another thought entered his head. He was almost certain it had entered his mother's.

It had. "Who's to say she's not some gold digger out to bleed him dry?"

She hadn't sounded like a gold digger, either.

"I'll put my people on it, but you'd better drive down right away."

"You have spies on him?"

"Not spies, informational staff."

"Call them off. If there is a problem, I'll take care of it." And that's when Peter realized he was sitting in an office discussing affairs and his eyes were wide open; the rest of him buzzed with interest. And he hadn't yawned once.

═

It was dusk before Dani heard Lawrence return. She'd just climbed down from the stepladder where she'd been dusting the top of the breakfront when Lawrence strode through the archway.

"About time you showed up. Somebody called while you were gone."

"Did you answer it?"

"Yep."

"Ah, I should have told you to let all calls go to voicemail."

"I didn't know if you had voicemail."

"I don't actually. Just don't answer next time. Who was it?"

"Not a clue; he didn't give his name. Where have you been? The only reason I even bothered answering it was because I was imagining you having an I've-fallen-and-I-can't-get-up moment and this was a cry for help."

His mouth twisted, and she was afraid she'd hurt his feelings. Then he coughed out air, a sound that Dani was beginning to recognize as his laugh.

"What did he want?"

"He didn't say; just asked to speak to you, then asked who I was."

"What did you tell him?"

"That you were not available and I was the cleaning lady."

"You are something else."

"Well, I didn't know who he was and it was none of his business. I was afraid he might be the tax man."

"Good girl."

Dani rolled her eyes.

"Did you bring any hard copies of your photos?"

"What?" She was so astonished at the non sequitur that she didn't answer at first. "Yes" finally came out, as she held her breath, hoping he would ask to see them.

"The original photos?"

"Uh . . . I think so. A few, but I also have them in the cloud."

"Bring them up to the den if you're not too busy." He nodded to her dust cloth.

"I just finished. At least, what I can do without several gallons of paint and a crew of six."

She caught the sudden gleam in his eye.

"Oh no. No painting. I'll get my stuff." She gathered up her cleaning supplies and hauled them off to the broom closet.

"No hurry," he called after her.

She hurried anyway, afraid that he might change his mind before she could retrieve them.

She grabbed her laptop, her portfolio, and a cardboard box. Congratulating herself on her last-minute idea to include the shoebox of old photos she stored in her closet, she ran up the stairs to the den.

The door was ajar. Lawrence was sitting at a long oak table set against a row of heavy drapes. There were two rectangular work lights placed at each end. She'd spent hours in that room the night before and hadn't even known there was a table there, the rest of the room had been so dark.

Hugging her bundle, she slipped inside, pushed her butt against the door to close it, and crossed to the table, where she stood waiting.

He glanced up. "Well? I can't really see them if you don't take them out."

She slid the laptop onto the table and unzipped the portfolio to reveal a large, slick notebook with her logo on the front; very high-end, very forward-looking, very so not anything she was feeling right now. She slid it across to him, fighting the urge to pull it back and tell him she wasn't ready.

But he pulled the portfolio away from her.

"These are mainly just copies of larger works. And these are just intended as a sort of catalogue for presenters, like a—"

"Be quiet."

She snapped her mouth shut.

"You would try the patience of a saint."

But you're no saint, are you? "Sorry."

He flipped quickly through the book, then pushed it aside.

The gesture stung. Why had he told her to bring them up if he wasn't going to look at them properly?

"What's in the box?"

"Some prints. I sometimes like to go back to the actual print to get a fresh take and . . . you know . . . the nuances that you don't always get on-screen."

"Hallelujah," he mumbled, and reached out his hand again. This time he didn't bother to look up.

He was staring down at what? The desk, the wood, his lap? He couldn't meet her eyes for some reason?

Dani lifted the box, but was reluctant to relinquish it to his outstretched hand.

"Some of them are really old; I didn't know what I was doing exactly. But I keep them for old times' sake."

He pushed her professional portfolio out of the way and dumped the old photos onto the desktop.

"They're RAW images," Dani explained. "I mean they were photographed digitally but with—"

"I know what RAW is. I haven't been living in a cave for the last . . . some odd years."

He could have fooled her. The whole room was dark except right around the long table. Last night the only light had been the flicker of the television. Today she couldn't even see it in the gloom. There were heavy drapes behind him, but they probably wouldn't help now. The light had started to fade an hour ago.

"They were just taken in the moment."

He gave her such a quelling look that she gulped down her next words of explanation and excuses.

He was frowning at one of the photos, but she couldn't see which. She eased closer to get a better look. But he brushed her back again. She moved to the end of the table and watched as he spread the loose photos around like they were cards in a game of Concentration.

It seemed she stood there for hours, but it was probably a half hour before he dropped his latest perusal to the table and looked at her directly.

"Why did you want to become a photographer?"

Dani was struck dumb. She shrugged. "I just did."

"I can't teach you anything as long as you keep evading the truth."

"What truth? What is the truth? I don't know why I did. Is this a trick question?"

Lawrence held up a copy of one of her latest gallery exhibits.

Dani leaned over to look closely at the shot. She remembered the day she'd taken it. The first of spring, sunny, but still with a chill in the air. It was a pretty standard shot, the reflection of a woman and a goose in a Central Park pond that she'd stretched and compressed until it had wrapped itself into an orb, like the earth. Only nestled in caramel corn—the prize in a box of Cracker Jacks. She saw now she could have taken it even further.

He didn't say more but rummaged through the box of RAWs until he found its first-generation mate. He slapped it down on the table next to its final incarnation.

"I look at this and I can tell your mind is already somewhere else." He tapped the original. "There was a picture here, a story, a connection. You came close but you missed it. Didn't you?"

Dani bit her lip. She'd thought she'd made it even more than it was.

"Maybe you were just hungry and were thinking about where to have lunch, but my guess is you were probably thinking about how you could make it better, even as you were taking the shot. Add this, stretch, manipulate, and obfuscate, and fancy it up until people are 'wowed.'"

She'd thought it was pretty darn clever until now. "It got

good reviews. Even a photo in *American Photographer. They* were wowed."

"So you take pictures to wow people?"

"No—I . . . I just took it, okay?"

"Sure. Go home and be happy." He started gathering up the photos.

"Wait. What did I miss?"

He didn't answer, but riffled through the photos in the box. Chose several four-by-sixes from her earliest years.

"Those are just my first tries. I keep them just to remind myself where I came from." She didn't add, *In case I have to go back there and run a bar for a living.*

"And these are what give me hope," he said enigmatically. "They were taken with a good camera."

"A Nikon D60. I didn't really know how to use it. Someone left it in the bar one night. My parents own a neighborhood bar in Brooklyn. We posted notices but they never came back for it, so my dad let me keep it but only until someone claimed it. No one ever did."

"So you started taking pictures."

"Yeah. It just seemed like a cool thing to do. I was twelve and, you know, not such a great age. It was an expensive camera, a digital so I didn't have to buy film or anything. I started fooling around with it and, well, then it just became something I did."

"At twelve?"

"Well, yeah."

"You took this at twelve?" He showed her a print of a building or something, she couldn't remember. "Around then, I guess." And then a thrill effervesced up her spine. "I do remember. That's a detail of the city court building. I was waiting for a bus and I just turned and saw this candy wrapper caught on the corner of the building. And I took a picture of it. Huh." She looked at it for a long while, kind of impressed that her preteen self had caught the angles and shadows and the way they rose upward out of frame, and folded out onto the sidewalk while the wrapper clung to the building's edge.

"Did this wow your friends?"

Dani thought back; she couldn't really remember her friends. She knew she'd had them. They were always making fun of her for taking pictures.

"They thought I was weird. They weren't all that great. I guess I wasn't that great of a friend, either. I spent more time with the camera than with them. But it was all I needed."

He just looked at her, waiting. Waiting for her to get to where she should go, even if she didn't know where that was.

"Things just made sense through the lens. You know?"

Lawrence slowly nodded.

"Everything. Everything I saw around me made sense. That's what I saw in your photographs in the antiques barn, wasn't it? I saw them and they made sense. They didn't wow me, like mine wow people, they just made sense, and I knew that I wasn't making sense anymore."

"Because you stopped looking."

Dani's breath caught. "Did I? I did. I've been trying to get it back, but I can't seem to—it's the gerbil wheel, isn't it? I'm taking a shot and I'm already planning on what to do with it. What gallery will show it. Who they can sell it to. What am I going to do? If I stop doing this, I won't have a career. Then what will I do? I don't want to work in my parents' bar."

Lawrence inhaled and expelled a long, jaw-cracking yawn. "So close," he said and began gathering up the photos again.

Dani stretched out her hand and grabbed his wrist to prevent him from giving up on her. It was bony and sharp. She could see the pink of his scalp through the fine strands of hair.

"Don't give up on me. I'll figure it out. Just show me what I have to do and if I have to pull beer to do it, I will." Because she couldn't go on doing what she was doing the way she was doing it. It wasn't just imposter syndrome. Her current photos were a fragile house of cards. One breath and . . .

"I don't want to be a fake!"

"What?" Lawrence's voice came to her from far away. He was irritated? Impatient? He knew, and he was finished with her.

"Fake!" she yelled, panic rising in her throat. Was the man hard of hearing?

"You're really the tax man?"

"Stop it. It isn't funny."

"No, it isn't, it's absurd." Lawrence shut down the computer screen and gathered up the prints. It was such a final gesture, Dani reeled on her feet. "Don't send me away! I'll try harder!"

Lawrence pushed to his feet. "God almighty, Mother of— Sorry, Mary Catherine, but this girl—" He scowled at Dani. "You're not a fake, but you can be pretty damn annoying. I don't want you to try harder. I don't want you to try at all. I just want you to look. Only look with your innocent eye. C'mon. I'll make us some sandwiches." He started across the room.

"But my photos."

"They're not going to get up and walk out the door. Hurry up. I'm working up an appetite with all this high drama."

Dani glanced at her life's work, abandoned on the table. Looked back at the man who held her future and who was opting for making sandwiches. She wouldn't be able to eat a thing. But she wasn't about to let him go without her.

She descended the stairs behind him, slowing her pace to

match his. And realized that in the brief time she'd been here, she'd forgotten that he was an old man. He was bright and agile and interesting. But she had to make herself not add . . . *for an old dude.*

He sat her down at the kitchen table and made peanut butter and jelly sandwiches. They'd be out of bread soon, she thought. She'd have to go to the store again. Her stomach rumbled.

Well, it couldn't be too bad if she was hungry, right? Or maybe that sound was just the acid eating her stomach lining.

He slid one of the sandwiches in front of her before sitting down across from her.

The silence grew. She was getting used to it. She was almost afraid that he would say something and it would be *I can't help you. You'll have to go.* And she realized that, except for Manny's worried calls and texts, she hadn't thought about her life in New York at all.

There was something she should be getting out of that realization, but tonight she was too tired. Too raw. Too . . . scared to sort it all out. Didn't know if it was even worth sorting out.

And somehow her sandwich disappeared, and the glass of seltzer he'd served was empty.

Lawrence stood up. "I'll clean up."

"You used paper plates," she pointed out, but with half the enthusiasm his inanities usually aroused.

"Huh. Tomorrow we'll find out if you're a genuine fake, or just got lost in your own cleverness. Now, go to bed."

Dani stood, too. "You can't deliver a zinger like that and expect me to sleep."

"If you have trouble, look for the pea under your mattress."

"What?"

He gave her a disappointed look.

Pea. "Oh, you think I'm acting like a princess." Not getting a reaction, she huffed out a "Fine." And took herself to bed.

7

Dani didn't expect to sleep. It seemed like maybe her last thread of hope was about to be severed. So she was surprised when she turned over in bed and was startled by daylight.

She felt for her cell on the bedside table. Swiped it open. Nine o'clock. What the hell?

She sat upright, certain she was late for a shoot, slowly realized she was in her housekeeper's bedroom in Lawrence Sinclair's old mansion, which made her panic all the more. How could she have slept so long with her future hanging in the balance?

Avoidance, a tiny voice in her brain whispered. She shoved it aside along with the bedcovers. She jumped in and out of the shower in record time, dressed in her "work" jeans and a Keith Haring sweatshirt, shoved her feet into her running shoes, and headed for the kitchen, where she was greeted by the aroma of fresh coffee and a note. *Bring your coffee upstairs.*

The condemned man's last meal.

"Snowflake," she mumbled, then poured a large mug of coffee and ascended the stairs.

The rain had departed completely and the morning sunlight followed her from the kitchen and up the stairs, until gradually giving up the fight and disappearing completely at the landing outside the den door.

Dani took a fortifying breath, knocked, and went inside. Into total darkness except for the glow of *two* computer screens.

"Ah" was all he said, and motioned her over.

She advanced, reluctantly, wondering where all these computers were coming from and building up her courage to hear his judgment, which was no doubt waiting on the screens. She nearly tripped over some unseen object, which sloshed her coffee perilously close to the table and all its prints and papers.

She put her cup down. Nerves making her rash, she blurted out, "I don't know why you insist on all this gloom. If you opened a window we could both see a lot better."

She reached for the drapery cord and gave it a good pull. The heavy hardware creaked as the draperies lurched open a foot.

"Don't," he said, but with no conviction.

Dani tugged again, taking her anxiety and frustration out on the hapless pull cord. As she pulled, hand over hand, the drapes opened, revealing a huge picture glass window and a blast of sunlight that was painful to the eye.

"There," she exclaimed, squinting against the brightness.

Lawrence didn't turn around. Dani blinked until her eyes focused on the blue sky and puffy white clouds that filled the window. She stepped closer. Below them, an overgrown garden flanked a neglected lawn that led down to a rocky bluff overlooking a dazzling sea.

"Shit!" she said in dumb surprise. Of all the things she might have expected to see, it wasn't this. The only thing she could think to say was "Is that Old Murphy Beach?"

"God no," Lawrence said without turning around. "Old Murphy is before you get into town. It's just that . . . old, like everything else here, including me. It may still have a bathhouse and a clam shack, not sure."

"Is it your beach?"

"Are you going to keep asking superfluous questions all morning?"

"Maybe. Do you ever go down there?" She moved closer to the window. "There's somebody down there now."

"Probably the students from the art school."

"There's an art school?"

"The nuns run it. Are you done now?"

She wasn't, but she stopped for now and returned to the worktable to look over his shoulder at the computer screens. The first showed the original of a photo she'd taken a year ago, the second was the enhanced version that had sold for a tidy sum.

"Look at these."

She looked.

"What do you see?"

"In which one?"

"My point exactly."

"Jeez, I wish you wouldn't talk in enigmas all the time. They're two different things."

"True."

"The first one is a moment I caught when I was just walking down the sidewalk in Flushing. These three kids were peering in a broken window of a burned-out house."

He didn't say anything so she moved to the final version.

"This one. Well, I started playing with an idea. I mean, what were they looking at? So I increased the mystery. See, in the original you see a sort of shadow behind the glass of the window. Right? I thought, so what could I make those shadows into? Demons. Everybody is afraid of demons, so they fly out at the viewer and grab their attention."

"Then why are the kids even in the photo? They don't even seem to see them."

"Right, because . . . they're too innocent to know they're evil, which is even scarier."

Lawrence chuckled. "You just made that up, didn't you?"

"No, I— Well, maybe. But you just pointed out something that was there all along."

"But not in the original photo."

"It is. I just showed you. It just wasn't obvious. Isn't art supposed to inspire the imagination?"

"Can't argue with that."

Dani waited for him to drop the other shoe, the one that always came after an unspoken "but."

"So why not trust the viewer with the original photo?"

"Because it's— I don't know . . . It was just a photo."

Lawrence took a long, controlled breath, while Dani listened, each squeezed-out sound making her own throat drier.

"So what are these things?" He moved the cursor over several glass geometrics that stuck out of the wall of the house.

"The broken glass of the window."

"Clever. What does it all mean? Now, think about this before you answer. Was this in the original photo, or did you come up with it when someone asked you what it was about? Or worse still, you overheard someone talking at the gallery, or read a review in an art magazine."

Dani thought back. It was all a big blur, exciting and challenging; long hours before a screen, longer hours celebrating, drinking champagne, dancing—not drugs, her dad would kill her if she took drugs—but living the lifestyle. Why wasn't it enough to enjoy the ride, as long as it lasted? Why did this seem so important?

Lawrence turned suddenly, catching her off guard. "Look, there's nothing wrong with playing with photos as long as you don't forget the reason you took the photo in the first place. You start playing with things and think that's interesting. Then someone comes along and says 'cutting edge,' so you do more, because, hell, once you're cutting edge, somebody is just behind you to push you off it."

He held up his hand, stopping her possible reply. "So you keep doing more, and more, and everybody's telling you how wonderful you are, so that you get awed by your own cleverness, until you are so far away from what you discovered, what it originally said to you, what you wanted to share, that you don't even know how you got there."

Dani felt his words down to her gut. Was that what had happened to her? Was that why nothing made sense anymore? Was it what had happened to him?

She looked back at her original photo, three children, looking into the dark. What were they looking at? It had made her wonder, too. And then she started playing the what-if-I-did-this? game. He was right; she had put window dressing on her photo—lipstick on a pig, she'd read in a review for someone else. She'd agreed with the reviewer. Was she guilty of the same thing?

What if her photo was the pig?

She looked more closely.

She couldn't tell if it was good or bad, not anymore. She told Lawrence exactly that.

"But I can," he said.

"How?"

"Just by watching you look at it."

"How?"

"When you looked at the original photo, you moved closer. It pulled you in. The second one bombards you with stuff, pushing you away."

"But everyone wants the 'stuff.'"

"Everybody wants ice cream for dinner."

"I just thought it would look cool. Everybody's working that way. You have to be able to compete, to be just a cut above, a little more out there." She pointed to the original photo. "Who's going to look at that when they're being overwhelmed by the extraordinary?" She wound down. She was afraid she was sounding hysterical, but she was afraid. "It's the new trend, like pop art, or conceptual art, or postmodernism. What's wrong with that?"

"Nothing under the sun. And if that's what you're working for, you're doing great. You didn't need me after all."

She just stared at him; that now-familiar sick feeling roiled through her stomach.

"You think I'm selling out."

"I doubt that. Not at all, unless that's what you're doing. Only you can know that."

"How can I know that?"

"I don't know, Dani, You tell me."

She bit her lip, trying to keep the tears at bay.

"I've stopped looking at things, haven't I? That moment in time that is different than all the others." She held up her hand. "No, that wasn't a question. I can see that. I haven't been looking for what they are but for what I can do with them . . ." She trailed off. She'd been standing this whole time; she felt weak, but instead of sitting in the extra chair, she turned toward the window, squinting from the light reflecting off the sea. Rested her forehead against the cool glass. She'd stepped so far out on the edge, there seemed no place to go.

She was slightly aware of Lawrence opening and closing a drawer, then he nudged her and held out a camera.

"Ever work with one of these?"

"What is it?"

"An old Nikon 35-millimeter. Try taking some photos with it."

Dani took it and held it carefully in both hands. Looked over the controls and looked again. "It's a manual."

Lawrence smiled. "And it uses this." He held out a rectangular cardboard package.

"Film?"

"Think you can handle it?"

"Sure," she said uncertainly.

"So here's your first lesson." He held the film in his palm. "It contains thirty-six exposures. That's all you get . . ."

She nodded. She often took more than that, but sometimes less. She could get something good in thirty-six exposures.

"Six subjects, six photos each."

She looked up at him as the instructions sank in.

"And the photo stops there. What you get is what it is. No postproduction allowed."

Postproduction. She didn't even know where to get it developed. Actually . . . "I'm not sure how to put the film in."

"That's why you have Google."

"Really? I thought I wasn't supposed to depend on the computer."

"All right, all right. See that little button?"

"This one?"

"No, that one. Push it just like you would for your SD card."

Dani glanced at him from under lowered lids. He might not take photos anymore, but he at least kept up with the advances in the business.

She pressed the button, and the back of the camera swung open. It took only a couple of times to get the film cartridge in place and the film lined up properly in the sprockets. She closed the cover. Took a minute to play with the focus and the other buttons. It was fairly simple once she got the film in place, and she quickly familiarized herself with the mechanisms.

Lawrence had been watching her closely. Evidently satisfied, he said, "Now get going." He leaned over to shut down the computers.

"Lawrence?"

He glanced back, still bent over the table.

She pressed the button, the camera whirred. "Smile."

Lawrence frowned. "Thirty-five exposures left."

"I'm not sure I can get perfect shots in six tries," she confessed as he herded her down the stairs and into the kitchen.

"Good, I don't want perfection. And you shouldn't, either. I want what you see. Perfection is completed. Boring. So stop striving for perfection. Beauty, though. Beauty is the lack of perfection. The thing that draws the eye. The balance between flaws and flawless is what you want to see. You want some breakfast before you go?"

Dani shook her head as anxiety suddenly welled up inside her. It was almost enough to make her put down the camera and run for her car. Beauty and flaws and . . . The way he talked made her feel weird. She prided herself on always being out beyond the others, catching the unexpected; capturing an image, then playing with it, then playing with that image and the next. Always moving. But this camera and its thirty-six, now thirty-five, exposures sounded so slow, so passive. So final.

"Just be ready to see, don't go looking for it."

With that, Lawrence shooed her out of the room, leaving Dani feeling like she'd just been handed a pop quiz for a subject she'd never opened a book for.

Well, to hell with it. She wouldn't learn anything standing here. She went back downstairs, grabbed a seeded roll from the counter and a bottle of water from the fridge, and hurried to her room for her backpack. Two minutes later she was walking out the side door and into the yard. It was a sunny day, warm, but with just a touch of crispness that told her fall was not far away.

Instead of going into the woods, which, until the view this morning, she'd thought surrounded the house, she struck off to the left, skirting the trees until she stepped at the edge of— She could hardly call it a lawn, at least not in its current state. What grass that was left had been taken over by tall beach grasses and other weeds. A sandy path had been cut through them, and she followed it downhill toward the beach.

Some of the grasses grew as tall as her head. Dani was suddenly hyper aware of texture. Scaly stems caught at her sweatshirt. Feathery plumes swayed over her head like Egyptian palms. The arrowhead shapes of fronds aimed at the sky. Several times she positioned the camera, adjusted the focus, held her finger over the shutter button, but then moved it away without taking a photo.

Only six tries per subject.

She tripped on something, probably her own lack of understanding. Lawrence wanted her to "see." She wanted to see. She wished he'd come with her to guide her hand, her eye. But he hadn't offered, and she knew that if she'd asked him, he'd have refused. And that, she thought, was as much about him as it was about her.

Why did he no longer take pictures?

Had he stood one day, as she was now, waiting for photos that just wouldn't come? She tried to recapture her own excitement, the sense of wonder when she'd taken her first exuberant shots with someone else's camera, the sheer pleasure that it had brought.

These days she worked with fierce intensity. But not with the same sense of wonder.

"Are you going down to the beach?"

Dani whirled toward the voice, nearly losing her footing in the soft sand.

It was the nun from the other day, her head appearing over the tops of the grasses, making it seem as though she had supernaturally appeared out of the landscape. Though as Dani got nearer, she saw that the nun was sitting in an aluminum beach chair.

"Dani, isn't it? I didn't mean to startle you." She smiled ruefully. "I guess I did anyway."

"I was thinking."

"I could tell. I'm Sister Mary Catherine. We sort of met the other day." She fell quiet, beaming at Dani like the sun overhead. "Are you out on a shoot?"

"I'm supposed to be."

"Getting any good shots?"

"I haven't taken one yet."

"Ah," said the nun, sounding awfully like Lawrence.

"Pretty much," said Dani. "Lawrence gave me this camera and said that I only had six chances to make the perfect shot. Now I'm afraid of taking any shots and not having enough left to get the perfect one."

Sister Mary Catherine pursed her lips. "Did Lawrence say, 'Perfect shot'?"

Dani sighed. "No," she admitted. "He said that he didn't want perfect, that perfect was . . ."

"Already completed," the nun suggested.

"Yes." Dani moved closer. "That perfection depended on flaws or something like that. I kind of understand, but I wish he'd just tell me what to do."

Sister Mary Catherine laughed gently, like a soft breeze. "Lawrence doesn't always take the most direct route, not anymore at least."

That sparked Dani's interest, but before she could press the nun to tell her more, she continued, "Trust in yourself. So what if you miss what you think was a perfect shot . . . or a perfect life, for that matter. There is no such thing. And you will have many more chances to find the beauty in our imperfection. Not everyone is so lucky."

She folded her hands over her lap. "The beach should be an inspiration. Our students certainly find it so."

Dani followed her gaze to the beach, small and shaped like a melon slice and overhung by a rocky bluff, the top of which she'd seen from the window. Scattered across the coarse sand, people of various ages and sizes stood in front of easels or sat cross-legged on the rocks with sketchpads in their laps.

"They're all from your art school?" Dani asked. "Lawrence told me about it this morning."

"They are . . . for now anyway."

"Do you close down in the winter, too?"

Mary Catherine laughed softly. "Like the Excelsior? Oh no, we're full-time nuns. Well, full-time retired nuns, but there are only three of us left, and the diocese is selling the mother house."

"That beautiful white house next door? That's terrible."

"Oh, it's too big for us to keep up anymore. And it is prime beach real estate. We'll be moving at Thanksgiving."

"But where will you live?"

"We're planning to share a house in downtown. It used to be our outreach center, before it moved to a larger diocese. And will be more accessible to our community arts program that's currently housed at the convent. We're bursting at the seams with budding artists, musicians, writers, quilters, knitters. We've been trying to find a space to lease large enough to house our many classes.

"That's foremost in our thoughts now. The program provides the opportunity for all ages, children, adults, seniors, and those with special needs to make art surrounded by the glories of God's world. Which is all fine and good; it's the zoning laws, cash flow, adaptable locations, accessibility, all the external things that make it a challenge. But we'll find a way."

So even nuns had their challenges. Somehow that wasn't as comforting as Dani thought it would be.

"Well, good luck," Dani said. "I better get back to my assignment."

"Enjoy the day and the wonders around you—the imperfect wonders around you." Sister Mary Catherine smiled as if all was fine, closed her eyes, and lifted her face to . . . heaven.

Dani aimed the camera and took her second shot.

She started across the coarse sand and pebbles that made up the beach. She stopped to watch a couple of painters but wasn't moved to take their pictures. She finally made her way to the granite boulders that formed a wall at the other side of the beach. Glacial deposits? They didn't look man-made.

She found a flat place to sit. Set her camera carefully beside her on the granite and reached into her backpack for her water and roll. The breeze gusted and let up only to gust again. The last throes of summer. Soon she would have to return to New York. Her life was there. She picked up the camera. Her time was running out.

She climbed along the boulders, exploring their nooks and crannies, wondered what was on the other side. Above them the roof of Lawrence's house pointed above the bluff like a witch's hat.

And somewhere along the way Dani began to photograph. She tried not to think, not to look directly at anything but rather let things catch her eye, six subjects, six photos. The gleam off what turned out to be a bottle cap in the sand. The expression of one of the seated sketchers when a gull swooped down and captured a piece of pastel in its beak, only to drop it in the sand several yards away. A crevice in the rock with a vein of silver that disappeared like a ribbon into the stone.

When she finally trekked back to the house, it was almost dinnertime. She was hungry, maybe a little sunburned, and was covered in sand, but she'd used all thirty-six chances in her camera. She had no idea if any of them were any good.

And no idea how one went about getting film developed.

She put the camera carefully on the dresser in her bedroom, showered, then carried it through the kitchen and into the foyer, where she stopped and listened. Hearing no sign of Lawrence, she went into the parlor. No Lawrence, but the *Times* lay on the floor by the club chair. She didn't bother to glance at it. She hadn't even looked at it online since she arrived.

She'd been here less than a week, but already she was losing track of the days. This couldn't be good for her career. Every night her phone was filled with emails from Manny, gallery owners, equipment ads, copies of reviews. She tried to ignore it all.

She found Lawrence in his office, only the top of his head showing above the computer screen.

"Playing solitaire?" she asked.

"The ponies," he countered smoothly, and the glow of the screen blipped out.

"Really?"

"No, just some business."

"What business do you do, by the way?"

"Retired. Did you finish the film?"

"I did. Now what? We can't look at them."

"We just have to develop them."

"Where? Do you have a darkroom?"

"Nope."

"Please don't tell me we'll have to mail them somewhere."

"No. I know a guy. But first what's for dinner?"

"For a skinny guy, you sure think a lot about eating," she said, following him out of the room.

"Do I? Never did before."

"You mean until I got here."

"Pretty much."

"It can't be my cordon bleu cooking. But what about my photos?" She waited expectantly. He didn't answer; the future seemed to hover above them.

Lawrence sighed.

Dani gave him a look.

"Okay. We'll go now. Just let me make a call."

8

Ray's Photo and Art Supply Shop was tucked into a side street in downtown Old Murphy Beach. The kind of place you had to know about or you would never find it. Luckily Dani had Lawrence in the passenger seat of her SUV. She'd insisted on driving after a lengthy argument. Having won the argument, she canceled the GPS and magnanimously asked Lawrence to give her directions. Which he did . . . for every pothole, blind drive, and solid yellow line in the seven minutes it took to get to downtown.

There was a parking space on the street right in front of the shop. Actually, there were several. It wasn't even sundown and most of the stores were already dark. Lawrence held the door for her, and she stepped inside a bare-bones rectangle sparsely filled with photographic supplies, several display racks of poster-size photos, and one corner stocked with general art needs, drawing paper, paints, crayons. Just the basics.

A glass counter ran along one side. A man sat on a stool behind the counter. In his sixties, Dani guessed, overweight, with sparse red curls and freckles sprayed beneath a pair of horn-rim glasses. He was talking to a woman holding a Tupperware container. She was as thin as he was hefty, with pageboy-length hair pulled away from her aquiline face by two combs. She saw Lawrence and dropped the Tupperware onto the counter.

"Lawrence," she exclaimed, holding out both hands as she

came to meet him. "Ray said you were coming down and I had to come see for myself."

"Hello, Ada." Lawrence kissed both her cheeks.

She noticed Dani and smiled, then lifted her eyebrows at Lawrence, who was looking a little at sea.

Dani stuck out her hand. "Hi, I'm Dani."

Lawrence cleared his throat. "She's got some film that needs developing. Ray said the darkroom was available."

"When isn't it?" Ada said.

"Always available to you, Lawrence," Ray said, sliding off the stool. He said this in a gravelly, slightly Italian accent. He was much shorter than his sitting presence had indicated. Ada stood a whole head taller. "I'll just get you set up."

"I'll bring down some coffee," Ada said. "You're in luck. I just made a nice cherry crostata." She hurried away.

Ray watched fondly after her, then turned to Lawrence and Dani. "She's a wonder, is my Ada."

He led them to a back room, unlocked the door, and reached in to click on the lights. A deep red hue barely lightened the dark. He stepped inside, right into a wood partition. They followed him to the left and to another partition and right again and into a square room.

Shelves ran along the wall above a stainless-steel counter with cabinets below. All were sparkling clean and held several machines, some that Dani recognized and others whose function she could only guess at. And it occurred to her that she had no idea what the process would be. Only a few large bottles and jars sat on the shelves. "Do you get many people still developing their own film?" Dani asked.

"You'd be surprised. I have a couple of old-timers." His eyes cut toward Lawrence and slid away.

"And I'm getting more and more people who are interested in learning. Enough that it's kept me from retiring. I mean, how can I leave a whole new generation of true photographers in the lurch?"

Ouch, thought Dani. It was the first time she'd ever heard that attitude. She supposed it was like those music lovers who had rediscovered LPs and swore the only "real" clarity of sound was to be found there and not in electronically balanced and amplified recordings.

Ray reached up and brought several jars down to the counter, reached underneath and pulled out colored trays, and slid them onto the counter.

"Ever developed your own photos before?" Ray asked.

"No," Dani said. "Actually, I don't have a clue as to how to do it. I started with a digital camera and never needed to actually use a darkroom." She glanced at Lawrence. "Until now."

"Well, you've come to the right place." Ray chuckled, a sound that shook his generous stomach and made Dani smile.

"Came to the only place," Lawrence said, which only made Ray chuckle more.

"Learned it from the best, my uncle Louis Barbosi. He owned the shop when it was on Main Street. Photographers came from miles around. Those were some days, weren't they?"

"Huh," said Lawrence.

"Uncle Louis brought me over from Italy to help him. I must have been . . ." Ray scratched his head. "Fifteen maybe. Best thing that ever happened to me. Out of the fields and into the darkroom. And then, of course, there's my Ada. Now, who's got the film?"

Lawrence reached into his jacket pocket and handed Ray the plastic canister. Ray took it, looked from the container to

Lawrence. "Huh," Ray said. A look passed between the two men, but Dani was too impatient to think much about it.

"I'll just explain as we go, okay? This is the first step." He picked up a stainless-steel canister. "This is a developing reel. The film goes in here, but it can't be exposed to light. Any light. Capisce? I'm a bit of a control freak, so I do double darkness, and I'm going to do it for you, this first time. Next time I'll help you do it yourself. That okay with you?"

Dani nodded. She didn't know if there would even be a next time.

"Good. Oh, you're not afraid of the dark, are you?" He chuckled, and the lights went out.

His voice rose out of a blackness so deep she couldn't see a thing.

"Now that we're really in the dark"—that chuckle again—"I pry off the film canister and thread it into the reel."

The sound of the canister being placed on the counter, liquid pouring, and a few seconds later a red light began to glow.

"The safe light. Now just agitate this for a minute." He handed her the filled reel and twisted her wrist up and down. "If you get tired, change hands, but don't stop."

Dani stared at the reel and began to turn it back and forth. Ray began pouring solutions into three different glass jars, and lined them up on the counter. Lawrence had moved off to the side and was perched on a stool on the far side of the room.

She didn't get his lack of interest. She tried to imagine him leaning over his work, deftly handling the film, making decisions that ended in the photos she'd discovered in the barn. And how many more? She knew there must be a few floating about, but none that she'd actually seen herself. Where had all those photos gone, and why had he stopped?

"Agitate," Ray reminded her, and she redoubled her efforts.

Between agitating the reel, emptying the reel, filling it again, emptying, filling, then washing, Dani didn't know how much time had passed when Ray at last opened the reel.

"Don't touch." He rolled the film out and held up the tiny negative images of her subjects.

"Wow," she said on an exhale of breath. "Now do we turn them into hard copies?"

"Now we wait for them to dry."

"How long will that take?"

"Depends on how we dry them."

"And how do we do that?"

"Well, we could hang them up, check the humidity, let 'em dry overnight, and come back in the morning to see how they did."

"The morning?" Dani repeated, nonplussed.

"That's the way we used to do it. I used to hang mine in the second bathroom. Ada didn't like that much. Too many kids to only have access to one bath. Or we could just hang them in the drying machine over there, adjust the temp and humidity, and let it do the work."

"How long will that take?"

"Well, let me see." Ray rubbed his chin while he calculated. "What would you say, Lawrence?"

Lawrence, looking bored, said, "You're the boss, but I'd guess about, say, hmm, fifteen minutes?"

Dani was beside herself with impatience, but she couldn't tell if they were kidding her or not. "Is it better to let them dry overnight?" she asked, hoping that it wouldn't come to that.

"God, no," Lawrence said. "Put them in the damn machine."

Ray clucked his tongue. "You photographers, always in a hurry."

This time Dani caught the twinkle in his eye.

"Lucky for you, I didn't sell this off with the other equipment when we moved to the smaller store."

She watched as he carefully set the negatives to dry, then closed the door. He started the timer and shooed them to the exit.

"Don't worry. They'll be all right and tight. Now, go on out, Ada will be back by now and she'll expect to feed you. I'll just clean this up and join you momentarily."

Ada was sitting at the counter talking to a middle-aged man with long, stringy hair and a Vandyke beard. He and Lawrence exchanged hellos. He eyed Dani with curiosity, and with a salute to Ada, took his purchase out the door.

"Lawrence, go turn over the Closed sign."

He went, but Dani noticed he was walking slowly and his stoop was back, something that she hadn't realized had disappeared since her arrival.

Maybe all that sitting was bad for him. Though he could tromp through the rain and woods with no problem at all, she reminded herself.

Ray joined them minutes later, and Ada poured thick coffee and cut wedges of her "incomparable" cherry crostata.

The three of them were obviously old friends. And the conversation was lively enough as they ate and sipped strong coffee. Lawrence seemed to perk up under Ada's constant attention.

But Dani couldn't join in with much enthusiasm. Her mind kept wondering about the negatives drying in the darkroom. Fifteen minutes seemed to be taking a ridiculously long time, and she kept surreptitiously glancing at her phone to make sure the minutes were actually going by.

But when fifteen minutes finally came and passed, and Lawrence and Ray made no sign of returning to the darkroom, she began to get really impatient.

It was a hell of a way to develop photographs. All this waiting. With digital you could take thirty-six shots and see them immediately. Hell, you could take a hundred and it wouldn't take any longer.

She knew that wasn't the point. Or perhaps that was exactly the point, no immediate gratification, only anticipation and patience required. But it was even more than that.

While she had been in the darkroom, she'd been mesmerized with the process. And that was the point. Do the process, appreciate the end result. She began to understand that her "lessons" had begun the moment she'd first walked into Lawrence's house.

She would pay more attention from now on. But she really wished she could see the photos tonight and see if she was learning what he had to teach. She crossed her fingers that printing them tonight wasn't dependent on one of the pieces of equipment that Ray had sold when he moved the store to this location.

"I think you've tortured the poor girl long enough," Ada said.

Dani looked up gratefully.

Ada shook her head, smiling fondly at the two men. "These two get together and they lose track of time. Now, shoo and get some prints for me to see."

The men got up, reluctantly, Dani thought, but she didn't care. She just wanted to see her photos.

Ray had set up the next step before coming out to join them. Now there were three plastic trays, yellow, red, white, lined up across the counter. Each had its own color-coordinated plastic pair of tongs. There were three beakers of processing fluids sitting behind each tray.

Dani went straight to the counter.

"Not so fast," Ray said. "First we get the negatives out."

Fortunately they were dry, and Ray proceeded to place them in plastic sheets. Then he motioned her over to a large machine. "Now we print out a contact sheet."

"And you choose one of each subject to print," Lawrence broke in. "One."

"But . . ." Dani began.

"One." Lawrence crossed his arms and sat down on the stool he'd been perched on before.

Ray widened his eyes in an exaggerated expression of surprise. "Then let's get to it."

The next half hour was spent developing the contact sheet and choosing just six, though standing close to Ray, she whispered, "Plus the two of Sister Mary Catherine and Lawrence."

Ray nodded and winked at her. "Ready to do a test print?"

"Yes, please." Dani glanced over at Lawrence but his eyes were closed. She hoped he didn't nod off and fall off the stool.

The white lights went out and the safe light came on.

═

Lawrence opened his eyes. He was trying not to be interested. To ignore the process marching inexorably toward the finished photograph. But he couldn't help himself. It was as if Dani's enthusiasm was siphoning into him. She was so intent as Ray explained about filters and how to make that first, all-important test sheet.

The look on her face when the first real print took shape as she stared into the developing tray . . . She was mesmerized—and mesmerizing. And he couldn't help but smile, thinking of all the prints he'd developed and all the times he'd felt just the same way.

And he pushed the feeling away, forced his gaze to follow. But it kept coming back to Dani and her delight at something he and his contemporaries had taken for granted.

It was well after midnight when the lights finally were restored. Maybe he had been dozing, because Lawrence had somehow lost track of time. Dozing, or perhaps, remembering.

He got stiffly off the stool. Dani was holding an envelope. For as much as Lawrence distrusted shortcuts, tonight he was thankful for all those shortcut machines. He didn't think making Dani go back to the dark ages just to prove a point would do either of them any good.

"Well, let me see," he said, trying not to hobble toward them.

Dani turned away, pulled out a print, and held it up. The look of hopefulness on her face almost melted his heart. He took it from her, walked over to one of the drawers, took out a magnifying loupe. Ran it over the image. It was a black-and-white eight-by-ten. What you saw was what you got. And what she'd gotten was good.

He took his time, relishing a feeling he hadn't felt in decades. So simple, so naked, so vulnerable. She was intuitive. Something the best photographers had naturally. She didn't need him for that. But he wasn't about to tell her that. Not just yet.

He grunted, nodded. Returned the magnifying loupe. Turned back to Ray and Dani. "What do you think, Ray?" Lawrence asked, forcing a frown. "Think she's off to a decent start?"

"I'd say pretty good," Ray answered.

"Just so you know," Lawrence said drily, "Ray's a sucker for budding photographers."

"I am." Ray winked at Dani. "Good going, kid. And not to worry. It's a great start. We can scan the rest to digital if you want to see them."

"But not tonight," Lawrence said.

They left after that, Dani gently holding her envelope of prints. Ray walked them to the street. Ada surely had gone to bed hours before.

Lawrence climbed into the SUV and waited for Dani to get in the driver's side. She handed over the manila envelope to him and they just sat for a few seconds.

"I know. It's all just part of the process. I didn't realize everything would take so long. All the drying time, and the different chemical baths, and the . . ." She sighed. "But when that first photo emerged like a ghost from the developing fluid, it was better than any app I've ever used."

Lawrence cracked a laugh.

"I mean it. It was magic. Did you feel like that every time you developed your film?"

"Sometimes," Lawrence said, mainly just not to have to think about the things he used to feel. "Mostly it just took a long time."

═

Dani started the engine. "I can't believe you developed all your photos that way."

"Everybody did," Lawrence said.

"Thank you. I would never have known." She turned to make sure the street was deserted before she started to back out and just to take a moment to appreciate her passenger. Her mentor, his face carved in deep lines above that wispy sorcerer's beard. If she'd had her camera she would have fired off several shots.

He glanced at her. "What?"

"I hope you weren't bored."

"Just hungry. Is it too late for dinner? Ada's coffee will keep me up all night."

They stopped at the only place still open that late, a diner by the name of Ruth's Café, where the food was substantial and tasty and everyone knew Lawrence by name. The diner, the photo shop, the convent—so not such a recluse.

But still an enigma.

9

Peter left early Saturday morning. His mother escorted him all the way to the front door, reciting a list of advice, and would have followed him all the way to the curb if he hadn't gently closed the door before she could.

He'd packed an overnight bag, on the outside chance there was really something to the story of his grandfather losing his grip. At least that's what he told himself. He couldn't actually make himself imagine Lawrence Sinclair as anything other than smart, talented, and ahead of the game in almost everything except how to love his family. But his mother wouldn't be satisfied until Peter took control.

The cleaning service was a good sign. It meant he cared about his surroundings, which was more than he had done the only time Peter had made the trip to visit him after the funeral. It had been Peter's first year in college. They'd spent an awkward hour together, trying, he supposed, to recapture their past closeness. Between the raw grief of the funeral and his mother's ensuing hostility, it was a near impossible attempt; they had lost too much. The visit ended suddenly when Lawrence said he had no intention of coming between Peter and his mother and showed him to the door.

Peter tossed his bag onto the back seat of his BMW and drove away. It was less than a three-hour drive, and with no beach traffic, Peter made good time. Not good enough to prevent him from thinking all the way down, thinking that turned to worrying about what he would find, which turned to anxiety about actually confronting his grandfather, who had once been "Gadda" when they were together, "Grandfather" when in company, and "Lawrence" since the funeral.

Peter drummed on the steering wheel. Now that he was on the road, he couldn't for the life of him remember how he'd agreed to make the trip. It was bound to lead to more ill will.

God, how he used to look forward to coming to the old house to stay with Gadda and Ganna Kissie, called this since Peter had been slow in conquering his *r*'s. Though he was given strict orders by his parents not to venture down to the beach at all, of course Gadda ignored them, and they splashed in the waves until their teeth chattered, explored the rocks, until Ganna Kissie called them in to dinner. In winter they would all bundle up and go down to build a fire on the sand and make s'mores and hot chocolate. Or sit in the dark and just count the stars.

In those days his grandparents spent most of the year traveling and photographing, and in Krista's instance, writing poetry and being a free spirit. But every school break and most holidays they were home for Peter, full of love and enthusiasm, which they showered on him while his father and mother were climbing their way to the top.

Peter didn't mind in the least. Here with his grandparents were freedom and fun and exploration. And though he'd known even then he was destined to take his father's place, just as his father and grandfather had done, in those days it seemed like an eternity away.

He found himself driving into Old Murphy Beach way before he was ready for the reunion to come. He slowed down just to prolong the inevitable. A lot of the stores had closed for the season, though the gas station and the old Excelsior Hotel were still open for business. A bellhop was unloading a pile of luggage belonging to a couple in a Mercedes.

The town passed by way too quickly, but it had to be done, and how bad could it be?

Pretty bad, he conceded as he turned into the drive and found, instead of smooth pavement, a drive riddled with erosion and crowded by unpruned shrubbery.

But as a prelude, it didn't do justice to the actual house, the haven of his boyhood.

The place was a dump.

He pulled to a stop in front of it. A. Falling. Down. Dump.

How could that have happened? Lawrence had never been one for fixing things, but this was ridiculous. And didn't bode well for his grandfather's state of mind.

There were two SUVs parked outside. Both cars were fairly late models—state welfare reps came to mind.

Maybe his mother had been wrong, and his grandfather wasn't being pursued for his money, but had lost it all. He wouldn't be the first person to blow a lifetime of accumulation.

Still, Peter couldn't prevent the sense of "being home" that settled over him as he walked up to the door.

Peter knocked, boldly. Not boldly enough. Either his grandfather wasn't home or he didn't hear him. Peter rang the bell. Leaned forward, listening. Heard . . . laughing? Who would be laughing?

The door opened and he jumped back.

Then the figure stepped into the doorway. A spirit right out of Halloween—the devil with a pitchfork. Tall and cadaverously thin, with uncut white hair and beard, holding a . . . not a pitchfork, but a broom, straw side up. There was a large cobweb stuck to one side of his face.

His grandfather peered back at him. "Peter?"

Peter could only nod, dumbfounded.

"They sent you? Christ. Who died?"

Peter's mouth opened. He managed to stammer, "Nobody," before he shut it again. That was the one thing, of all the thousands of thoughts he'd had on the drive down, he hadn't considered. What was he going to say when he finally faced his grandfather?

"Well, that's a relief. Must be important. Your mother usually emails when she needs my vote." Lawrence looked back into the house. "You might as well come in."

Peter stepped inside and saw someone on the far side of the foyer climbing down from a ladder. At first he thought it was a boy, dressed in jeans with what appeared to be an old T-shirt wrapped around his head. He saw Peter and yanked the covering off, revealing dark spiked hair with electric purple highlights.

It was a girl—a young woman. This was the cleaning lady? She didn't look very experienced. She'd been grinning but now she frowned. Not exactly angry, but wary?

Peter's mind leaped to all his mother's worst imaginings.

She came over, and Lawrence passed the broom off to her like a drill sergeant. She took it without even looking.

"Spiders," said Lawrence.

"Spiders," she echoed.

A look passed between them; Peter was hit with a stab of jealousy.

What had he expected? That his grandfather had made no friends since he'd cut his grandson off?

But *cleaning lady*? This hipster goth might not be some mercenary woman after his grandfather's fortune, but he seriously doubted she would know one end of a vacuum cleaner from the other.

As for Lawrence, he'd changed. He was older, sparer, but he didn't seem senile, just surprised to see Peter.

And he pulled himself together faster than Peter did. "Dani. This is Peter Sinclair. My grandson," he added after a long interval. "This is Dani Campbell."

"The cleaning lady." The girl waved her dust rag, setting off a cloud of dust motes. Then grinned in a slightly demented way that made him wonder if hiring her was an act of charity on Lawrence's part.

Lawrence finally brushed the cobweb from his cheek. "I suppose you came to talk business?"

Was Peter that obvious? "What makes you think that?"

"Besides that I haven't seen you in years, and no man wears a jacket on a Saturday who isn't here for business?"

He was right, Peter thought, feeling the heat rise to his face. He'd armored himself with an effing jacket, dead giveaway, despite the wrinkled linen and the rolled-up sleeves.

"Well, what is it?" Lawrence demanded.

It was hard to think about business confronted with his grandfather and this half-pint centurion with the weird hair.

Dani Campbell was eyeing him with open interest. And not in a good way.

Peter bristled. His grandfather expected Peter to carry on business here in the foyer in front of the hired help? "It's awkward."

"Well, if you're awkward talking about money, you've chosen the wrong profession."

"It isn't money . . ."

"Then what is it?" Lawrence asked, clearly losing patience.

"I don't know what I'm supposed to call you."

Lawrence stared at him.

"How about Grumps?" the girl chirped.

Peter and his grandfather snapped their attention toward her.

She shrugged. "It seems as good as anything. Now, can you please close the door? You're letting the bugs in."

Both men looked at the open door.

Bossy, too, Peter added. Peter looked away, but not before he saw a glint in his grandfather's eye and a returning twinkle from the upstart kid. He slammed the door, effectively shutting the bugs out, and just as effectively, he realized, trapping himself inside.

"Well, come in and take off that jacket," Lawrence said. "No one's here but us chickens."

He didn't care if the interloper was pinning him with a speculative laser eye. They were almost black, those eyes. Peter shook himself and shucked his jacket in record time, just like decades before when he'd been dropped off in a limo straight from school. And there would be Ganna Kissie at the door, saying, *Take off that jacket; no one here but us chickens.*

There was no Ganna Kissie now. Just a black-eyed goth and a stranger who had been his grandfather.

"Hell," Lawrence exclaimed, looking him over. "When was the last time you ate?"

"Last night," Peter said, taken off guard. "I didn't have time for breakfast before I left this morning."

"Did you hear that?" Lawrence said over his shoulder to the cleaning girl in a way that made it sound like a secret code.

She nodded seriously.

Peter shuffled uncomfortably. Were they goofing on him?

"Better make the man a sandwich if he's going to wring

concessions out of me." Lawrence turned and walked toward the door of the old library, leaving Peter and Dani Campbell looking at each other.

Before Peter could even take his leave, she said, "We've got ham and cheese, chicken salad, or PB and J."

"Whatever."

"And fresh-squeezed lemonade. I squeezed it myself." She did a quick biceps show with both arms. They were pretty muscular. Possibly lethal.

Maybe he was the one losing his mind, not his grandfather.

She made a twirl of her broomstick, then dragged it behind her out the door.

When she was gone, Peter turned toward the library and followed Lawrence inside.

Lawrence was seated behind a large wooden desk that Peter remembered. Only now there was a large desktop computer taking up the center. Lawrence swiveled it aside. "Have a seat and tell me what's going on."

Without the cleaning sprite, Lawrence's demeanor had become all business, a little harder, but less energetic, as if a spark had gone out. Was she responsible for that other Lawrence Sinclair? And was Peter's arrival responsible for this one?

Peter took his time pulling a chair up to the side of the desk, and sat down. He'd meant to come here, check out his grandfather's mental state, vet the cleaning lady, and report back to his mother.

Now that he was here, he realized he just wanted his grandfather back. But that was out of the question. His mother would never forgive him. His grandfather probably would never forgive him for letting his mother rule their relationship all these years. And Peter couldn't blame him.

Finally, Lawrence looked up. "Well?"

═

Dani dragged the cold cuts and chicken salad out of the fridge and slapped them on the counter. Good thing she'd made that grocery run, though she'd been buying for two—not three. She wondered how long Peter Sinclair planned to stay.

Grandson, huh? Here she'd been thinking Lawrence was all alone in the world with only the nuns next door to keep an eye on him. But he had friends in town, a grandson. Were there more?

Where were the rest of his relatives? If he had a grandson he must have had a wife. Probably divorced, possibly dead. The photo of the young woman standing on the cliff appeared briefly in her mind.

And if he had family, why didn't they at least hire someone to take care of him? Not that he actually needed taking care of. He'd left her in the shade on their walk through the woods, didn't think twice about going out in the rain. Stayed up to all hours at the photo shop, followed by the diner, and was up again this morning without a complaint. He climbed the stairs several times a day, and she'd never seen him out of breath.

She fetched mayonnaise and mustard from the fridge. Grabbed the jelly, mainly out of spite. "Whatever," he'd said. What kind of answer was that? Maybe if she'd said, *Tuna and marshmallow fluff*, he would have shown more interest. As for Dani, she couldn't abide tuna. Or marshmallows. And she would have let her hostess know it.

What a wuss. And no sense of humor. Did he really think she was the cleaning lady? Did she look like a cleaning lady? Hell, maybe she did. Something to think about . . . later. Right now, she had sandwiches to make.

She stood on tiptoe to reach the bread. It was on the top shelf, the only shelf with room for it, since the old breadbox was filled with cookies. She really should reorganize the cabinets so she could reach everything.

On the other hand . . . She was getting a little carried away with this wax-on-wax-off thing.

Lawrence had seemed pleased with a couple of her photographs last night. They hadn't discussed her successes or her failures. She'd hoped to get a full review this morning, but first there had been the spider episode and now this grandson business.

They were definitely estranged. Regardless, she hoped they would get their business done quickly, and she and Lawrence could say goodbye to Peter Sinclair. She'd felt a change in Lawrence the minute he opened the door. Even Dani had done a double-take, recognizing a young Lawrence in the lean face of Peter Sinclair. Not a bad face as far as faces went. He was tall and lanky like Lawrence but uptight and stiff, not like Lawrence at all.

Dani made several sandwiches, cut them in half, and considered cutting them in quarters and trimming off the edges just to be annoying, but it was more trouble than she had a feeling Peter Sinclair was worth. What kinds of concessions could he possibly wring out of Lawrence? And what kind of person didn't know what he should call his pop-pop? Her family was messy, loud, opinionated, and often a pain in the butt, but they were always family and she'd never trade them for one as stilted as these guys.

She retrieved a big tray she'd seen in the pantry and arranged the plate of sandwiches, two dessert plates, and the pitcher of lemonade and glasses. When she attempted to pick it up, she staggered under its weight.

Hardly the entrance she'd want to make. On the other hand . . . She hoisted the tray. Leaning in an uncomfortable acrobatic backbend to counter its weight, she backed out the kitchen door. By the time she reached the office—thank goodness they'd left the door open—her arms were shaking.

She shuffled the tray to the desk and dropped it on the least cluttered space.

It made a bit of a clatter, and Peter Sinclair jumped as if she'd goosed him. She cut half an eye roll in Lawrence's direction, but he was looking at Peter, and she didn't like his expression.

This guy better not wreck her time with Lawrence. Manny was having a cow about not knowing where she was or exactly when she was coming back. She'd finally turned off her phone just to concentrate on her mentor time with Lawrence. And now this new interruption. Ugh.

"Will that be all?" she asked in her most subservient voice. And when Lawrence nodded, she made an exaggerated curtsy, snatched up a ham and cheese half, and left.

Neither man even seemed to notice.

She didn't go far, merely around the corner of the door, where she stood munching her sandwich while she waited for one of them to say something.

"Who is that girl anyway?" Peter asked.

Dani stopped chewing to listen.

"Have a sandwich." The rattle of a plate. "Didn't you hear her?"

"Yes, but you can't tell me any reputable service would send someone like that. Have you counted the silver yet?"

"You sound just like your mother."

Dani gave a decisive nod. *Take that, Peter prodigal grandson.*

"Actually," Lawrence continued, "she showed up one day, on the run, I suspect, desperate for work, and needing a place to lie low. What could I do but take her in . . . out of the goodness of my heart."

Dani's mouth fell open. She peered around the edge of the door and met Lawrence's amused eyes.

She made a fierce face and disappeared again.

He was having his fun; she just hoped that his grandson didn't call the police down on them. Though Manny would probably be ecstatic with the publicity.

There was another prolonged silence while presumably the two men ate their lunch. Dani finished her sandwich and lost interest. She'd ask Lawrence to give her an update after Peter left. She just hoped it would be soon.

10

This was his grandson? Lawrence couldn't stop looking at Peter, who was dutifully eating his sandwich. He'd chosen peanut butter and jelly, of all things. He'd grown up to be a good-looking guy, tall like all the Sinclair men, with that ruddy brown hair. The same color as Lawrence's own before life and sorrow had turned it white.

As he watched, time slipped away and Peter was a ten-year-old, sitting there devouring his PB and J. The bright smear of jelly across his cheek as he exclaimed through a sticky mouth, "They never give us peanut butter at school." And Kristy standing beside him, beaming her love all over the little guy as if she could make up for all the lonely nights away from home . . .

Lawrence had to look away to control the lump that was climbing up his throat. He blinked several times, looked back at Peter, and saw the boy in the man he'd become.

But Peter was no longer a boy and he hadn't come from a desire to see his grandfather. They were long past that. He'd come because there was something going on in the company and he wanted to make sure he could count on Lawrence's support. Lawrence couldn't see his brother, James, in the midst of a power struggle. James enjoyed his lifestyle too much. Peter and his mother? God forbid.

Lawrence had to stop his fist from banging on the desk. A

family that distrusted each other, tied together by a legacy that had wrecked most of their lives in one way or another. And now another generation that was ripe for the picking.

The kid was not even thirty, but already looked years older than he was. And his brow creased in a seemingly permanent frown. The eyes that once could practically knock you over with their excitement because of some found beach treasure or a falcon swooping right above their heads . . . Those eyes were shuttered now. He'd seen it happen in his son and now his grandson, and probably in himself if he had dared look.

Peter also had a nervous way of tapping his fingers whenever he wasn't engaged. Lawrence had noticed it within seconds after he'd sat down. They'd all developed one nervous tic or another working their lives away. Lawrence couldn't remember what his had been; he only knew he'd lost it as soon as he left the business.

First this girl photographer, and now Peter. He'd have to ask Sister Mary Catherine if their appearance was a punishment for his sins or a chance to redeem himself.

"I haven't had peanut butter in ages," Peter said.

"Very nutritious," Lawrence said, fighting not to say, *It was always your favorite.*

They dropped—hell, they free-fell—into silence again. Maybe it was best just to get the business out of the way.

"Where did you find that cleaning lady?" Peter asked. "She's not really a fugitive, is she?"

Depends, Lawrence thought. But he said, "No. Just kidding you. Why are you so interested in her?"

"Just wanted to be sure you did your due diligence on her. You can't be too careful . . ." Peter trailed off.

"Too careful of what?" Lawrence wondered if Dani was still listening outside the door. He had no intention of telling Peter why she was really here. He didn't want her to get mixed up in the convoluted machinations of the Sinclair family. Maybe he was afraid to mess with the delicate circumstances of their relationship. She was talented, but lost. She'd come to him for help—no one had done that in years—and he didn't want her to be hurt because of his family. God knew they had done enough hurt as it was.

"Just wanted to make sure she was vetted. Cleaning people are notorious for helping themselves to whatever they can."

Disappointment slammed into Lawrence's gut. He sighed, resigned. "Was this your mother's idea or yours?"

Peter, who had been reaching for another sandwich, slumped back in his chair. "Whose do you think?"

Well, that was easy. The kid had caved pretty damn quick. And Lawrence felt a tiny little ray of hope that the tired demeanor of his grandson was not self-inflicted because of his desire to get ahead, but from being beaten down.

How the hell could you look this defeated and be so young? Lawrence shouldn't have left him to the piranhas.

"You can assure her that the girl isn't stealing from me." He saw Peter's expression change, and he knew there was more. He'd beat him to it, just to save the kid from further humiliation. "And you can also tell her that she isn't some gold digger trying to cheat me out of my fortune."

"She's worried about you."

"She's worried that she won't get my vote and you won't get my shares. You could have those right now if I thought it would do any good."

Peter jumped from his chair; the plate fell off his lap and hit the carpet. "God, no!"

Lawrence felt like singing hallelujah. He hadn't been wrong. He'd felt it the moment Peter had chosen peanut butter and jelly.

Don't even think about messing with his life, Lawrence told himself. *You might do more harm than good.* Lawrence had no intention of getting involved, but, as it turned out, he did happen to have the perfect person to do it for him.

Perhaps Sister Mary Catherine was right, and the Almighty did work in mysterious ways.

Peter had retrieved the plate and put it back on the tray. "Well, I guess I'd better be going, then." He stood up.

Let him go. "Why don't you sit down, stay for a while?" Lawrence must be out of his mind. After eschewing people for at least a decade, he'd invited two people into his life in the last week. "Catch me up on what you've been doing. I heard you passed the bar."

"I did, first time I took it," Peter said, still standing.

"Impressive. It took your father three times."

"It did?"

"Yep, but in his defense, he took them so close after graduating, he didn't really have a chance to study properly."

Lawrence pulled back a little. No reason for him to get involved now. The kid was living the company tradition. Which was okay if he loved it. God knew Elliott had, and Lawrence couldn't have been happier. Selfishly, it had let him off the hook. James had already carved out a comfortable place in the company, and seemed content to let Elliott take the lead. Elliott had soared in the company environment. And burned out like a supernova.

Peter had slowly taken his seat again. He reached for another sandwich. "It was pretty intense. But I had spent two years clerking with Judge Wembley in Boston. He prepped me pretty well."

"Sounds like you enjoyed working for him." *And how did he ever convince his mother to let him take that much time before taking over?*

"I did," Peter said. "Though it wasn't actually useful for setting me up for the Sinclair legal department. But it was . . . I don't know . . ."

"Satisfying?"

"Yeah, but more. It was fascinating. And Wembley was so tuned in to people. He'd just get right out there and duke it out. Metaphorically, of course." A grin broke on his face, and he looked like the twenty-eight-year-old he was. "Though sometimes I thought he might actually roll up his sleeves and have a go at some of these lawyers. Hypocrites and self-serving vipers, he called them."

Peter straightened a bit. "It was a good experience and I'm glad I got to do it."

Yep, Lawrence thought. What this kid could use was a good dose of Dani Campbell. He'd ask Peter to stay for dinner. A few extra hours just to give him a chance to breathe. She'd done it in less time for Lawrence and he was a pretty hard nut to crack. She might even learn something from Peter.

Hell, they might be good for each other. God knew they were good for Lawrence.

═

Dani gave them half an hour, then she sauntered back into the study. Both men looked startled. "Will there be anything else?" she asked. "Maybe a cup of coffee for the road?"

Peter frowned at her. Either that was his permanent expression or he was trying to suss her out.

"Milk? Sugar?" she continued. "We don't do cream."

Lawrence snorted out loud at that one. She glared at him. Since he hadn't bothered to correct the cleaning lady charade, she was playing it to the hilt. What was with that anyway? She'd concocted the cleaning lady story in a panic over the phone. She couldn't understand why Lawrence was carrying it on. Unless for his own entertainment, which she thought was a bit mean-spirited of him.

"What's with the 'we'?" Peter blurted out.

Dani looked to Lawrence, but he had hidden himself behind the computer screen. She was not amused. "The royal we," Dani explained.

Peter's head swiveled back and forth between them like a cartoon character's. She would have laughed if Lawrence hadn't already pissed her off.

She sank into one hip, and in her best Brooklyn accent said, "Do yah wanna coffee or not? I can probably find a thermos for the trip. Wouldn't wanna throw you off your busy schedule." And she added a few choice Brooklyn expressions that she didn't say out loud.

"Okay, enough, enough," Lawrence said, emerging from behind the computer screen, his lips tight, which she knew meant he was fighting a smile. Amazing what you could learn about a person just by spending a few days with him.

"No need to hurry off," Lawrence said, smoothly interrupting the two glaring adversaries. "Actually, I was hoping you could help me with something while you were here."

That got both their attention.

"You remember the sisters at the convent across the woods?"

Peter nodded. "I saw three of them on the drive on my way in. By the way, what happened to the pavement?"

"Flash flood. Happens every several years. Last time I just left it."

"About the nuns?" Dani said, curiosity getting the better of her.

"Right," Lawrence said, and turned his full attention to Peter. "The diocese is selling the property. They plan to live in a house in town. The parochial school has been merged into a larger one miles away. But they've made no concrete plans for the community arts program. A lot of people in town participate in that program."

"Man," exclaimed Dani. "Are you about to get condos next door? So typical. Pave paradise—"

"Do you mind?" Peter spat out.

"The nuns are perfectly willing to be resettled as long as it's nearby so they can continue with the program. They need to find a suitable building to house it, but unfortunately they have to relocate by the end of November. In the meantime, they're drowning in paperwork. I thought perhaps you would be willing to give them some advice."

"I'm not licensed to practice law in Rhode Island," Peter said.

"Oh, that explains it," Dani mumbled.

Peter cut her a caustic look.

"Just explain the process to them, possibly help them with some forms and such," Lawrence continued, unruffled. "I'm sure Sister Mary Catherine and the others would be so grateful."

"I don't think—"

"You could talk to them after breakfast."

Dani's jaw dropped. She shut it so hard she might have cracked a tooth. She didn't like the idea of this self-centered legal shirt crowding their space and taking her time. Even if he was Lawrence's grandson. Besides, she was paying for it. And she and Lawrence were just beginning to find a groove.

"I suppose I could," Peter said, turning his shoulder away from Dani, effectively excluding her from the conversation. "I can get a room at the Excelsior."

"Can't. It closed after Labor Day," Dani volunteered.

"No it didn't. I saw people checking in when I drove through."

Dani's head snapped toward Lawrence. He shrugged innocently.

Damn. He'd lied to get rid of her. He thought she would just pack up and leave him alone. Well, how did that work out for him? She was living in his house. Temporarily, but still . . . Guess she'd won the first round.

"No need to go all the way into town," Lawrence said. "There's plenty of room. I'm sure we can find a spare toothbrush around here somewhere."

The fight seemed to drain from the guy, but Dani couldn't tell if it was concession or relief. Weird. She couldn't figure out the dynamic here at all.

"Actually, I brought an overnight bag in case there were things to be discussed."

For two whole days? Dani thought. What was she missing here? This wasn't a *Hey, Gramps, it's so great to see you. Can I take you and your cleaning lady to dinner, maybe laugh about old times? Tell you my plans for the future?*

This sounded more like the dude who once had shown up trying to talk her dad into selling the bar because they were planning to gentrify the neighborhood. Mike Campbell had sent him packing—him and his briefcase—easily enough. Though she didn't think Lawrence would appreciate Dani grabbing his grandson by the collar and wrestling him out the front door. If she could even reach his collar to get a good grip.

"It's all settled, then," Lawrence said, before Peter or Dani could object. "You get your things from the car; I'll telephone over to the convent to see when it would be convenient to meet with them."

To Dani's dismay, Peter didn't argue, just stood up and walked out of the room.

As soon as she heard the front door close, she turned on Lawrence. "What the hell? Why didn't you tell me your grandson was going to show up? I didn't even know you still had family. Are there more?"

"None that you need be concerned with."

"Oh, well, pardon me."

"It's complicated."

"It always is," Dani said.

Dani had lifted the tray, but now she dropped it back to the desk. The china and silver rattled.

Lawrence grimaced. "Can you cut him a break? It's only for a day or two. I think his mother has him too— Well, never mind that. Let's just say she's a woman who knows what she wants, and right now she is carrying the torch of the Sinclair legacy."

Dani tried to imagine her own mother carrying the torch to save the Campbell bar. She might take a broom to some of the rowdier patrons, but as far as the legacy of Mike's Shamrock Bar . . . her parents were thinking of selling and retiring to Florida.

"What's his story anyway? If it's any of my business."

"I'm not certain. We haven't stayed in contact." He held up one long finger. "Which I'm sure you'll get out of me one day. But not today. He's just taken his place in the company hierarchy and I think he's just had a rude awakening."

"Did you ever have a place in the company hierarchy?"

"Like I said . . . But for now, do we have anything for dinner? He looks like he could use some home cooking."

"Isn't there a fancy restaurant around you could take him to? He looks like he could afford it."

"Did you bring fancy restaurant clothes?"

"No, but I don't have to go. I think you two might have things you should work out alone."

"Chicken."

"No, I mean it."

"You know, Dani, we're all balancing on that lunatic fringe most of our lives. Give him a chance. He was always a good kid."

Dani thought he acted more like a mama's boy, but Lawrence sounded so sincere that she relented. "If he's your grandson, I'm sure he's fine." She hoisted the tray. "I suppose you want me to keep playing the cleaning lady. He doesn't believe me."

"It's no wonder. But it has been entertaining. Do you want me to tell him why you're really here?"

Dani thought it over. She certainly didn't need to be outed when she was trying to save her career. "Nah. None of his business."

"Good. Though, Dani, perhaps it's best not to bring up photography."

11

A mystery, thought Dani, as she stood at the library window watching the interloper—a great title for a photo, if only she'd had her camera at hand. He'd brought luggage just in case there was business to discuss. What business?

Something to add to the already mystifying, mysterious mystery of Lawrence Sinclair. As if she didn't have enough on her plate as it was. If they were estranged, why had the grandson shown up now of all times? He couldn't have waited a week or two?

But no, it had to be now, when she needed Lawrence's total attention.

And what was with the "Don't say anything about photography"? Was she going to have to play cleaning lady for the duration?

And the big question. How long was the dude going to stay? Already she'd lost an afternoon with Lawrence that she'd meant to spend doing a full critique of the prints they'd made last night.

And what about tomorrow? "After breakfast" could easily turn into all day, and there would be another day gone.

Was she being selfish? Maybe. Well, okay, definitely. But she needed Lawrence. Her everything was on the line. Lawrence hadn't even talked to his grandson for who knew how long. Couldn't it wait for just a few more days?

She pressed her nose to the window. What was he getting out of the car? A briefcase? *And* a suitcase. What about her photographs? They were supposed to analyze them today. *Please don't let him take all of Lawrence's weekend.*

With Manny breathing down her cell phone and time barreling ahead, she was jealous of every moment taken away from her quest of honest, soul-full photos.

Not to mention she had to be back in New York for the Five X Five gala. She didn't have a choice. She would just add it to her time off. She wasn't done with Lawrence Sinclair yet. He wouldn't get rid of her that easily.

And then there was the business with the perfume people. Getting that account would be a huge coup. And though she wasn't really interested in selling products, even high-end perfume, it would look good on her CV and paid extremely well. Especially for a newbie who hadn't made a name for herself outside the art, photo, and media world.

Ugh. Maybe if she was nasty enough, he'd leave first thing in the morning. Nah, that wouldn't be fair to Lawrence, who seemed to be happy to see him.

Peter shut the trunk, hoisted a designer duffel, and headed toward the front door.

Dani grabbed the tea tray and fled back to the kitchen.

═

Peter took his time carrying his things back to the house. There was definitely something shady going on here. He had half a mind to call his mother. But she'd be down here in a flash with a cadre of lawyers and papers to sign. The thought of that made him sick to his stomach.

Besides, if they wanted him to assume his role in the company, he'd better start making decisions for himself.

Who was he kidding? He would do just about anything to prevent the confrontation between his mother and Lawrence. No one really knew why his mother blamed Lawrence for Elliott's death. Great-uncle James had once suggested it was because Lawrence was still alive and Elliott wasn't. Whatever it was, it had been festering for sixteen years. Even before that. It would be catastrophic if it ever came to a head.

It would be better for everyone if Peter just accepted his fate and took over Lawrence's shares and votes. Even Lawrence was amenable to the transfer. It seemed like everyone would be happy . . . except Peter.

He paused at the front door, his hand on the knob. There it was. He just wasn't ready. He pushed away the traitorous thought that he might not want to be ready. The outcome might be inevitable, but he couldn't bring himself to do it. Not yet, though only a miracle could put the brakes on his predetermined future.

But it was apparent that he did need to deal with this "cleaning lady" situation. Damn, he'd almost wanted to believe it. But the spiked hair and flashing eyes gave her away. Dani Campbell was no more a cleaning lady than he was. Which led to the question: Just who was she and what was she to his grandfather?

He might be naive—he'd actually spent more time studying than partying at college. But even he knew that old men wanted beautiful, cultured arm candy. Not some creature with weird hair, snappy eyes, and an attitude. And a mouth.

And what a mouth. He'd meant her choice of vocabulary, but as soon as he thought it, his mind went to her actual lips and the way they pursed slightly while she was thinking of her next awful thing to say.

Lips or not, he felt duty bound to stop her from getting her claws into his grandfather, her purple glitter–polished claws. Though they weren't claws at all, but cut short and rounded as if she typed a lot. They were still purple, and he didn't trust them—or her.

But where had she even met Lawrence? He never went anywhere that the family was aware of. A brief image of his grandfather dressed in a trench coat, entering a private club under an alias, sprang comically into his wayward thoughts. Though disguise might be the only way he could escape Marian Sinclair's spies. Ugh, she actually was having his grandfather spied on.

Lawrence was no fool. And Dani Campbell? Whatever her subterfuge was, Lawrence seemed to be a part of it. And was enjoying it.

And that was a problem.

The door opened before Peter finally turned the knob.

"Oh, there you are," Lawrence said. "I'll show you upstairs to the guest room. If we're lucky, maybe we can get Dani to make up the bed for you."

"In your dreams," came the echoing voice from somewhere down the hall.

Was she spying on them, too?

His grandfather grinned. Actually grinned. Peter's stomach did a flip, then a flop. Something was definitely going on here.

"I'll walk you up and you can unpack while I call the convent."

Peter climbed the stairs, moving slowly so as not to outdistance his grandfather until Lawrence passed him and said, "Maybe you should get more exercise." Peter hurried after him.

Peter had intended to pump Lawrence for an explanation about the Dani situation, but she obviously had no compunction about eavesdropping. He'd have to wait until she left for the day.

He changed into jeans and a polo shirt and met Lawrence on the landing a few minutes later.

"She said to come on over. They have their Saturday community program going on, but she'll have a few minutes free."

"What does she need exactly?" Peter asked.

"A lawyer."

"I explained that I can't actually represent her."

"I know. Just listen to her, if you don't mind."

Dani was sitting on the front steps when they left the house.

"She's coming, too?" Peter asked under his breath.

"It's a nice walk," Lawrence said. "Ready?"

Dani stood up. She didn't look ready, she looked annoyed.

And she didn't get any more approachable on the walk through the woods to the convent. She ignored them completely, stumbling behind them like she wasn't watching where she was going. The few times Peter glanced her way, she was looking off in some other direction, a slight furrow between her dark eyebrows.

Finally he gave up trying to figure her out and just relaxed into a sense of familiarity. He'd spent a lot of his childhood in these woods or down on the beach with his grandfather and Ganna Kissie. The thought made him smile, sadly though, since shortly after his father's death, Kissie had kissed them all goodbye, metaphorically at least, and departed for somewhere else.

Peter had been the last to know, which seemed to usually be the case with him. He was never told why, not even as an adult. His grandmother had become one of those skeletons the Sinclairs didn't speak of.

He remembered her, though, a true light in his life of boarding schools and absentee parents. He didn't mind any of it, because when his parents were gone, he stayed here with Gadda and Ganna Kissie. And this was home. "Huh."

"Something on your mind?" Lawrence asked.

"Just remembering," Peter told him.

Lawrence merely nodded and kept walking.

The convent was one of those buildings that seemed to smile at you. There were people strolling the lawns. Easels were set up in a semicircle, and several would-be artists were attempting to capture the landscape under the tutelage of a middle-aged man, probably a priest on loan from the parish. Others were taking selfies with the pre-fall foliage.

The sun was shining and Peter was glad when they stepped under a wide porch overhang and rang the bell to the main building. He'd been concerned about Lawrence making the long walk, but Lawrence seemed less affected by the trek than Peter or Dani, the goth cleaning lady.

Sister Mary Catherine greeted them with a tilt of her head, welcomed Lawrence, then Dani like she was already a member of the family.

"Thank you for coming, Peter."

"Good to see you, Sister," Peter returned.

"I know Lawrence has explained our predicament. But before we retire to my office, I thought you might like a quick tour to see what is provided here."

She led them down a short entry hall to a main corridor.

"The chapel is at the back near the ocean and has a separate entrance, but we've turned most of the rooms in the house into usable community space.

"We run year-round classes in various techniques for all to enjoy—young and old, children and seniors, those with special needs, and just plain folks who want to learn something about art.

"It's the only outlet that most of these people have; it enriches everyone. The community depends on us."

Sister Mary Catherine pointed out various art rooms as they walked; sometimes doors were open and they could see students bent over their work.

"We have meeting rooms and a large hospitality room and this"—she stopped at a double door and reached inside to turn on the lights—"is our art gallery." It was a long room painted an off-white and lined with paintings and sketches of all kinds, large and small, near professional to stick figures. Several pedestals held statues and modern sculpture, and cabinets held an array of ceramics.

"This is our budding artists room. It's a rotating exhibit. Every one of our students gets a place, just not all at once."

"It's nice that they all get a chance to shine," Dani said.

"And to give of themselves to others," Sister Mary Catherine added.

"What's in there?" Dani pointed to an archway with a Closed sign taped to the adjacent wall.

"For decades we've presented a special exhibit during our annual Harvest Festival. Last year it was handmade quilts of New England. Unfortunately, it became too expensive to continue. But we plan to fill the space in joyous celebration of this year's Annual—and perhaps last—Harvest Festival."

Sister Mary Catherine gestured them back into the hallway and turned off the lights. They retraced their steps to the distant chords of an organ, accompanied by the steady beat of a hammer up ahead.

They found the source of the hammering in the next corridor, where a carpenter was replacing a warped baseboard and another nun was overseeing his progress. Sister Mary Catherine introduced her as Sister Eloise.

The carpenter looked up. "Morning, Lawrence. How's it going?"

"Not bad, Watkins," Lawrence said. "I see the nuns have got you busy."

"Yeah. A burst pipe in the wall, undiscovered until it had done its damage."

Sister Mary Catherine sighed. "It needs those who can care for it properly."

"You've taken good care of the old place," Watkins said. "I just hope the next folks do half as well."

Sister Mary Catherine smiled and turned to Dani. "Would you like to look in on some of our classes in progress? Sister Eloise, would you show our friend Dani around while I do a little necessary business in the office?"

"Gladly," said Sister Eloise, gesturing to Dani to accompany her. "This way."

═

When Sister Eloise and Dani left and Watkins took up his hammering, Sister Mary Catherine showed Peter and Lawrence into her office and shut the door.

She gestured to chairs and then sat behind a battered wooden desk. "I don't know how much Lawrence has told you, but the upshot is . . . the diocese is selling the property, and I seem to be completely befuddled by all this paperwork." She inched a stack of folders across the desk toward the two men. "Lawrence said you might be willing to give us some advice. We do have a small budget for such things."

Peter waved his hand, embarrassed. "As I told Lawrence, I'm not licensed in Rhode Island, but I'm happy to take a look. I can only give suggestions and help you fill out the proper forms, but not as a legal advisor, just as a—a . . ."

"Friend," Lawrence supplied.

Peter nodded. "If there is any legal action involved, you'll have to find a local lawyer to represent you."

The sister blinked. Then looked to Lawrence. "Will it come to that?"

"Let's not think ahead," Lawrence said. "Let Peter take a look."

Under the intent eyes of the two, Peter opened the top folder. For a simple sale, the stack was almost the size of his last corporate case.

Now that he thought of it, what was the church but a giant corporation? He riffled through the documents. After a few minutes, he closed the folder. "May I take these? I'll look them over more closely, but it appears fairly cut-and-dried. They're selling the property and . . ."

He paused, looking at the woman in a new way. *How would it feel to serve the church all your life and be turned out when you were no longer needed?* ". . . terminating housing and all other activities associated with the Sisters of— Pardon me if this is none of my business, but don't they have a retirement home for nuns?"

Sister Mary Catherine folded her hands on her desk. "They do. But Sisters Eloise and Agnes and I are planning to move into town. We've been living in one of the retreat cottages on campus, but it will go with the rest of it."

"I'm sorry."

"Oh, we will do. It's been a good life, but we are too few and too old to keep everything running. The elementary school has already been consolidated into another in Providence."

"That's a rather long commute."

"I imagine most of our students will be absorbed into the local public school." She sighed. "We've lost the school; we've turned the food pantry over to another local church. We understand that we can't afford to keep it as things are now. And the church will be able to use the income for other good works. But there is still work to be done. And we do have what they call a 'footprint' in the community."

Peter looked down at the folders, then back at the nun. "If you're not against the sale and the school has already been transferred, what is it that you need me to do?"

"We've accepted our displacement and the closing of the convent. But please, please, help us save our art school."

═

Dani followed Sister Eloise down the hall and into a large, bright room where a table with an arrangement of seasonal fruits was surrounded by serious-looking artists of various ages. Some stood in front of easels working in oils, watercolors, and pastels; others sat in chairs, two of which were wheelchairs, with large sketchbooks balanced on their laps; while others still crowded around a table with paper and crayons.

"We have still-life classes on Saturdays and Wednesdays," Sister Eloise explained as she stopped and made suggestions at one easel, then bent over to nod at a seated artist.

"You've captured that pear to perfection, Vera."

A rather pudgy middle-aged woman twisted her neck to smile up to Sister Eloise. "I looked real close like you told me," Vera said.

Sister Eloise patted her shoulder and moved away from the

circle to another open door, and into a smaller room where a group of seniors, mainly women, sat in a circle knitting and crocheting.

"Our needlework is as much a chat group as a needlework group, but they have a good time and make prayer shawls for the elderly, which are always appreciated."

They passed out of the room into a smaller corridor. "At the end of this hall are sculpture and photography studios. We're very proud of those, but they are only open two evenings a week. Not ideal, but we just don't have enough staff to oversee things, even with our volunteers.

"And this is our newest addition." She opened a door into another square room, the windows shaded and several workstations and computer banks emitting glowing auras into the semidarkness.

"Our media lab." Sister Eloise gestured to several workstations where single users or small groups crowded around fairly advanced equipment. It was impressive, but Dani couldn't help but wonder if they should have spent more of their funds on fixing up the place than on electronics.

The sister guided Dani over to a work desk where one student was going through a series of twists and shoulder rolls as he hunched over a multiscreen setup.

"Logan, we have a visitor. Would you like to tell her about your project?"

Logan was tall and thin. A high schooler, Dani guessed. He was working his way through a sophisticated line drawing of a dragon fighting an as yet to be identified adversary.

It took him a while to switch gears and come back to the land of reality. Dani totally understood. And she was sorry they had interrupted him.

"Yeah, well," he said, shifting on his stool so that his knees arced like a metronome while he spoke. "It's a thing I'm working on. A story. A comic, like." He glanced back at the screen as if to make sure it was still there. And it did look real enough, even in a half-completed state, that it might jump off the screen. There was also a fully rendered dragon in an oversize spiral drawing tablet on the desk beside the console. And it was remarkable.

"You're transferring the line drawing to a drawing program?"

"Well, yeah. I don't have any of this stuff where I live, so . . ." He trailed off.

"It's amazing. Both of them. What program are you using?" Dana asked.

"Uh, Corel Painter."

"Good one," Dani said. "I use it sometimes, too."

"You do? Are you a graphics geek?"

"Mostly I take photographs, but I sometimes . . . play with the images."

A kindred spirit, thought Dani, though Logan was totally immersed in his work, lost in his own ideas, when she had merely gotten lost along the way. She wondered what Lawrence would say about this sprouting wizard.

"Cool. I'm saving up for a Wacom tablet. It might take a while."

"It has a good rep. You're planning to animate it?" Dani asked.

"I guess. Maybe someday." He glanced at Sister Eloise, who stood patiently by while they chatted. "I'm having trouble just trying to figure this one out. There's kind of a learning curve," he admitted.

"What's hanging you up?"

Dani listened as he elaborated on his vision of the frame.

"You need to start with a little less complicated background vector. You can always layer more." She eased toward the computer. "Want me to show you?"

"Don't delete anything."

"No," Dani promised. She nudged him over. Other graphics students began to drift over, and soon there was a group of them leaning over her and asking questions.

Dani had completely lost track of time when someone said, "Ah, there she is."

At the sound of Sister Mary Catherine's voice, the students parted like Moses and the Red Sea. Dani's head jerked up to see Lawrence, Peter, and the two nuns gathered before them. She had totally forgotten about Sister Eloise.

And Lawrence.

Lawrence. And here she was playing with graphics.

Guilt slammed the air right out of her. "I was just—" How could she have been so stupid to blithely go where she wasn't supposed to go? Her little attempt to help Logan could jeopardize her relationship with her own mentor.

Sister Mary Catherine beamed at her. "I see you've found our master cartoonist."

Lawrence said, "How you doing, Logan?"

"Good. She knew how to fix the background so I could lay down dimensions."

"Just glad I could help." Dani risked a glance at Lawrence. She couldn't tell if he was angry, disappointed, or what.

She glanced back at Logan. "Guess I'd better be leaving. Thanks for the preview." Dani moved away from the computer.

"Maybe you could come back sometime," Logan stammered.

"Yeah," said a girl who had been one of the first to come over and had asked several intelligent questions. "I need help, too."

"So do we," said one of the others, gesturing to his two comrades.

"I'd like to, but I don't know if I can."

"Please," they said in chorus. "Sister Mary Catherine, tell her to try."

"Now, now, Ms. Campbell is just visiting and I'm sure—"

"I'll try," Dani said over her shoulder. "But no promises." If Lawrence was angry, she might be on her way home before she could say "vector graphics."

"I enjoyed my visit. You guys are great."

"That was kind of you," Sister Eloise said as they followed the others out.

"I enjoyed it. They were all so engaged. And Logan. He's got that special something."

Sister Eloise sighed. "If he stays out of trouble."

"Cartooning should keep him busy."

"He doesn't have the equipment at home."

"I don't doubt it. You've got a pretty major setup."

"It was all donated to the school," Sister Eloise said. "But I suppose it will have to be sold along with the rest if we can't find a place to relocate."

"What's the problem?" Dani asked.

"I don't know. Sister Mary Catherine has taken on the responsibility of"—she took a second to cross herself—"finding us a miracle."

Oh dear, Dani thought. If she was consulting with Lawrence the town recluse and his "estranged" and she might add "strange" grandson, she really would need a miracle.

Both sisters accompanied them to the door.

The lawn that had been bustling with visitors when they'd arrived was more sparsely populated now. A few painters were still hard at work; the last of the families were gathering up their children and coaxing them toward the street.

"I hope we didn't keep you too long," Sister Mary Catherine told Dani. "They can be an insistent bunch. But oh so eager to learn."

"Once they settle down," Sister Eloise added.

"I didn't mind. You have a really cool program."

"And you're very knowledgeable; you managed to bring Logan out of his fantasy world for a minute."

"Actually, he pulled me into his," Dani said, and glanced at Lawrence. When he didn't respond, she added, "Thanks for the tour."

"Our pleasure," Sister Mary Catherine said. "If you're going to be here for a while, we would love for you to visit again. I'm sure the kids would appreciate your help."

"I don't think I'm all that good with kids," Dani said.

"She'd love to," Lawrence interjected.

Dani did a double-take.

Peter, who had leaned against the wall and was frowning at a bundle of papers he'd acquired during the visit, straightened at that, and turned his frown on Dani.

The nuns waved goodbye and went back inside. Dani, Lawrence, and Peter started across the lawn, Peter walking ahead, the bundle of folders under his arm, head down, preoccupied.

"So how did it go?" Dani asked Lawrence.

He shrugged. "Bunch of legal stuff. Greek to me."

"Will he be able to help them?"

"He took all the papers. Said he'd look into it. I guess we'll see."

They didn't stop until they'd almost reached the house, then

Peter turned and thrust out the files to Lawrence. "Can you take these inside? I thought I would take a walk down on the beach for a bit. If that's okay?"

"Sure, sure," Lawrence said, taking the stack of folders. "Just what the doctor ordered. Dani can go with you."

12

No need," Peter said. "I know the way."

Lawrence looked from Peter to Dani.

Dani widened her eyes at him, and seeing his expression, added a chin jut for emphasis. It did absolutely no good.

"She'd enjoy the walk," Lawrence added.

Peter was already moving away. "Thanks, but I'm sure she would like to get home," he said over his shoulder.

"Yes, I would," Dani said. "Thank you."

Peter took off, and Lawrence turned to Dani. "You could at least be hospitable."

"Why? I'm the cleaning lady. And if you want your dinner, I have to go see what's in the fridge."

"We could order out."

"No, no, and no," she said as they watched Peter navigate the path down to the beach, nimble-footed, as if he did it every day.

Lawrence let out a long sigh.

"What?"

"Would it hurt you to be a little nicer to him? He acts like he has the weight of the world on his shoulders. Though why would I be surprised? The Sinclairs hold you down while they drain you of life."

Dani looked up at that, wondering what the Sinclairs had done to Lawrence. She hadn't asked before, because she hadn't realized it was such a big deal. She'd come from a fairly wacky but loving family; they kept odd hours, raised their children in the back of a Brooklyn bar, sent them to public school, and sent the ones who wanted to go to state college. Dani hadn't been one of those. But they didn't push her to "further" her education, just follow her dream.

How were they to know how fragile her chosen dream was? If Lawrence Sinclair couldn't help her, it would implode. She couldn't keep on going the way she had. She'd be burned out, used up, unemployed and unemployable before you could say, "Guggenheim."

As if reading her thoughts, something it seemed he was perfecting, Lawrence said, "I think he may be going through a career crisis, too."

"Okay, but what am I supposed to talk about? You said not to mention photography. And BTW, why shouldn't I talk about photography? I can't exactly tell him I'm not the cleaning lady; he'll ask why we've been lying. And discussing the weather will take all of two minutes."

She could see Peter's head bobbing through the sea grasses as he neared the beach. Actually, a few minutes at the beach might be nice.

"Ask him about his ideas for the convent. Hell. Just be good company."

Dani rolled her eyes.

"Ple-e-e-ease."

She snorted out a laugh. "You are such a manipulator."

"Learned it from the best."

"But you owe me."

She stalked off after Peter, and Lawrence hurried into the house.

Dani didn't navigate the path quite as easily as Peter had. Unlike the path through the woods, this one paralleled the crag of boulders on the beach's far side. Not only was it steep, but it was filled with loose dirt and pebbles. She managed to reach the bottom after a few slides, but no mishaps, and stood for a second to take a breath and brush the sand off her hands.

Peter stood near the water, the tide perilously close to his expensive running shoes. His idea of living dangerously? So far he hadn't shown anything but downtroddenness—was that even a word? But Lawrence was definitely right about him. His shoulders even slumped at the beach.

So now what did she do? Stalk him in the background? Ease up beside him and try to make small talk? *Gee, lovely day, isn't it?*

She couldn't do it. It was one thing to make nonsense talk when you were furthering your career, but talking to someone who obviously wished you weren't there was a little dicier.

She'd just have to play it by ear. She trudged through the pebbles and sand until she was standing next to him.

"Lawrence made me come down. I'll just go sit on a rock over there and not bother you. Just let me know when you're ready to leave, so we can make a grand entrance together."

Peter glanced at her. "Don't feel bad," he said. "It's hard to hold out when Lawrence devolves into arm twisting. Sinclairs are used to getting their own way."

"Doesn't look like you're getting yours."

"I generally don't," he said, his voice even.

She'd been looking at the water, but his lack of gumption made her turn around. "What kind of attitude is that?"

"Life doesn't bode well for those who buck the Sinclair system."

"Huh." Dani raked her fingers through her hair. The ocean air was making her spikes curl, and Peter Sinclair's defeatism was pissing her off.

"What do the Sinclairs do, anyway?"

"Make everybody's lives miserable."

"Other than that," Dani said.

"You really don't know?"

"Why should I?" Dani looked to the sky and threw up her hands in supplication. "Do I need twenty questions?"

He laughed. Her head snapped toward him.

He looked as surprised as she.

Guess he didn't laugh a lot. At least he was looking better in the ocean air. Of course, it was too dark in the house to take in much detail of anything. And she'd spent the walk to the convent "looking" at other stuff.

Now she looked at Peter Sinclair. Tried to imagine him as a young Lawrence. He was tall, but not as tall as Lawrence. A face that was youthful behind the worry lines and frowning brows. His hair was darkish with a hint of red and had been ruffled by the sea breeze. She tried to imagine him as an old man with white hair and a thin white beard.

"What are you looking at?"

She jumped, the image dissipating as quickly as it had come. "Nothing."

"Just glowering at me."

"I wasn't glowering, I was thinking. Actually, I was trying to see a resemblance between you and Lawrence."

He shoved his hands in his jeans pockets and began walking along the edge of the sand. Since he was strolling, more than trying to escape, she hurried to catch up.

"Could you see it?" he asked without slowing down.

"For a second . . . maybe," she said.

"I used to spend a lot of time here with Lawrence and my grandmother. I haven't been down in a long time."

"How come?"

He cut her a sharp glance.

"I don't really care, I'm not the FBI. Just curious. If I had a grandpa with a beach house I'd be down there every chance I got."

"It's complicated."

"Yikes! You really said that? Seems like that little BMW of yours didn't have any trouble finding the way."

"God, are you always so—so—?"

"Pushy? Obnoxious? Nosy? Caring? Curious? Genuinely interested? A good conversationalist?"

Peter threw up his hands. "Okay, okay. I get it. How on earth did you ever become Lawrence's cleaning lady?"

Great. Now she was going to have to lie because she'd promised Lawrence not to mention photography, and photography was the reason she had come. And what was that all about? She really needed to find out.

"Just needed to expand my horizons."

"By cleaning someone else's house?"

"Hey, don't judge."

"No. I'm sorry. It must be a pretty overwhelming project."

"You could say that."

"You made him laugh."

They'd come to the end of the beach and turned around. Now she was the one at the water's edge.

"Is that so unusual? I know he's a grump sometimes."

"A grump?" exclaimed Peter. "He's a misanthrope."

"No, he isn't. He's a great pho— Funny person. At least he can be . . . sometimes." *Whew, that was close.*

"I remember he *was* funny sometimes when it was him and my grandmother." Peter smiled. "Gadda and Ganna Kissie—I couldn't pronounce *r*'s until I was in kindergarten; my grandmother's name was Krista, everyone called her Kristy, so . . . God, why am I telling you this?"

"Well, I think it's cool," Dani said, and liked him a little better than before. "So what did the three of you do?"

He stopped and looked over the small beach. His gaze scanned the rock boulders and lingered at the top for a moment before he jerked it away and pointed to a place on the sand. "Over there . . ."

But Dani's gaze had snagged at the top, and she wondered if the woman in the photograph was Kristy Sinclair. And what had happened to her. She certainly wasn't living with Lawrence.

"Sometimes, we'd bring blankets down at night."

Dani pulled her thoughts back.

"A real adventure requiring several flashlights; a basket of food; juice or hot chocolate, depending on the weather; a telescope; and several storybooks. We'd lie on the blankets and count the shooting stars. There were a lot of shooting stars some nights . . ." His voice trailed off.

"I don't know why I remembered that," Peter said suddenly, stuffing his hands into his pockets.

Or why he'd shared it with her, she bet. She didn't think the breeze was causing that faint flush across his cheekbones.

"It sounds like fun," Dani said. "My grandparents live in Brooklyn. In a basement apartment. The same apartment they lived in since they were first married. Wild, huh."

Peter had become silent. Was he still embarrassed, or was it something she'd said?

"Brooklyn?"

"Yeah, in New York. I guess that sounds weird to you." She looked up at the house above them.

When she looked back at him, his expression had changed

and he suddenly looked like the man she had met several hours ago, not the one she'd just been walking with on the beach.

"You're probably anxious to get back to your work, or home, or whatever," he said. "I think I'll stay for a while longer, if you can get back okay."

She couldn't really ignore that not too subtle hint. She'd done her duty. "Sure. See ya." She started across the beach back to the path, but at the edge of the sand, she turned to deliver one final wisecrack.

Peter Sinclair had disappeared.

═

Lawrence stood to the side of the den window; he could see the beach from here and he'd spent the last few minutes watching the two young people strolling along the surf.

For a moment he forgot they were a younger generation and he could see himself and Krista frolicking in the surf as if they didn't have a care in the world. But he did have a care by then. The reason he had given up their peripatetic life, he as a freelance photographer and Krista taking care of Elliott while they all lived out of a camper and she cultivated her spirit in a revolving kaleidoscope of meditation, sand painting, astrological studies, nature.

Krista, his free-spirit wife, could make a gourmet meal over a campfire. Laugh when the rain drenched the drying clothes hanging on a makeshift line strung between a car door and a tree. Carry a four-year-old on her hip and dance across the beach as if they were both light as air.

They'd been happy, then.

Moving back to Boston had sucked the life out of her. His family had done nothing to welcome Krista. And for that, he would never forgive them. And they would never forgive him for what came later.

So why was his grandson here now?

Lawrence held the curtain back and squinted down at the beach. What were they talking about? Were they getting along? It seemed like they were. And why did it matter to him?

Peter would go home to Boston. Dani would go back to her life as a hotshot photographer. And things would never change.

They'd both turned suddenly and stared straight up to the house, as if they knew he was there. He'd stepped quickly out of sight. But he couldn't move completely away.

Maybe he was a fool for even thinking those two could be good for each other. But being an old fool was one of the privileges of the aged. And he was definitely that. Though it seemed to him that he hadn't had an ache or pain since Dani had shown up at his door and bitched at him through the mail slot.

He smiled. He couldn't help it. He'd known that brassy Brooklynite for less than a week, and she was already like a granddaughter to him. A granddaughter he didn't have. Elliott and Marian had stopped after Peter. Lawrence had wondered why, but he was afraid he knew the answer. They were both too busy climbing their way to power.

He risked peering around the drapes. Dani was walking up the beach toward home. *Home.* This was no one's home. He reluctantly moved from the window and made his way back downstairs. It would only make Dani angry, and Peter distressed, if they knew he had been watching.

But hell, watching the two of them with their whole lives ahead of them, both on a precipice that would decide that future, he had hope that they would have better days ahead. That they would fulfill their dreams.

And a little flame of optimism ignited within him, and he thought, *Why can't they help each other get there?*

═

Dani scanned the beach, panic rising. Where the hell was he? People didn't just disappear off a beach. Not even for an alien abduction. *This isn't happening.* She scanned the beach again. The man was nowhere in sight.

She speared her pocket for her phone, but who would she call? Lawrence couldn't help, and what would she tell emergency services? *A man just disappeared from a beach.* No, there had to be a rational explanation.

Stay calm and search. Maybe he fell on the rocks and she just couldn't see him from where she was standing. She started across the beach looking in all directions. Searched the water; nothing floating. Besides, he hadn't had time to drown. She broke into a run.

She huffed to a stop at the base of the boulders. Called out, "Peter?"

Nothing.

"Peter! Where are you?" She braced herself against the rock and looked around the edge. More rocks rising at least twenty feet in the air. He hadn't escaped her that way.

The tide was pretty high, but there was still a thin shelf of rock at the base of the crag. She eased along its slippery surface, her back pressed against the granite, her fingers groping for purchase. Why would he have come this way? Unless the local tiki bar was located on the other side, and he'd stopped in for a drink. Still, she scanned the water, peered into the deep crevices of the boulders.

"Peter, dammit! This better not be some kind of joke. It isn't funny."

She cupped her hands to her mouth. Yelled, "Peter!" Yelled again, "Peter?"

"What?"

Dani yelped. Whooshed out a breath as her heart bounced around her chest like a tilted pinball machine. Her arms flailed for balance, and she was grabbed from behind. She twisted around to find Peter Sinclair's expression of alarm as he pinioned her arms to her sides.

"What the heck?" She broke away, but the effort unbalanced them both, and for a moment they teetered on the ledge. His arm slipped around her back, but it only sped up the inevitable, and they fell off the shelf, wrapped in an embrace . . .

All of six inches before their feet hit the sandy beach and surf rolled across their ankles.

"Really?" she said, attempting to climb back onto the ledge. "You scared the crap out of me. You wrecked my shoes. Where the hell were you?"

Peter stepped onto the ledge, blocking her way. "Just climbing around. Why didn't you go back to the house?"

"Because I turned around and you were gone. I was afraid you'd drowned or something. Where were you?" She tried to peer past him, to see where he'd come from, but it was near impossible.

"Don't get to the beach much in Brooklyn, huh?"

"Not funny."

"Come on. I'll walk you back." He reached for her elbow, but she snatched it away and sloshed through the water back to the beach. He got there before her and strode toward the path.

She stomped after him, shoes squelching and picking up sand.

As soon as they reached the house, Dani dumped her shoes

in the back hall and went to the kitchen in search of dinner makings. Peter strode straight past her, lingering only long enough to reach over her shoulder to snag a beer before continuing on his way, probably in search of Lawrence.

She wondered briefly when he would realize that the beer didn't have a twist-off cap. But he didn't come back; most likely there was a bottle opener in one of the many cabinets in the parlor.

Dani pulled out a last package of hamburger, not failing to notice that her hands were still shaking from her panic on the beach. Or maybe from her being so pissed off. The two of them were probably out there laughing about her reaction.

She slapped the beef package on the counter and got out an onion and some canned tomato sauce. There was just enough to whip up a batch of Mike's Thursday night special. Spaghetti and meatballs.

The idea calmed her, even brought a smile to her lips. She'd been enlisted to help form meatballs from the day she could reach the countertop. It had been a few years since her last meatball, but she was confident she could pull it off.

She got out herbs and a big yellow Pyrex mixing bowl. And by the time she started mixing the ingredients, she was almost back to normal. Her mother always complained that spaghetti was the daffiest thing to serve at a bar, where the light was dim, and after a few drinks, the patrons left with much of the spaghetti clinging to the fronts of their shirts. The floor was sometimes worse.

Dani paused to get her cell and send her parents a selfie of her in the kitchen. They'd get a big kick out of that.

When the meatballs were sautéed and simmering in the tomato sauce, she reached for a box of pasta. The kitchen door opened and Peter walked in. Stopped on the threshold. He was holding an empty beer bottle.

"Why are you still here?" he asked curiously.

"Making your dinner?"

"Why?"

"Well, Lawrence has to eat, and I confess I'm feeling a bit peckish myself."

"What?"

"Peckish, I heard it on a PBS series. Cool word. It means—"

"I know what it means. But why are you doing this? Are you also the cook?"

"Hmm. Most of the time. Though Lawrence makes a mean blueberry pancake."

"You share meals?"

"It must be because you're a lawyer."

"What is?"

"That you talk in questions. I'm serving spaghetti. Ain't fancy but it'll get the job done." She almost cracked herself up on that one. Straight from her dad's mouth. That was after he fired the short-order cook and before he harangued her mother into taking over the food service. Once she started cooking, the spaghetti became a local legend. Dani figured her own was somewhere in between. "I'll set you a place, but don't feel compelled."

He glared at her, snatched open the fridge, relieved it of two more beers, and left the room, the slam of the fridge door reverberating after him.

She should probably have gone easy on the salt tonight. The guy was stress on hormones. And no telling what his momentary disappearance had done to her.

They ate at the kitchen table like she and Lawrence always did. Conversation was minimal, with Lawrence tucking the napkin in his collar and eating with gusto. Peter, head down, ate fairly heartily after a slow start. No one made eye contact, but each secretly watched the others.

For herself, Dani didn't have much of an appetite. Mainly she watched the two men and wondered how she had landed in the middle of whatever was going on between them.

Finally Lawrence pushed his plate away, and Dani took this as her cue to extricate herself. "You two can do the dishes. I'm going to bed. It's been a long day." She took her plate and glass to the sink, then set off for her housekeeper's room.

Peter stood up, looked at his watch.

"Do you need a ride home? It's getting dark."

"I am home," Dani said, just to bust his chops. She was beginning to resent his appropriation of Lawrence.

"What?"

"I live here," she said smugly. "Didn't Lawrence tell you?"

She strode out the door to Lawrence's guffaw and dead silence from his grandson.

But if she'd expected to get any peace, that illusion was shattered when her cell phone rang. It had rung several times that day, almost all the calls from Manny. She couldn't avoid him any longer.

She took her laptop and phone to the bed and returned his call.

"Where the hell have you been? Why aren't you returning my calls?"

"I'm sorry, but some unexpected things came up today. I was busy, but I'm returning them now. What's up?" Dani pulled up her iCal, checked the schedule.

"You haven't forgotten Five X Five this Friday. Being one of the five, your appearance is not negotiable."

"Got it right here on my calendar." She could drive down in the morning, hit her apartment for some fashionista time, and drive straight back after the event. She'd be here by dawn.

"And the perfume people want to meet Saturday before they go back to Milan. They want to pass some ideas by you."

And so it begins, Dani thought. This would be her first commercial shoot, but she'd heard enough horror stories to make her want to turn tail and hide. Decisions by committee. A committee for every step of the process. Tears, and tempers, and more tears.

"Dani? Are you listening? If you're getting cold feet, don't. You're perfect for this campaign. And I'm going to get you a big contract, maybe multiple shoots. Don't let me down."

"Have I ever?" She wanted to say, *It's only a bottle of perfume*, but self-preservation held her tongue. She didn't even know why they wanted her. She didn't wear perfume; she didn't know many women who did. It seemed so last decade. But she would do it. She'd be a fool not to. It was a plum assignment. It would keep her in steam trays and takeout Chinese for a year—and keep her career on its upward trajectory.

It was a pretty bottle and smelled nice enough. She'd put it on a white table, and then . . . for once she didn't have an idea in the world.

"Oh, and the publishers want your next packet of *G and J* photos."

"But I—" She stopped herself before she confessed that she hadn't even given the *Junque* project any thought. She'd think about it tonight. But getting all these projects taken care of could take days in New York. A week even.

Her new photos were sitting in an envelope on her dresser. That was what she wanted to be working on. Not perfume, or antiques, or even gallery openings.

How could she leave now when it seemed like she might be making a breakthrough?

She would just have to make it work. "Don't worry, it's all good. I'll see you on Friday."

"Make it Thursday. Come early. Meet me for lunch. Chez Diner. Two o'clock."

"Wouldn't miss it," Dani said, feeling a heavy weight descend.

"We'll go over the shape of the next few months. Get things rolling after your little hiatus."

"I told you, I'm working on a project."

"Fine. What is it? I'll start booking."

"It's not ready."

"But it will be. The choice slots are already filling up for next summer. Ya gotta be in it to win it."

"I know, Manny, I'm good. I gotta go. See you on Thursday." She ended the call before he could make any more demands.

Thursday. Her time was running out. And so far all she had was a batch of photos on her dresser waiting to be critiqued, and the impediment to her success sitting in her kitchen.

13

Dani was the first one in the kitchen the next morning. Either the men were sleeping late or Peter had already left. She detoured into the library and peeked out the window. The BMW was still there.

Her spirits did a little flip and flop; first up, then down. Lawrence was happy that Peter had come, Dani could tell, but what was going on between them? Was she the one in the way?

To hell with that. She stalked back into the kitchen. If Peter Sinclair thought he could waltz in here like a VIP, then . . . She pulled eggs out of the fridge and carried them to the counter. Peter was family and she was . . . just shit out of luck. She cracked the first egg on the side of the bowl so hard that it shattered in her hand.

"Maybe you should take it easy on those eggs."

Dani screeched in surprise and the eggshell jackknifed into the air.

Peter barely managed to dodge in time. He recovered quickly and stooped down to scoop up the damaged shell.

He dropped it in the sink and wiped off his hands. "Are you planning to juggle every egg in that"—he peered into the bowl—"omelet?"

She scowled at him. She wasn't even pissed; it just seemed to be the expression he elicited from her.

"Mind if I make coffee?"

"Help yourself," she said begrudgingly. She'd meant to make that first, but she'd gotten waylaid by the whirlwind of jealousy she'd felt on seeing his car.

He went straight to a cupboard and opened it. Looked inside.

"I moved the coffee stuff closer to the coffeemaker," she said. "Left-hand side of the sink. Cups are on the second shelf."

"The glasses used to be there."

Dani gritted her teeth. "They're in the next cupboard over."

He got the coffee and filters down and poured water into the coffeemaker. "How did Lawrence find you? I don't think he's ever had a cleaning lady or housekeeper since I can remember."

"Just lucky, I guess." And where was Lawrence? She couldn't keep playing truth dodge all morning. As soon as they were alone again, she was going to make him explain why he insisted on the ruse.

Peter turned on her, gesturing with the coffee canister. "Why don't you ever give me a straight answer?"

"Why don't you ever stop cross-examining me?"

"I'm not that kind of lawyer."

"What kind of lawyer are you?"

He suddenly slumped and turned back to the counter to position the filter. "I wish I knew."

"Surely you know what kind of cases you handle. Family law, corporate contracts, ambulance chaser?"

"Man, you have a mouth on you."

"I'm from Brooklyn, remember?"

"No excuse."

The aroma of coffee began to fill the air. Dani got the package of local bacon out of the fridge. She'd been saving it for the weekend. She hadn't imagined they'd have to share it with the prickly relative.

The kitchen door opened. "Ah, perfect timing." Lawrence strolled into the room, looking more kempt than he had since she arrived.

For his grandson, no doubt, Dani thought, a flame of jealousy flaring up before she doused it again.

Dani and Peter both reached for a cup to pour him coffee. There was a momentary standoff, then Dani pulled back and caught Lawrence's eyes as they rolled upward. Was he enjoying this stupid situation?

As soon as he had his coffee, he sat down at his usual place and waited for Dani to serve him.

Dani concentrated on her eggs. She felt stupid; she and Peter were acting like two acolytes paying homage to the king. She had no idea what he and Peter had talked about after she'd left them the night before. They must have talked about something, but hardly any conversation passed between the two of them over breakfast. As for Dani . . . she might as well not have been at the table at all.

She bit back a stab of loneliness. The loneliness you felt when the other kids didn't include you. When the other artists resented you for your success. Odd man out. She brushed it away. Peter would be going back to Boston soon. And then she would have Lawrence to herself. At least for a few more days.

Peter left for Boston right after breakfast, and it seemed that both she and Lawrence expelled sighs of relief.

They watched from the porch until the BMW had disappeared down the drive. Watched long after he was gone, as if he'd left a sudden chasm between them.

Finally Dani ventured, "Too bad that he had to leave so soon."

"He got what he came for."

Dani cut him a quick look. His tone was so dry and lifeless

it frightened her. Then he turned to her and started laughing. "Sort of."

She whooshed out a breath. "You had me worried for a second. Maybe he just wanted to visit his grandfather?"

"Unlikely. Sinclairs never do anything without an ulterior motive."

"Is that why I'm cleaning your house and making your breakfast?" she asked, surprisingly stung by his words.

"No, not this Sinclair, not always. Peter was a good kid. I think he still is; he's definitely carrying out orders, but chafing at it."

"That's why he came here this weekend?"

"Oh yes, but I'm glad he did. It gives me hope. A bit anyway." He turned to go back into the house.

"So why *did* he come?" Dani asked, following him in.

"To find out if you're after my money."

Dani stopped dead. "What? That is so far from— How did they even know about me? That rat! How dare he suggest such a thing. I hope you called him on it."

"Nope."

"Why not?" She'd started to walk again, but came up short. "Wait a minute. You don't have any money."

"Sure I do."

"More than a Social Security check?"

"A bit more."

"Then why am I paying rent and buying groceries and cleaning your house for free?"

"Because you offered." He grinned at her. "It's all part of the wax-on-wax-off thing."

"I wish I had never mentioned that stupid movie."

"Come on. Are you going to stand here all day grousing, or are we going to look over your prints from the darkroom?"

Peter maneuvered the BMW back onto the paved road toward town. The image of Lawrence and Dani Campbell standing on the porch as he drove away burned into his mind. Dani was definitely part of the household and Peter was the outsider; they'd made that clear. But what had he expected? To be greeted with open arms after he hadn't stood up for Lawrence when his mother turned on him at the funeral? Or any time since? Peter had intentionally stayed clear of him, just trying to keep the peace.

He was sorry for that. Not because Dani Campbell had usurped him in his grandfather's trust. That was Peter's fault. He'd never blamed Lawrence for his father's death. Peter knew his dad was driven in his work, completely committed to the company, and loyal to his wife and family. And a good father when he was around.

A bitter laugh erupted from somewhere deep inside Peter's gut. What had he been thinking? That he could make that trip and come back unscathed? He'd wanted to go. But not for the reasons he went. And he'd fallen right into the chasm between his mother and his grandfather without either of them having to do a thing.

A familiar emptiness fell over him. The clunk of his stomach, the sickly pit that thrust him into the past. The sight of the limo coming to a stop in front of the old beach house. Standing stoically, trying not to cry, while his summer bags were stowed in the trunk. Ganna Kissie kissing his forehead, Gadda giving him a brusque nod. The driver opening the back door and Peter stepping dutifully inside, afraid to look back to see their expressions. Driving through town; the trips for ice cream, the photography store, the library rushing through his mind as quickly as the actual places rushed by the limo's window.

As they were doing today.

He sucked in a breath. He was being totally ridiculous. That all had been years ago. Before Lawrence walked away from his family, and before Ganna Kissie walked away from him. Peter knew it would take him much longer before he gave up his own dream of being a lawyer, except as a cog within the company's legal department.

But he'd always been a slow learner.

And now he was returning to the fold without a definitive answer, not even any relevant information. He hadn't exactly come right out and asked Lawrence about Dani, but Lawrence knew what he was after. And it was humiliating for Peter to even look him in the face.

Peter had tried to observe her rationally and dispassionately, but she kept throwing him off guard. She was prickly and outrageous, and dressed like a poster child for the lost sixties. She didn't back down, didn't complain about the work, and most of all, she'd made Lawrence laugh.

She made his grandfather laugh.

Hell, she'd made Peter laugh.

Actually, she did something to Peter that left him floundering.

He'd been sent with two tasks. To find out if his grandfather was senile and to scare off any would-be gold diggers.

He'd found evidence of neither. His grandfather was perfectly lucid, and perfectly capable of taking care of himself—and probably the company if he wanted to.

As for Dani Campbell, Peter had no more information on

her than he had the moment he met her, except that her grandparents lived in Brooklyn and she could make a decent omelet.

The very idea of her cheating Lawrence out of his money was ludicrous.

What woman after a man's money acted like a punk, dressed in secondhand-store clothes, wore spiked hair and purple nails, talked like a Brooklyn street kid, and cleaned house with a T-shirt tied to her head?

And now instead of returning with Lawrence's power of attorney securely in hand, Peter had a fat folder of forms and real estate permits that he had promised to review for the convent.

═

Dani's cell rang on her way to retrieve the prints and her camera. Manny again. It was Sunday—what kind of business could he possibly be doing now? Anyone who was at any of the galleries or parties last night would just be getting up for a late brunch or still nursing a hangover.

No way was she going to answer it. Not now that she finally had Lawrence to herself to go over her prints. A vague slither of anxiety slid across her skin and was gone. Surely a couple of them would be good. She knew that you couldn't push the right shot. She'd always known that, but getting the right shot had never meant as much to her as it did now. Maybe at least one . . .

She tossed her cell on the bed.

It took less than five minutes to scrub her hands and dry them completely before she grabbed her packet of prints and ran up the stairs to the den.

The worktable had been cleared of papers; the computer screens had been pushed to the side. The drapes were open, and

Lawrence was standing in front of them looking out. He turned when he heard Dani enter.

"Well, that was fast," he said, and held out his hand.

Her mouth was suddenly dry but she handed them over.

Lawrence sat down. Dani stood where she was, not sure what to do. Would he send her to the other side of the room while he perused them as he had on her first visit?

"Pull up a chair, unless you're going to stand there breathing down my neck."

Dani pulled up a chair, sat down.

He tilted the folder; the prints slid onto the worktable. The first one was the first photo she'd taken of him. She sucked in her breath, held it. It was Lawrence; all the things she saw in him were there in his face, his posture, his essence.

He frowned at it. Tossed it into the wastepaper basket.

She stared at it. Moved closer to see the next photo and snatched it out of the basket. She held it behind her while he considered the photo of Sister Mary Catherine, face raised to the sky.

He gave Dani a look, then handed her the second print. "For your photo album."

"Now, let's see . . ." He spread the other six out on the desk. Looked them over. Picked up one and held it up.

"You let the sun burn off the shadows of this one." He shoved it to the side. Five left.

He looked at her, eyebrows lifted. She was supposed to choose the next one to get the axe? She licked her dry lips. It did absolutely no good. She leaned over the prints, picked up one, then another. Chose one and pushed it aside.

"Why?"

Had she picked the wrong one? *Trust your eye*, she thought. *Your innocent eye.* "No depth. No life. I was off."

"A split second can make all the difference. No one gets them all right. You only need one. There are four left. Which one do you keep?"

Dani's eye immediately went to one of them. She tapped it before she could change her mind. "That one."

Lawrence studied it. "Why?"

"Because . . . the values are right. How the light catches at the top of the chair leg and seems to run down to the sand, changing to a thin line, underlining the shadow of the person we can't see."

"Not bad." He pushed the others out of the way. "And without an app."

"So was I right?" Dani asked.

Lawrence shrugged. "Art, no matter what certain people will tell you, is more than a science." He tapped his chest. "Once you get rid of the obvious flub-ups, it's largely a matter of taste."

She frowned at him. "Which one would you have chosen?"

"Probably the one you did."

"You would have?" Dani asked, feeling suddenly as if everything was right.

"Who knows. It doesn't matter. Stop worrying about getting it right. Give in to the process. You're doing fine." Lawrence sat back, put his hands behind his head, and stretched. "How did you like my grandson?"

Dani climbed her way out of her momentary euphoria. "Peter? Other than the fact that he scared me to death yesterday, I guess he's okay."

"What did he do?"

Besides being generally a pain in the ass? She'd put up with his attitude until that prank on the beach. She wasn't sure why it had rattled her as much as it did.

"He sent me back to the house, because he"—she dropped her voice and made air quotes—"wanted to be alone."

She thought Lawrence would be amused, but he just looked pensive.

"Anyway, I started back to the house, but I looked back and he was gone. Just disappeared into thin air. It freaked me out. You go to the beach with somebody's grandson and they disappear? So not cool. So I ran back but he wasn't anywhere . . . and I went a little berserk. I mean, people just don't do that. Not even in New York."

Lawrence rose and went to stand at the window.

Dani joined him. "I called and called, looked in the water, and finally climbed around the rocks to see if he'd fallen. I was balanced there between that wall of granite and the surf when he jumped out of nowhere. Scared the crap out of me. He must have been hiding in those crevices. But it wasn't funny. He could have given me a heart attack."

Now Lawrence was smiling.

"Not funny."

"No," he agreed, "but gratifying."

"You want me to have a heart attack?"

"Do you have a waterproof camera case?"

Now what? "For my digital camera? Yes."

"Go get them. Meet me in the kitchen in five. There's something I want to show you."

Dani didn't wait for clarification. She hauled down the stairs, grabbed her camera and case, glanced at the cell still lying on her bed, and left it there.

Lawrence was waiting for her in the kitchen like always. Today he was holding a gnarled wooden walking stick that came almost to his shoulder.

Dani slipped her camera strap over her head so that it hung cross-body. "Where are we—?" She cut off her question, earning an approving smile from her mentor. She followed him out.

"We'll take the path through the woods," Lawrence said. But when they started off, he didn't head for the path that led to the nuns, or the one they'd created on her first outing. Then Dani recognized it as the one she'd taken down to the beach on her first day with the manual camera. They were going to the beach.

But before they had gone fifty feet, a figure emerged out of the woods. A knapsack was hanging from his shoulder, and he held a sketchbook under his arm.

"Isn't that Logan from the convent?" Lawrence asked. He raised his hand, and Logan stepped out of the trees.

"Good day, Logan. What can we do for you?" Lawrence asked.

It wasn't lost on Dani that Logan got a much friendlier greeting than she had when she'd appeared at his door.

Logan took a few tentative steps toward them and lifted up his sketchbook.

"I came to see— I wondered if you had a minute to help me with something."

Dani's excitement plummeted. Why couldn't she get two minutes of Lawrence's undivided attention? Time was running out, and Manny, Peter, and now Logan were all taking up valuable time.

"I'll just go enjoy the view," Lawrence said. "Good to see you, Logan." He wandered off down the path. Dani watched him go, worried that he might fall on the descent.

Dani turned to Logan, feeling a little impatient. "What's up?"

He opened his sketchbook. "I drew up an idea for the background but I couldn't make it work with the overlay; something's messed up."

"Couldn't any of the guys in the graphics room help you?"

"It's Sunday. They close it up on Sundays."

She thought of her laptop sitting on the dresser in her housekeeper's bedroom. It sounded like an easy fix, but dammit, this was her time.

"I'm kind of busy right now. How about tomorrow? Why don't I come over tomorrow and meet you there?"

"Got school, then work program."

"After that?"

"They— Sure, whatever."

"Sorry but I—"

He closed his sketchbook. "No worries. It isn't important."

And she let him wander back into the woods where he was immediately swallowed up by the brush. Pushing away the niggle of guilt she felt for shining him on, she went to find Lawrence.

Lawrence was waiting at the tall grasses at the edge of the woods. Just where Sister Mary Catherine was sitting when Dani had taken her picture. He stood, staff planted, looking out to the open sea. The wind lifted his hair and blew it away from his ascetic face.

Without thinking, Dani unsnapped her camera case, brought out her camera. An action so familiar she didn't have to look. She took her shot. Moved to the right, easing quietly through the bushes. Took another. Adjusted the distance and the focus for a close-up now. She wished she had brought a longer lens. She knelt down, got off another couple of shots before crashing back through the brush to join him on the bluff.

"Could you help him?"

"Tomorrow. It's a simple fix. It can wait."

"For you at least."

"Don't make me feel bad."

"I have no intention of doing that. Shall we go?"

He stabbed the sand with his walking stick and took slow but surefooted steps down to where the sand was packed from the most recent tide.

Then he struck off across the beach toward the rock formation.

Dani hoped he wasn't going to attempt those rocks, and she sighed with relief when he stopped where the base joined the sand.

"This is where I found Peter yesterday."

"I know." He reached out his free hand to the wall of rock, and between the wall and the staff, he navigated the shelf along the sea.

She thought he might try to make it to the far side, but he stopped suddenly, ducked his head, and disappeared into the rock.

She jumped ahead, stared into the space, and saw his hunched-over body squeezing between two boulders.

"Are you coming?" His words echoed back to her.

She hurried after him. God forbid he got stuck; how would she ever get him out?

She crept along behind him, until suddenly she stepped into sunlight. A semicircle of the secluded beach was surrounded by high walls of dark striated granite surfaces almost iridescent in the sunlight. The sand was finer here, and she could hear the tide rushing in and out from some unseen source. Above them, the sky shone like a round blue dome.

"Wow," Dani said, automatically reaching for her camera. "It's like Shangri-La."

"Nothing so mundane. A pirate's cove."

"You used to play here with Peter."

"A long, very long, time ago. I'm surprised he still remembered."

"How could he forget?" Dani asked, still a little awestruck.

"Needs must," Lawrence said enigmatically, and walked over to where the flat surface of a small boulder made a perfect seat. He lowered himself onto it.

"It's all yours," Lawrence said. He leaned back against the damp wall and closed his eyes.

Dani quickly got out her camera and took her first shot of her resting mentor. So she could always . . . She didn't think further than that. There would be an always.

She climbed over rocks, taking close-ups of the rough walls, wide shots from the far side of the cove. She photographed the whole incredible structure from every direction. It must be a glacial formation; no construction site could have dumped these rocks into such a perfect expression of nature.

She found tiny purple flowers that grew right up the wall, their succulent stems twining and tangling as they fought for existence. It was a world unto itself. She turned to share her excitement with her mentor, but he seemed to have fallen asleep. And she took another shot of Lawrence, holding his staff like Poseidon in khakis and a plaid shirt.

She turned back to the beach. The sound of the tide was stronger now, and she suddenly worried that they might be trapped inside. But a scramble over a cairn of rocks revealed a hidden pool. Just a semicircle washing onto a small bit of sand. The water wouldn't get much higher; she could see the tidemark.

She slid down, holding her camera carefully above her head. She took a stream of shots and was lost in the work when Lawrence's voice broke into her concentration. She looked up to see him standing above her.

He shook his head. "I hope your camera is drier than you are."

She was soaked from the thighs down, where she'd knelt to get a close-up of the sea-foam. "Yep." She handed her camera up to him, scrambled up after it, then stood dripping happily before him.

"This is amazing."

"It is, but I'm ready for my dinner."

"Dinner? We just had breakfast."

"Hours ago. Come on." He handed her the camera and, leaning heavily on the walking staff, moved slowly and stiffly to the secret entrance.

He shouldn't have been sitting out here for so long. "You should have called me sooner."

"Probably, but I was enjoying myself." He stopped for a last look around, raised his face to the sky. Smiled, then ducked his head and disappeared once more into the dark.

"That was a challenge," Lawrence said blithely when they reached the beach again. "The indignities of old age."

To her surprise, tears sprang to Dani's eyes. She linked her arm in his, and they started back across the beach. "I have to go to the city on Thursday."

"I thought that all these calls from your agent meant you were leaving soon."

"Just for a couple of days. There's this big event, Five X Five, five photographers to watch. I'm one of the five. I can't miss it. It would be an insult to beg off."

"Not to mention career suicide," Lawrence said.

"But I'm coming back as soon as it's over."

"Hmm."

"I've just started seeing things again. I know I have a long way to go. I can't do it on my own, not yet. I don't want to go, but I have no choice."

Lawrence didn't answer, so Dani plowed ahead.

"I'm afraid I'm not ready, I'm afraid I'll forget what I've learned so far, and . . . I'm afraid you won't take me back." Dani held her breath, the words that she hadn't meant to say hovering fragile in the air.

Then Lawrence laughed. "Why would I do that? You're finally learning to cook."

"What if I backslide? What if I—?"

"Dani, Dani, Dani. What did you just do all afternoon?"

She shrugged. "I don't know. It's in my camera." She groaned. "What if it's awful?"

"What if we try a little more wax on, wax off and get rid of all these what-ifs?"

Dani huffed out a sigh. "Life was easier when I was popular and clueless."

Lawrence laughed. "C'mon. Help an old man to the nearest beer." He put his hand on her shoulder and they made their way back to the house.

14

Peter had just reached the outskirts of Boston when he realized he wasn't ready to return home. No doubt his mother would be waiting for a report, and he didn't have that much to tell her. At least nothing he wanted to tell her. She wouldn't understand, would make the worst conclusions. As far as Peter was concerned, the jury was still out.

He didn't blame her for being overcautious. She had taken up the banner to save her son's position in the company, but her constant vigilance was driving him crazy. He'd tacitly agreed to accept his fate and try to live up to the Sinclair name. Besides, there was plenty of life to live outside the company.

Who was he kidding? The company consumed the Sinclairs. Had destroyed his grandfather's happiness, led his father to a stubbornness that ultimately killed him. Only Great-uncle James seemed to balance his life with work, and Peter knew that was because he just wasn't very good at either.

Peter shouldn't have left the beach until later. Then he would be stuck in end-of-weekend traffic instead of already a few blocks from home. He made the next turn and got back on the highway. Called Rashid.

"Hey, how was your weekend? Slay any evil money-grabbing femmes fatales?"

The very thought of Dani Campbell in that role kicked

a laugh out of Peter. "She turned out to be the cleaning lady. A young cleaning lady, but . . . Nah. I think it was a false alarm." Though she *was* living in. But there were a handful of scenarios for that. Unhappy home life. Couldn't afford rent. And the nuns seemed to like her, though hadn't they said she was visiting, or something like that?

He should have taken notes. He definitely hadn't been in his typical lawyer mind all weekend. And now the only things that stuck out in his mind were the beach and Dani Campbell in his, albeit unintentional, embrace.

"Where are you?"

"A couple of blocks from your house."

"Come on over. Game's on. I got beer. Door's open."

Peter ended the call, took the next exit, and five minutes later he stopped in front of Rashid's place, an early "brick and ivy" row house in a neighborhood of upwardly mobile midlevel executives.

Peter always thought maybe he would move here if he could just "cut the old umbilical," as Rashid often suggested. But it was more complicated than that. And yet his grandfather . . .

Rashid looked up from the couch when Peter let himself into the townhouse. He muted the commercial on the wide-screen. "So what's the upshot?" he asked, and handed Peter a beer.

"The upshot," Peter said, putting his briefcase down and popping the top, "is my grandfather lives in a dilapidated mess of a house, the gold digger turns out to be a local goth with an attitude, and I'm representing a group of retired nuns who are being evicted from their convent."

"Busy weekend. You hungry?" Rashid held up a bag of pretzels.

The image of Dani eviscerating that eggshell brought a reminiscent smile to his lips.

"Uh-oh," Rashid said, helping himself to some pretzels. "I don't think that smile was for these pretzels or the nuns, so . . . tell me more about this local goth."

"Well . . ." Peter sat back on the couch and indicated the television screen. "Game's starting again."

"Uh-uh." Rashid flipped off the TV. "Tell me about this goth. 'Cause that was definitely a hot-chick smile."

Peter groaned. "You are so un-PC."

"And you are so deflecting the point."

So Peter told him, forgetting that he'd had no intention of even mentioning Dani when he returned to Boston. Her crazy spiked hair, her flashing, take-no-prisoners eyes, her purple nails, her slim petite body. Her mercurial switches of personality, how she took time to help the kids at the convent. How she seemed to genuinely care about his grandfather.

"How old is this paragon?"

"I think in her twenties maybe? It's hard to tell because of her . . . energy, I guess."

Rashid cracked a laugh. "Most people have energy; you're just so overworked you've forgotten what it feels like."

Peter sighed. "I know. But before I deal with my situation, I have to figure out what to do about Lawrence's."

"Which is?"

"My mother wants to declare him senile and assign me power of attorney. She'd planned to use the gold digger as evidence, but since that just went to shit, she'll somehow figure out how to use this girl as the proxy, whether there is any truth to it or not."

"Your mother . . ."

"She isn't bad," Peter said. "Just overzealous."

"Is that what you call it? That woman is ferocious."

"She has this thing about keeping it all intact for my father until I can take over. Which she is determined I do as soon as possible."

"She needs a hobby," Rashid suggested. "Or a boyfriend."

"Fat chance. She's placed my father on some kind of pedestal."

"That's depressing. I'd rather hear about the goth. Did you run a background check on her?"

Peter frowned. "No."

"Google?"

"I started to and then I got busy." He reached for his phone, tapped the Facebook app, and typed in "Dani Campbell." The name came up right away. A list of several variations but only one simple Dani Campbell. He opened that one first and scrolled to the latest post. "Great Night at Beauty and Essex @DaniCampbell Photography."

"This can't be her profile," Peter said, scrolling through a few more posts, all of weird artistic types at posh events.

"With my good friend Dani, at the opening of her first New York solo show." And a group shot of wildly but expensively dressed arty types, laughing and posing, and in the middle Dani, wearing shiny black tights, a metallic blue shirt cut low in the front and high at the sides, her hair spiking like jagged black diamonds. And the vague sense of unease that had settled in his stomach morphed into a stiletto of this-can't-be-happening. "It can't be."

Peter dropped his phone, got his laptop from his briefcase, and typed in "Dani Campbell Photography" and got a microsecond of blank screen before DANI in white letters hurtled forward. When it grew too big for the screen it dissipated into a shower of needle-thin color explosions, leaving a more conventional landing page of Dani Campbell Photography.

"Click through to her bio," Rashid said.

Peter did.

And there was Dani, the cleaning lady, looking sleek and sophisticated and in charge of her world.

"Shit." Peter was having a hard time wrapping his head around the dichotomy. He peered at the screen trying to make sense of why the woman on the screen would be playing at cleaning lady at his grandfather's house.

Only one thing came to mind. Not his money. But photography. The stiletto in his gut twisted. Gold digger—hell, almost anything on earth—would be a blessing compared to photography, the one thing that had ultimately torn the family apart.

He and Rashid spent the next few minutes checking out her photographs: weird, scary, distorted . . .

"Post-postmodernism?" Rashid suggested when Peter ran out of words to describe them. "Kind of like Dalí on steroids."

"Or drugs."

"You think she takes drugs?"

"No," Peter said automatically. She didn't act like it, just mouthy, clever; she kept him off-balance the whole time he'd been there. If there was a drug involved, Dani was it.

He clicked on Coming Events. There were quite a few in several cities, and even more in the past. Blurbs about how "Fresh, inquisitive, unsettling" she was by critics in established magazines and newspapers.

"Shit, she's like famous," Rashid exclaimed. "Are you sure this is the same woman?"

Peter nodded slowly. "But it doesn't make sense."

"Maybe they met somewhere?"

"Where would they have met? He never goes anywhere. And—jeez." He slammed his laptop closed. Stood up, paced to the wall, came back, sat down, and opened it again. She was still there. Haughty, yeah, he could see the resemblance. But for the life of him, he still couldn't see her hobnobbing in high heels and tight pants with the A-list of art aficionados. He was obviously missing something.

She had to have an ulterior motive. So what the hell was he going to tell his mother?

═

Dani pulled random packages out of the fridge. A bunch of left-overs and too much lettuce. She really didn't care about eating at all. She was anxious to take a look at her photos from the cove. And when Lawrence walked through the kitchen into the rest of the house, Dani sneaked at peek at her camera viewer. Impossible to tell. She needed a larger screen. Even her laptop would do, but what she really wanted was to see them on one of Lawrence's big screens. He had several. And what did the man do with so many computers? Most eighty-ish people were still trying to figure out their emails.

But she knew better than to appear eager. He'd end up having her scrub the stairs with a toothbrush or something equally annoying. Though she had to admit that cleaning had never been so satisfying.

Usually, she'd do just about anything to get out of cleaning. Until she met Lawrence. She wasn't learning any karate moves from scrubbing counters, but she was learning to pay attention; to look deep, to see with a mind focused on the task and not on the end result. Paying attention.

With a sponge in her hand, she could concentrate on a congealed blob of jam in ways she never did before. Normally she would either ignore it until it hardened and had to be scraped off with a knife or she'd take a picture and leave it to congeal and harden while she played with different ways she could create out of a blob of jam.

This afternoon had been different. She'd lost all track of time, which wasn't unusual, but what was, was that for long stretches, her mind had been empty as her eye bypassed the thought process.

Maybe she was kidding herself; that was always a possibility. But maybe that was what she'd been missing all along, and instead had been hiding her lack of whatever that thing was by clever manipulations.

"Stop thinking, you're making me tired," Lawrence griped.

She hadn't heard him come back into the kitchen.

"I'm *making* your dinner. And how do you know what I'm thinking?"

He wandered over to the counter, looked over the bottles of wine she'd bought. "What goes good with pizza?"

"You eat pizza?"

"Why wouldn't I?"

"I don't know; my grandmother gets heartburn."

"I don't eat peppers. How old is your grandmother?"

"I don't know. Eighty-ish, I guess. My dad is almost sixty—he was the youngest of four—so she'd have to be in her eighties."

"How can you not know how old your grandmother is?"

"Well . . . because she always lies about her age."

He barked out a laugh. "I think I like her." He chose a bottle of cabernet. "You have decent taste in wine."

"My dad owns a bar, remember?"

"I remember. We have three bars in Old Murphy Beach. Not sure any of them even have a wine list."

"Ours is in Brooklyn," Dani said.

"Ah, that explains it," said Lawrence. "Anything you don't like?"

"Anchovies, pineapple."

He made the call. "Hey, Tony. Yeah, good, been busy, yep, and a salad, something nice." He listened for a second. Glanced at Dani. "Yeah. Yeah, and Peter, too. Full house. Yeah. Thanks." He ended the call.

"You're famous," he said to Dani. "Don't be surprised if you start getting people interested in your cleaning services. Maybe you should put up one of those tear-off things at the grocery store."

"Not funny," Dani said, beginning to put everything back in the fridge. "What did you get? Do I have to pick it up?"

"My usual. And no, they deliver. Now, go get your camera while I open this bottle of cabernet, and meet me in the library. Not as good as upstairs but we can hear when the pizza gets here."

Dani threw the rest of the leftovers back in the fridge and hurried to her room. He was waiting for her when she and her camera speed walked into the library.

While they waited for the pizza to arrive, they cleaned off the desk, whose surface seemed to have sprouted even more folders over the weekend. She wondered if that had something to do with Peter Sinclair's surprise visit.

Getting Lawrence's effects in order? She shuddered. He wasn't *that* old. He could take care of himself. Peter better not be trying to take advantage of him. Though she couldn't imagine how. Maybe he wanted to sell the house. It was next door to the convent that was being sold. She had a horrible flash of the pristine white convent and the spurious-looking old gothic being replaced by rows of upscale condos, tennis courts, and Olympic-size saltwater pools.

The pizza arrived on that thought. Lawrence poured the wine while she slid slices onto plates. It was hot and delicious.

"As good as Brooklyn?" Lawrence asked, his mouth full and a string of cheese caught in his beard.

"Of course not," Dani said. "But it's pretty darn tasty."

As soon as the first piece was consumed, Lawrence wiped his hands on his trousers and opened her photo file.

He clicked on the first shot of the series. An establishing shot of the grotto walls, the smooth, the jagged, the spires and crannies. A study in light and shade and texture.

It wasn't bad, Dani thought, relieved.

The next shot. A little different angle. She'd caught just the right position to bring out the dimension and color. And with no special equipment. The sunlight had done that. She had just captured it.

The next and the next. Some worked, some didn't, but all were honest, especially the few shots of Lawrence sleeping on his throne of rock like Poseidon, a very skinny, gothic version of the sea god. These he skipped over with a grunt or total silence.

But they made Dani smile.

They took a break to eat more pizza, not bothering to reheat it. They opened the tin of salad and ate pieces with their fingers and drank more wine. Then Dani cleared it all away, brought back fresh towelettes she found under the sink, and they wiped their hands more expertly before turning back to the screen.

When the last photo scrolled from the screen, she looked at Lawrence. He didn't comment. He didn't need to. She saw that he approved. She also saw that he was a little sad, and the pizza burned in her gut. How could a total stranger, an old misanthropic man, come to mean so much to her in a few brief days? And how could she return to her real life without him?

Zoom, she told herself, *email, text*. She could visit. It wouldn't be the same, but Rhode Island wasn't that far away. Once you got out of Manhattan.

But that was a long time off. *Yeah, Thursday*, she reminded herself. But she would come back. She still had a lot to learn.

She felt safe to explore her art here. To be herself. The old self that lurked somewhere inside the one she put on for show, which was just about as phony as her photos had become.

But how long could she really stay? She'd just come out of curiosity. She slammed down on that lie. She'd come for the holy grail, and she'd glimpsed it. But she knew it was ephemeral, tenuous, and remembered how intrusive lifestyle was to your actual photography. It was one thing to spend a week away from it all and capture some good photos of boulders on a quiet beach.

She might even sell a few copies at a street fair. They might keep her in pizza, but without the cachet.

"You'll figure it out," Lawrence said, interrupting her thoughts.

"How do you know what I'm thinking?" she said petulantly. It was so irritating how he kept reading her thoughts.

"Because we've all been there at one time or other. The good ones. The discontented ones. The ones who grow. Even the ones who don't. And now, it's past my bedtime." He pushed stiffly from the chair. He'd had a strenuous day, she realized.

They said good night, but when he reached the door, she said, "Lawrence."

"Yeah?"

"Thanks."

He just nodded, then walked slowly out the door.

═

Lawrence stood at the window looking out at the moon, the beach below hardly more than a dark emptiness, a black hole that might suck up the world in a breath. He didn't look out often. Mainly because during the day the sun hurt his eyes; in the afternoons he was busy with other things and rarely came upstairs even to nap, which, until Dani arrived, he'd done in the club chair in the parlor. And as for the nights . . . he went to bed early. At least that was what he would tell people if anyone had asked. No one had . . . until Dani.

But something had drawn him here tonight. Maybe seeing the pirate's cove. Watching Dani climb over the rocks, so intent on her work, and remembering a young Peter scampering over the rocks, waving a stick and yelling, "Shiver me timbers!" Several times he'd had to stop himself from calling out to be careful, Dani and Peter, the present and the past, melding in his mind.

Photographers hated being interrupted, even if it was to prevent them from hurting themselves. At least he had. But he hadn't thought about that in a long time.

Tonight, the view seemed to teem with energy, and for the first time in decades, his fingers itched to pick up a camera.

Too late, you old fool. It's all too late.

He should never have opened the door to Dani Campbell. She'd badgered him into actually giving a shit about life. He'd been amused at first, thought for sure she'd give up and rush back to her high-tech fame and friends. But she was like an eel or a pinpoint of laser light, slippery, ricocheting, elusive.

He'd miss her when she left. After today, it was clear she was on her way to "that thing she'd been missing." She could probably do the rest without him. She could have always done it without him; she just needed to be pointed in the right direction. Wax on, wax off. What a clever, clever technique. Well, he would enjoy the last few days of her energy before she said goodbye. Because she inevitably would; she had a world to conquer, and he had . . . memories.

In his isolation, he'd given up on people. Assumed the

younger generation were all like James's grandchildren. He'd refused to make any judgments on Peter.

He knew Peter better than he knew the others, only by default because his parents had been just too damn busy and the company always came first. Generation after generation, it chewed up the Sinclairs and spit them out to start on the next.

And now it was about to do the same with Peter. The boy was clearly torn, and he couldn't be blamed for not having the backbone to tell them no. He hadn't gotten much guidance from anyone, especially Lawrence, on what to do. Because Lawrence had caved to the family and the company, and it had taken away everything he held dear: his wife, his son, his photography, even his grandson—his reasons for being.

It was too late for him. His Krista was long gone and several years dead. His only son dead. His great-nieces and -nephews sending cards at Christmas and his birthday. He sent them checks in reciprocation. Not that they needed the money.

Even Peter had stopped visiting. Until this week. Unannounced and looking years older than he actually was. He already had the Sinclair stoop, and Lawrence had no illusions about why he had come. Marian was making the push, and oh, it would be so easy to give in to her, to saddle his grandson with the onus of being a Sinclair. Out of pure selfishness, he'd been loathe to do it so far. And after this weekend, he knew he had been right.

He'd hold out and give the kid a chance to reclaim his life. It would mean outright war, but Peter needed to have the chance to choose. And if ultimately he couldn't pull the trigger, then Lawrence would do what Marian wanted. But not just yet.

He should have turned over his shares to Marian in proxy for Peter right after the funeral. But he'd held out hope that finally one of them would be set free.

He'd made a mess of his life. At least he could give Peter a chance to save his. Because if he knew Marian, Peter would be making a return visit.

Lawrence was trusting, if not in God, at least in the nuns next door to help see him through.

═

Peter stayed so late at Rashid's that even his mother had given up and gone to bed by the time he'd crept upstairs in the wee hours. Of course, after several calls and texts from her, he'd texted back that he would be very late and not to wait up. He really had to figure out how to get his own place without having her packing her bags to leave before he could. They were two prisoners shackled by an idea, who would both be free if they'd only just walk out the door.

Rashid thought Peter should call her bluff. But Rashid didn't have to live with this family. Since childhood, Peter had witnessed enough of family games, ultimatums, and cold shoulders to last a lifetime.

So Peter wasn't surprised to find her waiting for him when he crept back downstairs the next morning, before heading to the office.

"I've been thinking," she said.

Peter, who had almost reached the door, turned back. "Mother, we talked three times on my drive back to Boston. I told you. He has a cleaning lady." (He'd omitted the part about her living in and being a famous photographer.) "And he is perfectly sane and able to take care of himself."

"And did you discuss having him turn over his vote to you?"

"No. And I'm not going to. He's done everything you've asked of him. You can just be patient."

"I'm only doing this for your own good. What if something

happens to him? Things could be tied up in court for God knows how long."

"As long as probate takes. I'm sure Lawrence has taken care of that."

"How do you know? How do you know he even has a will?"

Peter didn't. "Because he's a Sinclair."

His mother winced.

He put down his briefcase and laptop, took both her arms. "You have been running this company ever since my father died. If anyone gets Lawrence's shares it should be you."

She pulled away and held up a hand as if warding him off. "It's your birthright."

"And what if I don't want it?" Peter blinked. Okay, he was losing his mind. It didn't matter what he wanted. "Look. I've got to get to work. Everything will work out. Let's just keep the status quo for a while longer. Okay?"

Marian's jaw tightened. God, she was a stubborn woman. Peter wished he had half her determination. And maybe he would, if he cared about something enough.

"Love you. Gotta go," he said, and hurried away.

Where were all these traitorous thoughts coming from? He thought he'd buried them so deep they would never dare rear their enticing heads again. It must have been the trip to the beach. He'd prepared himself to find Lawrence old, feeble, and unkempt. In other words, miserable.

What he'd found instead was Lawrence as wild-looking as ever, even when in the office, but dynamic and bright. All the things his mother's spies had said he wasn't. Unless they were totally incompetent—and his mother would never hire anyone but the best—Lawrence's reclamation could only be due to one thing. Dani Campbell.

15

It started to rain during the night. The wind howled outside Dani's window, befitting the old gothic house. She could even hear the waves crashing on the rocks below. It was the first time she was aware of being so close to the sea.

And the moment she put her feet on the floor, she knew that the weather had turned cold. Autumn would soon be upon them, which raised the question . . . Did the house have heat?

That was a cost that gave even her pause.

She dressed hurriedly in jeans and a sweatshirt, added a zip-up hoodie over it and woolly socks that she always traveled with to keep her feet off hotel carpets. She padded into the kitchen, aware of a slight headache and a vague feeling of discomfort that she couldn't name.

Lawrence came down a few minutes later, wearing a heavy cardigan and looking thunderous. When Dani asked if he was feeling okay, he merely grunted and sat down, waiting for Dani to pour his coffee.

"I expect I'll have to start curtsying soon," she told him as she put a cup of steaming coffee in front of him.

That didn't get a rise out of him, and it occurred to her that maybe he was acting this way because Peter was gone. Which gave her a little prick of something that she refused to call jealousy.

Peter was his grandson, after all, even if they had been estranged. They seemed to be on okay terms by the time Peter had left.

Dani made breakfast, cleaned up while Lawrence retired to the parlor to read the paper, which, she realized, he had delivered every morning. Canceling that would be a good way to cut corners if he needed money for heat, with winter coming on.

Surely his grandson would make sure he didn't go without.

Why had he even come, just to turn around and go back the next morning? She wanted to ask, but didn't want to risk putting Lawrence in a worse mood. Besides, it was none of her business. Her business was to glean everything she could from Lawrence before she had to go back to the city.

She spent the morning cleaning out the back hallway, calling on Lawrence for his opinion about what to throw away. She pulled out an old crabbing net whose handle was stuck between two water-damaged cardboard boxes, which promptly broke and spilled a variety of gears and cogs and stuff onto the floor.

Which set off a panic in her brain. "Shit!" she exclaimed.

Lawrence's head appeared in the doorway to the kitchen. "You all right?"

"Yes," Dani said, dropping the net and brushing off her hands. "I just remembered that I owe Manny more *Gems and Junque* photos."

"What?"

"Just this idea for a book that my agent pitched. Someone bought it and now I have to shoot it. How could I forget?"

Lawrence shrugged and went back inside.

There was plenty of stuff here. Just because it wasn't for sale . . . The light was pretty uneven, as in most old places, but it could work.

She hurried to her room. Washed her hands and picked up her camera. She picked and chose a few shots and finally just fell into randomly following where one photo led into another. She had a good selection of odd objects in the camera when Lawrence's voice called her back to the present.

"If you're planning to go over to the art school, you better eat something and go."

Dani blinked a couple of times. Reoriented herself. Right, the art school. She'd promised Logan.

"Thanks." She hurried past him to change clothes; when she came out again, he was waiting in the kitchen with heated soup and a sandwich.

She sat down. "Did you eat already?"

"Yep. I think I'll see what damage you've done to my hallway." And he left her to her lunch.

As soon as she finished, she fetched her laptop and went to find Lawrence. The hallway was empty, so she looked in the parlor. He was sitting before the empty grate. Sleeping?

She eased closer, and he looked up.

"Will you come, too?"

"Maybe later." He closed his eyes.

She slung her laptop and camera cross-body and went in search of the rain poncho she'd worn the other day, then set across the woods to the convent. The weather was raw, though the rain had stopped, and the drip-drip-drip of droplets running off the leaves added to the feeling of chill. Back in the city, the gallery shows would be in full swing. She told herself it didn't matter. But she knew that there was a scene among the photography art world, and you couldn't afford to let it happen without you.

And the commercial-product stuff? Man, it was the most

cutthroat. You couldn't turn your back for a moment. She'd been gone for far too long.

And yet . . .

She cut across the grass, the wet blades grasping at her ankles. Her sneakers were soggy—again—by the time she rang the bell at the convent entrance. A nun she hadn't met answered. She was even older than Sister Mary Catherine and Sister Eloise. This must be Sister Agnes. Dani explained why she'd come; the nun let her in and turned to lead the way down the hall. At a snail's pace. Dani had to take slow-motion baby steps not to trample over her.

When they reached the main hallway, Dani thanked her and said she knew the way and not to bother taking her all the way down.

The nun said it was no bother, and they started on their snail's pace once more. Fortunately, Sister Eloise was coming out of one of the rooms ahead and came to meet them. "Thank you, Sister Agnes. I'll show her the rest of the way."

Sister Agnes smiled and nodded and continued on her way. "She's our oldest, past ninety, we believe, but she still has the vigor to serve."

Dani smiled and followed Sister Eloise to the media room.

There weren't so many students today.

"Most have work programs or part-time jobs or chores. Logan is here, though. He normally has work program on Mondays but he says there was a change in his schedule this week."

At the sound of his name, Logan looked up. He'd pulled his lanky hair back into a ponytail today. He rocked slightly and blew out a breath as if he'd been running.

Dani pulled up an extra chair.

"So let's see what you've got."

═

The sun was headed toward sunset when Lawrence made his way across the convent lawn. He'd kept busy most of the day with normal stuff, but he kept coming back to his computer and Dani's photos. She most definitely had the eye—the soul. He could see it clearly now. She didn't need him to help her; she just needed to stop listening to everybody else.

In a few days she would be on her way back to New York, and he was trying not to think about it. And not just for himself, though he had to admit she'd brought a whole new vitality to his existence.

It baffled him how he'd ended up spending part of a weekend with the only two young people he really cared about—and he did care about them in his way. Strange that they were both poised on a tiny sharp pinnacle, not of success, though that was part of it, but of choice, surrounded by slippery slopes on all sides. And they had both come here.

He'd been on that same point when he was younger. With no one to guide him except those who already had decided where his future lay. Had he really chosen, or merely caved to their will? He wasn't sure now. He hadn't known what an unforgiving choice it had been. Unfortunately, he could see it clearly now that he was too old to change course. But it wasn't too late for them.

Sister Mary Catherine was in the garden retying the stakes of the last of the season's green beans. He stood for a moment just to watch and marvel at how she bent down among the plants as if she wasn't pushing eighty. The climb down to the beach to the pirate's cove had taken all his concentration and exhausted him.

Sister Mary Catherine stood, a little stiffly, he thought. She saw him. She put her tools in a basket, tossed her gardening gloves after them, and came to meet him.

"And what brings you here on a Monday afternoon?" she asked.

"Thought I'd see how Dani is doing in the art class."

"Shall I take you inside?"

"Not yet. If you can spare a minute."

"Certainly. I think it's dry in the gazebo." They walked down the path to the octagonal building. A place of welcome to contemplators, painters, writers, and visitors just needing a respite from the sun.

"Peter took your papers back with him, I said it was okay."

"Thank you for volunteering him. I hope it didn't depend on too much arm twisting."

"No. Not at all."

"I was surprised to see him."

"So was I," said Lawrence. "His mother sent him to see if I was senile enough to grab power of attorney." He chuckled. "And to see if Dani was an adventuress after my money."

"Oh dear. He told you that?"

"Not outright. But it was obvious."

"Well, I hope you set him straight."

"I told him she was the cleaning lady. And she played along. I'm not sure he was convinced."

"Lawrence, why not just tell him the truth?"

"What truth? That she was here because she has some misguided notion that I could help her with her photography? Just the mention of the word would have had him running for the closest court order."

"Perhaps you don't give him enough credit. You were always close when he was a child."

"But not since . . . Elliott died. Somehow his death got equated with me and photography and who knows what else."

"Well, I have hope for that young man, and I will pray for him to find his way. And for you, too."

"Even if it's the Sinclair way?"

She didn't answer right away. How could she? When he and Krista had first come back, Sister Mary Catherine had been a member of the order for over ten years.

It had been strange living next door to his childhood sweetheart when he was married and she was married to God. Now it seemed the most natural of all possible worlds.

"It's his decision," Sister Mary Catherine said. "You can only give guidance from love, not from what you would do if you had it to do over again."

"I know. And I don't even know if I would choose differently given the chance."

She placed her hand briefly over his.

"I don't think he was happy having to do it. Or perhaps he was just embarrassed . . . I don't know; he didn't seem happy in general."

"I wonder if this is an unexpected opportunity?"

Lawrence smiled at her, not surprised by her question. "Truth be told, I was kind of hoping that myself. But to what end?"

"For you to help guide someone you love. As for Dani, I think maybe you can learn a little bit from her. For us, she's been a godsend. Sister Eloise says she has the whole teen group enthralled. And Logan, well, what a difference a little interest makes."

"She's leaving."

"When?"

"In a few days. She has some event she has to attend."

"Does she plan to return? She was going to help hang the art exhibit for the festival."

"She says so. But once she gets back into that groove, I doubt we'll see her again."

"We'll all miss her."

"Yes," said Lawrence. Indeed they would.

Sister Mary Catherine stood. "Shall we go see how they're doing? Classes are almost over."

Parents were already waiting at the door for their children. And when Lawrence and the sister entered, they were met with an exodus of young artists and their supplies.

"You seem to have added a few pupils," Lawrence said.

"We're growing by leaps and bounds. Now if we can just arrange for a way to keep them."

"I'm sure Peter will find a way. He's a very clever boy."

"Young man," Sister Mary Catherine reminded him. "And if he's half as clever as his grandfather, I'm sure we are in good hands."

The door to the media room was open, and it was so quiet that Lawrence thought they must have already left for the day.

Only one workstation was still occupied. Dani sat next to Logan, her shoulders angled slightly toward the young man as she pointed out something on the screen.

And Lawrence felt his age, his isolation, his sense of being left in the past.

"Maybe I've been wrong," he said, barely above a whisper, so that Dani wouldn't hear and perhaps Sister Mary Catherine would.

"I doubt it," she said just as quietly. "Perhaps half wrong, which means you're half right."

He looked down at her and smiled fondly at the girl she had

been and the woman she had become. "You always had a way of seeing things."

"And you didn't always agree with them," she said.

"No."

Dani looked up, and after a brief discussion, she gestured them over.

"Check this out," Dani said enthusiastically. "I predict an up-and-coming cartoonist."

"I can see," Lawrence said, and after a frown from Dani, added, "Very impressive."

"But that's enough work for today," Sister Mary Catherine said. "I believe you need to get home, Logan."

Logan looked at his phone, exclaimed, "Shit," followed by "Sorry, Sister," and hurriedly packed up his sketches.

He looked at Dani.

"You go ahead. I'll save everything for you."

"You'll be back tomorrow, though." He was already backing out the door.

"I will, yes. See you tomorrow."

And he was gone.

Dani spent several minutes closing things out, and finally the screen went blank.

"He has a lot of potential," Dani told them as they made their way outside. "Isn't there someplace he can get more advanced training?"

"This is it," Sister Mary Catherine said.

"Maybe you could check in on him while I'm gone?"

The question was directed at Lawrence. He immediately shook his head. "I don't know anything about digital."

"Ha," exclaimed Sister Mary Catherine. "I would use a phrase that I would regret, so let us just say that you are telling a fib. You can't tell us you haven't kept up with the business even if you stubbornly refuse to take photos yourself.

"And . . ." she continued before he could argue, "while Dani is gone you can visit the photography class. You won't have to prepare anything, just talk about life and photography."

"I—"

She cut him off. "And we need a model for the after-school drawing class. They're getting tired of drawing the three of us."

"I think that's an excellent idea," Dani said.

"We'll see." Lawrence had no intention of doing any of those things, but he knew better than to take on both women at once.

They said goodbye and walked back across the lawn to the house.

"Why do you refuse to take photos?" Dani asked, staring straight ahead.

"For my sins. Now, come on. It's getting late and I want my dinner."

═

Peter closed out the Schickley file. It had been a simple search and disclosure. His job so far was finished. Older and much more experienced lawyers than he would use his information in the case. It didn't bother him. He really had no interest in the outcome, which was an indictment against his commitment to Sinclair Enterprises. Bid on a smaller company, add it to its list of acquisitions, or lose the bid and go on to the next acquisition. It was all paper and stocks. Just the thought of it made him yawn.

He tapped his pen on his desk. It was late enough that he could actually leave the office without any guilt. His mother had left an hour ago to have her hair and nails done, which he knew because she stopped to tell him where she would be.

So if the whole company fell apart while she was being shampooed, she was just a text away and could return to save the day.

No, that wasn't fair. She was good at running the company. Actually, she should be running the company. If she just would and let Peter . . . do what? Continue to run searches and prepare disclosures on potential acquisitions?

His mind drifted back to his time with Judge Wembley. He worked all day for the judge, spent evenings researching, and even managed to fit in a few night classes on various legal issues. When two years was up, he reluctantly said goodbye and passed the bar exam. Looking back, he didn't know how he'd even made it through. Both clerking and studying, as it turned out, were full-time jobs. But somehow the two fed on each other, pushed him to learn more. He could have stayed with the judge, would have happily worked as a clerk where his research often led to life-changing results.

But what he'd really loved was sitting in the courtroom, listening to the two counsels. Prosecutors and defenders work with the facts, sometimes manipulating them, sometimes stretching them to just within the boundaries. People's lives were affected directly by those cases.

Even then, Peter knew that would never be a career path for him. He'd only convinced his mother to not thwart his going to law school by promising to study corporate law. Good old Uncle James had backed him up. "Always room for a good lawyer in our legal department."

So he was reprieved from a Wharton degree in business. He'd

even managed to sneak in a few courses in family, environmental, labor, litigation, and civil law.

Looking back, he was amazed that he'd actually made it and passed the bar exam on the first attempt. Maybe that was why he felt tired all the time. He was still running on adrenaline and the future.

He logged out of the business site and pulled the stack of manila folders Sister Mary Catherine had given over to his care.

From the bit he'd scanned in her office, it appeared that they had as yet not entrusted their future to a private attorney, expecting the diocese to take care of things for them.

Peter didn't know diocesan law, but if it was like other law, they would do what was best for the diocese, and if that was relocating a few retired nuns and closing a couple of programs, the outcome seemed inevitable. Things weren't looking good for the art school or its three lady overseers. The nuns had a serious problem.

He should have expressed his sympathy and then refused to help them. God knew his inbox was filling up with paperwork.

But as soon as Sister Mary Catherine had begun to explain in her innocent, God-moves-in-mysterious-ways way what was happening, Peter knew it was just the kind of problem that he could get his teeth into, the kind of problem he didn't see in his office at Sinclair Enterprises, ever.

And the temptation was just too great. He could look things over in his spare time and at least might be able to give them some advice. Point them to a good local lawyer. Maybe Lawrence knew of one.

Peter could kick himself for the way he'd left Sunday morning. It was obvious that Dani Campbell, whatever the reason she was staying with him, photography or something else, was not looking to be arm candy. Lawrence's fortune was secure.

Though did any of them know what Lawrence did with his money? He lived like he was destitute. Surely that was by choice. Peter wondered just how tightly his mother kept track of Lawrence's activities. There was something offensive about spying on a member of your own family—he added *by marriage*, because his mother had ingrained that into him since birth. It was his responsibility to carry on the family interest. And her duty to serve as steward for her son.

Peter closed the folder, pushed the stack away, tapped his desk with his pen. Pulled the stack back.

It wouldn't hurt to spend a few minutes . . .

It was almost ten when he looked up again. He locked the convent notes in his file cabinet, checked his phone. Two calls from his mother. He texted her back. *Working late at the office.*

That should satisfy her for a minute. Was it too late to call that real estate agent? Deciding he wasn't up for that particular fight, or even getting his butt kicked in racquetball, he packed up and left for the night.

═

By Wednesday, Dani had the whole media class working on projects and turned her attention completely toward Logan. He was an amazing artist who just needed the equipment to take him to the next level. She warned herself not to get too excited. That this was how it started with her. More gadgets, more playthings, more—more—more until she could barely find her own art.

She didn't think that would happen to Logan; he was so clearly embedded in his fantasy. But he was only fifteen, and it was a steep, slippery slope. He'd tuned in to the drawing program, got her when she showed him a few of her shots from the pirate's cove. But she had no business trying to determine how he could make it work.

He seemed totally surprised when she reminded him that she wasn't coming in the next day. Then disappointed and a little angry.

"But I . . . Who's going . . . ? Oh, never mind, it doesn't matter."

"Of course it does. But I have to go to New York for a big art gala."

"But you're coming back, right?"

Was she? She wanted to. She felt . . . safe here. Lawrence had made her realize so many things about her own photography. He hadn't actually given her any technical tips, just sort of kept her stumbling along in the right direction. Could she do that on her own?

She'd have to. But was she ready now? She didn't know.

Logan just stood waiting for an answer. She could already see him preparing for her to say no.

She couldn't disappoint him, but she couldn't promise that she would come back. It would be worse to promise and then renege. So she just said, "I hope so, but you can do this now. Just keep at it."

"Sure. Thanks." He slid his knapsack off the table and shuffled out the door.

"And Lawrence will be here to help you if you get stuck."

But he was gone, and she stood in the empty media room and thought, *Please don't let me screw this up.*

Dani meant to leave that evening, but she'd stayed late at the art studio with Logan, then kept putting it off until it was too late. Manny had scheduled a meeting to discuss the perfume shoot

Thursday afternoon. So she waited until after breakfast on Thursday morning, timing her departure so she'd miss rush hour on her ride down the coast. As long as there were no long tie-ups in traffic, she would make it in time for a late lunch with Manny.

Lawrence saw her to the door, and at the last moment she balked. "What if—?"

"You'll be fine."

"I can come back, right?"

"I'm not going anywhere."

That didn't exactly answer her question. She'd packed all her equipment and cameras. After all, she would be gone several days. But she'd left a few things, a pair of jeans and a couple of T-shirts, to let him know she wasn't finished here yet.

"It may be a few days."

"Take your time."

She glanced at Lawrence, taking in every detail, the way his clothes didn't hang quite so loose on him. The way he stood a little straighter than the day she'd arrived. Was it because of her?

"I left stuff in the fridge."

He laughed. "I saw. I won't starve."

She'd stayed up late into the night preparing meals for a few days. It seemed the natural thing to do. All those years growing up in the bar must have rubbed off on her. Turned out she did know her way around the kitchen, and she actually enjoyed doing it.

But not in the city when it was too easy to get takeout, and time was always at a premium.

She drove away, glancing back at Lawrence, who stood on the porch until she rounded the bend in the drive. And then Lawrence and the house were out of sight and she was on her way back to Manhattan.

Except for the usual delays on the Cross Bronx, she made

pretty good time. And pulled into the garage near the river in the early afternoon. Snagged a cab across town and climbed the two flights to her apartment on East Fifth Street with time to spare.

She felt a bit of relief when the door finally opened and she maneuvered her gear and duffel into her small living room. She dumped everything on the couch and went immediately to open the window. She got a little rush of familiarity when a bit of air slipped in along with honks and yells and a general buzz of city life. It was good to be home in her own space, her space, her . . .

She turned from the window, looked around. Same as she'd left it. She wandered into the kitchen. When had it grown so narrow? Opened the fridge out of habit. Empty like it usually was. There was a dirty pan in the sink. She couldn't even tell what it had held.

Back into the living room, where she grabbed her duffel and carried it into the tiny bedroom barely large enough for her bed and a bookshelf crammed with books, equipment, and overflow clothes from the closet. She squeezed into the bathroom, whose door was prevented from fully opening by a pile of laundry she'd tossed on the floor before she left for Rhode Island. She wandered back to the bedroom and just stood.

Everything was just as she'd left it . . . everything but her.

Her cell rang.

She answered automatically. "Hi, Manny, I'm home. Yep . . . yep. Two o'clock. No, sure, that's fine. See you there."

She looked around. All she had to do was change into her city clothes and take a cab.

Her city clothes were pretty much always the same: black on black with a splash of intense color. Today she added a big leather carryall, mainly to carry her heels and a point-and-shoot camera.

She stowed her camera and equipment in the false bottom of

the futon couch and triple locked her door, then went downstairs to hail a cab.

Chez Diner was a mid-century diner refitted with a nod to Bauhaus and run by two Algerian brothers from Hoboken. It was a favorite place for meetings among the arty set, especially if you wanted the news of the meeting to spread quickly. There were a few tables and chairs outside, but if you wanted to hear the person across the table from you, you chose the inside, where the light was even but not harsh and the decor minimalist so as not to get in the way of the wheeling and dealing.

As for the food, it was nouvelle, expensive diner food that was delicious and rarely tasted among the wheeling and dealing.

Manny was waiting for her at what he liked to call "his" table, as if he were Sam Cohn at the Russian Tea Room. It had started as a big joke that he'd thrown out and had since become a reality. He stood when he saw her, tall, still pretty fit, with black hair slicked back into a man bun. He was wearing an Italian suit over an off-white silk Henley T-shirt. No question that he was a successful agent.

Air kisses ensued.

"Country air agrees with you," he said, and not waiting for a reaction, added, "Did you get me my shots?"

"Shots?" She caught herself just in time. The damn *Gems and Junque* shots. She'd forgotten about them again. "Something better."

He leaned forward, carefully placing his linen-clad elbows on the immaculate tablecloth.

"Not telling," she said coyly.

"I'm intrigued," he said, in a way that invited her to continue.

Dani shook her head and smiled.

"Come on, Dani. When's it going to be ready for show? All the choice spots are booked through next spring. You snooze, et cetera."

"Yeah. I'm on it. You'll have the *Gems* photos next week."

"Great. So about this perfume spread . . ."

16

After several days of trying to concentrate on company business and pushing the previous weekend and his grandfather, the nuns, and Dani Campbell—especially Dani Campbell—out of his mind, Peter gave up.

He'd been forcing himself to concentrate on Sinclair Enterprises business, but invariably ended up sneaking peeks at what he was calling "the Nuns' Dilemma" file. After reassuring his mother several times that Lawrence's mental capacity was in no way diminished and no one was taking advantage of him, Peter himself was having a hard time pushing away the suspicion that maybe he had missed something else.

Well, he'd definitely missed a chance at connecting with his grandfather after all this time. And he had to admit that if he had looked more closely at his own motives for going there, he would have realized he'd been hoping that things could be good between them again.

An impossibility with the spiky-haired beauty—scratch that, the spiky-haired interloper—butting in every time he had a minute alone with Lawrence. And as far as his grandfather was concerned? He didn't seem at all ruffled by Peter's unannounced appearance. Unruffled and uncaring? Peter had left feeling a sense of disappointment that he'd first tried to pretend he didn't feel, then persuaded himself he hadn't felt at all. And failed at both. He did care. He hadn't realized how much until his grandfather had opened the door holding that broom, looking older but happier than Peter could remember.

By Thursday, Peter knew he had to make some changes. Just going with the Sinclair flow had done nothing but get him stuck in a place that he wasn't sure he could stand. He didn't want to be CEO of Sinclair Enterprises. It didn't need him. But there were people who did. He glanced at the nuns' folder.

He tossed down the pen he'd been tapping on the desk—a habit that his mother insisted he overcome—and leaned back in his ergonomic, highly uncomfortable executive desk chair.

His phone buzzed.

"Mrs. Sinclair on line one."

"Claudia. Did I not ask you not to put my mother's calls through?"

Silence at the other end of the intercom.

"Claudia?"

"Just a minute. I'm still trying to figure out the double negative."

"Just don't put her through anymore." He stabbed the End button.

Her voice came back on. "I can't do that."

Peter relented. "How about every third call? Just tell her I'm busy."

"I'll try, but your mother can be very persuasive."

"Tell me about it." Peter ended the conversation.

He sat for several seconds trying to figure out how he'd gotten himself into such a weird situation. No self-respecting man let his mother rule every aspect of his life. Of course, they didn't have

Marian Sinclair for a mother. She'd ruled his father the same way. Only his father had basked in her attention, been empowered by it. He'd been perfect for the position of Sinclair heir.

Peter was not. He didn't want to be. He had never wanted to be. But it never seemed he had a choice.

Something had to give. He picked up the phone. Put it down again. Better to do this in person. Show some initiative for a change.

Claudia looked up in alarm when he strode past her with a quick "I'll be back in a few."

He walked down the hall and into James's outer office.

"Mr. Sinclair." James's secretary also looked mildly alarmed.

"Is . . ." There were too many Sinclairs in the Sinclair company, Peter thought. Conversation was like a clown car. ". . . your boss in?"

"Mr. Sinclair? Mr. Peter Sinclair to see you."

Peter rolled his eyes. "A clown car," he said. And left the secretary staring openmouthed behind him.

James Sinclair looked up from his desk, suspiciously clear of paperwork, Peter thought.

"Pete, my boy, how can I help you?"

Peter cleared his throat. He should have thought this out. Too late now. "I've closed out the Schickley disclosures. I'm momentarily between projects and thought this would be a good time to take a two-week vacation."

James didn't respond for a moment.

"I haven't taken any time off for years," Peter said, hearing his mother, his father, and every Sinclair before him telling him, loud and clear, *Your time is the company's time.*

"No, no, you haven't," James said finally. "I've often said that to Marian. That she—we—were pushing you too hard."

He looked steadily at Peter. Why did his agreement sound like he was talking to a child? Or was it just relief that he wouldn't have to help Peter "get acclimated," as his mother called it? Peter didn't care as long as he got his vacation time.

"Two weeks, you say?"

He didn't wait for Peter's answer, but plowed ahead. "I think that's an excellent idea. I've been thinking about taking a few weeks myself. When would you go?"

"Tomorrow after work."

"Oh. Well . . . I'm sure it's fine."

Do not ask me what Mother thinks, Peter thought.

"What does your mother say?" James asked.

"I haven't consulted her. I'm sure she'll be fine with it."

The two of them looked at each other. Neither one thought that Marian would be fine. And for the first time Peter sensed an understanding between them. James would happily let Marian continue to run the company the way she'd run it for over a decade. Peter's ascendancy, especially if he was successful in securing his grandfather's backing, would make life a lot more complicated for James. Status quo was his motto.

"Well, enjoy yourself. We'll hold down the fort while you're gone. Going someplace special?"

"Yes," Peter said. "Well, I'll let you get back to work." And he strode out the door.

═

Lawrence sat on the stool feeling uncomfortable; his butt was too bony for wooden stools and if he sat for longer than ten minutes, he was too stiff to stand up. It had been Sister Mary Catherine's doing, and Dani's. That a recluse of his age suddenly let himself be bossed around by two women at once was ridiculous. Though as Sister Mary Catherine observed, the kids were happy to have a new model. But when one of them insisted he looked just like Gandalf, and Sister Eloise added that she thought he looked more like Moses, for the first time in years, Lawrence thought of shaving his beard off.

So here he sat, holding a broom bristle side up like a devil's pitchfork. More like the old farmer in *American Gothic* with his hay spear. Lawrence sighed. Or just a silly old man, chasing a spider with a broom while a girl, young enough to be his granddaughter, screeched and giggled and made him feel alive again. And helped to dispel the shock of opening the door to Peter.

Lawrence missed them both. If he could change time he would have done more to keep Peter close. As for Dani, he was just happy that she'd ferreted him out. He would miss her. But his grandson . . . He didn't know if he and Peter could ever mend their relationship.

Someone tugged at his sleeve. He looked down.

A little girl who couldn't be more than eight or ten stood at his knee. He remembered Mary Catherine pointing her out as having talent. She thrust a tall purple cone of paper at him. It was deftly done, but for the life of him, he couldn't figure out what he was supposed to do with it.

"It's a wizard's hat. Put it on . . . please."

Lawrence suppressed a grin—the hell he would. He looked ridiculous enough just sitting here with the broom. But she was still holding out the hat, looking determined and cute as all getout. Another one who knew her own mind. He took the hat and pushed it on his head.

She looked up at it seriously.

"I'll draw the decorations on it on my paper," she informed him, and went back to her place.

Lawrence did manage to stand up at the end of the session, but he couldn't begin to move for several minutes.

"Arthritis," Sister Mary Catherine said, coming to stand with him. "It does tend to catch up to us all."

═

Dani was up early Friday. With the sun streaming through her bare windows, the traffic from the street below, the sheer energy that seemed to seep in under the doors, she couldn't stay asleep. And besides, she'd gotten in the habit of getting up early to fix Lawrence's breakfast. She jumped out of bed before the pang of whatever that feeling was took hold. She dressed, grabbed a coffee and buttered roll from the corner deli, then hit the streets.

It was close to five before she staggered up the two flights to her apartment burdened with dry cleaning, a two-liter bottle of spring water, a "vintage" camera, a zoom lens, and several rolls of film.

She showered, wrapped herself in a towel, then went to the fridge to pull out the containers of leftover Chinese from the night before. She ate cold moo shu pork and garlic green beans standing at the kitchen window. Then she carried her water into her living room, set her phone alarm to six, and pulled up the photos she'd taken in the last few days.

She was studying a series she'd taken of Lawrence. On the sly, of course. He was a terrible subject when he knew you were taking the shot. But when he was oblivious, he became totally intriguing.

She'd even grabbed a photo of Peter from his Facebook page.

She told herself she was looking for a resemblance between them. And she guessed she was in a way—looking for that spark Lawrence kept hidden and the same spark in Peter that perhaps he just hadn't discovered yet. The only time she'd glimpsed it was that moment on the rock ledge. But it was only for a second. It had disappeared almost immediately and refused to show itself for the rest of the trip.

She became aware of an annoying buzzing sound. Her alarm. She reluctantly clicked out of the shots and went to dress for the evening.

An hour later she stepped out of the cab, gelled, manicured, made-up, and dressed into the next century—and four inches taller than she'd been when she stepped out of her Rothy's that afternoon. And to think a day ago she was wearing boyfriend jeans and muddy sneakers.

The sidewalk outside The Space was crowded with the overflow crowd sipping champagne, smoking, and expounding about art, business, and the latest scandal.

"Dani!" Cleegas Ding, another photographer being feted that night, called from the crowd.

The others turned, applauded her entrance with what enthusiasm they could manage while juggling drinks, smokes, programs, and purses.

She stayed to mingle a bit and then made her way inside.

The place was packed. The music was loud. Well-groomed waiters balancing trays of champagne flutes and canapés managed to weave their way through the room without mishap.

Dani squeezed through the group near the door and headed for the arch where a neon sign flashed FIVE X FIVE in several colors. Things were a little less loud and crowded in the actual exhibit room, a long, narrow rectangle featuring the honorees' works.

Enlargements backed on cardboard ranging in sizes from inches to feet were arranged simply on the walls. Slide shows bounced around the walls like trapped butterflies. Dani took her time trying to check out the other photographers' work, but couldn't see past the shoulders of the invited guests, most of whom had already turned from the exhibits and to one another.

Her selections were near the back on the right side and had attracted a respectable group of viewers, all of who seemed very intent on describing what they saw.

Manny was there. She straightened, lifted her chin, as well as a champagne flute from a passing tray, and went to meet him.

"And here she is," he announced, when Dani was still a few feet away. The next few minutes were dedicated to air kisses and exclamations of how wonderful they all looked.

Of course, half of those smiles harbored secret desires for the others' failures. Some of them, she knew, were directed at her. She just smiled and thought, *God, my feet hurt.*

═

Peter stopped his SUV at the front of the beach house but didn't get out immediately. What if he had jumped the gun? What if he wasn't welcome? What if Lawrence and Dani had breathed a sigh of relief to get rid of him; they might be annoyed at his reappearance. Well, let them. He had every right to reconnect with his grandfather, and if Dani Campbell was part of that . . . well . . . fine.

He got out, pulled bags and briefcase out of the car, and strode up the steps. It would be harder to turn him away if he was carrying luggage. He rang the bell. Knocked on the door. Wondered whether Lawrence or Dani wearing some weird getup on her head would open it.

The door opened a crack, then swung wider. Lawrence stood in the doorway, not moving, just looking from Peter to his cases. "Have you run away from home?"

Taken off guard, Peter forgot his planned explanation and sputtered out a laugh. That was exactly what he was doing.

"I'm taking a two-week vacation. I was hoping you might have room for one more."

"Then come on in. This B-and-B thing is becoming a lucrative venture."

"I'm not intruding, am I?"

"No, not at all. I was just making dinner. Can you cook?"

"A little bit. Where is Dani?"

"Gone."

That one word hit like an anvil to the midsection. "Gone?" Peter exclaimed involuntarily. "Where?"

"Back to where she came from."

"When?"

"Yesterday. You just missed her."

"Is she coming back?"

Lawrence took a long time to answer. "I don't know."

"Why did she leave?" Peter asked, trying to ignore the fact that he was way overreacting to the news.

"Had things to do. Why are you so interested in where she is?"

Peter wasn't ready to look at that too closely. He forced himself to swallow. "Look. I know who she is. And what she does."

"Ah."

"Why the hell did you let me think she was a cleaning lady?"

"I don't know. We thought it was funny. And once we started, well . . . it was easier . . . and less painful for all involved."

"Because of the photography thing," Peter said.

"Bound to set your mother off, though contrary to her opinion, I bear her no ill will."

"And what about me?" The words were out of his mouth before Peter even knew he was thinking them.

"Don't be absurd. You're my grandson. Nothing can change that. Now, are you gonna come in, or are you just gonna stand there asking questions I can't answer?"

He stepped back, and Peter lugged his stuff inside.

Lawrence had already started toward the kitchen, so Peter left his bags in the foyer and followed him.

Lawrence opened the fridge and got out two beers; handed one to Peter. "You'll need a church key. No screw caps in this household."

Peter thought he sounded a little sad. Was it because Dani was gone? Was she gone for good?

Lawrence rummaged in a drawer and pulled out a can opener, opened his beer, and handed the key to Peter.

"Why did she come? Did you invite her?"

"I'd never even heard of her. *Veni, vidi*, et cetera . . ."

"She conquered," Peter finished for him.

Lawrence chuckled. "She certainly seems to have gotten your attention. But tell your mother all is well."

"She didn't send me . . . this time," Peter said, propping one hip against the counter. "You were right. I have kind of run away from home. I was hoping . . . I don't know . . ."

"Maybe you could find it here?"

Peter shrugged and took a swig of beer.

"Dani left some food. Are you hungry?"

"Yeah, maybe."

"Yeesh." Lawrence went back into the fridge, pulled out

several rubber containers with labels. "Let's see, mac and cheese. Chicken-ish."

"What is that?"

Lawrence frowned at the package. "Don't know. Either the label got smeared or it's a description of how it turned out."

Peter raised both eyebrows.

"She's not the best cook. But she's improving."

"Wait. She's really staying here; she's actually cooking and cleaning for you. Dani Campbell? She of the next century website and exhibits all over the place?"

"Yep, that one."

"Why?"

"Not sure."

"Are you paying her?"

Lawrence shook his head. "She's paying me."

"To work for you?"

"Yeah, don't that beat all."

"Did she have some disastrous financial loss?"

"Not that I know of. None of her checks bounced." Lawrence shrugged. "I don't have Venmo."

"Are you . . . having financial problems?" Peter hated having to ask.

Lawrence pulled out a covered plate. "Deviled eggs. She's good with eggs."

"I've seen her egg technique," Peter said drily. "But I don't understand. Are you sure you're not in trouble?"

"I'm doing quite well, thank you. In fact, you might say I've done more than well. The one useful thing I learned working for Sinclair Enterprises was how to invest."

"Then why is Dani paying you? For what?"

"For room and board. And cooking and cleaning."

Peter sank into the nearest kitchen chair. "I don't get it. It's crazy."

"It's simple. She searched me out wanting some advice. Evidently she found some of my early works in a junk store and thought I could help her. She's having some kind of career crisis. Something I imagine you both have in common."

Peter looked away.

"She wanted me to . . . I don't know . . . help her see things better. I said no. She was persistent, to say the least."

"That I can believe."

"She offered to pay rent to stay. We haggled over the price."

"You didn't."

"I did. I figured if I kept upping the rate, she'd give up and go away. I gave in at nine hundred dollars a week before she offered more."

"Bedlam." Peter guzzled the rest of his beer.

Lawrence handed him another and the church key. "She thinks I'm destitute. I guess I haven't really kept up with repairs lately. She thought, actually still thinks, she's helping me out."

"You have to tell her the truth."

"I will—eventually. Can you imagine how refreshing that is? Someone actually wanting to do something for me rather than manipulating me to get what they want."

"Like your family," Peter said, feeling duly chastened.

"Among others. I couldn't resist. But don't worry. I'm keeping a running tab; I'll return it to her when I see her again."

"So she *is* coming back."

Lawrence shrugged again and got down two plates. "I sure as hell hope so."

"Didn't she say?"

"She said she was, but the girl's got her groove back. She doesn't need me anymore."

Peter sat back; that would make reporting back to his mother much easier. So why did he feel like the air had just been sucked out of him?

"Why didn't you just tell me this to begin with? Then maybe Mother would have crawled off. She thinks you're beset by gold diggers."

"Well, don't tell her why Dani was really here. The only thing worse to Marian than a gold digger is photography."

═

Dani spent the next two hours meeting and greeting. Manny steered her through the crowd like the captain of a high-speed craft, whispering details on the way from one to the other. "This is Mr. and Mrs. Thackery. Big donors to PBS. Really more into painting, but they're thinking of producing a new series. Integrating the arts. *Integrate*," he repeated just as they reached the happy couple.

They admired her work. She was delighted to see them. *Yes, we should encourage more integration of the arts*, and on to the next.

Instead of dying down as midnight rolled in, the crowd was still going strong. Dani was just thinking about finding a quiet place to get off her feet when Manny came over with another couple. Brilliant stars among the other brilliant stars.

"Dani, I want you to meet Irina and Adrian Koppel. The creative minds behind some of the world's greatest perfumes."

Dani pulled on a smile and forgot about her aching feet.

"My dear. Adrian and I are very much interested in talking to you about our new launch. Alizée. It's a play on the French word for trade winds. We think you would be perfect for the print campaign.

"Manny and Adrian have been in talks to make it happen. I want you to meet with editorial. Getting them together is always a feat of sheer determination. So many projects, you know. But possibly as soon as next week or the week after. We'll let Manny know, and he and Adrian can iron out the details."

Dani glanced at Manny. This was happening very fast. She didn't even know what the shoot would entail. "I'm not sure of my schedule—"

Manny smiled his shut-the-f-up smile. "I'll figure it out."

"The art department already has some ideas about locations for the shoot," Irina said, ignoring the two men. "We have a production team in place, so just let them know what equipment you'll need and it's a go."

"Just the bottle and whatever," Adrian said. "No airhead models to screw things up."

"We want to focus on the form of the bottle," Irina continued. "The breath of sea air, the . . ."

Dani had to resist the urge to back up from the advance of the steamroller that was Irina Koppel. She stood a little straighter. A little more aloof. *Never appear too eager. And never appear dismayed.*

Irina rattled on, and Manny and Adrian snagged the nearest waiter. Took drinks for themselves and turned to greet two passing art critics.

Dani was left completely alone with Irina. She didn't care about any of this stuff. She wouldn't know what to do with a production team, a cadre of lighting equipment, and an editorial committee making the decisions.

Nor did she think she wanted to. But she wouldn't burn this particular bridge without talking to Manny first. The clusters of people standing nearest to them had grown quieter during their conversation, and she knew that by tomorrow, the word would be out that Dani Campbell had snagged a gigantic account. Some would congratulate her the next time they saw her, whether they meant it or not. The others would badmouth her to anyone who would listen. It was the nature of the business.

She knew other photographers who worked print ads. They were always complaining about the committee mentality. It took a special kind of resilience, patience, and talent to get ahead in commercial photography. It sounded like a nightmare to Dani.

But she should at least try it. It was good money. They'd sent over a mock-up of the bottle weeks ago. Decent shape and depth to play with. Which was probably not what they had in mind. She could manipulate it until it looked like it was flying or exploding, or lost its shape entirely. But you couldn't make a product unrecognizable, like those commercials during the Super Bowl when at the end everybody said, *Genius, but what was it selling?*

She came back into the conversation on Adrian's "We'll talk."

Hands were shaken and they all moved on. Conversation ticked back up. And a slew of surreptitious looks were cast in Dani's direction.

"Good, good," Manny said, perusing the crowd. "Go enjoy yourself." Meaning, *One job down and I have other clients to attend to.*

Dani headed for the wall where she at last had room to really look at the art.

Among the five were some good photographers. She wasn't sure she was one of them. One of the others had definitely slept his way to a career, but the other three were good. Cleegas Ding's work was precise, leaving the viewer on that tiny edge between ecstasy and pain. Stacy Abramovich's was stark; she had a story to tell, and possibly an axe to grind. Her photos had been compared to Arbus, but Dani thought that was missing the point. There was influence there but her perspective was forward-looking. And Will Chaplin had pushed the parameters of simple, dissecting a shot to the point of geometry: clean, perceptive, pristine.

All three of them were true to themselves. But even so, none of them had the zing, the pure innocence of those five old photographs in Ye Olde Antiques Barn.

As she moved from one enlargement to the other, she wondered what Lawrence was doing. Hell, she even wondered what Peter was doing, and if the two of them would ever reconcile. If they would remember her, or if she would become just a blip in their history. *Remember that girl who showed up at my door that summer? What was her name? Sounded like a boy's name—yeah, the one with the weird hair.*

"Dani?"

Dani bobbled her champagne flute.

"Hi. Did I interrupt a moment of creativity?"

"No, not at all," Dani said automatically.

A broad hand was stuck out before her.

"Gary Estes. I don't know if you remember me, but I'm a contributing reviewer for *Photography Revolution* magazine." Gary was maybe thirty-five, medium height, wearing the obligatory turtleneck and dress jacket, topped by curly hair.

"This show is amazing. I love the direction you're going in. I'd love to do a spread, Dani Campbell in her element. Catch you at home, at work, where you get takeout. All the things that make you . . . you." He smiled enthusiastically.

It was a nice smile. A man who loved his subject. "Would you be interested?"

"Absolutely." Dani knew better than to say no to anything before running it past Manny.

"Not sure how soon it would happen, I haven't pitched it yet. But I didn't want to pitch it if you weren't interested." He laughed quietly. "A catch-22."

Dani smiled back, desperately trying to stifle a yawn. It had been a long day, with too much champagne as an ending.

"Great. Well. Talk to you soon." He backed away and headed for the door. Lucky him.

Dani turned back to the guests and their wild array of fashion, talking and gesticulating, now unabashedly competing with the artwork, as they became the display and the exhibits merely a backdrop to their animation.

Dani smiled, laughed, kissed cheeks, listened intently-ish, repeated it all again. As midnight began to fade, so did Dani, in energy and in presence. She knew if she left, people might briefly notice but figure she was on her way to an after-event private party—and normally she would be—and she would be forgotten just like the artwork behind them.

By one o'clock it was just another raucous party.

A little after two a.m., she finally kissed Manny good night and he put her into a cab. She had it take her straight to the garage where she parked her car when in the city. It would take only a few minutes to get back to her apartment, pack, and she would be on the road again. She just needed to grab her camera and laptop and throw a few changes of clothes in her duffel. She'd left the most important thing at Lawrence's.

17

It was still mostly dark, the sun just a promise on the horizon, when Dani pulled into the long drive to the house. The house was dark, the yard a play of deep shadow, and she shivered thinking how dead it looked. But not for long. Right now she just wanted something to eat.

She grabbed her cases, tripod, duffel, considered making two trips, but she was just too damn tired. She lumbered up the front steps with the load and managed to reach for the doorknob. Locked.

Luckily she had the key in her pocket. She'd cleverly wrested it from Lawrence the first day she'd had to leave the premises to buy groceries—in case he changed his mind while she was out. He'd never asked for it back.

It took some concentration but at last she maneuvered her cases and her person through the door. Then, trying not to wake Lawrence, she went straight to her room and dumped everything on her bed before heading to the kitchen. She was starving, but there should be plenty to eat. She'd left him enough for days and days in case her trip took longer than expected. It hadn't, and there would be hell to pay when Manny found out she'd done a late-night scarper.

But for now she just needed food.

She groped her way through the kitchen to the light switch.

Instead of the switch, her hand touched another hand.

She screeched and jumped back; the owner of the hand screeched, too. Not Lawrence.

The light popped on and her wild eyes met the wild eyes of Peter Sinclair, holding a candlestick above his head.

She whooshed out a breath. "I thought you were a burglar!"

He lowered the candlestick. "Me? You're the one who broke in, and made enough racket to wake the dead."

"I didn't break in. I have a key."

"Why am I not surprised? Just . . ."

He trailed off as if he'd lost his train of thought. He was staring at her with an expression somewhere between astonishment, loathing, and déjà vu.

Maybe because she wasn't wearing jeans and a sweatshirt. She'd been so anxious to get back she hadn't even changed out of her gala clothes before she'd left. She should have changed, but how was she to know they would have company? She crossed her arms as if that could hide the metallic blouse and the skin-tight leather jeggings. At least she'd ditched the larger-than-life Nigerian bead necklace.

Not exactly the wardrobe of a Rhode Island cleaning lady.

"If you're going to stand there gawping all night, look at my back. I'm hungry." She turned away and yanked open the fridge. Pulled out several Tupperware containers and put them on the table. Went back to the fridge, reached for a beer, opted for an Evian water instead, and closed the door. Got a fork out of the drawer, held it up in question.

Peter shook his head.

"What are you doing here?" he said, following her to the table.

"I live here. Do you mind putting down that candlestick?"

He looked at the candlestick, quickly put it down on the table. "You left. And you don't live here."

"Who says? What are you doing here?"

"Visiting my grandfather."

"Wow, twice in the last decade. Wonders never cease."

She saw him flinch. It was a direct hit and she should feel vindicated, but she could only manage mildly rueful. "Okay, low blow. I don't usually stoop to them. But something about you just pisses me off."

"The feeling is mutual," he mumbled.

She sat down and opened the plastic containers. Half of her somewhat successful chicken was left. A similar portion of the mac and cheese and green beans.

Peter began to pace.

"If you're determined to work off calories, could you just reach into that basket and hand me some bread?"

He tossed the loaf toward her. She caught it. "That was easy."

He turned on her. "I know who you are."

"And I know what you did last summer!" she returned in her most ominous movie voice. While inside she was thinking, *Oh shit, now what?*

"And if you think—"

The door swung open. Lawrence, wearing a ratty flannel robe, his hair sticking up in all directions like Scrooge on Christmas morning, stood in the doorway.

"Could you two keep it down? Is it really necessary to argue at the top of your lungs? It's enough to wake the dead. Which as it so happens I'm not . . . yet."

Dani gave him an eye roll and stuffed a forkful of mac and cheese in her mouth. After her initial scared-spitless reaction to

Peter's appearance, she'd been sort of glad to see him. Which was stupid, since he was trying to get rid of her. Was that why he'd come back? He'd fleshed out her true identity and had come to save Gramps from the . . . what?

Lawrence already knew who she was. Had always known. Had Peter raced back to warn Lawrence that his cleaning lady was an imposter? Dani choked on her chicken.

Lawrence, who was standing closest, patted her on the back.

Peter glared.

When the tension couldn't get any tighter, Peter leaned on the table. "I don't know why you both thought it was funny to pull this cleaning lady crap on me. I was genuinely worried about you."

"Huh," Dani said.

Lawrence patted her back again, not so lightly this time.

"We weren't being fair," Lawrence said. "But . . ." He shrugged.

Dani took the initiative. "But we knew you'd report back to your mother that Lawrence had . . . a . . . a . . . kept woman."

Peter barked out a laugh. "I doubt if anyone could keep you."

"They wouldn't dare try." Her eyes met Peter's. Oh yeah. He wanted a fight? He had no idea. She slipped into kid-of-a-Brooklyn-bartender mode. Jabbed her finger in the air. "You've been warned."

This time it was Lawrence who burst out laughing. "It's so nice to have kids in the house again. Is it too early for breakfast?"

"Yes!" Dani and Peter snapped.

"Then I suggest you finish eating and we all get back to bed. Or in Dani's case, to bed. We've a busy day ahead of us."

"We do?" Peter said, before Dani could.

"Yes, come on and leave Dani in peace. Good night. Glad you're back."

Peter reluctantly followed him toward the door.

Dani turned her attention back to her food, waiting for a parting shot from Peter, but the door just closed behind him.

═

The sounds of pots and pans and men's voices slowly crept into Dani's consciousness. She rolled over and checked her cell. Ten o'clock. Five hours' sleep. Not bad on a gala night. Another half hour would do it. She pulled up the covers—a particularly loud metallic clanking jolted her completely from sleep.

Fine, whatever. She got up, and after a quick shower and change into her "country" jeans and sweatshirt, she padded into the kitchen to inspect the damage.

The sudden cessation of conversation on her entrance made her think the two men had been arguing. About her? Was Peter going to try to get rid of her? Just let him try; she would put up such a fight. It seemed everyone wanted a piece of Lawrence for various reasons, including her, she acknowledged uncomfortably, but at least she'd given a little back, hopefully more than monetarily.

The kitchen was a war zone of pans and utensils. There was definitely the smell of burnt eggs? Milk? Toast? All of those things?

Coffee was made. She poured herself a cup. Took a preliminary taste. Not awful. She carried her cup to the table and sat down.

The two men looked at her.

"Don't pull that poor male look on me. Carry on."

They carried on.

And at the end of a few more clanging, smelly minutes, she was served extremely crisp bacon and limp toast, and having given up on the eggs, they presented a plate of cheese and cold cuts.

She wasn't hungry but she ate. They sat down, and soon the conversation turned to the plans for the day. Which seemed to start and end with a visit to the convent.

Dani had planned to go over anyway. She wanted to see how Logan had done on his own, and check on the progress of several of the other groups in the media lab.

"I looked over all the papers," Peter said, rolling up a slice of ham and folding it into a piece of toast. "It doesn't look like they've made much progress, if any at all. I sure hope they weren't planning to leave it in someone else's hands."

"Yours?" asked Lawrence.

"Actually, I was thinking of a higher power."

"I'm sure that plays into some of it, but Mary Catherine is pretty down-to-earth. She just has a lot on her plate."

"I'll forgo saying anything about collection plates," Peter said.

"How bad is it?" Dani asked.

That got both men's attention.

"Why? You planning on bankrolling them?" Peter asked drily.

"I'm not that successful, but I could sell a photograph or two and donate the proceeds or something."

A look passed between Lawrence and Peter that Dani almost missed; an idea niggled at her mind. But it was gone so fast that she couldn't begin to interpret it.

"I mean, are people contributing more than their usual Sunday morning dollar?"

"I'm afraid it would be too little too late at this point," Peter said. "The buyer wants them out by Thanksgiving."

Dani put down her cup. "But that's less than two months away."

"It's been in the works for a long time. I think the nuns were waiting for a miracle."

"But where will they go? What will happen to the school? They can't let that just cease to exist."

"Their living space is provided for," Lawrence said. "The diocese owns a small house in town that was used for their outreach program, when they were still a functioning convent."

"They still look functioning to me," Dani argued. "They have classes running all the time."

"By the nuns who do it from the kindness of their hearts and from donated equipment which is rapidly becoming obsolete. And by local businesses and parents who provide paper and art supplies. They've cobbled together a small"—Lawrence held up his hand to silence her—"but functioning program because they didn't have to worry about rent and utilities. But the building has been sorely neglected as of late."

Dani couldn't help herself; she glanced around the dated kitchen.

"Yeah, like some others, I admit. But even if they could keep the current space, renovations to bring it up to code would be prohibitive."

Dani sighed and pushed her plate away. "What will happen to the kids and the seniors and the special needs people?"

Lawrence looked at Peter, who frowned. "I'm sure the county or state have some kinds of programs to fill the void."

"Bull. They should have a fund for a new school building."

"A little late for that now," Peter said. "Their best bet is to find a place to rent that needs less upkeep and . . . let's face it, none of them are getting any younger. Maybe they would enjoy not having the pressure of running such a broad program."

"No!" Dani and Lawrence exclaimed.

Peter opened his hands. "Okay. I'll go over and talk to them today. See if anyone has any brilliant ideas. In lieu of that, I suggest they take a second look at the three viable rental spaces they listed in the dossier and have them inspected, then have their accountant crunch the numbers. They do have an accountant?"

"I'm sure the church will . . ."

"And that's something else they have to consider. Will it still be under the supervision of the church? Who is going be responsible for legal issues that are bound to crop up? And—"

"Okay, okay. We'll go over there as soon as we clean up." Lawrence pushed away from the table. "I'll call over and tell them to expect us. Are you going with us, Dani?"

"Of course I am. I want to see how things are going in the media room." *And make sure Peter doesn't try to talk the nuns into really retiring.*

═

Once the dishes were done, more or less, the three of them set off for the convent. Peter carrying his computer and briefcase; Dani loaded down with camera, laptop, and tripod; and Lawrence using a gnarled wooden walking stick that came almost to the top of his head.

"Are you feeling okay? Are you up to the walk?" Peter asked, suddenly concerned for his grandfather's health.

Dani just grinned at Lawrence and strode ahead, her equipment banging against her hip with each step.

Another inside joke, Peter thought, feeling an unusual moment of resentment. Here he was trying to help out Lawrence's friends while putting up with the brass-mouthed fashion disaster and they were making fun of him. He was sure of it.

He hurried after Dani.

"What's with the walking stick?" he asked quietly, nodding back toward his grandfather.

"Gandalf," she said, and strode ahead.

When they got to the convent, Dani immediately left them for the media room, and Peter and Lawrence turned toward Sister Mary Catherine's office.

They passed the carpenter, who seemed to be pretty much in the same place he'd been the week before.

"Slow work," Lawrence said.

The carpenter grunted. "Can only get here on the weekends. Between you and me—"

"I'll go on down," Peter said, sensing a commiseration session. There was too much work to be done.

Sister Mary Catherine was expecting him. He went through the financials and advised her to get inspectors and an accountant. When she seemed to hesitate, he volunteered to ask around town for some recommendations, a professional who would work for a fair price. Lawrence must have friends somewhere.

"I see that you didn't include an inventory of your equipment, supplies, or exhibit pieces. You need to have them valued, unless the diocese is responsible for that and will continue to take responsibility."

Sister Mary Catherine shook her head.

"While you're working through that process, you need to get Sister Eloise and Sister . . . ?"

"Agnes," she supplied.

". . . to do an inventory of what you have, what you will keep, and what you will assign to the trash."

"Oh dear . . ."

"What?"

"Sister Agnes wanders somewhat in her mind."

Peter groaned inwardly. Stopped himself. What was he complaining for? This was exactly the kind of case that interested him. And the fact that his first case since becoming a lawyer was representing three nuns, he took as a good sign.

Not that he could represent them. He'd have to find someone local who was willing to do pro bono work. Someone good. Someone who was willing to let Peter take the lead. He wasn't about to turn over his case to someone who wasn't up to par.

Lawrence came in a few minutes later, while Peter was asking the sister a series of questions he'd compiled to better familiarize himself with the actual state of the case.

A few minutes later there was a knock at the door, followed by the carpenter.

"Oh, hello, Watkins," Sister Mary Catherine said. "Please don't tell me you've found more leaks."

"Not yet, Sister, but I have to run into town for a minute to check on another job, and I just wanted to ask Mr. Sinclair here . . ."

Peter waited patiently for him to finish, then realized the man was looking at him. Peter raised his eyebrows and pointed to himself.

"Yes sir. Your granddad tells me you're a lawyer. Do you have an office in town? I'm having a dispute with this client refusing to pay for work I did. Figured out some clause about finish dates, that was backed up because of the supply chain problem. I'd told him in advance what was happening, and he agreed, now he's saying I didn't finish in time, and—"

"I'm sorry, Mr., uh, Watkins, but I don't have an office in town. I'm licensed in Massachusetts, not Rhode Island."

"Oh, I see." Watkins looked at Sister Mary Catherine. Nodded. "Sorry to bother you."

"But I'm sure he'd be glad to take a look at the contract and give some unofficial advice," Lawrence said. "Wouldn't you, son? Mr. Watkins is working for the convent for free."

Peter glared at his grandfather. Not because of the work it might entail, but for manipulating him. He'd been manipulated by his family his entire life, and he was pretty tired of it. Still, Mr. Watkins obviously needed help. "If you bring it by on Monday, I'd be happy to take a look. Just as a courtesy, not as a binding legal arrangement."

"I'd be grateful, I would. Thank you. I'll see you on Monday, then. Sister Mary Catherine, Lawrence." And he was gone.

"Thank you," Sister Mary Catherine said. "We've kept things together thus far by the kindness of people's hearts."

"Why isn't the diocese paying him for repairs?"

"Because the buyers will probably just tear it down to make way for whatever their project is."

"Then why fix it?"

"This building has been our home for our entire adult lives here. It's seen baptisms and deaths, watched children grow to novitiates, take their vows, and dedicate themselves to service and to prayer. It deserves our love and attention to the end."

And what could Peter say to that? A lovely idea, one that didn't hold much truck in the business world, the legal world, or the daily world of most of the planet. But if the nuns wanted new pipes, then so be it.

"If you have the time, I'd like you to give me a more in-depth tour of the art school, and then my— Lawrence and I might take a look at the prospective spaces."

"Certainly."

The three of them started in the gallery space. Lawrence insisted on coming, his walking stick tapping along the hallway with the steadiness of a metronome. Peter took some photos and talked into his cell as Mary Catherine explained who owned what.

═

"We could consolidate if need be. We've just gotten spoiled with all the space. Oh, and the lawns and the sea. Perhaps one of the new spaces will have a park nearby."

"You're welcome to use my property anytime," Lawrence said.

"You're sure to lose a few kids in the wilderness if you do," Peter quipped.

"Ah, but there will always be someone to lead us out."

Peter hesitated as he worked out her meaning: oh, *the* wilderness, duh.

"Also, it will be an insurance question," he added to Lawrence.

By way of answer, Lawrence led them into the next room, where two dozen children were busily drawing and painting several superhero action figures posed on a table in the center.

Several heads turned when they walked in. Their expressions changed quickly from curiosity to excitement. One little girl ran toward them. "I decorated the hat. Come see."

And to Peter's amazement, she took Lawrence's hand and pulled him to the group, most of whom were already on their feet and surrounding him.

"I . . . don't . . ."

"I know," said Sister Mary Catherine. "Completely out of character. Come."

She led Peter over to where a dozen depictions of an old guy with a beard and wearing a pointed hat were displayed along the wall. Some beards reached nearly to the floor, others grew straight out like they were beset by strong headwinds. The hats were of all different colors. There were grassy backgrounds, mountains, the sea, fire. Elves and trucks and dinosaurs surrounded the figure.

They were all his grandfather.

"They're very imaginative," Peter said, somewhat overwhelmed.

"Indeed. Lawrence was just the catalyst they needed. He's set them on a journey, reluctantly and grousing the whole time." She watched for a moment, then added, "And they have set him free."

Peter didn't know about that, but Lawrence looked twice as young as he had sixteen years ago. The children pulled on him, yelled to him, whispered in his ear, all at the same time while he stood bent nearly double, listening and nodding and showing off his staff. He didn't need it. It was a prop. "But how?"

"It was Dani's doing," Sister Mary Catherine said. "She made him come sit for them while she was back in New York." She smiled.

"You knew about her? What she does for a living?"

"Of course. You forget, Lawrence and I go back a long way."

"They told me she was the cleaning lady."

"And you resent that."

"Well, it makes me feel foolish. I *am* an adult."

"And if you'd known she was a photographer what would you have done?"

It was an odd question, and yet he knew what she meant. He would have been furious, for reasons he didn't want to examine too closely. He would have immediately told his mother and she would have gone ballistic. For all her business savvy, her rational, consistent grip on the world, she blamed photography and Lawrence for her husband's death. It was the one crazy thing she allowed herself. And Peter, without thinking, would have nourished that hatred.

"I guess it was the smart thing for them to do."

"Don't feel badly, Peter. He wasn't making fun. He was protecting himself . . . and you."

"And Dani?"

"Oh, she's a breath of fresh air. But yes, I think he wouldn't want her to be caught in the crosshairs of the Sinclair feud."

"You think my mother is a monster."

"She's just a very unhappy woman who cares deeply for her son and will fight to make sure he gets what is his due."

"Even if he might not want it?"

She looked up at that. "Oh dear. Are we making it harder for you?"

"No. Just clearer."

They left Lawrence surrounded by a now quieted class thanks to the timely appearance of Sister Eloise. Neither of them continued the conversation about Peter's future.

It wasn't until they reached the media room that Peter realized that he'd been anticipating this part of the tour. He wanted to see Dani in a new light, not as an adversary but as someone who might actually care about his grandfather. And the students. Or was she just better at manipulation than he realized?

As soon as they entered the room, Dani stood up from a cluster of teenagers and headed their way, almost as if she'd been waiting for them.

"Sister Agnes said that Logan hasn't been coming to class. Is that true or is she just confused? He isn't here today. Doesn't he usually come on Saturdays?"

"She isn't confused. Logan hasn't returned since you left. His phone is off. I called his foster home. There was some kind of altercation with another boy. It seems Logan has run away."

18

"Run away?" Dani exclaimed.

Sister Mary Catherine motioned her out of the room. Dani was only slightly aware of Peter ducking out after them.

The sister continued to walk until they were well away from the door. "This session will let out soon. I was hoping he might show up for the afternoon session, but his foster mother just called. She's coming over at two."

"Foster mother? I didn't know," Dani said, feeling sick.

"She's a very nice lady. She already had four fosters. Logan lived with his grandmother, but she had a bad fall and had to be moved to a semidependent facility. She's not able to have him home yet.

"The county asked Mrs. Johnson to take him in temporarily while they waited for a decision on whether to place him or send him back home after his grandmother's recovery.

"Mrs. Johnson was already fostering a full house, but she's friends with Logan's gran so she agreed to take him in. Evidently the crowded conditions have been difficult for one of the other kids. There was an altercation. It seems Logan skipped school and his work program. She had to inform the state when he didn't come home. But she'll explain everything when she arrives. I'll ask her if she minds if you sit in. She mentioned how much Logan was responding to your work with him. That's what makes this all the more tragic."

"Yes, please, I would like that." Dani glanced at Peter. "And so would Peter."

"Wha—?" He formed the question but never got it out, before he realized her intent and shook his head.

Sister Mary Catherine brightened. "Oh, that is excellent. Perhaps you can see a way out of this predicament. We don't want to lose him to the system. As much as they do try." She made a sweeping sign of the cross.

Up and down the corridor, doors opened and students of all ages began to file out.

"Maybe he'll show up," Sister Mary Catherine said. "Oh, here comes Lawrence."

The sister quickly apprised him of the situation. "The dragon artist?" Lawrence said. "That's not good."

"No."

They stood by the door until the classes had changed over. Hardly anyone left the media room. Only two new students came in.

"Our most popular workshop, even before Dani came," Sister Mary Catherine said. "Now that you're here, we have a hard time getting them to leave at all. Bless you."

While they waited, Sister Mary Catherine brought Lawrence up to speed on Logan's disappearance. When it was obvious Logan wasn't going to show up, Dani grabbed her things from the media room, promising a speedy return, and the three of them accompanied Sister Mary Catherine to her office.

Peter held Dani slightly behind. "I cannot get involved with this boy's disappearance. I shouldn't even be helping the convent or Mr. Watkins."

"Who is Mr. Watkins?" Dani asked.

"The carpenter. He got cheated on a contract."

"Will they put you in jail for helping them?"

"You wish. But yeah, they could if I'm not very careful."

"Well, that should be easy. Just be very careful." She grabbed his sleeve. "You will help him if you can . . . without getting in trouble. He's a good kid."

"You've known him for all of two days."

"More, but I can tell."

"Because he draws dragons?"

"Yeah. You can tell."

They'd reached the sister's office. He stopped Dani at the door. "I'll see what the situation is. Not promising, okay?"

She nodded and they went inside.

It was nearly twenty minutes before there was a knock on the door and Sister Eloise entered, bringing another woman with her.

Sister Mary Catherine stood. "Mrs. Johnson, come in. Have a seat."

Mrs. Johnson shuffled across the floor, carrying a bundle and biting her lip. Short and overweight, she was wearing ill-fitting double-knit pants and a T-shirt partially covered by a tight-fitting cardigan. Thin gray hair was pulled back from her face with a plastic bandeau.

She looked quickly around. Sister Mary Catherine relieved her of her bundle and put it on her desk, then helped the woman to a seat.

"You haven't seen him?" Mrs. Johnson asked hopefully.

Dani couldn't take her eyes off the woman. It was hard to imagine young children living with her. She seemed so tired, as if she carried a heavier burden than the one she'd just been lugging. Dani's fingers itched to reach for her camera. That face had been lived in, had stories to tell, was telling one now. How could she possibly take care of several children? Dani tried not to think about Logan living with this poor soul.

She glanced at Peter and knew he was thinking the same thing.

It was impossible to tell what Lawrence thought. His expression was something to be unlocked.

Sister Eloise went for a glass of water, while Sister Mary Catherine pulled her desk chair around to sit next to Mrs. Johnson and took both her hands in hers.

Eloise returned, and Mrs. Johnson drank a little water.

"Poor boy . . ." she began. "But I couldn't say no to taking him in. I know his gran. I'd never forgive myself if they let that boy go to a group home. And now look what's happened." And Dani felt a little guilty for her snap judgment of the woman.

Sister Mary Catherine patted her hand. "Just tell us from the beginning."

"Wednesday afternoon he came home late. He was in a mood—not aggressive, he never got aggressive. He went right to his room. Said he was working on something. But see, I had to double him up with Shawn. Shawn wasn't too happy having to share his room. Neither was Logan. He liked quiet; Shawn just blared that music all night. Finally had to buy him a pair of earphones. But they were the two oldest boys and I was out of space.

"Then I heard this ruckus. They were fighting, really going at it, fists and everything. I got 'em separated and tried to find out what had happened, but they were both pretty riled up, then I saw these."

She reached across to her bundle and pulled a handful of torn paper from between the folded clothes.

Dani recognized what they were right away, what they had been. Logan's beautiful intricate dragon drawing had been ripped into pieces.

"I tried to make Shawn apologize, but he wouldn't. That's when Logan lunged at him. Shawn stumbled back and hit his head. I guess Logan grabbed his backpack and ran. I was looking after Shawn and didn't see. He didn't even take his phone."

"Damn," Peter muttered beside Dani.

"I thought for sure he'd come back when he cooled off, but he didn't. I know I should have called services, but I just hated to think of him going back.

"When he still wasn't back the next morning, I was gonna call the school and say he was sick and then go look for him." She paused to do more biting on her lip. "I thought he might show up there. He liked school because it was ordered and quiet and gave him a place to draw his things in his book. But then Carey spilled the orange juice, and it made me late for getting the two little ones to preschool, and before I remembered to call, the school called to see why he wasn't there.

"I told them I had gotten busy and forgotten to call and he wasn't feeling well, that he'd probably be there on Monday. I didn't know what to do." She hung her head.

Sister Mary Catherine squeezed her hand. "Go on."

"So I went to look for him. To his gran's house, but he wasn't there. No sign he'd been there at all. To the nursing home, but they hadn't seen him. I drove around. I knew he had to be at work program or he'd be in real trouble.

"I waited for the bus to drop him off, but it never did. I finally called where he worked. He hadn't been there since Tuesday. They'd already reported his absence. He's in big trouble." She sighed and lowered her head. "I was hoping maybe he had come here."

She was clutching the remnants of Logan's drawings so tightly that Dani leaned over and pulled them from her fingers.

Mrs. Johnson didn't resist, just sat there chewing on her lip. "I know you shouldn't lie, only sometimes . . . It wasn't a bad lie, I didn't think."

"Told by a good heart," said Sister Mary Catherine sympathetically.

Mrs. Johnson nodded. "Thank you, Sister."

"I'm afraid he's been coming to art class instead of going to work program," Sister Eloise said. "He said his schedule had changed."

"He knew any infraction and they'd send him to group home, and he was guilty of several."

Dani saw red. As far as she was concerned Logan wasn't guilty of anything but loving to draw.

"Anywhere else he would go?"

Dani almost jumped in surprise. The question came from Peter.

"Any friends he hung out with? Arcades? Park? Coffee bar?"

Dani rolled her eyes.

Peter frowned, shrugged. "Diner? McDonald's?"

Mrs. Johnson shook her head. "No. I thought he might— I was hoping that— Could he be hiding out here at the convent?"

"We would have contacted you immediately if we'd seen him," Sister Mary Catherine said.

"I meant secretly. There must be places where you don't go every day."

"We will make a thorough search," Sister Eloise assured her.

Mrs. Johnson nodded jerkily. "I'd better get back; the neighbor's girl is watching the kids. But you'll let me know? I'll just leave his things here in case. It's just a change of clothes and his toothbrush." Her teeth once again captured her lip, as if to keep from saying anything else, and Sister Eloise guided her out the door.

The whole room seemed to exhale when she was gone.

"*Could* he be hiding out in the convent somewhere?" Peter asked. "Any unused storerooms? Basement? Outbuildings?"

"There's only the old barn, a garage, and the toolshed."

"You have a garage?" Dani asked, suddenly distracted.

"Oh yes, there is a car that we used to use for our outreach programs. We use our bicycles now." Lawrence and Peter were already on their feet.

"It hasn't been taken out in over a year," Sister Mary Catherine said. "I doubt if it even runs."

The car was still there, but there were no signs that Logan had been. They checked the barn, whose interior reminded Dani she had more work to do on the *Gems and Junque* photographs. There was a lot of interesting junk, but no Logan. And no room for him in the shed.

They gave up looking and went back to the convent.

By the time they returned to the house, the classes had ended for the day, and they stopped by the office for Dani to collect her things.

"I'll telephone if we get any word," Sister Mary Catherine said, and watched from the door as they started for home.

Dani struck off ahead of Peter and Lawrence. This was her fault. She'd known it the moment she'd walked in the door to the media room and he wasn't there. If she hadn't let them talk her into helping, if she hadn't gotten overexcited and started showing him all the things that he could do . . . Logan would be happily drawing his dragons the way he always had. He would go to school and to his work program and come to art class like he always had. She'd enticed him away from being satisfied and wrecked everything.

Just like she'd been enticed away from her own work, but with the outcome being success, not on the run and alone.

She whirled around, tightening her hold on the bundle of destroyed drawings as if she could protect them. Peter and Lawrence were yards away from her, and she had to wait before she burst out, "Where could he be? We have to find him."

"Calm down," Peter began.

And Dani lost it. All the anxiety she'd held on to while Mrs. Johnson related her story, while they searched the convent with no success. All the guilt bubbling up inside her came bursting out. "Don't ever tell a woman to calm down. It's not what we do."

She spun away and stomped across the grass into the woods.

═

"Well, glad we cleared that up," Lawrence said. He stopped to pick up a torn scrap of Logan's drawing that had fluttered out from the bundle as Dani had turned away. He shook his head and slid it carefully into his pocket.

"I was just trying to . . ." Peter said, walking alongside him.

"I know, but it's always better to wait until the tempest is quelled a bit before opening your mouth. And don't mention dinner. I think it's going to be takeout."

They reached the house to find Dani coming out of her room. Her purse was slung over her shoulder. "I'm going to the store."

Peter opened his mouth, but Lawrence grabbed his elbow.

"There must be an art supply store in town," she continued.

Lawrence thought. "No. Just the photo shop. Ray sells a few basic art things, but he doesn't have a big supply."

"But he'll have backing board? I didn't notice when I was there before."

"I expect so. What are you planning to do?"

"Put Humpty back together again." She headed for the hallway and the front door.

"I'll just call him and tell him you're coming," Lawrence called after her.

"We'll take care of dinner," Peter added. But she had slammed the door.

They both stood in the kitchen listening to her car drive away.

After the sound of the engine faded away, Lawrence said, "What do you say to Chinese?"

═

Ray and Ada were both waiting for her when Dani marched into the photo shop.

"Lawrence called," Ada explained. "I can't believe Logan would run away. He wouldn't worry anybody like that."

"You know him?"

"Oh sure," Ray said. "He gets his art supplies here. Well, some of them. I cut him a little bit on the price and he helps me out if I need to move stuff around."

Ada smiled fondly at her husband. "Which he seems to do whenever Logan is around."

"Lucky for me, with all my help grown up and moved away. Maybe we shoulda had a couple more."

Ada wagged a playful finger at him. "Sometimes Logan comes up and keeps me company in the kitchen when I'm baking."

"And she's always baking." Ray patted his substantial stomach. He walked over to the display rack and brought several pieces of backing board of various thicknesses to the counter. "This one is self-adhesive, easier to work with, but if the pieces are really bad, you'll be better off with this one and using a photo mount glue."

"I'll take both," Dani said. "I kind of ran out without planning ahead."

Ray reached under the counter and brought out a tray of accessories. "You better take a mat knife. I'm not sure if Lawrence still has any tools." He brought out another tray. "And a couple of micro-spatulas."

Ada held out a canvas shopping bag, while Ray added the tools to it.

Dani got out her credit card.

"You just bring back what you don't use and we'll charge Lawrence for the rest." Ray handed Dani the bag.

Ada slapped his hand.

"We will not. You fix that boy's drawing and that will be payment enough."

"But I don't want Lawrence to pay."

"Don't worry about it." Ray shrugged. "I'll just help you carry these out."

Dani thanked them both profusely, but she was a little concerned. They'd given freely of their time the other night. And now these supplies. But was Lawrence paying for everything? Surely his friends weren't taking advantage of him.

But as she backed out of the parking place, she saw them both standing on the sidewalk watching her go. No way could they be anything but the generous people they seemed.

═

By the time Dani returned, carrying backing board and the bag of other supplies, the two grocery bags from Wah Hun Gardens were sitting on the kitchen table, and Peter and Lawrence had cracked open their second beers.

She marched past them to her room.

A few minutes later she marched back into the kitchen and stopped at the table. "Sorry. It just makes me really mad."

She started pulling cartons out of the paper bags. "Didn't you start yet?"

"No," ventured Peter warily. "We were waiting for you."

She glanced up at him, but her expression was so thunderous that he decided not to say anything else. Merely went over to the cabinets and brought down plates and bowls, which he placed carefully on the table along with forks, spoons, and paper-wrapped chopsticks from the restaurant.

They'd barely passed the cartons around when Peter's cell rang. He pulled it out of his pocket, glanced at it. "I'd better take this."

"Business?" Lawrence asked.

"Worse. It's my mother."

He pushed his chair back and hurried away.

"I hope it isn't bad news," Dani said, concentrating on pinching a bean sprout with her chopsticks. "Why does he let her push him around?"

Lawrence paused with his chopsticks dripping with lo mein.

"It's a long story. She's doing her duty . . . duty according to Marian Sinclair. In Peter's defense, she's a force to be reckoned with."

"Why? She isn't even a real Sinclair, right? She married your son."

"God, don't ever say that out loud. She would agree with you. And that's why she's so fierce about protecting Peter's position in the company."

"What does the company do exactly?"

"A little bit of this, a little bit of that."

She frowned at him. "Toothpicks? Hedge funds? Real estate? Work uniforms?"

Lawrence looked over the beef and broccoli and lifted out a floret. "Pretty much." He shoved the broccoli into this mouth.

She wanted to ask if the company was so important, how could the family let Lawrence live alone and far away from the rest of them in this gothic horror of dust and poor lighting? Why wasn't he involved with the company? He was probably retired, but from the few things she'd overheard, there was something rotten in the state of Sinclair Enterprises.

After that, they studiously ate while trying to pretend neither of them was listening for snippets of Peter's conversation.

But Peter returned a few minutes later with Dani no wiser. Just that whatever had passed in that conversation had left Peter flushed—he stabbed a dumpling out of the container and practically threw it at his plate—and possibly angry? Well, there was a good sign.

She was really beginning not to like Marian Sinclair.

As soon as they'd finished eating, Dani put her plate in the sink. "I have some work to do. Can I use the worktable in the den?"

Lawrence raised both eyebrows. "Of course."

She stuck her head into a bottom cupboard, pulled out an iron. "Does this thing work?"

Lawrence shrugged. "Maybe."

Dani made a disgusted sound and left, dragging the iron's cord behind her. She went to her room, pulled a pillowcase off her pillow, and carried her purchases, pillowcase, iron, and Logan's ripped drawing upstairs to attempt to repair the damage while trying not to worry about where the teenager might be spending the night. Hopefully somewhere safe.

She plugged the iron in and turned it to low, then spread the pillowcase on the worktable.

Piece by piece, she slid the drawing inside the pillowcase, touching lightly with the iron and constantly checking that it wasn't burning the paper as she painstakingly pressed each one until they all were flat.

She arranged the mounting board and all of the accessories. Then spread out all the pieces on the worktable. Damn. There were a lot of them. The brat that had done this must have been very angry.

She found a corner piece, then another, guessed where they belonged, and slowly set to work to reconstruct the dragon drawing.

One hour slipped into another. Her back was aching and her eyes were dry from squinting at the minute edges of the tears. It seemed like an interminable job. But she couldn't quit.

She was carefully positioning a particularly difficult piece of the drawing into the puzzle when there was a light tap at the door, followed by Lawrence, holding a steaming mug.

"Thought you might want some tea. Herbal."

She nodded and went back to work.

═

Lawrence pulled a side table over and placed the mug on it, then stood back for a few moments just watching her work. So intense, so focused. And he felt a certain recognition that catapulted him back to a time when he had worked with such devotion.

And then it all was ripped apart as surely as the drawing that lay in pieces on the worktable. He'd been responsible for tearing his family apart. He'd never been able to put them back together, though to be honest, he hadn't tried very hard.

He hoped Dani had more luck with her picture and her career. At least she was trying to get back on track. Unlike Lawrence, who had given up everything he had to be everything he was supposed to be . . . according to his family. But instead of accepting and embracing his choice, he'd resented every moment of it. Poisoned everything around him with his grief for his lost art. Everything after that had dominoed. He lost his son, his wife, his grandson. Everything that mattered.

And then Dani Campbell showed up at his door. And somewhere in the last couple of weeks, she'd become more than an annoying intrusion, more than a student, more like a . . . granddaughter.

He'd meant to slip in and slip out, just a gesture to let her know she was supported, but instead he just watched her, head bent over her work, the lamp creating a cone of light around her. He moved closer to peer over her shoulder. She had reconnected a big portion of Logan's dragon. It was indeed impressive. Amazing what a pencil and a piece of paper or a camera in the right hands could produce.

His own hands were stiff, not as steady as they'd once been. But in this moment, this week, he thought he might have been given a second chance. Not that he'd ever pick up a camera again. But he could pass on what he could to Dani and even Peter—if the boy could just figure out what he really wanted.

"I think it's hopeless," she said into the silence, jarring Lawrence back into the moment. "Is it my fault?"

"Yours?" Lawrence echoed, slow in making the transition.

"It's what I always do. Nothing is ever enough; I push and push until I've wrecked it."

"I wouldn't say that," Lawrence said, fumbling for words to put to his thoughts, except the only thing he was feeling was pure panic. He could still talk about photography, but an emotional crisis was way out of his experience.

"He wanted to know how to work in the graphics program, and I showed him how to use a background vector, and things just exploded and it was exciting.

"But I shouldn't have done it. He'll never have a chance to succeed. It isn't fair."

No, it wasn't, Lawrence thought. But most of life wasn't fair.

"Where could he be? What will happen to him? When they find him, will they send him to some juvenile detention place?" Dani made a funny little noise and glanced up at him. "I can't even find all the pieces."

Lawrence was taken aback to see the tears swimming in her eyes. He reached in his pocket and fished out the scrap of paper he'd found on the lawn, slipped it into an empty space on the mounting board. "Will this help?"

"You found it?"

"Hmm, on the lawn," Lawrence said, his attention focused on the drawing. "Isn't that—?"

"Your pirate's cove. I showed him the photos I'd taken and he said it looked like a dragon's lair. I hope you don't mind. I let him use one of the photos to create a background vector on the graphics app. But he drew all this by hand."

She looked at him again, her features stark against the down light of the lamp. "I know I wasn't supposed to manipulate the photos but he was so excited—inspired—I couldn't say no. And look, it came out perfect.

"Please don't be mad. He'll need those kinds of skills."

"I'm not mad. What right do I have to be mad? I have nothing against technology when it's used by the artist. It's when the technology, and the opinions of others, use the artist. It's not about gaining new tools, it's about not losing the eye."

"That's what was happening to me," Dani acknowledged. "I see that now. You made me see that."

"Don't let anyone tell you what to do. Not even me." Lawrence tried for a smile, but he was sure it didn't look like one, because she just stared back, her expression unchanging.

"You'll help him, won't you? Take an interest in his work . . . even when I'm gone? Logan needs someone like you to guide him, like you're doing with me. Do you know how important that is? No hype, no manipulations, just someone you can trust. Who is always honest even when it hurts."

Lawrence cringed. She'd smashed his complacency, refused to leave, even insisted on paying him, because she thought he was poor and needed the money. She'd placed her faith in him. Trusted him. Against his best efforts, she had bored her way into his life, somehow inserted herself into his heart. And he'd let her.

"Promise."

You're a foolish old man, he told himself, and reached out to awkwardly pat her shoulder.

She smiled up at him and returned to her work, somehow assured that he would help. Perhaps Peter was right and it was time for him to confess that he wasn't the paragon she thought him. But he couldn't bear to break this precious cocoon of light that surrounded them. Not just yet.

Maybe tomorrow.

19

Dani had stayed up late into the night reconstructing Logan's drawing. She was dragging, but she got up in time to help with breakfast, which was eaten pretty much in silence. Lawrence seemed distracted and Peter seemed preoccupied; Dani was just plain tired.

"I don't suppose the nuns will want to discuss business on their day of rest," Peter said.

"I don't think they have a day of rest," Lawrence said. "The convent is open to the community on weekends, and they make themselves available for all those who come." Lawrence's voice had taken on a soft quality, which likely meant that last sentence was a direct quote from one of said nuns.

"So I should go over with my findings?"

"By all means. Mass has come and gone by now. The chapel has been opened for any congregant in need of solitude. And time is of the essence. What god wouldn't allow a little leniency under the circumstances?

"Besides, weekends are the only time Watkins can work for free. So you will probably be met with hammering and a copy of his contract."

"If you think so."

"Actually, they're expecting you."

As soon as the last dish was cleaned, Dani grabbed her camera and tripod and joined Peter as he left for the convent.

"Do you think Lawrence is okay?" she asked as they walked. "He seemed, I don't know, tired."

"We've kept him pretty busy," Peter said, striding through the woods.

Dani had to do a little skip step to catch up to him. "Are you in such a hurry because you have a plan to help Logan?"

"Who do I look like, the Red Cross?" he snapped, barely looking her way.

"So-o-o-orry. I don't know why you're such a grouch. You're on vacation."

"Some vacation. Restructuring the nuns' future, helping Watkins with a small claims case that I can't even try. And now this."

"Nobody's making you do those things. Nobody's even making you stay. It's probably not too late to get a ticket to Martinique."

"I don't want to go to Martinique."

They'd just stepped out of the woods to the sweep of the convent's lawn when Peter's cell phone rang.

"Dammit!"

He stopped so suddenly that she stepped past him. She stopped, too. Not that she wanted to listen to him debase himself to his mother, but like a train wreck . . .

He fished in his pocket. Looked at the phone as it continued to ring. Scowled, then refused the call.

"I think you'd better cool your jets before entering the solitude of the convent," Dani said primly.

Peter pushed his fingers through his hair, which, she noticed, hadn't been trimmed in at least five days. He was really letting himself go.

"You think I'm a pushover."

"You do seem to let people tell you what to do."

"My mother, you mean."

"Well, I did notice."

"She's a strong woman. She runs the company; my uncle James might as well stay at his golf club all day. But she's running it in the memory of my father. Running it until I can take over for *him*. She's relentless."

"When can you take over for him?"

"I could have done it already."

"Oh." Obviously she'd missed part of the equation. "So can I ask why you haven't?"

"Because, dammit, I don't want to. I never wanted to. But it's my duty. And I dread it."

Dani sucked in a breath. She'd never seen such intensity from Peter. Hadn't imagined he had it in him. It was interesting, but futile if he didn't grow a pair. And fast. Though she doubted it would be as simple as that. And it made her wonder . . .

"Is that what happened to Lawrence?"

"Not my story to tell." He started ahead again but she stopped him.

"Look, we're all going through stuff—can we take a minute to regroup and do a restart?

She walked toward the bench that overlooked the water, hoping he would follow. She was tired physically, mentally, and emotionally. But she'd come here to get rid of the bullshit, not to create more.

She sat on the bench and was glad when he sat down beside her.

"I didn't mean to have that outburst. Very bad habit in a lawyer."

"Why did you become a lawyer?"

"I always wanted to be a lawyer. I love the law."

"You do?"

"But not the kind of law I'm practicing for the company. That law has nothing to do with protecting people who can't protect themselves. About making certain that people have their fair shot. Business law is important. Necessary. But it's too abstract for me, too big, too inhuman." He turned toward her, a look of pure horror on his face.

"Do not repeat what I just said."

"Why not? Is it a secret?"

"Yes. More than a secret. It's treason to think like that. I didn't mean it. I'm just under a lot of pressure lately. I mean—I was fine, I'd accepted it. Then she sent me here to check up on Lawrence. He still holds the majority share and they need his vote. On everything."

"And your mother wants you to have it?"

He nodded, his head bent.

"And Lawrence refuses?"

He looked sharply at her.

"He's never said. She just assumes we'll have to seize power of attorney over an old man losing his faculties."

Dani jumped up. "The hell. There's nothing incompetent about Lawrence. You can't tell that?"

"Of course I can. But we didn't know. She sent me to find out. Especially when she heard a woman was living here. She thought you were a—" His mouth clamped shut as his eyes opened wider.

"A what?" Dani asked, her temper rising again. "A what?"

"I—I don't know."

"Or too chicken to say it."

"It's crazy. She blames Lawrence for my father's death. It wasn't Lawrence's fault. I think I understood that even then. She had a meltdown right there at the cemetery. Banished him from the family. I was twelve. It was awful.

"Though Lawrence was all too glad to go. The company had already wrecked his life. He ceded control to her until I came of age.

"I wasn't allowed to see him. I did go down once, but Lawrence didn't encourage me. He didn't want to cause any more rifts in the family."

"And he's lived in this crumbling old house, alone and broke, for all these years?"

"Broke? He's— It was his choice," Peter said.

"Does he know that's why you're here? To declare him incompetent, and take whatever he has left?"

Peter reared off the bench. "That's not why I'm here. That was never why I was here. Not exactly." He huffed out a sigh and sat down again. "I just wanted to get to know my grandfather again. I wanted him to help me hold out against them." His voice cracked and he turned away.

Shit, Dani thought. And sat still, waiting for the storm to pass.

"Forget I said any of this. And don't tell Lawrence." He jumped off the bench, this time like it was too hot to bear, and strode away. She strode after him.

"He helped *me*," Dani said.

Peter jerked his head no. "I'm not getting him involved."

"Because of your mother?"

"Look, she's doing what she sees as her duty, because my father can't, and Lawrence won't. I don't really have a choice."

"Yeah, you do." She had to run after him. "In the meantime, have your vacation and practice some of the law you do like to do. Maybe you can do something for Logan, too."

"I don't have a license here."

"So you've told us. Maybe you should get one."

"Do you know how hard it is to pass the bar?"

"I've heard nobody passes it on the first time."

"I did."

"Of course. Well, come on, genius. Let's see what you got."

Peter started toward the convent. "You're infuriating."

"So are you," Dani said. "And try not to be bitchy to everyone else because you're mad at me. They really do need your help, even if it's nonlegal."

"You're right, I'm sorry. It's just . . ."

"You've been holding it in for a really long time."

He frowned. "Yeah. I guess I have." Peter knocked, and they waited a few minutes in silence until Sister Mary Catherine answered.

═

"Come in." Sister Mary Catherine motioned them into the office. "I was just on the phone to Mrs. Johnson."

"Any news?" Dani asked.

Sister Mary Catherine shook her head. "He still hasn't returned, and services have already picked up his stuff to move him to the juvenile residence."

Peter crossed to the desk and began pulling folders from his briefcase, but Dani stayed by the door.

"If it's okay with you," Dani said, "I'd like to take some shots of the things in your storage shed. For a book I may be doing. Just close-ups of odd objects."

"And perhaps see if you can find some clues as to Logan's whereabouts?"

"Well, he must be somewhere. If I ran away, I would hide near someplace where I could keep working. The only place Logan has, according to everyone, is the media room. I know he gets some supplies from the photo shop, but Ray and his wife, Ada, said they wanted to help. I'm sure they would have let us know if Logan had shown up there."

"Then certainly, take your photographs," the sister said. "But do be careful around all that junk."

"I will, thank you." Dani started to leave, turned back around. "Maybe I could do some photos of the convent. For the Harvest Festival. We could make a celebration board."

"We had thought of doing something like that, but with the move and everything else . . ."

"Do you have archives? Maybe shots from over the years, and the nuns who lived and worked here. I bet people would be interested."

"I'm sure Sister Eloise could help you with that."

"What if I document some of the classes? Show all the great things that go on here. People might want to donate." Dani frowned. "We might have to get release forms. At least from the parents. Not sure how that works. Maybe Lawrence will know. If not, my agent certainly will."

"Sounds ambitious," Sister Mary Catherine managed.

"Great, I'll leave you two to plan for the future," Dani ended triumphantly. And she was gone, leaving Sister Mary Catherine and Peter staring after her.

"Well, she is certainly a whirlwind," Sister Mary Catherine said as soon as the door shut behind Dani.

"More like a tornado, leaving destruction in her wake."

"Really? Do you think she's doing harm?"

Peter put his briefcase on the desk and opened it. "Not destruction exactly, but she's certainly a disruption."

Sister Mary Catherine sat across from him. "Things were certainly less exciting before she came. Sometimes disruption can be a good thing."

"I suppose."

"You seem troubled. Is our situation a burden on your time?"

"No. No, of course not. I'm happy to help. It's just, I sort of had a conversation with Dani and I told her some stuff I shouldn't have. Not about her, though really, Sister, she'd try the patience of a saint."

"I imagine the two of you will work things out."

"I don't see how, but from your lips . . ."

"I believe that situation is in your hands . . . and Dani's? And how are things going with you and Lawrence?"

"It's hard to tell. I'm not sure what I expected. I just knew I didn't want things to continue the way they have since my father died."

"Lawrence can be a stubborn man, but that isn't always a bad thing. He's never given up on you forgiving him."

"He didn't do anything but give my father what he wanted. His chance to run the company. Lawrence sacrificed his calling and his family to the company. It's absolutely gothic. We sell stuff, we buy stuff." Peter stopped. "Sorry, Sister. I don't know what came over me. Please, let's tackle something we can fix."

He shuffled papers around just to try to collect himself. What was wrong with him? Complaining first to Dani and now to a nun. He must be out of his mind.

"I've been running some numbers." He slid a sheet of figures toward her. "Studied the local real estate valuations, zoning laws, and the like. Then there's insurance, utilities, salaries, maintenance, and other monthly expenses."

Sister Mary Catherine's expression grew more somber with each addition to the list.

"Every property you've already viewed has been out of your price range. Would you consider a smaller space?"

"We're already cramped for space, but I suppose if we must."

"Or move farther from the center of town?"

"We considered that, but we need a central location. A lot of our young people don't have access to transportation."

"Hmm. You may need to consider temporary quarters until a better opportunity arises."

"I suppose you're right." Sister Mary Catherine stood. "I've been preparing myself for that inevitability."

"Then let's look at some places that might be adaptable in time. Ask Watkins to advise us on repairs and bringing things to code. Is he here today? I promised to look over that contract he signed."

"Yes, he's in the kitchen. I'll walk you down."

Watkins was there, but half of him was hidden beneath the sink. He shimmied out when Sister Mary Catherine called his name.

"You're a plumber, too?" Peter asked as Watkins put down the wrench he'd been using and wiped his hands on a much-used rag sticking out of his coverall pocket.

"Only for family and my favorite nuns."

Peter explained about the newest plan for the relocation and Watkins agreed to lend his expertise.

═

"I brought over a copy of my contract. If you still have time to take a look at it."

"Of course," Peter said. "I can at least steer you in the right direction." Watkins went over to a chair piled high with handyman paraphernalia, then handed Peter a plastic pocket file.

Peter took it. "Do you have documentation of the history of the transactions? Emails, texts?"

Watkins screwed up his face. "I've got a file. I kept track of orders and deliveries and such. I'll see what I can find and I'll drop them off here tomorrow on my way to work. How's that?"

"Excellent," Peter said. "Anything that might be helpful."

Peter and the sister left Watkins crawling back beneath the sink and made their way back to the office.

They really didn't have anything more to discuss at the moment, and Peter suspected his reluctance to leave had more to do with putting off the inevitable confrontation with Dani Campbell. For the life of him, he couldn't figure out why he'd spilled his guts to the woman. He didn't trust her. Not completely.

How could he face her again? She already thought he was a mama's boy, and when he told Lawrence and her his evaluation of the nuns' predicament she would call him something worse.

Though why he should care what she thought was beyond him. She was from a different world, they had nothing in common, and he probably wouldn't think much of the people she knew or the way she acted there. She had purple tips in her hair, for crying out loud. But she was close to Lawrence, closer than Peter was, and what she thought of him might color Lawrence's opinion, too. At least that's what he told himself as he followed the sister into her office. There was no reason he should care, but he did care all the same.

"Peter, is it all too much?" Sister Mary Catherine smiled sympathetically.

"Not at all."

"Don't let Lawrence strong-arm you into doing something that you don't want to do."

"He isn't. Frankly, if I could practice law in Rhode Island, I would take this one pro bono." He went for broke. "Watkins, too."

There was a knock at the door, and Sister Eloise came in with another woman. Not Mrs. Johnson.

"Oh, excellent," Sister Eloise said. "Mrs. O'Dougal was hoping to see Mr. Sinclair before he left."

"Lawrence didn't come over today."

"Oh, not Mr. Lawrence but Mr. Peter. She just needs someone to look over her will."

Mrs. O'Dougal shoved the paper forward. "I got this off the internet and filled it all out. Jay Watkins said you might be willing to look it over and make sure I did it right. I can pay, if it isn't too much."

"No!" exclaimed Peter and she quickly withdrew the paper.

"I mean, I'll be glad to look it over, but I can't accept payment." He went through his not licensed explanation, the upshot being that Mrs. O'Dougal happily handed him the document and went on her way.

"This has the potential of getting out of hand," Sister Mary Catherine said, obviously fighting not to laugh. "Shall I ask Watkins not to volunteer you for anything more?"

Peter, still slightly befuddled at how quickly that had transpired, meant to agree. He really had no business accepting these projects. He should immediately refer them to a local licensed attorney. And yet . . . "I don't mind."

"In that case, maybe you should set up an office. I'm sure we have a spare room somewhere. In fact, there's an empty one right across the hall."

20

Lawrence had sighed with relief when Dani and Peter left for the convent. He'd somehow managed to make it through breakfast without confessing his charade to Dani. He told himself it was because she had too much on her plate to deal with his little joke. But really he was afraid she might despise him for deceiving her.

He took himself upstairs, a feat that until Dani Campbell showed up on his doorstep he had indulged in only twice a day. It seemed like since she had forced her way into his life, he was constantly going up and down, and hiking across to the convent, and climbing on rocks at the beach.

He went straight to the desk and turned on the work lamp. A bright cone of light spotlighted the dragon drawing.

The boy definitely had talent, and an eye and imagination. But he would need tools and training to make a career out of it. Lawrence should set up a scholarship fund for the school. If they were able to continue the school.

Hell, if the old house wasn't so ramshackle, the nuns could move themselves and the school in here. But it was too remote.

He looked up from the drawing. Dani was right. It was a dungeon in here. He couldn't even see across the room.

He turned to the window and yanked on the cord. The drapes jerked open a foot. Lawrence shut his eyes and drew them open until light suffused the room.

The couch and chairs, the books and media center, the bookcases, the work desk.

And the dragon drawing. The rock fissures of the pirate's cove transferred beautifully into a fantasy dragon lair. A hideout, a fortress, a safe haven.

He thought of other days when he and Peter sloshed through the tide, Peter running ahead and pulling him by the hand. The two of them crab-walking through the narrow fissure until they burst into sunlight again. They'd passed many adventures in the cove. "We're good pirates," Peter would say. "Like Robin Hood, only on the ocean."

They'd stay all afternoon, until Kristy, standing on the bluff above, the wind blowing her gossamer skirts, her long fine hair whipping about her face, would call, "Ahoy, mateys," when it was time for dinner. And they'd scamper like marooned men through the narrow schism of rocks and up the beach to home and sustenance for body and soul.

He and Kristy had always meant to have more children, more grandchildren, to grow old surrounded by eager young faces, to take them on adventures.

But Lawrence had killed all that. Kristy had been happy in their peripatetic life, living out of a caravan, just the three of them. She never took to life in Boston. His family were distant and unsympathetic to her freewheeling spirit. Most of the daily life was taken care of by servants. Elliott was put under the care of a nanny, bathed every night in a spotless enamel tub, dried in plush, expensive, four-hundred-thread Egyptian cotton towels. He ate wholesome snacks, served by the kitchen staff.

Lawrence spent most of his time at the office and didn't notice how it was slowly suffocating Kristy's spirit. She would never fit into a family with standing in the community, a place in society; with a husband whom she hardly recognized in a business suit and expensive haircut, who came home at night too exhausted and unhappy to notice that she was slowly withdrawing from them all.

After two miserable years, he'd moved her and Elliott up to the Rhode Island house, hoping to recapture the life they'd had when they'd been a real family. But he only joined them on weekends, weekends when the business didn't need him elsewhere. One of those weekends, she miscarried and was found, close to death, by her seven-year-old son, who had just learned how to call the operator for help. She almost died. The next year, Elliott was sent to boarding school like all Sinclair men.

Years later Kristy placed all her unappreciated love into Peter. Then Elliott was killed, Marian removed Peter from their lives, and Lawrence awoke one morning to find that Kristy had gone. She'd left a note. Lawrence didn't blame her. She'd lost her son and then her grandson. Lawrence had lost her long ago.

It was all down there on the beach: his life, the loss, the sadness. And hidden inside those formidable boulders of granite, one little bowl of happiness, forever safe from the world. He turned back to the drawing. Once a pirate's cove, now a dragon's lair. He hesitated, his finger arrested as it traced the dragon's head.

"I wonder," he said. And went downstairs to find out.

═

Dani headed straight outside from the convent office. Between Peter's overbearing competitive mother and Logan's lack of a mother, Dani felt an overwhelming desire to talk to her own.

She stopped when she was away from the convent and completely alone on the lawn.

It was early at the bar, though she knew both her parents would be there, prepping and restocking for the day.

"Mike's."

"Hi, Mom."

"Dani, what a surprise. Everything all right?"

"Yep. Just needed to hear your voice."

A few minutes later, Dani ended the call and shoved her phone in her pocket. She got out her camera, and, fortified with some good no-nonsense Brooklyn advice, she began her documentation of the convent.

She spent a few minutes just taking establishing shots of the grounds and buildings. She already had the presentation in her mind. The convent through the ages. The nuns young and hopeful and growing older, until finally only three were left.

A celebration of its history.

And its future? How could they not continue with the art school?

A lot to do, but first things first. She headed back to the shed, took a few "odd objects" photos, while keeping an eye out for signs that Logan had been here. But even that receded in her mind as she attempted to capture the special moments in the life of the convent itself.

She moved on to the gazebo, the distant view of the sea, wondered if the nuns ever went for a dip in the waves. And what they might wear. Turned back to the house, whose shadows were beginning to create geometric patterns in the lawn.

She took several photos of that, then she turned her attention to the little chapel. She opened the door, stopped just inside to make sure she wasn't disturbing anyone at prayer—or a skittish runaway.

It was smaller than she expected. Narrow, with whitewashed

walls and rows of wooden benches. And she tried to imagine it filled with new novitiates and older, veteran nuns, all who had committed themselves to a cloistered life.

But they weren't cloistered, she reminded herself. At least Sisters Mary Catherine, Eloise, and Agnes were out in the world feeding, teaching, and bringing people together.

A shaft of light slanted through the clear chapel windows to illuminate the simple altar. Dani backed up to get a better angle, took a shot, backed up again. Another shot, another step back. The camera whirred in a comforting, familiar feeling. Another shot, another step, until she was in the far corner of the chapel.

A crunch under her foot. She carefully lifted her foot away, and looked down hoping it wasn't something of religious importance. It was a cellophane wrapper, the kind snack cakes were wrapped in. She slowly looked around. She was pretty sure the nuns wouldn't eat snacks during the morning Mass. And she was pretty sure they no longer offered Mass to the public. Even if they did, no one would eat in church. Ergo . . .

Photos forgotten, Dani got down on her hands and knees and began searching the wooden floorboards for evidence of a runaway boy.

She had no success, though on further investigation, she did find an unlatched window in a little room in the back, a sacristy maybe. She pulled the window open, hoisted herself up until she could look outside. An agile teenager could easily have climbed in.

Dani gently closed the window and tiptoed back into the chapel proper. Listened, taking shallow breaths, and heard nothing. Had he heard her coming and fled? Or was it more likely that he'd been sleeping here at night when there was no fear of being found, and leaving early to hide out somewhere else during the day?

Further search yielded no more information, and Dani decided to return to the media room. Maybe one of the kids had an idea of where he might be. Maybe she'd been around long enough for them to trust her.

But no one was there. Of course. They didn't have classes today.

But maybe . . .

"Logan?" she called softly. "Logan, it's Dani. I'm alone."

But no one appeared.

She sank onto the chair in front of the console she'd been using to show Logan how to transfer his work into vectors. *Where are you? Please be safe.*

She booted up the computer. The screen filled with the background for the dragon drawing. Her photo of the pirate's cove. She sat up. What had she told him about the cove? About Peter disappearing and slipping out behind her and scaring her so that she slid off the ledge. They'd laughed at that.

She'd told him how it had been a private place away from the world. All to make it more fanciful, more inspiring. But she hadn't told him where it was. She wouldn't have to. He was a bright boy.

The pirate's cove. It was possible. It was at least worth a look. She slipped her camera over her head and ran down the hall to the office to see if Peter was still there.

═

It wasn't an easy trek. Even with his "Gandalf" stick, named by the kids when actually he'd bargained for it in a Peruvian market decades before. It had been sitting in a spare closet ever since.

Reminding himself that he'd just made this trip only the day before, he started down the path. Of course, then he'd had Dani with him. Not that she could have saved either of them, if it came to that. He slid a few times but managed to reach the beach without mishap.

He started across the sand, his body gradually falling into a rhythm that had once been second nature to him. By the time he reached the glacial ridge, he was moving like a natural. Well, maybe a slower, less agile natural.

He reached for the side of the rock, rough against his own rough hands. With one hand guiding him along the rock and the other holding fast to his staff, he stepped onto the ledge, made his way around to the opening.

The entrance seemed narrower today. And for a moment, he wondered if anyone would find him if he fell inside.

Stop acting like an old man, he told himself, and realized that he didn't feel so old these days. And he had his cell for emergencies. He was tempted to just yell out Logan's name. But he didn't want to frighten the boy. He turned sideways, squeezed through the opening, and felt his way through the chasm and into the daylight inside the cove.

Memory rushed at him from the carved walls, their nooks and crannies alive with caught echoes of the past.

But now another boy sat here. He saw Lawrence and pushed back against the rock, clutching his backpack to his chest, his feet grappling in the sand as if he was trying to disappear into the very rock.

"Logan, the dragon creator, I presume," Lawrence intoned.

"Who says?" came the belligerent answer.

"I'm Lawrence Sinclair. We met briefly the other day. I live in the house up on the cliff. I'm a friend of Sister Mary Catherine's, and everyone is very worried about you."

"I'm not going back there."

Lawrence stepped forward, Logan shrank farther back

against the rock even though Lawrence was a good ten feet away from him. "I'm not going to make you do anything you don't want to do." Lawrence walked over and lowered himself on a rock next to him.

Logan scooted around to face him, wary, and something else—speculation, maybe? Planning to make his escape.

"I hope you're not going to run. I came down to find you. I might need a little help getting back up the hill."

"How did you know I was here?"

"Well, I saw your dragon drawing and recognized the cove."

"No, you didn't. It got torn up."

"I know, but Mrs. Johnson came to the convent looking for you, she brought the pieces, and Dani put it back together."

"Dani? She left."

"She did, but if you had stuck around, you would know that she came back. And you could have saved us a whole lot of trouble."

"I just . . . I just want to live with my gran." Logan dashed at one eye and looked away.

"When is she supposed to get out of the rehab place?"

"I don't know. They don't tell me anything."

"Well, you know, my grandson is here and he's a lawyer. Maybe he can help you."

"Can't afford a lawyer."

"Well, he wouldn't charge you and he can't represent you in court, because he can only be a lawyer in Massachusetts."

"That's stupid."

"Yeah, it kind of is," Lawrence agreed. "But he might be able to find some things out. You've been sleeping here nights? Don't you think it's getting a little cold for that?"

Logan shook his head. "Been sneaking into the chapel after everyone goes to bed and leaving before they get up."

"What are you doing for food?"

Logan glanced at the paper bag. "I bought some soda and chips from the deli."

"Man. Bet you could use a hot shower and some lunch. We've got cold cuts and leftover Chinese food up at the house. And hot water and soap," Lawrence added as he got a whiff of four days of rough-living boy.

"What's in it for you?"

"I'm not sure," Lawrence confessed. "I just know a lot of people are worried about you. And Dani was really looking forward to working with you."

"She was?"

"She still is. She went over to the convent this morning to see if you had turned up. So what do you say? I'm too old to sit on this hard rock much longer."

"You won't let them send me back?"

Lawrence didn't have a clue as to the boy's future. He wouldn't lie.

"Can't promise. But we'll try."

The boy hesitated.

"You don't want to be a runaway. You want to be an artist." Lawrence held the staff and motioned to the kid. "Give an old guy a hand, will you?"

Logan slowly got up, stuffed the paper bag in his backpack and threw it over his shoulder, then extended his hand.

He only gave a little when Lawrence hoisted himself to his feet.

"Did anybody ever tell you that you look like Gandalf with that stick?"

Lawrence laughed. "A few." And he bent over to lead Logan out of the safety of the pirate's cove and into God knew what.

21

Dani ran down the hall and reached Sister Mary Catherine's office just as the door opened and Peter stepped out.

"Oh good, you're still here. I think I might have an idea where Logan is."

"Where?" Peter asked.

Dani hesitated as she realized she hadn't told him about Lawrence taking her to his special cove. Would he be angry? Hell, let him be angry.

"Pirate's cove. Lawrence showed it to me, and I told Logan about it." She was afraid to look at Peter. "I hope you don't mind. I'm going there now. I'll let you know." Dani took off down the hall toward the exit.

"Wait up," called Peter. "I'll go with you."

Dani heard Peter's footsteps behind her, but she didn't slow down. Images of terrible disasters were bombarding her brain, from drowning to being crushed beneath a fallen boulder. The fact that the boulders had been stationary for thousands of years didn't assuage her fears.

He caught up to her halfway across the lawn. Kept pace through the woods. But when she turned toward the beach path, he stopped her.

"Let's put this stuff in the house first."

She looked down at her camera, his briefcase. *Ever the pragmatist*. "Okay, but we have to hurry."

She burst into the kitchen. She could see Lawrence sitting at the table. "I think I know where—" She skidded to a halt.

Peter knocked into her. And they both stood panting and staring.

Logan sat at the table across from Lawrence, looking clean and clothed and eating leftover Chinese food and an array of other things from the fridge.

"Where have you been?" Dani demanded.

Logan's whole body tightened. Fight or flight. He was going to bolt.

"Wait! It's okay; we're not going to turn you in."

"You can't promise that," Peter mumbled beside her.

She cut him a look that dared him to say otherwise.

He just glared back at her.

"Why don't you both sit down," Lawrence suggested. "Want some lunch? Logan here has made a dent in the moo shu pork, but there's plenty of cold noodles and more cold cuts in the fridge."

"You should at least call the convent," Peter said. "And then Mrs. Johnson before we do anything."

"And we will, but first we need to make some decisions."

Peter opened his mouth to argue, but Dani nudged him toward the table.

Lawrence grinned. Logan relaxed his hold on the fork he'd been ready to use and lifted a heavy tangle of noodles to his mouth.

Peter put his briefcase on the floor by his chair and sat down. Dani sat next to Logan, and put her camera on the table.

"Now," said Lawrence.

"Before you go any further," Peter said, "you realize that we will have to contact child services."

"And we will. All in good time."

Logan glanced at him, but kept eating.

Peter looked at his watch. "Before end of day."

Dani huffed out a sigh. "You're going to help him, aren't you?"

"He's broken the rules, Dani. There are procedures for that. And he's possibly broken some laws. And that's serious."

"That's why you have to help him."

"The court will appoint a lawyer, if it comes to that."

"But you—"

"Jeez. How many times do I have to say I. Am. Not. Licensed. To practice in Rhode Island."

"Why can't I stay here?" asked Logan. "You have plenty of rooms."

"Because—" Peter began.

"Nobody has to know. I'll be invisible. You won't even know I'm here. I can even stay in that room behind the kitchen where I took the shower."

Lawrence shot Dani a rueful look. "I didn't think you'd mind."

"Sorry, that's my room," Dani said.

Logan stopped mid-chew. "Your room?"

"Yep."

"Whoa, they have all these rooms and they make you stay in the servant's quarters? That's pretty lame."

"Yep. Plus I have to pay rent."

"Man, that's really lame."

Dani saw Peter shoot a look at Lawrence. And realizing that this might be embarrassing to Lawrence, she added, "I insisted. He's helping me with something."

"I—I don't have any money."

Now she shot Lawrence a look. "He can do chores."

"No." Peter slapped the table. "This is not a game. There are laws that have to be followed. And we would not be a qualifying household. Even for emergency placement."

"Well, that's stupid," Dani snapped.

"I won't go back," Logan said. "I won't." He pushed his chair back.

"Don't even think about running or they'll send you to juvie," Peter snapped.

Logan sat down so hard that his chair rattled.

Peter turned his frown on Lawrence.

"What if I call Cyrus Turner?" Lawrence said, already retreating toward the door.

"Who's he?" Dani asked.

"A guy I know who happens to be a lawyer. He's retired but he hasn't closed his office yet. He might be willing to take on one more case."

"It's not really a case . . . yet," Peter said.

"I don't have any money," Logan reminded them.

"Mainly filling out forms and maneuvering it through the system expeditiously," Peter explained.

"We'll work it out. I'll just give him a call." Lawrence slipped out of the room.

The other three watched him go.

Dani had been around Lawrence long enough to know that he had a plan, which probably would require some strong-arming, which was probably why he left the room to call.

"I'm sorry, Logan," Peter said. "I'd like to be able to help you. I really would. But laws are laws. And I'm not even that well-versed in family law. I'll just call over to the convent and tell them you're found."

"Don't let them rat me out. Please."

Peter cleared his throat.

But Dani beat him to it. "He would never," she said, glaring at Peter. Then to Peter: "Maybe he can stay at the convent for a day or two. I mean openly."

"What about Mrs. Johnson, just until—"

"No!" Logan said. "She's a nice lady, but those kids are awful."

"Absolutely not," Dani echoed. "Oh, we retrieved the pieces of your drawing thanks to Mrs. Johnson. Did Lawrence show you?"

"No."

"Want to see?"

Logan nodded.

"We'll be upstairs. Don't decide anything without us," she said to Peter. She motioned to Logan, but Logan just looked between her and Peter.

"Come on, you can trust Peter, maybe. And you can definitely trust Lawrence."

Logan still hesitated, then finally stood, and the two of them left the kitchen.

═

Trust me, maybe*?* Peter glared at the closed door. She had a lot of nerve. He wasn't the one who let her think he was down to his last dime. He didn't encourage her to cook and clean and wait on him day and night. He was the one who had been suckered into doing odd-job lawyering, though he had to admit he'd found even the simplest will fun to do. The look on Mrs. O'Dougal's face when she left, the aura of relief and . . . trust—which brought him back to his list of grievances against Dani Campbell. It was Lawrence, not Peter, who was the one playing the poverty card on her.

He called the convent and was just ending the call when Lawrence returned to the kitchen.

"They're upstairs looking at Logan's refurbished drawing," Peter said. "Will your friend take the case?"

"We're in luck," Lawrence said. "He said he'd do it as a favor to me, as long as you deal with the paperwork and see that it moves through the system expeditiously." Lawrence smiled with satisfaction.

"Really? And what's he going to do?"

"Sign the papers when you're done. Unless you're planning to pull a Rhode Island law license out of your pocket."

Peter grimaced; he'd thought of that more than once already today.

"Oh, come on, you're interested, aren't you?"

"In a pro bono case that consists of reams of fill in the blanks and hope for the best?"

"For a pro bono case that will save a kid from a whole lot of hurt."

Peter slowly nodded. "Yeah, I am."

"It's okay, son. You'll figure it out. And I'll pay Cyrus for the use of his signature."

"Which reminds me," Peter said. "Dani told Logan that he could trust you, and me, maybe. Don't you think it's time for you to come clean about your financial situation?"

Lawrence held up his hand. A gesture that broke time, and they were standing in the kitchen decades ago and Peter had just asked for ice cream before dinner. "I will, it's just there's been no time, with real estate and runaway teenagers and trips to New York. Besides, it seems to me that I'm not the only one who needs to come clean."

"Me?" Peter asked incredulously.

Lawrence patted his shoulder. “Let’s go see what those two are up to and figure out what to do with Logan.”

And me, thought Peter as they climbed the stairs together.

═

Dani watched as Logan drew his finger lightly over the reconstructed drawing. “That’s really wild. You can hardly see the tears. What did you use?”

“Something Ray Barbosi turned me on to. The board and the adhesive came from his photo shop. He asked about you.”

“He’s pretty cool. And so is Mrs. Barbosi. And a great cook. One day I’ll pay them back for all the food and discount art stuff they gave me. Mr. Barbosi said it was the frequent customer discount, but I know he doesn’t have one.”

“He’s very generous,” Dani said. “He showed me how to develop photos in the darkroom. It took forever, but somehow it was super exciting, you know?”

“Like drawing by hand instead of with a graphics program.” He sighed.

“It was a shit thing that happened to your drawing, Logan, but there are more paper and pens and graphic programs.”

“Not if my grandma doesn’t get better.”

“She will,” Dani assured him, though she had no idea if she would or not. “What happened to her?”

“She fell. She didn’t break anything, but they had to do something to her ears because of her balance.”

“Well, that doesn’t sound too bad, does it?”

He shrugged. “It’s taking a really long time.”

They would just have to find somewhere for him to stay. “Peter will figure it out.” She would make him.

"What's taking them so long?"

"They probably have to make a lot of calls. You want to go back downstairs?"

He cut a look toward the restored drawing.

"It'll be okay here. I still need to add a finisher to reinforce the edges."

"Okay."

They went back downstairs, paused at the bottom to listen for sounds from the library.

"You want something to drink?"

Logan shook his head.

"Me neither." They both sat down on the bottom step to wait.

It was a long wait. Dani was about to go knock on the door when it opened and Lawrence came out.

"Well," Dani said, jumping to her feet. Logan got up more slowly. Dani could feel him quivering beside her. "Don't you dare bolt," she whispered.

"I won't go back."

"Everybody relax," Lawrence said, striding forward. "Peter's still hashing things out with the authorities."

"What things?" Dani asked before Logan could.

"I don't know, lawyer stuff. Can we go into the parlor where it's more comfortable? I've had a lot of exercise today and I am not going to subject my old bones to the stairs. Or on second thought, Logan, have you ever seen *The Karate Kid*?"

"Not tonight." Dani jabbed her finger toward the parlor and herded them out of the foyer.

Peter was gone so long that Dani almost wished she'd agreed to the movie. At least it would have helped pass the time. Logan just sat with his elbows resting on his knees and constantly kneaded his fingers.

"You're going to wear those things out," Lawrence said. Logan stopped. Then Lawrence started tapping his foot.

Dani was ready to scream when at last she heard the library door open. Peter stepped out at the same time they heard a car approach.

"No!" cried Logan, and jumped from the chair.

"Just stay put!" Peter ordered in a voice that shocked Dani. He went to answer the door.

Dani moved closer to Logan. It would just make it worse if he tried to run. What did they do with runaways?

They heard voices from the foyer, then Peter returned with another man.

"Oh good," Lawrence said, and hoisted himself out of the chair.

Ray Barbosi lifted a hand in greeting. "Well, Logan, I hear you've been giving everyone a worry and a half."

"I guess," Logan said. "I didn't mean to."

"Yeah, I heard. No more of this running away and acting out stuff, right?"

Logan didn't react.

"If you're going to stay with me and Ada for a bit, you have to promise."

Logan's mouth opened, but still he said nothing. Finally . . . "Really? With you and Mrs. Barbosi?"

"Well, at least for tonight until we can get all the paperwork done. But I don't think there should be a problem. As long as you're not the problem."

"I won't be."

"I didn't think so," Ray said in his phlegmatic way. "Go to school every day. And the work program."

Logan looked quickly toward Dani.

"Promise him and we'll work something out," she said to Logan. Though what, she didn't know. She would have to go back to the city soon.

"Let's just take things one step at a time," Ray said. "Right now, I think we could all use a nice rest. Get your stuff, and tomorrow we'll see about getting your other things back. In the meantime, I'm sure there are plenty of clothes at our place that will fit. And you won't be at a loss for art supplies."

"Okay." Logan headed for the kitchen, Peter on his heels. Always the lawyer even if he "wasn't licensed in Rhode Island."

"This is amazing," Dani said to Ray. "Logan and I were talking about you upstairs, and I was thinking maybe you could take him in."

"From your lips . . ." Ray said.

Dani doubted it, but she was thankful that someone's prayers had been answered, even if only temporarily.

"But how did they agree to let you foster him? Aren't there a bunch of things like background checks you have to go through?"

"There are. But this is a small town, everyone knows us, and we've done this on an emergency basis before. You might say we're on their call list."

22

Peter left early the next morning to meet Ray and Logan and take them to social services to fill out paperwork. Dani and Lawrence lingered over coffee, then walked to the convent. Dani was feeling optimistic and Lawrence strode alongside her, his walking stick, which had become his trademark among the young students, swinging in a steady cadence to match their steps.

Fall was definitely making an entrance. The leaves that had been trying to hold on to the last greenery of summer were showing hints of yellow, orange, and red.

Dani felt revitalized. Maybe it was the relief of finding Logan and knowing that he'd have a place to stay. Or being back after her adrenaline-inducing trip to the city. Or it might just be the fresh air of the morning.

She owed this feeling—this new way of looking at things—to Lawrence. She'd taken a chance, giving over her trust, her future, to him. Hopefully she had done something for him in return. If nothing else, he was healthier and more energetic since those first days.

He and Peter seemed to be getting along. Peter had even insisted on paying for this week's groceries. Which would hardly make up for ignoring Lawrence's welfare for who knew how long. But it was a beginning.

She thought about her own messy, crazy, sometimes off-the-wall family, but they never lacked for love or food, or a soft place to land. She'd always taken that for granted. Not anymore.

The two of them split up as soon as they were inside, Lawrence to discuss finances with Sister Mary Catherine, and Dani to the gallery to meet with Sister Eloise. Dani had agreed to help organize the hanging of the various art exhibits for the festival. They had decided to go all-out and include the media room projects, which would mean setting up extra electrical and making certain the cords were secure and would not overload the circuits. And in the grand tradition of small towns, Watkins, the carpenter, "knew a guy."

This morning the convent was abuzz with talk and laughter. It seemed to Dani that every room held some committee gearing up for the final few weeks before the celebration. The refreshments committee was meeting in the children's drawing room, and was having a lively discussion about sugared drinks as she passed the open door. The hospitality room had been taken over by carnival games. Next to them, the needlework group was organizing stacks of handmade articles to sell, proceeds going toward the new art school.

Everyone was busy—a final burst of activity culminating in the last hurrah? So many years of dedication and devotion coming to an end. It was daunting, even to Dani, who never thought much about longevity or devotion. But she understood dedication, and she would do her part to make this final tribute as meaningful and spectacular as she could.

═

One day slipped into the next. The festival was coming along, but the real estate prospects were not. Dani's time was divided between helping Sister Eloise, working in the media room, and accompanying the others on real estate recces, taking her camera to document the pros and cons of each space.

They considered houses, showrooms, storefronts; nothing was quite what they needed. Too big, too dark, too derelict, too remote. Anything that seemed the least bit adaptable was too expensive. It seemed like every place for rent or sale was too everything, except too perfect.

Even Sister Mary Catherine, who usually could find something to be thankful for about the most dilapidated buildings, was beginning to flag. "Oh dear," she said as they all stood outside the convent after a particularly disheartening day.

"Maybe you should rethink your needs," Peter suggested.

"Or raise a lot more money," Dani countered.

Lawrence and Peter both gave her a quelling look.

"Well, it's the only option we—you—haven't discussed. And I don't think selling hand-knitted prayer shawls is going to do the trick. I could sell some photographs, but that would only be a short-term solution and might pay a few expenses, but not much more."

Dani cut her eyes toward Lawrence, but even if they could find photographs he'd taken in the past, he'd been out of the business too long to fetch higher prices. Besides, how would they ever attract buyers to a harvest festival in a convent in a little town in Rhode Island?

But she wasn't giving up. There had to be a way to raise the needed funds. A sale? A fund-raiser? Pass the hat?

She tried pitching several ideas to Peter as they walked back to the house. He waffled between agreeing to one idea, then immediately countered with questions of the legalities of fund-raising, of the limitations of profit or nonprofit status. Insurance. Renovations. Maintenance costs.

"It's hopeless," he said. "Just getting the paperwork together will take at least a year."

"Fine," said Dani. "That will give you time to pass your Rhode Island law exam and for me to figure out how to get some art patron donors."

He didn't bother to contain his reaction. "And where are you going to be all that time?"

She'd been ready to do battle, but she hadn't anticipated that question. "I'll be working my butt off, so I can become one of the art patrons who donates to the school."

═

The next day, Sister Mary Catherine met them with a hopeful smile. "Nina Greenwood just called. A place just came on the market; it's downtown, central location, not in the best shape and small, but she said if we're interested, she'll meet us there."

"Tell her we'll drive over, then call her if we want to see more," Lawrence said.

He didn't sound all that enthusiastic, but after lunch they all piled into Dani's SUV and drove into town.

The new listing turned out to be a derelict wood-framed house whose porch had been turned into a storefront with big plate-glass windows, one of which was dissected by a jagged diagonal crack.

They got out of the car but stopped on the sidewalk. Even Sister Mary Catherine couldn't think of anything good to say.

"I'd be surprised if it could even pass an inspection," Peter said.

"Besides being too small," Sister Mary Catherine said. "But it is well located."

They'd started to climb back into the SUV when a sign across the street caught Dani's eye. Half buried beneath the fall foliage, so old and faded that Dani could just make out PROP 4 SALE.

"Wait a second. What's that over there?"

Partially hidden by weeds and a line of struggling trees was a brick building, obviously abandoned some time ago. And Dani was hit with the same reaction she'd had upon first seeing Lawrence's dilapidated gothic horror house. *And look how that turned out*, she told herself.

"Don't even think it," Peter said, following her gaze.

She started across the street.

"Dani, stop! It may not be safe."

Mary Catherine shook her head. "Peter's right. It may be dangerous."

Dani grinned at them. "That's why he's coming with me."

Dani was practically bouncing on her toes in anticipation while she waited for Peter to trot across the street. *A whole building . . . Lots of space. The possibilities were . . .*

As soon as he reached her, Peter gave her a look that said what he was thinking. But she gave him back her best I-really-don't-care expression and turned toward the weeds, knowing he would have no choice but to follow her.

"You two be careful," Lawrence called after them.

Dani raised a thumbs-up and stepped into the underbrush.

"Hold on, dammit," Peter called after her.

"Hurry up." Dani pressed ahead, past the For Sale sign, through the weeds, until she stepped onto a narrow paved parking lot that ran along the front of the building. "Plenty of parking," she announced, and took her camera out and fired off several shots before she plowed ahead. "And plenty of space," she added, taking in the façade of what at one time must have been a factory or warehouse.

She was already seeing it as a vibrant art center. And it had a double door right in the center. It was metal now, but doors could easily be replaced with something more welcoming.

She marched straight across the lot and tried the handle. Locked. Tried it again with no luck.

Undeterred, she picked her way through the weeds, broken glass, and other trash, and, cupping her hands to the first window, peered in. The interior was an immense, high-ceilinged rectangle. Another row of tall windows lined the far wall. Lots of light—once they were cleaned.

This was perfect! A little prodigious elbow grease and they could have light most of the day. There would be enough space for a gallery and separate workspaces and classrooms.

A frisson of excitement sparked up her spine. She moved to the next window.

"Dani, wait!"

"Come look!" she answered.

Peter carefully made his way over and peered inside.

"It's big and it has light."

Peter didn't bother answering.

She continued along the building, looking in windows, until she came to a smaller annex set back from the main building with another door and two large plate-glass windows. "Gift shop!" she exclaimed, and tried the door.

This door was also locked, but Dani took a few more shots through the windows, then took a couple of Peter before he put up his hand in front of his face to stop her.

"What? Didn't I get your good side?" Dani quipped, suddenly feeling optimistic. "This looks really promising."

Peter rolled his eyes. "This looks like a calamity."

"Come on, Eeyore, let's go see if we can get the key."

═

Pipe dream, Peter thought as he tromped along behind Dani back to the street. But he had to admit, even he could see the potential. Unfortunately, even if the price was right, renovations would be a black hole.

On the other hand, time was running out. Maybe he and Lawrence could donate the down payment. As soon as he thought it, his mother's image invaded his good intentions.

She would have a fit, not because he chose to invest in real estate—Lord knew the family had plenty of it—but because it didn't serve any purpose toward advancing the Sinclair name or fortune.

Maybe he could change his name. The idea actually tore a laugh out of him.

Dani spun around. "What's so funny? Don't kill this before we even take a closer look. You guys haven't been all that successful so far. And I have a vision."

"So join a—" He stopped himself from saying "convent." Totally inappropriate. But jeez, the girl couldn't be controlled. That wasn't what he meant, either. She was just so . . . infuriating.

She'd already reached the SUV.

Lawrence looked up. "Dani thinks we should take a closer look at this place."

Was he expecting Peter to throw the spanner in her plan? No thanks. Lawrence could do his own dirty work. Besides, in the process of stalking back to the car, some of the enthusiasm radiating off her had stuck on him. The building did have potential, but it would need a shitload of money.

Then again, the Sinclairs had a shitload of money.

Of course, most of it was tied up in the business, making it impossible for any of them to lose a fortune, even a bit of a fortune. Also making it impossible to use it for anything that didn't make more. Was it better to nix the idea right up front or take the chance of the building being perfect, then having to be the one that burst everyone's bubble?

"It does looking interesting," Sister Mary Catherine added.

"I guess it's worth a closer look," Peter said reluctantly.

The look Dani shot him was so filled with emotion that his heart thudded, then skittered around in his chest, before a deep breath settled it back where it belonged.

"I'll call Nina and see if she can bring the key," Lawrence said.

Nina arrived five minutes later.

"Probably champing at the bit to unload this pile of rubble," Peter grumbled. On the other hand, the brickwork looked fairly sturdy. The windows were unique.

"And a historic site," Dani added, though no one had said a word.

"It used to be a moccasin factory decades ago, then an antiques mall. Hasn't been used for years," Nina explained as they followed her to the double doors of the building. She unlocked the door. The hinges creaked as she pushed it open. "Careful now," she warned, and led the way inside.

They all stopped just inside the door, except for Dani, who strode several steps ahead to look up at the ceiling that was at least two stories, except at one end where a metal staircase led to a second floor.

Sister Mary Catherine came to stand beside her.

"It's perfect," Dani said on a sigh.

It was a mess, Peter thought. The room was littered with the skeletal remnants of display booths, collapsing shelves, wooden crates, pallets and hand trucks, cardboard and leather remnants that he was sure provided nests for an untold number of rodents. Unrecognizable trash lay abandoned as if they'd left in a hurry.

As Peter thought this, a ray of sun cut through the window to bathe Sister Mary Catherine in an aura of light.

"Oh my," Sister Mary Catherine said. "How glorious!"

Oh shit, thought Peter. *They'll take this as a sign and empty their bank account into the black hole.* Even Lawrence stood, mouth partially opened, as the light continued to move across the floor.

Sister Mary Catherine turned back to the others.

She didn't have to say a word. It was written on her face, in the whole carriage of her body.

Peter groaned inwardly and cast a quick SOS look to Lawrence.

Lawrence just smiled into the mid-distance, a smile that made a sense of fait accompli run up Peter's spine.

He looked around for Nina, hoping she would contain the oncoming flood of enthusiasm, but she was on her phone, head down. Probably figuring how much wiggle room she had for a deal, and what her commission would be.

Mary Catherine picked her way through the garbage to join Dani. And conversing almost head to head, they started across the floor.

Peter and Lawrence followed, with Nina, still on her phone, bringing up the rear.

In the next half hour, Dani and Sister Mary Catherine explored the space from one end to the other, exchanging comments and occasionally looking around. And they would have climbed the flight of stairs to the second floor, if Peter hadn't firmly put his foot down.

For once Dani didn't argue, though she did take her time studying the layout before she acquiesced.

He just caught a wisp of her sentence as the two women passed him going the other way. "A gallery balcony and . . ."

He hurried after them. They seemed to have forgotten the others were even there.

This did not bode well. Peter could understand Dani being all excited as she studied space after space, taking photos and consulting with the sister. It was what she did. But he didn't know how to stop her, and to be honest, didn't know if he really wanted to.

Occasionally, she would stop, look around in a full 360, take a few steps back, then strike off in another direction, Sister Mary Catherine right by her side.

As Lawrence started after them, Peter grabbed his elbow. "Someone needs to curtail this before it gets totally out of hand. She's never taken this many pictures of any of the spaces we've looked at before. And it's so out of the range of what the sisters can handle even if they could afford it."

Lawrence merely answered, "Hmm."

Peter pushed on. "Not to mention renovations and equipping the space. There's no elevator if they decide to use the upstairs."

The slight smile Lawrence had been wearing broadened into an almost grin.

Peter was getting a bad feeling about this. "She's already making plans, and she's seducing Sister Mary Catherine into unaffordable dreams. She's so irresponsible."

"Maybe," Lawrence said. "But she's right."

That landed like a kick to Peter's gut. Not because of what Lawrence said, but because the longer they stayed there, the more he was having to admit that it was an ideal space for an art school and gallery. Perfect—for someone who had unlimited funds. A big corporation or a well-endowed arts organization.

The nuns were three retired old women with a desire to help their community.

He would just have to make them understand that . . . in a sympathetic, nondismissive way. But not in front of the others. When they got back to the convent, he would take Sister Mary Catherine aside and explain the reality to her.

After another few minutes of exploration, they moved on to the annexed building, which was reached by another set of double doors.

They picked their way through more abandoned junk to the far side of the room, Dani taking multiple photos.

"Office space." She indicated a far corner, made a quarter turn. "And a gift shop." Another quarter turn, her arm outstretched like the hands of an old clock. "And retail. Arts supplies and crafts for kid and adults. That would be some income."

"Dani, stop it," Peter commanded. "You're way ahead of yourself."

She spun around and said simply, "Avant-garde," before turning back to the room.

"She's got you there," Lawrence said, breaking into an unrepentant grin.

"Are you going to bankroll this fiasco?" Peter asked, expecting to wipe the grin off Lawrence's face.

He merely shrugged.

"You can't." His mother would declare Lawrence incompetent for sure. If he even had the money.

Peter had to think. "Ladies, it's getting dark and we've taken enough of Nina's time today."

"Not at all," said the real estate agent. "If you're really interested, I'll have someone in the office follow through."

"Why don't we discuss it and get back to you tomorrow,"

suggested Peter, earning him a dark look from Dani, who had reluctantly joined them.

"It is a lovely old building," Sister Mary Catherine said as they made their way back to the car. "But it must be very expensive."

"It's been on the market for a long time. I'll see what I can do," said Nina. "That is . . . if you're really interested."

"Yes, please do."

Peter cringed and started to protest, but a look from Lawrence stopped him and he had to be content with glaring at Dani, who had blithely opened this can of worms.

They dropped Sister Mary Catherine off at the convent.

"What an adventure," she said. "Thank you all for coming, but I must run or I'll be late to Vespers."

"I'm sure you'll find a suitable property eventually," Peter assured her.

"Oh, I believe we already have." She nodded to him, smiled at Dani, and gave Lawrence a look that spoke volumes before slipping through the doorway.

No. Just no no no. Peter's whole world rocked. Even if Lawrence had that much money, if he threw Sinclair money into a project so unprofitable, it would be a disaster.

Surely Lawrence understood that. Peter's mother would have him declared incompetent, grab power of attorney and his voting shares, and they would all wind up where they least wanted to be.

Peter in the boardroom of Sinclair Enterprises and the nuns without a school.

23

"What do you think you're doing?" Peter demanded as soon as the door closed behind the sister.

"Trying to be supportive," Dani said patiently.

"Maybe this could wait," suggested Lawrence.

"By encouraging her to join in your pipe dream?" asked Peter, ignoring him. "Why would you even suggest this? It's way out of their financial range, and even if it wasn't, who do you think is going to run an enterprise this large? The ladies' auxiliary? The knitting group? They're three old nuns looking forward to retirement. And you're setting them up for failure."

He'd taken Dani's elbow; now she shook him off. "Do you do anything other than try to burst people's bubbles? Just because you're miserable doesn't mean the rest of us have to be, or that we can't dream. Jeez."

"At least I don't encourage people to do things that could ruin everything they've worked years for. You're impetuous, reckless, and living in denial."

Dani jutted her chin at him. "Everything you're not, except for the denial part."

"And thank goodness for that. Lawyers need to be precise, meticulous, with a firm grasp of reality. And a logical train of thought. To prevent people like you running roughshod over helpless people."

"I wouldn't go so far as saying that," Lawrence attempted halfheartedly.

"You've encouraged them to think about doing something that can't possibly work out." Peter tried to stop but he'd gone too far. "You come traipsing in here expecting everybody to follow your lead like you were some kind of Pied Piper. Right into bankruptcy and living on Social Security for the rest of their lives."

"Which they won't have to do if they keep the school running."

"On a smaller scale that they can handle," Peter insisted.

She whirled on him, throwing him literally off-balance. "And how small would you suggest? Twenty students? Ten? Five? Who would you turn away? Logan, who has so much talent? Or Vera, who will never be able to live on her own? Which one of them will you turn away?"

"It's a good question," Lawrence said.

"Better than no one getting a chance," Peter snapped back.

"Spoken like a typical spoiled rich kid. You don't know what it's like having to scrap your way through the world. My parents were always supportive and I was lucky, I found an unclaimed camera at the bar, but I had to learn how to do this on my own. If I'd had a place like the art school with people who are accepting and encouraging and could guide me, I wouldn't have made the mistakes I've made along the way.

"Or maybe I would have, but I was lucky there, too, to find a way to Lawrence, who was willing, under duress, I admit, to help me. And the nuns who gave me an opportunity to help others find their way.

"If the school closes down, these kids won't all be so lucky.

They should have a safe haven, to learn and grow and be artistic. They just should." She finished that with a sniff, because her nose had started to run.

A handkerchief appeared in front of her face. She took it from Lawrence. "Thanks."

"Great, when all argument fails, pull out the waterworks," Peter complained.

"These aren't tears; they're liquid anger."

"Well, when you get over your liquid anger, let me know and we'll continue this conversation like two adults."

"Says the mama's boy."

And at that moment Peter's phone rang.

Dani burst out laughing. "Perfect timing. You better take it."

Peter snarled at her and strode away.

"That wasn't very nice," Lawrence said.

"I know. And I might feel a little remorse, but later. Just when I start to think he's okay, he does something that makes me so angry. One moment he's all helpful and filled with ideas, the next he's so . . ."

"Practical."

"Well, yeah, but not just that. Pessimistic. He won't even stand up to his own mother. That's sick."

"It's not his mother as mother. It's his mother as CEO. And keeper of the dreaded Sinclair legacy. It's an ingrained habit, constantly nurtured in us from birth, one generation to another; they never let up."

They'd come to the woods. Peter was nowhere to be seen.

"*You* said no," Dani said, as they stepped beneath the trees.

"And look where it got me."

She turned in surprise. "Is this such a bad place to be?"

He nudged her on. "Not at the moment. And it will be even better with my feet up and nursing a cold beer."

Dani followed him into the house, stood by while he collected a beer from the fridge. But when he started to carry his beer to another room, she blurted out, "Was he right? Did I get Sister Mary Catherine to hope where there's no hope?"

"Oh brother, that doesn't sound like you. Do we have to watch that movie again?"

Dani shook her head.

"Clean out the kitchen cabinets?"

"No. And don't make fun."

"I'm not. I'm assaulting your insecurities. Peter has his mother, but you have your own self-doubt."

She followed him into the foyer. "Still?"

"We all do. It's something you don't grow out of."

"Even you?"

"What kind of question is that?" He raised his beer and carried it upstairs. He didn't ask her to join him.

═

Peter strode as far away as he could before he answered the call. He was already feeling sick from the one-two punch, first from Dani accusing him of being . . . exactly what he was. And now his mother. God only knew what she wanted now.

As much as he'd tried to curb the enthusiasm for the building today, he'd caught a bit of the fire himself. It wasn't until later that sanity resettled in his brain and he made a stand.

He took a calming breath. And answered.

"You haven't been returning my calls."

Peter winced—not even a question that he could answer or

make an excuse for, but a direct statement. It left any answer he might make superfluous. But knowing she expected him to stumble through some kind of explanation, he said, "I'm on vacation, everything is fine. I don't have time to talk right now."

"What are you doing that you're so busy?"

"Just vacation things." Rashid was right. Dani, damn her, was right. He was a wuss.

"Are you getting *anything* accomplished there?"

Lots. Looking for runaways, helping a carpenter with a contract dispute, an older lady with a will, and three nuns looking for a building they can afford. He could have said all those things, but he didn't. "Mother, I'm on vacation."

"When are you returning to the office?"

"At the end of two weeks."

"It's already been ten days and—"

"Two weeks, that's fourteen days."

"Well, I hope you're at least having a good time."

Why did she make it sound like an indictment? Actually he was having a good time. Intense, sometimes infuriating, but good. Yeah, it was good.

"I am. Thank you."

"And what about your grandfather?"

"I think he's having a good time, too."

"Don't be cute. I mean about his votes. His power of attorney."

"We haven't discussed it."

"What? Do you even have a plan?"

"I'm on vacation." Did he sound desperate? He felt desperate. Just to get back to what he'd been doing before she called, even if it was fighting with Dani.

"Peter, darling, you have to learn to never let things slide. You need to begin as you mean to go on. Everybody's wondering how you chose to take a vacation when you just started working. It isn't a good look. Your father—"

"Don't, Mother. Do not bring him into it."

Evidently she didn't hear him, because she plowed on. "He never let things slide." *Maybe he hadn't even spoken the words out loud.*

"Even when he was on vacation."

"I don't remember him ever taking a vacation." Certainly none that Peter had been a part of.

"He didn't let anything stand in the way of him and his work."

Yes, Mother, we both have cause to know that.

"Even when he knew it might be dangerous, he knew his duty. He didn't have to go to that meeting the day he died. But he was that loyal and faithful to his responsibility. Unlike some people in this family. If only Lawrence—"

A hard seed of an unnamed emotion suddenly burst in Peter's gut and rumbled into this throat. He felt the words forming on his tongue. He was helpless to stop them.

"No, Mother. It wasn't Lawrence's fault. My father alone insisted on flying a twin-engine in a rainstorm when he could have postponed the meeting. But he was too enamored with his own sense of being irreplaceable."

Peter finally managed to clamp down on whatever else he would have said.

The silence at the other end of the call was cataclysmic.

He tried to form an apology but it wouldn't come. And finally, as people in power often did, his mother took up the narrative where she'd left off, his outburst deleted, and with it Peter's sense of self.

"James explained that your inefficiency was caused by not having a break after school. I understand that. I've been pushing you, but only for your own success. But you can't run a business virtually. It doesn't have the same power as in-person advocacy. Especially when you're just starting out."

And for the first time in his life, Peter wondered if it wasn't his grandfather's lack of interest but his mother's insistence on excellence that sent his father up in the air that day.

And it finally hit Peter that he was going to have to make a choice. A real choice. Possibly for the first time in his life. There was no outcome that would make them all happy.

And he wasn't quite ready to put it to the test.

═

When Peter didn't return, Dani climbed the stairs to consult Lawrence about what they should do about dinner.

She tapped at the den door. Getting no answer, she knocked louder, and a weird sense of something akin to panic took hold.

She opened the door wide enough to stick her head in.

Lawrence was standing at the window where the drapes were open. It was growing dark.

"Lawrence?"

He didn't answer.

"Peter hasn't come back. I wondered if I should start dinner?"

Lawrence didn't turn, just pointed his beer to the window. "He's down there."

Dani came to stand beside him, looked down on the beach. Peter was sitting on one of the lower boulders, his elbows resting on his bent knees.

"Guess his phone call didn't go well," Dani said, feeling a stab of contrition for her parting swipe about his mother.

Lawrence sighed.

"Will it help if I go apologize? Though, if I may point out, he started it."

"Do you think you can without getting into an argument?"

"I'll contain myself, though it won't be easy."

"Why not? You're both going through crises. He needs support, you need support. Why not support each other?"

"What crisis is he going through, besides separation anxiety?"

"Has anyone ever told you you have an attitude?"

"Yes, and much worse. It's the only way you can . . ." She hesitated. She had been about to say, *It's how you stay on top in this business,* but she knew what she really meant was *It's how you protect yourself.*

"You can help each other."

"He's tied to by-the-book methods. I'm an artist, creative. I've made it this far by breaking the rules."

"Not necessarily. You got there by being good at what you do. But there is something to be said for being able to create within a framework."

"Like the law?"

"Why not? You think free spirits are the only ones who have something to contribute to life?"

Dani winced. "I didn't say they were."

"I know."

"Okay. I'll go talk to him. I'll try not to judge, or argue, but you have to make dinner."

"Deal."

She left the den, dragging her feet to let Lawrence know that she wasn't excited about what was before her. And she wasn't sure how she was going to actually talk to Peter without totally losing her temper. Especially if he started up about her misleading the nuns again.

She climbed doggedly down to the beach, trying to figure out an opening line. *I'm sorry I called you a mama's boy*? That was bound to set him off again, particularly since it was true. But mom as boss did have a chilling ring to it. She tried to imagine her own mother as CEO of some big corporation. She was definitely the boss in the Campbell household and at the bar. Everybody knew it, and she knew it, but she never lorded it over them. Never acted like anything other than a mother and a partner.

Unlike what Dani was learning about Peter's mother.

By the time she reached the boulders, she still hadn't figured out what to say. She'd just have to wing it.

He flinched when she sat down beside him. And she thought for a moment that he might stand up and walk away.

"I came to apologize," she blurted out.

"For which of your many putdowns?"

She gritted her teeth. What many putdowns? She thought she'd been very patient. And what about his?

"Okay, I admit I may have gotten carried away in the old antiques building, but Sister Mary Catherine is no dummy; she's not going to run amok and buy something she can't afford."

He looked up at that.

Dani managed not to snap, *And if you were such a hotshot lawyer, you would have learned that about her by now*. But she stifled herself. "And I shouldn't have called you a mama's boy. I guess life isn't easy when your mother's your boss. But jeez, she calls a lot."

"Unlike Manny," he mumbled.

"That's different. Manny is my agent. Photography is a fluid, volatile business, and we need to be in communication." She didn't need to explain herself to Peter. Manny was always working to get her new gigs. Manny negotiated her contracts and was in charge of her livelihood. Timing was important. A necessity. But as the justifications racked up in her mind, the more she realized that most of the time, Manny told her what to do. He was good at his job and she trusted him to go all-out for her. And before this perfume thing, the shift to push her into high-paying commercial jobs, she wouldn't have questioned his choices. But that was before she'd met Lawrence.

She didn't know about Peter's dilemma, but she did know that he seemed much happier doing these local consultations, even though it must be infuriating not to be able to practice law here.

Maybe their situations weren't so different, except she loved what she did, and Peter didn't seem to even like what he did. But she didn't say any of those things.

They sat in silence for a minute or two.

"I guess your phone call didn't go so well."

"You could say that."

"You want me to have my mom talk to yours?"

A funny sound escaped through Peter's tight lips.

Dani hoped it was a laugh, which was what she was going for.

"My mother would eat your mother alive."

"I doubt it. Brooklyn, remember."

He turned so suddenly that she reflexively leaned back.

"Are they making you run the family bar as a way of life?"

"Hell, no," Dani said in sheer surprise. "Oh. Let me make a wild guess. You don't want to work for the family firm."

"I *want* to want to work for the family firm, but . . ."

"Okay, that's already too complicated."

"Tell me about it."

"If there were no family firm, what would you want to do?"

"The family got me where I am, paid for law school, gave me every advantage to get ahead."

"And you owe them."

"Ya think?"

"Actually, no. That's what families do to the best of their abilities; yours just had access to more than most. Doesn't mean they own you. But you didn't answer my question. What would you do?"

"It's academic."

"You want to be a teacher?"

Peter growled. "Sometimes you're so infuriating."

"The feeling is mutual. But I'm not a mind reader."

"Okay, you want to know? I'd be a lawyer. I love being a lawyer."

"But not your family's kind of law?"

"Not corporate shenanigans law. I want to practice the kind of law that I've been pretending to do here."

Dani frowned, thinking. "People law."

"Not exactly a legal term, but yeah."

"I think that's an excellent idea. You can start by figuring out how to make the art school happen."

"So let me get this straight: You want me to convince the nuns to undertake something they're not equipped to do, not to mention the other obstacles that stand in the way. If we can even get permits for the building. And you expect me to fix everything."

"Well, yeah. You're the lawyer." She grinned at him, but it was getting dark, so she wasn't sure he saw. "And that building we saw today would be perfect."

"I know it would," Peter admitted. "So would the Taj Mahal; so would a dozen other more local places, all unaffordable and unsustainable.

"I might even pull it off, but I'm not so irresponsible as to lead them into territory that could ruin them."

"Or make their dreams come true."

"Great. This isn't a Disney movie."

"Okay. That's it. I was trying to be nice. But you don't let up."

"Neither do you."

"Fine." Dani pushed to her feet.

"So you're just going to walk away because I don't live up to your expectations."

"Whoa!" Dani turned so fast the sand spurted beneath her feet. "Is that what this is all about? Family expectations?"

Peter slumped back. "It always has been."

"Lawrence broke away."

"Yeah, and look what happened to him."

Dani's stomach tightened. Lawrence had said pretty much the same thing. "What did happen to him?"

"My mother banished him from the company and from our lives."

"What? She couldn't do that."

"Well, she did."

"Why?"

"It's a long story and not mine to tell."

"Tell me anyway." Dani sat back down beside him.

Her cell phone rang.

24

Dani caught the edge of Peter's tit-for-tat expression before she walked away to take the call. Far enough not to be overheard.

Wrong.

Manny started at a level-four storm. Not even the breaking surf could mute his strident "Where the hell are you now?"

Dani stopped to let him finish his tirade.

She was still standing on the beach when Peter passed by her on his way to the house, hands in his khaki pants' pockets, and wearing the most annoyingly supercilious expression.

Well, hell, if it made him feel superior, fine, she could handle that. She let him go and turned her attention to Manny's demands.

When he finally wound down to gale force, Dani slowly started toward the house. Still, she had to stand in the yard for him to calm as she gave him assurances that she was his, and ready to work anytime. Even after they parted with her promise to answer all his calls and reciprocal "ciaos," she had to stand while waves of anxiety washed over her. When they eventually dissipated into a low murmur, she went into the house.

She found Lawrence and Peter sitting at the kitchen table perusing takeout menus.

Fine by her. She wasn't going to volunteer to cook. She suddenly had a whole load of organizing to do while she waited for Manny's "red alert" call.

"We're thinking barbeque," Lawrence said.

"Fine," Dani said. She got out her phone, sat down at the table, and started making a list. First off, check on Logan and finish his partially restored drawing in time for the Harvest Festival exhibit. While she still had the time.

"Ribs?" Peter asked."

"Whatever you guys want," Dani said, and went back to her list. By the time they'd placed the order, she had a hefty number of to-do tasks.

She leaned back, considered the two men across the table, and was struck by a mix of emotions that she didn't have time to deal with at the moment. Now she just had to get them to help her out. She sucked in a breath, expelled it.

"I have to go back to New York."

Dani's statement dropped like a bomb between them.

"Now?" Lawrence asked.

"No, but soon. A week, week and a half. It's the perfume people. I told you about the gig."

Lawrence nodded.

The smirk had slid from Peter's face. Probably realizing he would have to continue the building search on his own. He should be happy about that. She waited for his satisfied smile. It never came, so she continued.

"It's just for a production meeting or two. They're ahead of schedule on some shoot in California and are planning to come back early. But we know how that goes."

"Quickly to hell," Lawrence said. "I don't think I ever had a shoot that ended up ahead of schedule."

It took a minute for Dani to react. It was the first time he'd ever mentioned his career as a photographer, even tangentially.

She wanted to ask him more but not when Peter was there, and mention of photography was taboo.

"Fingers crossed for lots of snafus," Dani said. "That will give me time to keep doing my work for the festival, and I'll leave instructions in case it takes longer than a few days. I told Manny I didn't have time to come back, only to find out it was a false alarm." She cut a this-is-how-you-control-your-life glance at Peter, who was still wearing the same expression as when she'd first said she was leaving.

"There's a lot to do. Sister Eloise is coordinating the committees as well as formatting the art exhibit, but it's a major undertaking, and Sister Agnes is . . . well, she's enthusiastic but not the most focused worker. And I don't want the media room to fall apart. They need guidance about their work and setting up the equipment for their part of the exhibit."

"But you're coming back?" Peter asked. "The festival is only a few weeks away. You've sort of taken over the whole thing. To desert them now—"

"I did not. And I'm not deserting them."

"It looks like—"

"Stop it, both of you," Lawrence said. It wasn't loud, but it was commanding, and they both shut up.

Dani snapped her mouth shut. She would never desert them; she was coming back. Why wouldn't she? Lawrence expected her to return. She'd just taken it for granted that she would be back in time to take up her part of the plans again. And she hadn't taken over. She was just helping. She just knew how to do things faster, more efficiently. Even if something happened and the perfume people needed her in the city, they'd be fine without her.

"It should just be a couple of days, max. But—" She stopped her words before she blurted out what was really worrying her.

"But what?" Lawrence asked.

But what if she wasn't ready? The thought slammed into her. She wasn't sure she'd ever be ready. One day she'd have to go back to the city for good.

Dani glanced at Peter, back to Lawrence. She didn't want to admit that she was scared. This was her first commercial shoot. What if she blew it and they hated her work and wrecked her future? Or worse, what if it was a success but wrecked her life? She knew it could happen. She'd heard stories about others whose careers had flourished, then crashed and burned over a product placement. And she knew from one look at Lawrence that he'd heard those stories, too.

She couldn't say any of these things in front of Peter, especially not after the way she treated him about his own insecurities.

Why did things have to be so hard?

The food came. A plate piled with slices of brisket, ribs, coleslaw, and beans was set down in front of her. She moved it to the side and kept entering things into the phone.

"You'll need to keep the media room on track while I'm gone." She stared at Lawrence until he looked up from his plate. "Promise me."

"I promise. Eat."

She picked up a spare rib. "And that you'll keep sitting for the kids while I'm gone. They're really looking forward to it, and I don't want them to lose momentum."

She put the rib down without taking a bite. "And Logan, supposing they let him come back to class. He needs mentoring."

Lawrence pointed to her plate.

She picked up the spare rib again and took a bite. Chewed,

trying not to think of anything but her list. Because with each passing moment came a sliver of fear that this was the end of something too important to let go.

She'd almost made it through the meal without exploding into a full-fledged panic when Peter said, "I guess it's a pretty important gig."

She knew he was just making conversation, maybe even a peace offering, but she heard, *I guess you don't care about the people who you have been nurturing for the last few weeks.*

That was what fear did to you. She recognized it. And she realized that it was something she hadn't felt a lot of since coming to Old Murphy Beach.

"Pays well?" Peter pressed.

"Huh? Oh yeah, lots. So you don't have to worry, I'll leave a check in advance for the rent before I go." She'd meant it as a joke but it came out exactly the way she felt. Defensive and suddenly back to not knowing who or what she was.

"I don't know why you're always so volatile," Peter snapped.

Across the table, Lawrence dropped his forehead to his hand.

"Probably because you're always so . . . so . . ." Dani couldn't think of a word. At least fighting with Peter kept her from thinking about her own situation.

"Dull," Peter said for her. "Ambivalent. Spineless. Immature—"

"I wasn't going to say that." She cut him off before he could say any more. "I don't think you're any of those things. Well, maybe a little too careful."

"Someone has to be."

"I've had enough," Lawrence said, and left the room.

"Now see what you've done!" Dani cried and ran after him.

He was halfway up the stairs when she reached the foyer.

"I don't know what to do," she called after him.

He stopped. Turned a bit to look down at her.

"I'm right back where I started. Not knowing what to do. Afraid I'll screw up." She didn't care if Peter was listening and gloating. "Should I go? I mean, I have to, but all the stories I've heard. These shoots destroy egos and self-belief."

"I think yours is strong enough to survive."

He motioned her up, then lowered himself to a stair, patted the place on the steps beside him.

She climbed up and sat down.

"You just have to stay focused. Keep slightly aloof, and don't let yourself be drawn into the inevitable brawls that break out continually." He sighed. "Art by committee. They'll change their mind several times. Then change it again. They'll hold up the shoot while they argue over stuff that doesn't matter. Rearrange lighting and sets until you can feel your hair grow. It must be worse for those poor souls working in the movies."

Dani finally took a breath. "Okay. Stay aloof."

"But make it look like it's because you're totally involved in your work," Lawrence added. "Or they'll accuse you of being impossible to work with."

"Did that happen to you?"

"Nah. I did two shoots and opted for nature. I'd rather face the unknown than the debilitating predictability of a commercial shoot."

"You think I should turn it down."

"Not at all. You should try it out and see if you like it. Some people do. Some thrive on it. Just try to be patient. And don't get embroiled in the fights. Then when they've yelled themselves out, *you* tell *them* what they want, but in a way that makes them think it was their idea.

"Do not lose your temper. And whatever you do, don't cry."

"I wouldn't think of it," Dani said with more bravura than truth. She just hoped it wouldn't come to that. And that was when she saw that Peter had followed them out, and was standing below them staring straight up at her.

She straightened her shoulders and returned his gaze, expecting to find him gloating over her insecurities. But what she saw was total sympathy. And that was harder to take than his worst sarcasm.

He understood what she was going through, and that connection was as frightening as all the rest. They had both come to Lawrence with their lives ticking toward a place where they'd have to choose the next step, all choices fraught with risks. Knowing whatever the possibilities, they would have to take the chance of suffering the consequences of a wrong choice.

In other words, life.

═

"They're always picking at each other," Lawrence complained to Sister Mary Catherine one afternoon as they sat on the bench enjoying the vista. "It's like having teenagers in the house."

"Teenagers? What do either of us know about teenagers?"

"True. Elliott was at boarding school most of his teen years, just like I was and Peter was."

"And they're not teenagers," Sister Mary Catherine reminded him. "Those two are very much adults and very much trying to figure out what direction their lives should take. And I suspect all that bickering, besides being the natural expression of insecurity, might have something to do with vying for your attention."

"What? Now they really sound like teenagers."

"Don't act like a clueless old man. You're not. At least not all the time. You're worthy of people's respect, which is evident from everyone who knows you."

"Not my family. I'm certain Marian sent Peter here to keep tabs on me."

"The first time, maybe. But if I know anything about human nature, he returned on his own, and I think he'll have a hard time going back."

"I don't think he's cut out for a company man."

"And he's smart enough to know it. I'm guessing that's why he's staying on here. Among other reasons . . ."

"Being?"

"Well," said his childhood friend. "I'd say you have the makings of a new beginning."

"You think those two . . . ?"

"I think those two both love you and you love them, though I doubt if you'd admit it. You're going to miss them when they're gone."

"It will be a lot more peaceful."

"Come now, Lawrence."

"And a lot lonelier," he admitted.

She patted his hand. And he thought how much younger hers felt than his own. And for a second, a bare flash of time, they were young with all the world before them.

"Well, I'd better get going," he said, drawing his hand from beneath hers. "They'll be bickering over what to have for dinner if I'm not there to officiate."

Dani set her mind to organizing her responsibilities for the festival in preparation for what she had begun thinking of as "the call." Hopefully it wouldn't come for another week or two, but just in case, she took everyone's emails and phone numbers, so she could keep in touch while she was away.

She delegated duties to people who could be trusted to carry on in her absence. Sister Eloise was happy to let her do it; it freed the sister to see to her other duties, which seemed to be just about everything else, since Sister Mary Catherine's time and energy were directed at the preparations for moving and finding a new location for the school.

Lawrence still came over most days to sit for the children and had begun to appear in as many drawings as the three sisters.

Together Dani and Sister Eloise began to choose which artwork would go where. There would be the short wall at the entrance portraying the convent's history, a large poster-size long shot of the convent surrounded by a collage of historical and current photos blown up to eight-by-tens, interspersed with the typical five-by-sevens and Dani's current ones, all arranged in a loose timeline through the decades.

One group of teenage cartoonists had agreed to print programs and include snippets of a comic they were working on. They wanted to print and sell the actual comics and donate the sales to the new school, but Sister Mary Catherine gently persuaded them to wait and take advantage of a blitz campaign right before Christmas.

"Well, we couldn't have them taking people's money when we don't even know if we'll have a school . . . completed," she added, keeping up her inevitable trust in things working out. "I agreed to let them print a teaser inside the front page as long as it was G-rated, with a place to sign up for notifications. I shudder to think what the bishop would make of it."

Considering the amount of money the church raked in every

year, Dani didn't think that he should be too upset. But she didn't offer her opinion.

As far as finding a new space, Dani was pretty much in the dark. She knew Nina had dropped off the specs of the antiques mall building and the price with the good news that the owners were willing to negotiate. "I think they're tired of paying the taxes," Nina informed them. Which necessitated a trip to the records department.

Dani also knew that Peter, despite his personal opinions, would be diligent in his research. He spent long hours studying the specs, speaking with inspectors, not sharing any information or asking anyone's opinion, but secreting himself away with Sister Mary Catherine several times a day.

The room he had moved into across from the sister's office saw a steady flow of people needing help with forms and navigating bureaucracy.

"I don't know how they find out that I'm handing out advice. I finally had to write up a disclaimer that I am not—"

"Licensed to practice law in Rhode Island," Dani and Lawrence quoted together.

Dani continued to push for the antiques mall, but not too hard. They might disagree on just about every subject on earth, but she knew Peter would do his due diligence.

He was getting more frequent calls from his mother, but Dani stopped making snarky comments about them. She was well aware of the comparison between his mother and her agent.

Dani spent several days choosing which of her own photos she wanted to exhibit and decided to stick to her favorite candid shots she'd taken of Lawrence, the three sisters, and some of the kids. Sister Eloise wanted her to take a whole wall. "It will be good publicity for you," she said.

"Thank you, but this is about the convent and the school and the women who made it what it is."

After the hurry-up-and-be-ready phone call from Manny, she'd heard nothing. The California shoot, as Lawrence predicted, had run into a snag.

Logan had come back to help in off hours. He was still living with Ray and Ada and going to his work program, but with Ray's help, he was working on getting his dragon drawings ready for the exhibit.

When Dani had chosen her final photos, she took them down to the photo shop to be enlarged and mounted. She insisted on paying Ray. He argued. They compromised on him giving a donation to the new school.

"Have they found a place yet?"

"One that I like, but it may be out of reach." She told him about the old antiques mall.

"That would be perfect," Ray said. "Convenient neighborhood. And only three blocks from here. I might think about expanding my art supplies section."

It didn't look like he could cram much more in the space he had. A brief image of an expanded photo shop and art supply store situated on the site of the art school popped into Dani's mind.

"How is Ada doing?" Dani asked, dispelling the expansion image.

"Well, we're working with the county to get Logan assigned to the photo shop for his work program. Even when his grandma is home, and he goes back to live with her. Ada's in hog heaven having another mouth to feed. She'll have a hard time when he leaves."

He shrugged. "Knowing my Ada, she'll be insisting on joining the permanent foster roster."

It was after five when Dani finally returned to the convent just to do a final check on progress before they ended for the day. She gathered up her things and headed for home.

She ran into Peter coming out of his office.

"You're here late," she said.

"So are you."

"Trying to finish up before 'the call.'"

"Yeah, me too. My vacation is almost up. As I'm reminded daily, sometimes twice a day."

"Ask for an extension. I mean, you're one of the bosses, aren't you? They can't fire you."

"I wish."

They walked out of the convent and across the lawn. The leaves were ablaze with color; there was a real nip in the air. Evidence that time was passing. Too fast for Dani's liking.

"You seem a lot happier than when you first came," she commented. "Man, were you a grouch."

"I am. And I know I was . . . distrustful."

"Of what? Not me?"

"Well, let's just say everything. I'd hardly seen Lawrence since my father's funeral. I didn't know if I'd be welcome. And then I saw you in that ridiculous getup."

"I was dusting."

"I know, but I wasn't prepared."

"Are you always prepared for things?"

"I try. But I wasn't for this. I really feel—I don't know—unfettered here. But I can't play hooky forever."

"If this is your idea of playing hooky, I'd hate to see you busy. You're working your butt off. For strangers. For free."

"I like it," Peter said, looking past the trees to the ocean. "I'm not even real—"

"Yeah, I know. But it's the next best thing. Someone just to lead them through the forest, you know?"

"Sort of." They literally stepped out of the trees and Peter said, "Do you want to walk down to the beach?"

"Sure."

They veered toward the beach path, walking single file. As soon as they reached the sand, Dani said, "Maybe you're trying to tell yourself something."

He gave her a look. "Let's not go there."

Dani shrugged. The breeze had whipped up and ruffled her hair, which had grown too long and heavy to support her city spikes sufficiently, even with double gel. She'd finally given up. It was an odd sensation to have hair flying near her eyes.

She pushed it back from her forehead, which did absolutely no good. "You know, you're going to have to face it sooner or later."

"Huh? Oh yeah. And probably sooner. My mother is beside herself. She thinks Lawrence is corrupting me." Peter cut his eyes toward her. "And seducing me away from my responsibilities."

"He is."

"Do you think so?"

Dani started walking across the beach. "Not intentionally. You may not know your grandfather, but he doesn't tend to tell you what to do. He made me wash dishes and clean the house before he'd even start helping me with my photography. And it wasn't just because he needed the money—"

"About that," Peter began.

"It was his wax-on-wax-off technique. Do you know that movie?"

"Yeah, but . . ."

"No buts. The point is, he didn't tell me how to change my life. He created a way for me to change it myself."

"How did you even find him?"

"It wasn't easy. But I saw some of his photos in a glorified junk store, and I could see that he had something that I didn't. I didn't know what it was. But now I think I do."

"What?"

"Soul."

Peter nodded, looked up at the rock wall before them. "He does. I remember his photographs. My dad actually liked art. He never did it himself, but he surrounded us with paintings and sculptures and stuff. He had several of Lawrence's photos that he hung in places of honor. I think he must have looked up to him."

"You have photos that Lawrence took? There are hardly any prints left."

"Mother took them all down after my father died."

"What happened to them?"

"I have no idea. I was away at school."

"Maybe they're in your attic; you should look for them."

"I think I will."

They'd reached the opposite side of the beach and were standing at the foot of the boulders.

"Would you mind if we went inside the cove?" Dani asked. "I know it's yours and it's special, but Lawrence took me and I'd just like to be there again before I go back to the city."

"That sounds like you're not coming back."

"I am. I have a duty to the festival."

Peter gave her a curious look. "Come on."

The tide was up and they had to wade ankle-deep across the slippery shelf of rock to the entrance.

Peter held her elbow as she bent over to slide between the boulders, then followed close behind.

Inside the cove, the setting sun was blocked by the wall of granite, draping the rough-grained stone in deep shadows.

A draft of sea air blew in suddenly, whipping through the cove and disappearing again like the swoop of a seabird. Dani crossed her arms against the chill.

"Too cold?"

She shook her head and sat down on the flat rock to prove her point.

He sat down beside her.

"What exactly do you do for Sinclair Enterprises?"

"Legal department lackey. And on the board of directors, soon to be chairman."

"Gack. That's sounds pretty, uh . . ."

"Awful, boring, and ungrateful of me to say so."

"I don't think so. A person should do what they do best *and* makes them happy."

"Sorry, but we're not exactly in the same position," Peter pointed out.

"I realize that. I totally get it. And so does Lawrence."

"Huh," said Peter.

And they just sat, letting the spell of the pirate's cove wash around them. And in that moment, Dani felt a connection, and she thought maybe things would turn out all right for both of them.

When they got up to leave, a final gust of wind swept in again and was gone. Not a farewell gesture, Dani thought, but an invitation to come again.

25

"The call" came on a Wednesday afternoon. Dani and Sister Eloise were spreading out a group of drawings and paintings on two large tables, deciding how to place them on the children's wall. Dani had just picked up a crayon drawing of the three sisters dressed in *The Sound of Music* habits, with flying red capes à la superheroes—Lawrence's influence—and fat yellow halos floating above their heads.

"I think we should make this the centerpiece," Dani said.

Sister Eloise cast her eyes heavenward, and that was when Dani's phone rang.

She knew what it was without even looking. She pursed her lips, looked at Sister Eloise.

"You'd better get it."

Reluctantly, Dani accepted the call.

"They're taking the red-eye tonight," Manny said without preamble. "They want to meet with the production team first thing tomorrow morning."

"Manny, I'm in the middle of something."

"Well, drop it. If you leave now, we can meet tonight and go over some strategies."

"Manny, I have things to take care of. People who—"

"You can call them from the car."

"That's insane. What if the plane is late? They won't be in any shape to talk ad campaigns."

"Not yours to question."

"So help me, Manny, if I get there and they've changed their minds . . ."

"You'll swallow it and think of the money."

"I can leave first thing in the morning."

"Now." Manny's voice was strident. "Throw your camera in the car and get back here tonight. We're not going to lose this plum assignment because you got stuck in rush-hour traffic. This could catapult your career to a whole different level. Capisce?"

"Yeah, okay."

"Call me when you're on the road. And call me when you get to Manhattan. I'll make reservations somewhere. Chop, chop." He ended the call.

Dani held the phone for several moments longer. "I have to go."

"I heard," Sister Eloise said, sounding so calm that Dani thought she might not have understood.

"There's so much work to do—what if I don't get back in time?"

"All will be fine. You just do your best."

"I'll touch base with you every day."

"We'll manage. You do what's important for you. Now shoo. And Dani, drive carefully. We'll be here when you get back. *Deo volente.*"

Dani nodded—it was all she could manage—then she ran out of the gallery and all the way home.

She heard voices coming from the kitchen and she burst into the room. "I have to go."

Lawrence looked up, startled. He was wearing a fur hat with a raccoon tail hanging down the back. He snatched it off his head, leaving white wisps of hair standing out like a halo. *Too many angel images.* She hoped it wasn't a premonition.

"I found it in a trunk upstairs. Davy Crockett."

Dani could only stare.

"King of the wild frontier?" Lawrence dropped it on the table. "I thought the kids might get a kick out of it."

"Good. Listen, Manny called, I have to leave now. You're going to continue sitting for the class while I'm gone. And I'll need you to oversee the media room, too. Like we agreed. Right?"

"How soon do you have to leave?"

"Now. Manny said to call him as soon as I got on the road."

"Then I guess you'd better hurry up and pack." Lawrence pushed to his feet. "I'll make you a sandwich to eat on the way."

The image of Lawrence making her a sandwich, after bullying her with those wax-on-wax-off chores for so long, flooded over her. And suddenly she didn't want to leave, she wanted to stay here where things made sense.

"Go," Lawrence said over his shoulder. "I don't want to be responsible for giving Manny a stroke."

"But I can come back, right?" *You won't try to lock me out like you did when we first met?*

"You know where we are."

Why wouldn't he look at her?

She looked at Peter for help. But he was just standing there staring at the tabletop like a big potato. Not a word of reassurance, or a "hurry back."

"Fine." Dani rushed out of the room.

It took less than twenty minutes to pack up her cases and put them in the car. She went back to her room, double-checked to make sure she had essentials. And also that she'd left enough of her belongings to claim her territory. She got out her checkbook and wrote a check for the next two weeks' rent. Just to be on the safe side.

She stopped in the kitchen where Lawrence and Peter still sat with their beers, just like they did every night, just like her life wasn't taking a cataclysmic turn.

"I'm leaving now."

Lawrence lifted his hand but didn't look away from his beer.

Peter's mouth was fixed in that defensive line she really didn't like. But for once she welcomed it. It yanked her right out of the sentimental tears she'd been about to shed.

"What?" she asked. Had they been discussing her? Were they angry at her? At each other? What was going on? She had thought she and Peter had come to a kind of mutual understanding and maybe something deeper, like real friendship. But now she wasn't sure. If he saw this as his chance to pull a fast one to get rid of her, he'd learn just how tough a Brooklyn girl could be. And her distrust came back in spades.

"Nothing, have a good time," Lawrence said.

Peter's lips tightened, if that was possible. But Dani didn't have time now to figure out why.

With a growing sense of unease, she pulled out her checkbook, tore out the check she'd written, and plunked it down on the table. "So you don't try to rent my room while I'm gone."

"Don't be ridiculous," Peter snapped. "Put it away."

"Don't be a buttinsky," she countered. "This is between me and Lawrence."

"Well, in that case, Lawrence has something he wants to tell you."

"You're going to watch after the media kids," she reconfirmed, feeling wary. "And the little kids. And adult art class. You promised."

"Yes, yes. You'd better get going. It will be dark soon."

"So what do you need to tell me?"

"Lawrence," Peter said. "It's time to end this subterfuge."

His words stopped Dani cold. She turned to Lawrence. "What subterfuge? Have you been lying to me about something?" Her talent, his friendship, his belief in her? She'd bared her soul to him, believed him about life and art.

"It's nothing," Lawrence said. "It's about making you pay rent. I made you that outrageous deal because I thought you would turn up your nose and leave me alone. But you didn't leave. I should never have done it. But I did. And then it just got complicated." Lawrence glanced at Peter. "But I kept track of every penny. I'll go get it now."

"But I thought—"

"That I was broke and too proud to ask for a fee. And I let you keep thinking it. I'm not derelict. I'm not even poor. In fact, I'm pretty rich."

"Extremely rich," Peter added, pointedly.

Dani shook her head, an automatic response to her heart breaking.

"And you've been laughing at me ever since."

"Dani," Lawrence began. But Dani didn't give him a chance to finish. She turned on Peter.

Peter threw up his hands. "I didn't know until I got down here. I thought . . . I thought something totally different."

"Oh my God," Dani cried, as the pieces all fell into place. "All that talk of power of attorney. But you really came racing down here because you thought I was after his money. That's why you called and wouldn't leave your name. You were checking up on me. Probably with orders to send me packing. I bet your mother has spies everywhere."

"Don't be ridiculous," Peter said.

And she knew in that moment that it was true.

"So you came running down to save him from me. God, how stupid I've been. It's a classic plot for every old movie I've ever seen. You thought I was a gold digger."

Both men visibly flinched.

"Well, set your minds at rest. I don't want your money, Lawrence. I never wanted your money. If I had even known you had money." *I wanted something much more important, your belief in me. And it was all a lie.*

"I'm sorry." Lawrence pushed her rent check toward her.

"Too late. Keep it, and if I owe more, just send the bill to Manny."

Her cell rang. "Dammit! You all make me sick."

"It's not Lawrence's fault," Peter said.

"You shut up." She rejected the call.

"You're not acting rationally," he snapped back.

"Evidently I never have, especially thinking you"—she jabbed a finger at her mentor—"really wanted to help me. Well, now I know."

She slapped her checkbook down on the table, scribbled out another check, tore it off, and tossed it next to the rent check.

"Here's another thousand to cover your fees for looking in on the media class. If you feel like you need overtime, like I said, take it up with my agent."

"Dani, don't be mad."

"And don't even think about tossing my stuff while I'm gone. I've paid in advance."

She stalked out of the kitchen, hurt, humiliation, disappointment clogging her throat and weakening her knees. She was afraid she might throw up before she made it to the car.

She made it to the car but didn't manage to drive away before the door was yanked open.

She tried to yank it back, but Peter stepped in front of it.

"Would you listen to reason?"

"Save it for the courtroom."

"I know this is all my fault."

"You don't know jack. This was between Lawrence and me. You were just the icing on the cake."

"If you would just—"

"You are a complete and total ass."

"Yeah, pretty much. But I didn't come down here to check up on you."

"For a lawyer, you're shit at lying." She grabbed the handle and yanked so hard, he nearly fell into the car. He stopped himself by grabbing on to the doorframe. It put him way too close for comfort.

She fumbled for the ignition.

"Give him—us—another chance."

"In your dreams." The ignition caught; she shifted into drive and stomped on the accelerator. The SUV lunged forward, knocking Peter backward. She didn't stop to see if he was okay, just drove, door hanging from its hinges until she rounded the bend, then she slowed down just enough to slam it shut—on the Sinclairs, her hopes, her trust—and sped away.

═

"Well, that was not one of my better ideas," Peter said, coming back into the kitchen.

Lawrence stood at the sink, staring out the window, though Peter knew he could no longer see Dani's SUV because Peter had stood in the yard doing the same thing until it was out of sight.

"She didn't deserve that," Lawrence said quietly.

"And neither do you," Peter said. "I'm sorry, Granddad. I thought it was the right thing to do. But I really screwed it up."

"No. I screwed this up all by myself."

"She'll be back when this perfume thing is over. Obviously the stress is making her a little oversensitive. I'll explain it when she's calmed down."

Lawrence finally turned from the window. "I'm afraid you don't understand. You can't explain this away. No one can. It's about trust. She handed me her talent, her career, her hope; put herself completely in my hands. And I betrayed that trust. I think I'll go upstairs."

Peter watched him go, no longer the vital, energetic man he'd been just an hour ago. Now he looked like the man Peter had expected to find. Old, resigned, forgotten, and alone.

Peter didn't know whether to blame Dani Campbell for leaving—or himself for making Lawrence tell her the truth. The one time he'd insisted on asserting himself, he'd totally screwed up. Maybe he deserved having to work for the company.

Dani was right; he was a complete ass.

═

A mile down the road, Dani finally gave up and pulled to the side and let the tears fall. Banged on the steering wheel. Railed at the irony of it all. The sadness. The humiliation.

The sheer emptiness.

She had come here because she'd been lost, trying to fake her way through something she didn't understand. She'd been clueless. But successful.

Now that she had begun to see, really see, her inner fire, it had been finally and truly doused. Now she only had success. Her desire to find the essence of her subject, stomped on. Made ridiculous.

A fresh hot wave of humiliation washed over her, leaving clear, hard light in its wake. *Get a grip. You're a success. Ahead of the herd, in several ways. Count your blessings and get on with it.*

She wiped her sleeve across her eyes, took another swipe at her nose, and pulled the SUV back on the road.

Her future was just a few hours ahead of her. She called Manny.

"I'm on my way."

And ended the call before he could ask how far.

She'd almost added "home." *I'm on my way home. Home.* Lately, she'd begun thinking of Lawrence's house as home. Boy, had she been wrong. Another surge of heat roiled through her. What secrets had she confided? What weaknesses had she exposed? As she'd bared her soul to him.

Her mentor, her friend, her Gandalf.

No longer. She now saw him for what he was. A bitter old man who didn't care.

She was stuck in traffic on the Cross Bronx when Manny called again.

"I'm on the—" was as far as she got before Manny broke in.

"Chill. The meeting's postponed. They missed the flight; they won't be in until Friday."

"That's days away," Dani said, but it seemed she really didn't care.

"So it'll give us time to work out strategy, since they haven't actually sent us a contract."

Not getting a response, he went on. "And you can make the rounds. You know the drill. Out of sight, out of mind, out of a job. In fact, you should be here in time to make a quick stop at home, change into something fabulous, and meet me in the Meatpacking District. We'll make the rounds."

"It will be midnight by then."

"The good stuff will just be getting started."

"Fine."

"Are you okay? You sound weird."

I just lost my mentor, ran out on my responsibilities, found out someone I thought might be a friend is really an ass, and if I had a dog it would have probably died.

"Just stuck on the Cross Bronx."

"That explains it. South entrance of the Whitney. We'll move on from there. Text me when you're on your way."

It was after twelve by the time the cab dropped Dani off in front of the museum. She'd changed into something trendy, but decided no way was she going to wear uncomfortable shoes. Not after all she'd been through lately.

When she stepped out of the cab, she was wearing an embroidered print polo tunic and satin gaucho pants, finished off by a pair of ancient hiking boots that she'd dressed up with some frilly socks. And she was done.

She was so done.

By the time Manny dropped her off at home, as the sun rose over the East River, she was numb. She dumped her shoes just inside the door, stripped as she walked through the room, and crawled into bed without even washing her face.

It was midday before she woke for real. She made coffee and called Sister Eloise to tell her about the changed schedule and check on the progress of the exhibit. Then she spent the rest of her day taking her camera and exploring her city, trying to get her rhythm back. Reestablishing her sense of place.

The next few days were filled with meetings with Manny and taking photos. Every evening she'd look through the shots of the day while eating takeout. Some of her shots were good and the takeout was definitely better than her or Lawrence's cooking. Thinking about Lawrence would bring on a few tears; thinking about Peter just made her mad. And something else that she didn't want to examine.

Later she'd dress herself in remarkable clothes, shoes, and accessories and hit the circuit.

Sometimes Manny would join her, sometimes she just worked the crowd herself. It was invigorating in its own high-energy way. She fell back into the rhythm of late nights and late mornings.

She called Sister Eloise every day to check on the progress of the exhibit. The sister was always "delighted" to hear from her. Logan was helping out at the festival as part of his work program. Lawrence was sitting for the children. But it wasn't until after several calls that Sister Eloise confessed that things just didn't have the same sense of completion and satisfaction as when Dani was there.

"It's like we've fallen into a habit of doing things—but not with energy or total joy. I think everyone misses you."

Dani promised to try to be back before the festival weekend. But she only promised to try. It was all dependent on the perfume meetings. If things didn't work out in time for her to get back, she'd send Sister Mary Catherine a check to help start the new school.

She began to get back in tune with the city, with the crowd, and her weeks in Rhode Island began to fade. But something was missing, and she was afraid that it might be something in her.

On Friday the perfume people finally blew into town. The meeting was everything Lawrence had warned her it would be. And more. Two hours late starting, while they waited for the head of production to arrive from Kennedy Airport. Then an immediate argument with the editorial representatives about where to accentuate the name of the product, at which point Dani tuned out, reminding herself to look distantly artistic and above it all, and not just bored, while her mind wandered to the art school festival and if she could figure out a way to return without having to see Peter or Lawrence ever again.

Lunch was brought in; work discussions stopped while everyone scarfed artisan cheeses and beluga caviar, washed down by Pellegrino, and colleagues caught up on each other's lives. At two, the meeting resumed, and so did the arguments.

It all seemed like an incredible waste of time, the clashing egos, the outbursts and storming from the room. The hiatus while someone ran after the injured party and talked them down from the artistic ledge and finally led them back into the conference room.

There were project boards, location ideations, spreadsheets and slide shows, coffee breaks and Red Bull in the fridge, and more arguing and mind changes.

And all the while, the clean, curved lines of the Alizée perfume bottle sat quietly in the middle of the conference table while ideas, food, chatter, and slide shows hammered out its fate. And when it seemed that the day's session was finally coming to a close, Dani announced that she wanted to take the bottle with her to study.

Complete silence. Then one by one, shakes of the head went around the table. Until it came to Adrian Koppel. "Impossible. We never let the product leave the building until the launch."

Dani thought calm thoughts and crossed her arms. "I must become intimate with my subject."

Someone snickered, and Dani gave him a look that could wither his chances of becoming intimate with any subject for a long while. Manny intervened.

They left half an hour later, with one single perfume bottle wrapped in velvet, then flannel, then bubble wrap in a wooden coffin and with the insistence that she show it to NO ONE.

And by the time Dani stepped back on the sidewalk, she'd come up with a plan.

26

That night Dani dressed to impress, as her mother used to tell her. Of course her mother's idea and Dani's were miles apart. All the same, her mother never led her astray. A quick "please squeeze me in" appointment at her hairstylist that evening, a steam tray from the deli for dinner that she ate standing up and staring at her laptop and the photos that she'd taken since returning to the city. Some of them were good. Really good. Maybe. Or maybe she'd been wrong about everything.

She shut down her laptop. No time for insecurity now. She went to her closet to put together the confident, successful, not-trying-too-hard, new Dani look. Still cutting edge, but sophisticated. Not so eager to be the flash in the crowd, but confident to lead the crowd. A move that she gambled people would follow—all the way to Rhode Island.

She knew what to do with this new Dani, because Dani knew herself—as much as she could with her heart breaking. She pushed away the last ties to Lawrence and Peter and went off to conquer the New York art scene—again.

From the moment Dani walked into the Oberon Art Show that night, she knew she belonged. And for the first time realized she didn't need the sophisticated clothes, or Lawrence holding her hand, or Manny showing her off. She was different from before. She felt it down to her very center, and whatever success or failure she had from now on would lie squarely on her shoulders and her honesty.

She suddenly had nothing to prove. She was Dani Campbell and they could take her as that, no more, no less. She could feel the air change as she walked through the space. Could tell the moment Manny saw her and hurried to meet her.

She wasn't sure how it had happened, but tonight she was just being Dani. She wished Lawrence could see her now. Peter too. She missed them both. But she didn't need them. Not for this.

She might not be the most sophisticated, most artistic person in the room, but she no longer felt insecure just being there. She was confident. Not of their approbation but of her own inner eye. And whether it made her a dime or not, it was all she wanted.

She'd be amazed at herself if she'd had a moment to relish the new her.

But Manny pounced. "You look . . . Wow, is this new look part of the secret project?"

"Just the beginning," she said, and went to work the room.

═

For the next few days, Dani worked nonstop, culling out photos to have printed for the Harvest Festival, calling Sister Eloise for an update on the festival and the building search, and trolling the city from Fifty-Seventh Street to Orchard Street in search of the perfect backdrop for the little bottle hidden away in the secret compartment beneath her futon. Alizée.

At night she attended openings, galas, parties, whatever was happening. It was the height of the fall season. Triumphs were played out in full view, disappointments relegated to looking daggers or mumbling in corners.

Dani mingled freely, only this time she knew where she was. Not at the top—the top was as elusive as fame—but a new Dani, still a work in progress. And for the first time ever, she wasn't quaking inside.

They all noticed the new look, the new energy, and wondered what she was working on. "Something different," she told them. "Something simple."

That got startled laughs. When they pressed her for details, all she would say was that she was planning a show of entirely new photographs. They went to Manny. He'd just shrugged in a way that sent them off thinking something big was in the works.

"You do have something big going, right?" he asked Dani one night after a particularly determined effort by one of the reigning critics to suss out her secret project.

"Big for me," Dani said, and kept moving.

It occurred to her that she might be guilty of using the Harvest Festival for her own gains, but since her gains were totally aligned with theirs, she thought she might be forgiven.

"It better be earth-shattering."

She didn't know about that, but it might get the convent their art school.

═

"It's been a week and not one word from Dani," Lawrence complained.

"Well, what did you expect." Sister Mary Catherine looked disapprovingly at Lawrence and Peter across her desk.

Lawrence shrugged like a guilty schoolboy. He didn't even look at Peter. It was hard enough being reprimanded without having your grandson witness it. He was a good kid, but he couldn't begin to understand the history of Lawrence and the family, Peter's father—or photography.

"You lied to her, Lawrence. Lied, then told Peter what you were doing, and the two of you let her keep believing she was helping save you from poverty."

"Peter urged me to tell her sooner. It just got harder the longer it went on. It isn't his fault, but Dani thinks we were laughing at her—which we weren't."

"I should never have forced you into that declaration," Peter said. "A terrible time to assert my sense of duty. She accused me of being a wuss. And she was right. I never stand up for myself; it always seemed easier not to."

"It's a Sinclair affliction," Lawrence said sympathetically.

"And when I did—"

"No excuses, either of you. You brought this on yourself." She sent a surgical glare at Peter. Then passed it to Lawrence. "Not only have you hurt Dani, and yourselves, you've hurt the rest of us."

It wasn't the first time Lawrence had been accused of a lack of humanity. But it stung all the more coming from his childhood friend, especially when she was absolutely right.

Next to him, Peter looked pretty miserable.

"I know. You don't have to tell me something I don't already know," Lawrence said.

Peter gave him a look.

"What?" asked Lawrence, diverted.

"Double negatives," Peter said. "It must be a family trait."

"I'd like to double negative the both of you," Sister Mary Catherine said.

"Time is running out, and since I see that Peter is still here . . ."

"I got a week's extension on my vacation," Peter said. "Thanks to Uncle James."

"Then put it to good use. We all miss Dani. She was a bright star around here, but you don't see us wallowing in self-pity. There's a job to get done, and I expect you to help."

"Maybe we should go after her," Peter said.

"And say what?" Lawrence said.

"That we're idiots and to please come back."

"She won't. If she comes, it will be on her own terms. And she may want blood." Lawrence tried and failed for a smile. "I created a monster."

Sister Mary Catherine folded her hands on her desk. "You did no such thing, Lawrence Sinclair. Dani came with everything she needed to fulfill herself. Maybe you helped her get there, but if anyone was creating around here, it was Dani. She has certainly changed the trajectory of your life."

"You're right," Lawrence said. He'd tried to help Dani, in his own inefficient, bungling way, and look how that had turned out. It seemed his every step, his every move, dug him deeper into hell. If he'd never let Dani into the house, he would still be shuffling along as the bitter old man he'd become. Was that what he would revert to if she never came back again?

"Why don't I just buy you the damned building?"

"No," Peter said. "Mother will have you declared non compos mentis."

"And she would be right," said Lawrence.

"Stop whining. This isn't about you." Sister Mary Catherine gave him a look so pregnant with the past that Lawrence was catapulted onto the playground where Mary Catherine, nee Lorna, had pinned him with her unique and laser-sharp adherence to what was right and what was wrong.

She'd never seemed to have any doubts about life, but he had, and he seemed to always choose the wrong side.

"Then I guess we'd better get to it." Peter stood. "You're sure about the antiques building?"

Sister Mary Catherine nodded.

"I'll contact Nina and have her start negotiations with the owners."

Sister Mary Catherine nodded again.

"I'll kibbitz as an interested party, while you feel them out about how eager they are to sell, then we'll hire a good real estate lawyer for the closing."

"Excellent," the sister said. "Now, let's get hopping."

Peter followed Lawrence out.

"I'm sorry," Peter said as they paused by the door of Peter's "office."

"Not your fault."

"I mean beyond that. About, well, everything."

"Also not your fault," Lawrence said.

"But the thing with Dani was. She was different than most of the women I know. She didn't take shit, and she was so straight shooting—"

"I expect she still is," Lawrence said. "But in New York."

"—that I didn't think about her getting hurt. What are we going to do?"

"What do you want to do?" Lawrence asked, his curiosity kindled.

"I want her back," Peter said.

Lawrence nodded seriously. "She'll be back; she won't leave the convent in the lurch."

"You're sure?"

"I'm sure."

Peter's face lit up like he had just discovered loot in the pirate's cove.

Lawrence slapped him on the back and Peter went inside. As soon as the door closed behind him, Lawrence broke into a grin.

Well, well, well, he thought, and hurried down the hall to become anybody those little kids wanted him to be.

═

Dani lay in bed following a crack in the ceiling that she didn't remember being there the night before. She'd been in the city for a week, and she should be up and dealing with things, but everything seemed to be on hold. The perfume shoot, her work on the Harvest Festival. The *Gems and Junque* book . . .

She wondered how Lawrence was doing. Peter would be back in Boston working at a job he obviously hated, and Lawrence would be alone again. Was he eating properly? Had he kept his promise of keeping an eye on the art classes, or had he withdrawn back into his dark, bitter life?

What a family the Sinclairs must be. Dani was lucky. Her family was wild, and sometimes pushy, but always supportive. They never once tried to make their children take over the family bar.

Of course, a bar in Brooklyn wasn't exactly the same as a big corporation. Strange that Sinclair Enterprises, which according to Google was just some company that bought and sold other companies, could hold such sway over its owners. How could you be loyal to that?

Her cell buzzed. She sat up, reaching for the phone. It was Manny. Not that she should have expected anyone else.

"Hi, Manny," she said, resigned for whatever crisis had broken today. She sat up at the word "Greece."

"What?"

"They're thinking about moving the shoot to Greece."

"When did this happen?"

"Last night, evidently; that was after they nixed Yugoslavia and Egypt."

"Do they even have trade winds in Egypt?"

"Huh?"

"Alizée? The perfume? It means trade winds in French."

"Yeah, well, Greece is the latest idea."

"And subject to change, I'm sure," she said. "Honestly, it's amazing ads ever get made."

"They were arguing over Athens and Crete the last time I was updated. Though Adrian did mention the Amalfi Coast."

"That's in Italy," Dani reminded him.

"Sure, either way, just have your suitcase packed and ready to fly."

Dani dropped her head back on the pillow. Greece was beautiful. A trip would take her mind off Lawrence's betrayal. But she had committed to the festival; she couldn't let the sisters down.

"When would this take place?"

"They're working on that now. Maybe next week. They want to get it in before Thanksgiving."

"Tell them I'm not available until the middle of November."

"Why? Because of this secret project you have?"

"Yes."

"Christ, Dani, you're not eloping, are you?"

"Of course not."

"You're not pregnant? Having medical issues?" A pause. "You're not cutting me out, are you?"

"No-o-o."

"Then what?"

"If you must know. I'm helping out some nuns with their art school, and they have a big art show in a few weeks."

Dead silence on Manny's end. Finally: "This is your big secret project rumor that is going around?"

"Yes, Manny. It's not my show, though I'll have a few simple snaps among everyone else's work just to be part of the team. But I'll thank you not to make that part public . . . at all."

"Are you trying to ruin us both? How can this possibly aid your career? If anything, it could fracture it. 'Dani Campbell does amateur art show.' Do you want to end up selling your photos in between art on velvet and handmade candles at street fairs? Just shoot me now."

That stung. "They need some benefactors to keep the school afloat. It provides important support in the community. I'm paying it forward, Manny. Something we should all do more of. Once the festival is over, the perfume people can send me wherever they want, but frankly, I hope to have something in the can that they'll like enough so they won't have to."

"Can I give them any hints? Something so they won't go batshit diva on me?"

"Tell them I have some ideas. I'll do some mock-ups and send them in to see if they like any of them. I don't need a huge production team, the sponsor haggling over shots and lighting, the editorial staff looking over my shoulder. It will be a simple shot. The rest I'll do in postproduction.

"That's what I do. That's why they hired me and not somebody that is a veteran of location shoots."

"All right. Let me think of the best way to spin this. I'll get back to you."

"Fine, but I'm going back to Rhode Island first thing

tomorrow. Meet me tonight at The Space. I'll be ginning up some interest in a very low-key way. And Manny, if you want to drum up some patrons with wads of cash, be my guest."

"Without telling them where their money is going?"

"Knowing you, Manny, it will work like a charm."

═

That evening, Dani ran, almost literally, into the curly hair and bow tie of Gary Estes, the freelance writer.

"Hi," she said. "It's great to see you."

"It is?" he said as soon as he recovered from his surprise. "I didn't think you'd remember me."

"Of course I would, and I have a favor to ask."

"Sure, anything."

She took him by the arm and, leaning her head toward his, steered him through several curious bystanders.

"Oh good, but it's very hush-hush."

He leaned closer. So did everyone within earshot.

"For your ears only," she said, knowing that even if he stayed mum, somehow it would get out. "I'm doing a community project. Something special to me. To raise funds for an art school . . ."

"You mean like happening artist doesn't forget her roots?"

"Um, something like that." So what if she was born in Brooklyn, and she was pretty sure her family was Presbyterian. She gave him the date—and the address. "If you come a day earlier, I'll show you around so you can get a jump on the others." If there were others. She was counting on it.

She leaned even closer. "It's at a convent."

Gary's eyes nearly popped. She knew that the word had carried to several other sets of ears. She'd already primed them for it over the last week. But a convent . . . Imaginations would go full tailspin.

She hoped to hell she wasn't overplaying her hand. She was popular, she was selling, she was in demand. But she wasn't at all sure that she would still be by the time the Harvest Festival was an actuality.

She also wasn't so naive as to think they would fall for a bunch of local artists, some with no training at all, some merely children. But there was an angle there. She'd figure it out once she got back to the nuns and convinced them to turn their celebration into a fund-raising event.

As for the Alizée ad, she wouldn't be sure until she was back at the pirate's cove when the wind was up.

═

Peter threw himself into work. And he had plenty of it. Whenever he wasn't consulting the real estate agent about the antiques building, he was fielding the locals' small claims. It seemed that once he'd agreed to help Watkins with his contract dispute, word traveled and he was kept busy most of each day. Anything that needed real legal advice, he funneled into Cyrus Turner's office.

He loved the work, small or large, and if Dani had still been here, he would have been content. Strange how one person could drop into your life, into two lives, and change them so much and in such a short time. He wondered if she really would come back. And what it would mean. And what it would mean to him. And he found himself, in those moments, wondering about what it would take to pass the Rhode Island bar exam.

He'd actually gone so far as to look up the schedule for the next test, just out of curiosity, when James called. Peter immediately tensed. James was happy to let things continue as they had been going, and had readily agreed for Peter to extend his vacation.

So this call boded no good.

He answered anyway.

"Just wanted to give you a heads-up. Your mother is not happy with whatever she's hearing about what's happening down there. She's making noise about coming down to check out the situation for herself. I don't know how long I can hold her off."

"Thanks, I'll take care of it." Peter hung up. Who was he kidding? He was no match for her. He was beginning to think no one was.

═

It took more organizing than Dani anticipated, but finally she was heading north, her equipment and a suitcase of fall clothes in the back of her SUV.

She yo-yoed between excitement and trepidation, excited to see the kids and the nuns again, to help with the project that was foremost in her mind. Then wondered if Lawrence would even want to see her. Peter wouldn't be there, and she had to really work to ignore the empty pit in her stomach when she thought about him.

Neither he nor Lawrence had even texted to see if she had made it safely. Obviously they didn't care. Maybe they were even glad she was gone.

The weather had definitely taken a turn toward cold, the leaves were at their height of color, and as she drove into the outskirts of town, lawns had begun to sprout jack-o'-lanterns and other Halloween decorations. There would be none of these at the convent, as Sister Eloise had explained. They only observed All Saints' Day. And the yearly harvest.

She'd made a reservation at the Excelsior as soon as she'd arrived in the city. Though she'd hoped that Lawrence—or Peter—would have called and asked her to come back, they hadn't, so she stopped by the hotel to check in.

The Excelsior had gone full Halloween, with pumpkins and gourds and colorful fall arrangements.

"Oh yes, it's a big time for us," the receptionist said. "Between leaf peepers, the corn mazes, and the Harvest Festival, we do a good business."

Dani got her key but instead of taking her things upstairs, she called Sister Eloise to let her know she was back, and learned from her that Lawrence was currently at the convent.

It was a perfect time to grab the rest of her belongings and get her things without a confrontation. That would come, but later.

Dani had tried to stay mad at him, but her anger was hard to hold on to. She'd had such wonderful times with him, and had actually started liking Peter, before she found out he was a party to Lawrence's deceit. Maybe they could all start over one day, but for now it was better to keep her distance.

She drove straight to the horror house from hell and had never been so glad to see anything in her life. A misplaced euphoria that was quickly doused by the knowledge that once she removed her remaining belongings, it might be relegated only to her past and not to her future.

She slowed down. Trying not to remember the first drive up, the finagling with the unseen voice to let her in. He still had her photos from Ye Olde Antiques Barn—it seemed like a lifetime ago—but she wouldn't take the time to look for them now. Just get her stuff and get out.

It took only a few minutes and three trips back and forth before she carried her last bundle of summer clothes to the SUV.

And nearly dropped it when a black Town Car appeared in the drive and stopped in front of the house. The driver got out and opened the door to a tall, well-dressed woman who stopped dead when she saw Dani.

Then she marched forward, seemingly unhampered by her very high heels. And Dani felt a nanosecond of envy before the woman burst out with "Just what do you think you are doing?"

Dani was completely taken aback. For a New York minute.

"And what business is it of yours?" she retorted, even as a creepy feeling stole over her.

"I'm Marian Sinclair and my family owns this house." She looked at Dani's armload.

"Foster, call the police."

The driver slid back into the driver's seat. And Dani saw red. So this was the infamous Marian, mother, daughter-in-law, wife. It needed only this.

For a second Dani felt herself waver. Then she smiled, showing teeth, and her years of Brooklyn playground etiquette kicked in.

"These are my clothes . . ." she said quietly. "But if you insist . . ." She pulled a red midriff tank top off the top. "Lawrence always admired this. Tell him he can have it." She tossed it at Mrs. Sinclair and threw the rest of her things into the back seat.

"I know what you're up to," the woman spat at her. "You won't get a penny."

"Good thing I don't want one. They're all yours." Dani started to get in the SUV, changed her mind. What the hell. She'd gone this far.

"Actually, I have something to say before I go. You have blamed Lawrence, shunned him from the family, cut Peter off from his grandfather, and generally made their lives miserable for something your boneheaded husband insisted on doing years ago.

"No one could ever live up to your expectations, because they're driven by your bitterness. Have you ever even asked Peter what he wants to do with his life? He's really good at helping people, but I bet you don't even know that, do you?"

Dani gulped for air, but she'd gone too far to back down now. "And you're wrong about me. And it sure seems to me that you're wrong about a lot of other things. Maybe it's not my business, but at least I care about those two guys, and if you do, maybe you should give them a break.

"Goodbye." She jumped in the SUV and drove away just as Marian Sinclair reached for her phone.

27

James seemed to think she was on her way," Peter told Lawrence as they strode through the trees to the house.

Just as they reached the clearing, Peter thought he saw the flash of a light-colored vehicle speeding away. His heart blipped, then crashed back to where it belonged. His mother's black Town Car was parked in front of the house.

Her driver, Foster, was leaning up against the car. He saluted Peter, then pointed to the house.

Peter nodded and went inside.

She was sitting on the very edge of the sofa as if she thought the fabric was dirty, which it wasn't thanks to Dani. Peter shoved the pang of memory away. He metaphorically girded for battle and strode into the parlor, vaguely aware of Lawrence following.

She stood immediately.

"Mother, what a nice surprise." He gave her a buss on the cheek.

"Perfect timing," she snapped.

"Did you just arrive?" What the hell was she talking about?

"I just met what has been keeping you here."

"I'm not sure . . ."

"Spiked hair, bad manners, clearly out for what she could get."

"Dani was here?" Peter blurted before his self-preservation gene kicked in.

"Is that her name? Short for Danielle, I presume."

Actually, Peter had no idea. She was just Dani. "Is she still here?"

"Of course not. I gave her her walking papers."

"I doubt it," Lawrence mumbled behind him.

His mother's radar zoomed in on his grandfather. "This is your doing. You won't be satisfied until you destroy the whole family."

"Mother! That's enough."

Marian actually looked shocked . . . for about two seconds.

"Since . . . Dani . . . is gone, I assume you'll be cutting your extended vacation short and coming back to the office and the responsibilities you've been neglecting."

Lawrence had left after her spiteful remark, and Peter thought he was going to have to go this alone, but Lawrence came back in at that moment and said, "The rest of her things are gone."

"She was packing out when I arrived," Marian said. "No telling what she took you for."

"You're a spiteful, unhappy woman, Marian," Lawrence said. "I let you drive me away from my grandson once. I won't be a party to it again. You and Peter can duke it out and let me know the outcome. But Peter, I hope you know you're welcome here anytime you want." He walked away.

Peter noticed the keys in his hand. "Where are you going?"

"To find Dani."

"Just like Lawrence. Walk out on his family when things get serious."

"You're not being fair." Peter could hear Dani's scoffing voice. *Really? That's the best you can do? It isn't fair? Then tell her what is.*

"No?" Marian's eyebrows tilted up.

Peter slowly let out his breath. And did what he seldom, if ever, did. Said, "No."

Her expression didn't change, so he went on. "You threw him out of the family when Father died. Granddad was grieving, too."

"So it's 'Granddad' now, is it?" Her voice was sharp with bitterness. And he knew in that moment if he caved, he would one day be entrenched in bitterness, too.

"Stop it. You need to let go of this." Peter heard the words and wondered whom they were coming from. "He's my grandfather. A Sinclair."

He saw her face drain of color and could have smacked himself for what it implied: *And you aren't.*

"We were all grieving. He lost his only son, and everyone was blaming him. Even his own wife."

"If he had done his duty and kept his position, your father wouldn't have had to do everything himself."

"No one made my father go up in the plane but my father. He could have postponed the meeting. But he didn't. It was his choice, his idea of living up to his responsibilities. It was his stubbornness. It made him a good businessman, but he took his duty to the Sinclair name too far.

"It was his arrogance, pure and simple. He didn't need Lawrence. He had you, if he'd only recognized it. But he couldn't see past the company and I want none of it."

Peter stopped, his words cutting his throat like glass as he spoke them. A cold dread poured over him as his words reverberated back to him. He'd just said out loud something that he'd never even let himself think. And something he could never take back. He didn't even try. It was true.

It took only a second for Marian to recover. "It's that girl, isn't it?"

"What girl?"

"The one I discovered cleaning out the place."

Peter smiled in spite of himself, thinking that cleaning *up* the place would be more accurate, as he remembered meeting Dani, a T-shirt tied around her head and wielding a broom. "She had stuff here. She was just picking it up."

"You'd never even questioned your place in the company until you came here."

He had, he'd just never had the courage to admit it. And that, he realized, had been a huge mistake.

"Peter, I realize it's a big transition, but it's time for you to pack your things and come home. You're the head of the company; it's time to start acting like it."

She strode toward the door without even waiting for him to see her out.

It was now or never. *Just tell her you're not coming back.*

She turned abruptly. "You do want to be head of the company, don't you?"

═

Dani was shaking as she drove to the convent. What had she been thinking? She'd probably made things worse, but Marian Sinclair deserved it. Yet she already knew it was more than just Marian. It was Peter and Lawrence and the perfume people. She'd probably just wrecked everything. How could she ever face Lawrence or Peter again? She probably wouldn't get the chance once Mrs. Sinclair talked to them.

She knew she was taking a chance of running into them at the convent, but at the moment she just needed a safe haven. And she could at least warn them who was waiting for them back at the gothic horror beach house.

Sister Mary Catherine answered the door.

"Dani, you're back. I'm so glad."

"I am. I wouldn't let you all down."

"Well, come in. Sister Eloise was just asking about you. She seems to have more entries in the art show than she knows what to do with." They'd started down the hall. "And Logan brought over the photos you had Ray enlarge. They're in the gallery; we didn't unpack them. We thought you would like to oversee their placement."

"How is Logan?"

"He's still staying with Ray and Ada, working at the photo shop three afternoons a week and helping Lawrence in the media room since you left."

"So Lawrence has been coming?"

"You haven't talked to Lawrence?"

Dani shook her head.

"Peter?"

"No. But I met his mother. I thought maybe you could warn them."

"So she did show up," said Sister Mary Catherine. "They already have been warned. Lawrence's brother, James, called from Boston to say she was on her way. They left immediately. I'm surprised your paths didn't cross."

"I'm glad they didn't. I was getting my things and she accused me of stealing."

Sister Mary Catherine sighed. "We can only be patient and pray for that family. So much pain and bitterness." She crossed herself.

"I kind of said some things I shouldn't have, but she accused me of stealing. What a horrible woman."

"A very unhappy woman. Grief can be relentless. Some people are helpless to see their way through it."

"Now I feel really bad."

"Well, don't. I'm sure she's tough enough to take a little criticism. But why were you getting the rest of your things?"

"I'm staying at the Excelsior."

The sister tsked. "A couple of sad cases, those two. I guess this means you're not ready to forgive them."

"They let me make a fool of myself and laughed at me the whole time."

"Well, if it's any consolation, they're not laughing now. But I beg to differ about their crime. They didn't make a fool of you; they simply gave you the opportunity to show your most generous and caring self."

"That's *you* being generous," Dani said. "I had my own motives to agreeing to do it."

"Most people do. That family has been simmering with bitterness and recriminations and heartache for years. Things have been changing for the better since your arrival. And I know you will probably not believe this, but a big part of it was you offering to pay rent, and at such an outrageous price."

"I want it to be right again."

"I know, my dear. Just remember, people make mistakes."

"I know. I've made my share."

This inspired a little laugh from the sister. "We all have."

They had come to the gallery, but instead of going in, Sister Mary Catherine stopped and turned toward Dani. "I'm not sure what state the collection is in. You may have your work cut out for you. More entries than we have space. We're thinking about continuing it into the hall. But we were waiting for your return."

"Anything new on the building site search?"

"We've discussed it and have decided to make an offer on the antiques building. If they accept it, we would use part of it and rent out the rest until we can afford to expand. It's all dependent on getting them to lower the price considerably."

"I may be able to help there." Dani's mouth suddenly felt dry. "But it also may be one of those mistakes we were just talking about."

Sister Mary Catherine had reached for the door handle, but dropped her hand. "Do tell."

"While I was in the city, I had time to think about how we could ensure the school's future. And hanging out with all these rich art patrons and advertising people, it occurred to me that we could have a fund-raiser. Churches do it all the time. I Googled it. So I enlisted a little secular help for the festival.

"I sort of hinted that I was doing something special for it and would be showing it that weekend. And it isn't really a lie because this is special to me and to all of us. I might have gotten a little carried away, because I started a rumor that it was a secret project. Something entirely different for me."

"And is it?"

"Well . . . I don't actually have a secret project."

"Isn't that what all those boxes are for?"

"Not exactly. Well, not originally. They're just photographs I took while Lawrence was, I don't know, showing me the way. I was going to use them to be a part of something bigger than me. But I thought I could spin it to interest some outside donors. Unless that breaks some church rule, or you find it offensive. Then I can just email them and tell them it was a false alarm." She hesitated. "Though that will make them all the more curious. I may have created a monster. Or worst of all, I could bomb."

Sister Mary Catherine pressed her palms together and laughed. "Oh, we've missed your energy. Since this won't be a diocese venture, I say let's run it past our nonlegal legal advisor on how to do it.

"Now, shall we see how the art exhibit is coming along?"

They found Sister Eloise surrounded by tables covered with drawings and photographs and all manner of things.

"Who knew how prolific our students are? I'm not sure they will all fit, and I hate to leave anyone out. I've managed to arrange them as best I can, but I'm so glad to have you back. You are staying?"

"Of course I am," said Dani. "Let's see what we've got." They started on the convent history wall, unpacking the box marked Convent Pics, arranging Dani's new photos to align with the old, and hanging them in fairly chronological groupings across the wall.

Then they took a minute to stand back and admire their handiwork.

Sister Eloise sniffed. "It's been a good life," she said quietly. "A good place."

It was a good place, Dani thought. One that should continue in whatever way they wanted.

When Sister Eloise left to see to her daily convent duties, Dani took out a second box of new photographs, but instead of opening it, she laid it aside and reached for the larger, thinner package propped against the wall. She knew what it held. Photos of all three sisters—and Lawrence.

She carefully placed it on a table, slipped her finger under the tape that held the brown paper wrapper, and peeled back the edges. She turned over the first one, an eighteen-by-twenty-four photo, a strange calm sense of déjà vu overtaking her. The first photo she ever took of Lawrence, done with a manual camera she didn't even know how to work.

And it took her breath away. His action in a split moment as he turned toward her. His expression in an instant of time, unguarded, unplanned, like the slip lifting on the clothesline, the woman overlooking the cliff. The duck's nest. Her mentor.

She was barely aware of the door to the gallery opening.

"There you are."

She quickly turned the photo facedown, and covered it with the open wrapper.

Stepped away from the table, and waited for Lawrence to come into the room.

They both stood silent, waiting.

Finally he shut the door, and came toward her. "You have every right to be mad at me. I took advantage of you."

"It was a mean trick," Dani said, and bowed her head. She wanted to stay angry, but it was hard when she was so glad to see him.

"I know. Peter said so right away. He tried to convince me to tell you, but I wouldn't. Frankly, I couldn't take the chance that you would leave. I know that may be hard to understand, but when anyone comes to see me, it's always with their hand out. It had been so long since anyone actually wanted to give me something, I panicked. My first response was to send you away and get on with my life, such as it was. But you wouldn't leave.

"Then I saw your photos, and some of them were god-awful, but I saw what you had, what you could be, what I'd let die because of bitterness. I'd almost forgotten what it could be like. And then Peter came. And I was afraid to do anything that would change things.

"I was wrong, I'm sorry. Forgive me. Dani?" He reached out and lifted her chin. Snatched his hand back. "Are you laughing at me?"

She shook her head, flinging happy tears. She threw her arms around him, and when he awkwardly patted her back, she forgave him everything.

"Now that that's settled," Lawrence said, stepping back, "I left Peter to face his mother alone. He doesn't want to run the Sinclair company any more than I did. He just needs help pulling the trigger."

"Well, I'm not going to tell him what to do," Dani said. "It seems like his mother does enough of that."

"True," Lawrence said. "Are you ready to come back to the house now? It's getting late."

And it's time for your dinner, she thought fondly.

"Though maybe we should wait. She was there when I left. And I should go check in with the media room."

Dani hesitated. "I guess, but I have a reservation at the Excelsior."

"I'll call them and cancel for you. It won't be a problem."

"For a recluse you sure know a lot of people in town."

"I'm not a recluse."

"In that case, I guess I should tell you, I sort of had a showdown with Peter's mother. And maybe said some things I shouldn't have. She drove up when I was getting the rest of my things out of the house.

"She accused me of stealing and being after your money," Dani added, getting angry all over again. "That was a laugh. You were after mine."

Lawrence had the grace to look chagrined.

"Then I told her she had made your life miserable just because of something her boneheaded husband had done."

Lawrence groaned. "You didn't say 'boneheaded,' did you?"

Dani winced. "I might have, but that was better than what I was really thinking. No offense. He was your son. So not his fault; he probably inherited boneheadedness from you."

"True."

"And I sort of maybe went too far when I asked her if she had ever bothered to ask Peter what he wanted to do with his life."

"God, you're impressive sometimes."

"I may have made Peter's life worse than it already is, but . . ." Dani shrugged. "Maybe she'll actually ask him."

"But will he tell her the truth?"

═

"The strangest thing happened just before you arrived," said Peter, coming out to greet them when Dani and Lawrence got out of the SUV. Dani and Lawrence exchanged looks.

"What?"

"My mother asked my opinion of something."

"Of what?" Lawrence asked innocently, as they started unloading Dani's equipment.

Peter pulled several rectangular packages from the car. "Of what I wanted to do with my life. It was the strangest thing." He frowned at the packages. "What are these?"

"Fabric," said Dani. "A white silk, a peach silk chiffon. And a couple of other colors."

"For what?"

"So I won't have to go to Greece."

"What's wrong with Greece?"

"Nothing and I'd love to go, only not on a perfume shoot. I just don't think it's necessary and I have things to do here."

"Like what?"

Dani paused to roll her eyes, and Lawrence took the opportunity to ask, "What did you tell your mother?"

"Huh, oh. That I was pretty sure I wanted to be a small-time lawyer and not part of the legal department at Sinclair. Why would they go all the way to Greece to take a photo of a bottle of perfume?"

"Exactly what I said."

"So what did she say?" asked Lawrence.

Peter handed the fabric to Lawrence to carry and pulled Dani's suitcase out of the back seat. "She just looked confused for a moment, then didn't say anything. I think she needs time to assimilate it all. And did you convince them?"

"Hope so," Dani said as she loaded down her shoulder with camera case, tripod, and computer. "Manny is going to convince them what they liked about my photos was done in postproduction. Which is true. They hired me after seeing my Hamptons show. Some of the ones you really hated, Lawrence."

"I didn't hate them. It's just I saw the potential for something . . . different."

She glanced at him. "You of course will be looking over my shoulder to make sure I don't lose my soul."

"I don't think there's any fear of that, but I'll look anyways."

"So no Greece, just smoke and mirrors," said Peter as they carried her luggage inside.

"More like silk and sea breeze. The perfume is called Alizeé. Trade winds. I was hoping to use the pirate's cove for the shoot if that's okay with the two of you."

"Of course," Lawrence said. "We can run some wiring from the house down the opening and set up some lighting. If you need lighting. Ray has some equipment, enough to get decent surround anyway. And Logan and Peter can act as gaffers."

"Looks like that makes you production manager," said Dani.

Lawrence went dead still, then started up again. "Yeah, I guess it does."

28

As the opening day of the Harvest Festival approached, the convent took on a new look, with pumpkins and other gourds overflowing the garden and stacked in pyramids throughout the lawn. Cornstalks appeared like ancient Greek dancers circling the gazebo. Concession tents were set up, as well as a games area and children's maze made from bales of hay.

Announcements and articles appeared in the local paper, extolling the event and accentuating the art school and the hope that it would continue after the convent had closed. And a final note, encouraging those who were interested in keeping the program alive and well to send donations to the Old Murphy Beach Art School Fund.

Posters, designed by the media room teenagers and printed by Ray's photo shop, appeared in store windows and on telephone poles. Special invitations went out for the opening ceremony of the Harvest Festival Annual Art Exhibit.

And they still didn't have a building.

Dani spent most of each day putting final touches on the exhibit. Down the hall, Peter, Lawrence, and Sister Mary Catherine spent many hours in conversation with the real estate agent and the owners of the antiques mall.

There had also been several calls between Peter and his

mother. He didn't seem stressed, but he didn't volunteer what they were about. And Dani didn't ask.

On the first sunny blustery day, Dani collected her "production crew" and set up her perfume shoot in the pirate's cove.

"Feels like the old days." Ray grunted as he squeezed through the narrow opening to the cove. Above them, Peter and Logan stood ready to lower two large soft lights down to the floor of the cove.

With expansive arm gestures and orders of "Slowly now," "A little to the left," "Gently, gently," Ray guided them down. Then he untied the cable and Logan hauled the cable back up, only to prepare another load.

Dani was hoping to be able to use the available natural light, but Lawrence had convinced her to add the alternate source in case the weather didn't cooperate.

"Remember, it's an ad. All roads lead to that bottle. You want it to pop."

It was a side of Lawrence she'd never seen before. He knew his stuff, though she'd never doubted it. But to witness the transformation from the cantankerous old man who had tried to drive her away to the organized shoot manager he was today was amazing. She shouldn't have been surprised; he'd merely reached for what was already inside him, had always been inside him. And Dani spent a moment to appreciate her better understanding of what it was to be yourself.

It took two hours just to get the lighting equipment in place, while Dani tried to quell her fear that the wind would die down before she got enough shots and they would have to spend another day away from the festival preparations to do another shoot.

But at last they were ready. The bottle was placed in a niche of one of the several rock outcroppings that seemed to grow spontaneously from the sand. Perfectly situated to catch the light and lift it from the boulders behind it.

Dani adjusted the tripod secured with sandbags to prevent it from reacting to the wind. Peered through the lens. Straightened and took a deep, deep breath.

Lawrence spoke into his cell phone and Ada's face appeared on the bluff above. He smiled, and Dani wondered if he was remembering another day, another face who appeared there to call him and Peter to lunch.

"We're ready up here," Ada called. "The weather's perfect."

Sister Eloise and Sister Mary Catherine took their places next to her.

Dani gave them a thumbs-up. Took another deep breath. Turned to Lawrence. "Ready when you are."

Lawrence raised his hand, sliced it through the air just as a gust of wind whistled through the cove. A cloud of silk whipped above their heads, then floated downward, lifting and twisting in the breeze.

Dani's camera whirred. And when the bolts of silk were lying on the ground, they gathered them up and did it again.

It took all morning of adjusting, shooting, readjusting, rethinking, reshooting, when at last Dani declared she was satisfied.

"Now if the perfume people like it," she mumbled to herself.

"How could they not," Peter said, as he and Ray passed by on their way to dismantle the lighting equipment and send it back up to the bluff.

Ada and the sisters rolled up the silk and the sisters left soon after to return to the preparations at the convent. The others went inside to have lunch, which Ada had had the foresight to supply.

"Plenty of leftovers," she said.

"She's in hog heaven," Ray said. "Having Logan there to feed."

Logan just nodded, his mouth being too full of pasta to answer.

"We'll miss him when he goes back home, but we've convinced the county to let him do his work program permanently with us. And funny, but business has picked up."

"He's a natural," Ray added.

Logan managed a thumbs-up.

═

Days flew by, everyone working at warp speed. Dani and Sister Eloise forbade everyone from the exhibit except Logan and the teens setting up the video equipment. Mainly in order not to slow them down, but also due to sheer terror on Dani's part.

"Patience," Sister Eloise said to anyone who asked, and winked at Dani.

But at last they had to compromise, since there were so many entries by current students and the selections that had been archived over the years. In order to display them all, they had to extend the artwork to the hallway walls.

Sister Mary Catherine had invited Dani to have a special show of her own work, but Dani opted to display her work unobtrusively among the others'. One of the many.

She'd put herself on the line in her promise of a secret project. It was the only way she could think of to entice the art aficionados to come all the way to see her project.

There was an angle there, but she'd leave it to Manny to sell it. She just wanted them all to see what she saw in the works of Logan and Vera and the little girl who made the pointed wizard's hat. To see art through their eyes. The Innocent Eye.

She was counting on Manny to spin it into something that would get attention, create buzz, not for her but for the school.

After much negotiating, Sister Mary Catherine made their final offer for the antiques mall. "I'm afraid we're maxed out. We've received a few donations, but they're much too small to help with the building. Well, it's in the owners' and the Lord's hands now."

The owners turned it down.

═

With the fate of the school still in limbo, the gallery opening arrived. Refreshments, nonalcoholic, would be served, opening addresses would be delivered. Even the mayor was coming with his wife.

"Interesting look," Peter said, indicating Dani's appearance as they walked over the lawn toward the convent. She'd opted for a midi-length stretch knit-and-sequin sheath with a simple banded belt. It was glittery but not too splashy, classic, sleek, not so statement-y as to stick out from the locals, but not so local as to alienate the critics. She was wearing her sneakers and carrying her highest gallery heels in her hand to save them from the elements.

She sighed.

"What?" asked Peter.

"That's it?" Dani said, trying not to feel disappointed.

"You look like you. Only in a dress. A combination of surprising, intriguing, exasperating, and just the kind of person I'd like to be walking across the lawn of a convent with."

"Uh, maybe something in the middle?"

"You look great. I'm glad we've gotten to know each other. Let me carry your shoes for you."

That surprised a laugh from Dani. She shook her head, gave him something short of an eye roll, and handed over her heels.

"I'm trying to be gallant."

"And I appreciate it."

"I know it's been kind of rocky."

"I can do rocky," Dani said. "And the feeling is mutual."

They walked in companionable silence, but Peter stopped her before going inside. "Just a heads-up. My mother may show up tonight."

Dani's heart sank. "Oh man, why didn't you warn me?"

"I'm warning you now. But I didn't want you to be distracted. It's going to be fine."

Dani clapped her hands to her head, remembered her carefully coifed spikes, and removed her hands. "What were you thinking? She'll have my head."

"No, she won't. We've been in negotiations."

"You and your mother?"

He nodded. "I told her I was staying in Rhode Island. That I didn't want to be chairman of the board."

"Great. I'm so screwed."

"No, you aren't. She's getting used to the idea."

"I'm glad for you. I really am. But did it have to be tonight? She'll ruin everything." Dani snatched her shoes and went inside, where she headed straight to the gallery.

═

Dani had already begun to rue her overreaction to Peter by the time she reached the gallery. He'd finally stuck up for himself and she hadn't been supportive. But really, what was he thinking?

She'd apologize as soon as she saw him again—as long as Marian wasn't nearby.

Sister Eloise was waiting for her. "Don't you look lovely."

"Thanks, are we good to go?" Dani asked.

"Yes." Sister Eloise turned to the room. "What a wonderful tribute to the convent and all the children and adults who have been enriched by it."

"Yes," Dani said, trying to take it all in now that it was installed and ready to be viewed. Every wall was filled with the work from decades past, new ones mingled with the old. To one side, the media students' slide show slipped from one imaginative scene to the next. Tables of sculpture and quilts and jewelry and pottery took up all of the far end. And straight ahead, in a position of honor, the children's wall, and the title above it: THE INNOCENT EYE.

Dani blinked several times, until her emotions were under control and her mascara was out of danger.

"You run along to the reception," said Sister Eloise. "I'll stay here to open the doors. Now shoo."

Dani shooed. She slipped into the reception hall and stood at the back perusing the room, searching for familiar faces from the art world—and for Peter and possibly Marian Sinclair. She found Gary Estes almost immediately. Excellent . . . if all went well. She crossed her fingers behind her back.

Manny stood nearby, talking to two other critics whom she hadn't expected to see. Even better. She squeezed her crossed fingers tighter. She could depend on Manny to spin Dani's "new" direction.

And she really did have a new direction. Except that it wasn't new. It had just been ignored and forgotten until Lawrence had wrestled it out of her again. She searched the guests for his wild, long hair. And found him standing across the room, looking very artistic in a linen suit, his beard still long but trimmed. He seemed completely at home in the crowd.

Peter stood next to him, suitably lawyerlike.

Dani didn't see Marian Sinclair anywhere, which didn't mean she wasn't nearby planning a stealth attack.

Sister Mary Catherine stepped up to the microphone set at a dais at the front of the room. She welcomed the guests, gave a little history of the convent and the art school, and then thanked the many people who had helped make the festival possible.

"As many of you know, the convent and grounds have been sold, so this will be the culmination of our wonderful life of service here. But it will also be a new beginning. Sisters Eloise and Agnes and I will be staying in Old Murphy Beach." She paused as applause broke out through the room. "And I have particularly good news this evening. You may also be aware that we plan to continue the art school and have been looking for a suitable venue. And tonight I'm happy to announce that thanks to your generous donations and one particularly large grant from the Elliott Sinclair Arts Foundation for the inclusion and support of a commercial gallery for local artists, we have agreed to purchase the old antiques mall downtown."

"Bravo!" someone called, followed by enthusiastic applause.

Dani could hardly believe what she was hearing. Lawrence? Peter? She looked across the room and found Peter. He shrugged and mouthed, *My mother.*

The breath whooshed out of Dani. How was that even possible?

"And now something that has brought us all great pleasure over the years and particularly this year: our art show. And we thank Dani Campbell for her oversight and insight for something that has become the hallmark of our outreach to the community."

At the sound of her name Dani jerked her attention back to Sister Mary Catherine, and felt the beginning of the familiar quake she'd felt so many times before. Then Lawrence appeared at her side. And the quake vanished. She knew where she was now. It was where she wanted to be. Whether anyone else thought so or not.

The doors to the gallery opened behind them, and Dani stepped to the side as the guests flooded into the exhibit rooms.

Ray and Ada stopped as they passed. "Big night," Ray said.

Dani nodded. Ada took her arm. "Come along, you two. I can't wait to see." And she bustled the three of them across the hall.

A few people had stopped to observe the pictures in the hallway, but most had crowded into the exhibit rooms.

Sister Mary Catherine stood at the entrance looking at the sign that spread in an arc over their heads, THE INNOCENT EYE.

She clasped her hands, her smile wavering, her eyes glistening. "It's a perfect title," she said to Dani. "Like a benediction."

"For the new school," Dani said, her throat stinging.

"For the new school."

"And the gallery," Ada added. "That was certainly a surprise."

"That most of all. A new art gallery and the beginning of healing for a family too long torn by grief. It is indeed a wondrous night."

"Indeed it is," Ada said. "But we seem to be blocking the doorway."

They moved farther into the room, and Ada maneuvered them to the children's wall.

Gary Estes was already there among the spectators, talking quietly into his phone, recording his first impressions.

"Well, would you look at that?" Ada leaned forward to peer at the artwork. Pen and ink, charcoal, pencil, crayons or colored pencils, paints, even a few collages. There were renditions of every conceivable character in all kinds of moods. Pensive, frowning, calm, ferocious. From Moses to Wolverine, pirates to space aliens. And they all had one thing in common—a long white beard.

And in the center, her very first photo of Lawrence, caught as he turned, on the day he'd given her the manual camera.

"That's a wonderful photo of Lawrence," exclaimed Ada. "I'd recognize that look anywhere. You caught him perfectly."

Dani nodded, her heart filling to the brim.

"They're all Lawrence," Ray said, laughing. He pointed to a figure in skinny-legged jeans and a guitar, beard flying into the air like live wires. "Hey, Lawrence, you're a rock star."

"Among other things," Lawrence said, coming over to join them.

"And a ninja turtle," Ray pointed out. "A kind of all things to all people."

"Hardly," Lawrence said wryly, and shook his head.

But Dani's favorite was the one with his pointed purple wizard's hat and the gnarled wooden staff. Lawrence as wizard. As Gandalf. Her mentor.

Suddenly overwhelmed, Dani excused herself and made her way over to Manny, who was standing with several New York critics talking animatedly.

". . . exploration beyond the pack . . . hidden among the multitude like gems . . . a treasure hunt among . . ." Dani cringed and moved on, right into Gary Estes, who was looking eager as always. "Is that what you're doing? To me it looks like a pristine simplicity. Will this be your new direction?"

"One of many," Dani said. "I've just begun to explore." Only now when she manipulated photos it would be with a clear and innocent eye.

"Well, I like it. And I like the idea of a community arts school. Paying it forward, while you're still young and on your way up, instead of waiting until you're on your way down again. It's a great angle." He blushed. "And besides, it's just a good thing to do. More artists should be doing this. Maybe you've started a new trend. Again."

From your lips, thought Dani, and just smiled.

He looked up at the Lawrence wall. "I heard that Lawrence Sinclair is here tonight. Is that him in your photo? There were several others on the far wall over there. With the nun and student portraits. You shot those, too, I can tell."

"I did. I came up to . . . study . . . with him. You're familiar with his work?"

"Oh yeah, my dad has a bunch of Sinclairs. I didn't know he was still alive."

"Very much so," said Dani. "I'll introduce you."

She snagged Lawrence as he walked by, and while he talked with Gary, Dani took the opportunity to look for Peter. That was when she saw Marian Sinclair enter the room.

Dani slipped behind a cluster of several people and watched as Sister Mary Catherine went to greet her. Peter was not far behind. Lawrence was sidling crablike toward Dani.

There was a brief but what appeared to be amiable exchange, then Peter showed his mother inside.

They disappeared from view as Manny walked by with one of the stodgiest critics in their circle. They stopped by Dani and Lawrence. "Well, I wasn't convinced when I heard about this, but I must say, this new direction bodes well for your future."

Manny beamed, his expression a silent warning for Dani to smile and keep quiet.

"Brava for bringing us back from the edge and pulling us into the depths of intimacy."

Lawrence pressed his bony elbow into her side.

Dani, knowing not to try topping that one, merely put her hand to her heart and bowed her head.

Manny led him away, revealing Peter and Marian only a few feet behind. Dani's immediate reaction was to try to escape. But it was too late.

She lifted her chin, but she needn't have bothered. Marian came straight up to Lawrence. Dani braced herself, but surely even Marian Sinclair wouldn't create a scene in a convent with all these people about.

Lawrence moved to meet her, or most likely steer her out of the room, but they were intercepted by Ray and Ada, who apparently had the same thing in mind.

"Why, Marian Sinclair. It's been years," said Ada enthusiastically.

"Good to see you, Marian," Ray added.

"So nice to have had a chance to visit with Peter. You should come down more often."

Marian had a history here? Dani couldn't imagine it.

"Good to see you both," said Marian in a voice so stilted that Ada and Ray took the hint and moved on.

Marian turned to Lawrence. "I have something to say. To both of you."

Dani looked frantically at Peter, but he seemed unable or unwilling to stop her.

"Perhaps we should—" Lawrence began.

"Peter has informed me that he doesn't wish to take his place in the company."

"Marian, really."

"Lawrence, let me say this. It isn't the easiest thing I've had to do. I owe you an apology. I should have said this sooner."

Dani moved closer to Lawrence. She wanted to signal Peter to stop his mother, but she couldn't take her eyes off Marian.

"I never wanted you out of the family, not really. I just wanted my husband back. It wasn't your fault. But I needed someone to blame. I've held this position in the company in trust for Peter. But he has other plans for his future. Stubborn like all the Sinclair men."

Dani wondered what this was costing her, though she thought she detected a note of pride in Marian's acceptance of her son's defection.

"And the Sinclair women," Lawrence said softly.

She shook her head.

"Marian, you're as much of a Sinclair as any of us. You've taken the company to new heights. You've just as much right to the legacy as Peter."

"A subject for further discussion."

Lawrence nodded. "As far as that goes, James and I have talked. We planned to call a formal nomination committee meeting, but let me just say that we'd be delighted if you will continue to head the company."

Marian might have turned to stone; Dani had never seen anyone so still.

She recovered quickly. "I want what is best for the company and I'll abide by whatever the board decides."

"But do you want the job?"

For a moment no one spoke, the air humming with kinetic energy, as everyone waited for her reaction.

It was a long time coming.

"I would be honored."

"Excellent," said Lawrence.

Dani stood amazed. What next? A family chorus of "Kumbaya"? Dani would happily lead the singing.

Marian turned to Dani. Dani braced herself.

"I hope we'll have a chance to become better acquainted in the future," she said. "Now if you'll excuse us, Peter has offered to show me the exhibit."

Peter, who had been staring at Dani throughout the exchange as if attempting to mesmerize her into not lashing out, broke out of his spell and steered Marian away.

The little group let out their collective breath.

"Well, that went amazingly well," said Ray.

"Did you know about this?" Dani asked Lawrence.

"I knew they were in negotiations, but I stayed as far away from that one as possible."

He let out an extended "Whew."

═

It was an early night in the scheme of art openings, but the critics were in a hurry to get back to the Excelsior bar, or to catch the late-night train to the city. The locals had to be up early to man the booths or bring their children to the outdoor festivities the next morning.

Sister Mary Catherine stood in the doorway watching the last of the guests walk to their cars. "What a day, and it's just beginning. I wanted to thank you all for the work and support you've given. Especially you, Dani. People are very excited, we've gotten quite a few promises of donations, and it's going to be perfect weather for the rest of the weekend.

"And now Sister Agnes is trying to get my attention. Excuse me." She bustled off.

"Well, we're off, too," said Ray. "We have an early day tomorrow. Logan and the other media students have talked me into selling posters at the festival tomorrow. All proceeds to be donated to the school. All G-rated. Ada double-checked."

"Oh, Peter, we didn't get a chance to say goodbye to Marian, but tell her she's always welcome."

The Barbosis said good night, and Lawrence, Peter, and Dani started across the lawn toward home. And Dani realized that for the first time in memory her feet didn't hurt at an art opening. And then she realized why. She was still wearing her running shoes.

A Year Later

The night was clear and cold for the opening of the Old Murphy Beach Arts Center and Elliott Sinclair Gallery. The new hall was packed with artists and art patrons, dignitaries, journalists, and critics.

Sister Mary Catherine, Sister Eloise, and Sister Agnes in a new wheelchair greeted visitors as they arrived. Peter stood nearby with Rashid, watching the crowd's reactions.

"Impressive," Rashid said, looking around the reception hall. "I'm glad I made the trip down."

"The whole place had to be gutted, but it's coming together slowly but surely."

"Busy year."

"No kidding. Between the renovation, the bar exam, and setting up an office, it's been a marathon."

"Harder than being CEO of Sinclair Enterprises?"

"Absolutely, but much more satisfying," Peter said, marveling at the turn his life had taken in the last year.

"And you finally got your own place, even though you had to move to another state to do it. Looks like it was the right move."

"The best," said Peter.

"How are things going between you and the goth cleaning lady photographer?"

"Dani? She still has her apartment in New York, travels a lot for shoots. I used to think hours were long at Sinclair Enterprises, but when she's home, she can disappear into the darkroom for hours."

"Home, is it? Sounds like your apartment won't be just yours for long."

"We're in negotiations," said Peter.

═

Dani stood next to Lawrence listening to Manny wax enthusiastic to several journalists as they waited for the official opening of the Elliott Sinclair Gallery.

She was as excited as she'd ever been even for the most important New York opening. Because this one was bigger than her or a handful of photographers. It was about the next generation of artists, and the next, and she'd helped make it happen.

It had been a busy year for them all. And there was still work to be done on the center. But the school was open. Classes had begun several weeks ago. Ray and Ada were planning on moving the photo and art supply shop into the newly renovated wing.

Dani took a deep breath.

"Feeling okay?" Lawrence asked.

"Feeling great."

"No more doubts?"

"Always, but not about the things that count."

And she had Lawrence to thank for that. Not that he would ever take credit. But he'd saved her in his own inimitable way, taught her how to see that thing she'd been missing when she'd yelled at him through that mail slot a year before and badgered him into letting her stay. It had been a journey, but Lawrence had given her the tools to find her way. Her mentor. Her Gandalf.

Acknowledgments

As always, thanks to my agent, Kevan Lyon; my editor, Tessa Woodward; and my whole William Morrow team for all the wonderful work you do.

And to Lois, Gail, Nancy, Yvonne, and Irene. Carry on.

And especially my thanks to Jim Cooper for his expertise and for giving me insight into the world of photography. Any mistakes are solely my own.

And to my readers. You are the best.

About the Author

Shelley Noble is the *New York Times* and *USA Today* bestselling author of *Whisper Beach* and *Beach Colors*. Other titles include *Stargazey Point*, *Breakwater Bay*, *Forever Beach*, *Lighthouse Beach*, and five spin-off novellas. A former professional dancer and choreographer, she lives on the Jersey Shore and loves to discover new beaches and indulge in her passion for lighthouses and vintage carousels. Shelley is a member of Sisters in Crime, Mystery Writers of America, and Women's Fiction Writers Association.